THE ONE WHO GOT AWAY

"Tory," Chey said, her voice low and as threatening as it had ever been in her life. "You did not—" She could barely get the words out. "Tell me you did not—"

"She did." And if that voice didn't set Chey so far back on her heels that it almost planted her ass-first on the packed dirt, one look at Wyatt Reed as he stepped into the stables—her stables—sure as hell did.

"Hey, Cheyenne," he said, as if an entire lifetime of anger, pain, longing, friendship, and regret hadn't filled her every waking moment since he'd walked out of her life so very many years ago. He held her gaze directly, and she owed him a direct one in return. She owed him so much more than that. But meeting his eyes was a start. And it took everything she had to manage even that much.

He didn't look angry, or mad, or sad, or . . . anything, really.

What he did look was good. So incredibly, terrifyingly damn *good*.

Under a Firefly Moon

DONNA KAUFFMAN

ZEBRA BOOKS
KENSINGTON PUBLISHING CORP.
www.kensingtonbooks.com

ZEBRA BOOKS are published by

Kensington Publishing Corp.
119 West 40th Street
New York, NY 10018

All Kensington titles, imprints, and distributed lines are available at special quantity discounts for bulk purchases for sales promotion, premiums, fund-raising, educational, or institutional use.

Special book excerpts or customized printings can also be created to fit specific needs. For details, write or phone the office of the Kensington Sales Manager: Attn.: Sales Department. Kensington Publishing Corp., 119 West 40th Street, New York, NY 10018. Phone: 1-800-221-2647.

Zebra and the Z logo Reg. U.S. Pat. & TM Off.

First Printing: February 2020
ISBN-13: 978-1-4201-4933-3
ISBN-10: 1-4201-4933-4

ISBN-13: 978-1-4201-4934-0 (eBook)
ISBN-10: 1-4201-4934-2 (eBook)

10 9 8 7 6 5 4 3 2 1

Printed in the United States of America

To John
For being my drop-everything guy

Chapter One

"You're breaking my heart, Buttercup." Cheyenne McCafferty buried her nose in the gelding's mane and smiled when she heard him snuffle, even as she tried to blink away the moisture that continued to gather at the corners of her eyes. "Yeah, well, you might think the name is an indignity, big guy." She straightened and rubbed her palm gently over the horse's cheek, looking him straight in his weary, lackluster eyes. "But we both know it's perfect for you."

His ears flicked forward and Chey had zero doubt that this horse knew exactly who she was, despite the more than decade-long gap since she'd last seen him. Her heart squeezed in a painful knot as she tried, and failed, not to remember, with crystal clarity, the circumstances surrounding that last time.

"Well, I don't know what son-of-a-bitch let you get in such deplorable condition," she murmured, working to keep her voice smooth, calm, and the anger tamped down deep. "Although I have my suspicions. Don't you worry, though. Thanks to Tory, you're going to be fine now. And for all the rest of your days, too. I'm going to see to that." She laughed and sniffled at the same time when Buttercup nodded and snorted. "Exactly. I'm only sorry I didn't find out sooner." She rubbed his neck. "So sorry," she added in a whisper.

Chey didn't want to think about the reasons why she hadn't known anything about Buttercup's life once he and his first owner had left the rodeo circuit all those years ago. She'd eventually left it, too, gone her own way. She didn't want to think about the reason for that, either.

"You two getting reacquainted, I see."

Chey dashed at the dampness on her cheeks, unconcerned by the streaks of dirt her gloves left behind. She plopped her cowboy hat on her head, pulled the brim down, but kept her palm on Buttercup's neck as she turned. She wanted the horse to know she wasn't leaving. Not now, not ever again. A sincere smile on her face, she turned to look at her dear friend. "We most definitely are. Thank you," she said, those two words never more heartfelt. "For letting me know. I realize I keep saying I'll do better about staying in touch—"

Tory just laughed outright at that, and Chey knew she deserved it.

"As I may have mentioned in my previous, oh, four thousand e-mails and letters, there are these marvelous inventions you Yanks call cell phones for folks who hate to write," Tory teased, her British accent always a bit crisper when she was giving Chey a hard time. So, pretty much always. "You don't even have to actually talk to people, either. You can send these wondrous things called text messages."

"I've heard about people like you." Chey pretended to grumble, then chuckled along with her.

"I have to say, I was really surprised to hear about your new venture," Tory said. "You said you were working on a farm now but neglected to mention the part about owning it. And that it's a lavender farm, not a horse farm."

"Part horse farm," Chey corrected. "My part anyway. I didn't tell you about the lavender?"

"I believe I'd have remembered that bit."

"I could have sworn—anyway, I'm only part owner. I'm working with rescues, giving lessons, doing some training." She shrugged. "Pretty much the same thing I've been doing since I left the circuit."

Tory folded her arms and tilted her head to the side, her expression telling Chey she wasn't buying it. "You mean other than launching a lavender farm complete with pick-your-own lavender, a tearoom with a wonderfully diverse menu, offering classes in making your own lavender products, which you all also sell in your adorable little gift shop." At Chey's lifted brows, Tory's smile merely curved a bit deeper. "They also have these incredible new things called Web sites. You do know your farm has one?"

"Not my wheelhouse," Chey said wryly. "My guess is my partners had something to do with that."

"Have you even seen it?" Tory deadpanned.

"Why would I? I live on it."

Tory laughed, her expression making it clear she thought Chey was a hopeless case where modern communication was involved. She wouldn't be wrong. "Well, I might have drooled a wee bit whilst scrolling through it. It looks like a slice of mountain heaven."

Chey's smile warmed at the thought of home, and she felt her heart fill, just as it did every time she thought of her new place in this world. She missed Blue Hollow Falls. Even being away for just a few days. More than she'd thought she would. Which was saying a lot for a former vagabond. "I like it."

Tory merely shook her head, her smile rueful. She was the effusive one, not remotely staid or stuffy as one would assume based on the accent. Chey was more of the observational type, not into big displays or chatty exhortations. Not that she was shy. Far from. She simply didn't feel the need to fill up the space around her with words. She spoke when she needed to, said what she wanted to say. No less, but no more.

"Well, it looks like a wondrous new life adventure to me," Tory said. "And it looks good on you," she added, giving her oldest friend a once-over. "I'm happy for you, Chey. I know it hasn't been easy."

Chey nodded and was relieved when Tory didn't go any further. They both knew why Chey had left the circuit, left that life behind. It didn't need to be dragged out into the open and examined all over again. Chey had made her peace with her older brother's passing. Owning and running a lavender farm in the Blue Ridge Mountains of Virginia, far away from the life she and Tory had led out west, was part of that process.

Chey suspected Tory had figured that out, too, and re-membered again why they'd become so close when they'd been kids on the rodeo circuit together. Tory was a cham-pion barrel racer, as was Chey, or they both had been, back in the day. Where Chey was the assertive, in-your-face kind of competitor, Tory had been the darling of the circuit. Pretty, always cheerful, a friend to everyone . . . and a dogged competitor in the ring. Pretty determined outside it, too, as Chey had come to know all too well.

Even as a kid, when Victoria Fuller decided a person was worthy of her friendship, she went about making it happen, and then she stuck by them, through thick and thin. *Through years of not exactly being the best pal in return, too,* Chey's inner voice nudged. Of course, Chey hadn't asked for that friendship then or now. In fact, she'd actively done every-thing she could to shake the vivacious youngster who'd joined the circuit at age seven when she'd come to the States to live with the American side of her family, all of whom rode the circuit as well. Tory had been to-the-saddle-born in Sussex, England, but had taken to the western style of riding like a fish to a pond and immediately threatened Chey's title of reigning champion.

Tory had beaten her plenty inside the ring, but outside it, she'd been even more determined, pushing her way past every wall Chey could put up between them. And Chey had been a champion at that, too. Eventually it had just been easier to give in and let Tory have her way. A pattern that had continued ever since. Chey smiled to herself, knowing she was more grateful for her friend's persistence than Tory could possibly know. Then, and now.

When Chey's older brother Cody had been killed during a bull-riding competition, Tory had been the only one capable of shoving her way through Chey's fierce bluster and anger, pushing her to let the pain of her brother's death in, so she could then let the grief out. Not that Chey had been all that thankful at the time, and she'd let Tory know as much. What Tory didn't know, couldn't possibly know, was just how much her persistence and mere presence had meant to Chey. She owed her dear friend more than she could ever repay. Which was why she'd pretty much re-arranged her entire life and that of a few others so she could drop everything and drive all the way across the country when Tory had called and told her about finding Buttercup on the auction block.

Chey accepted the little stab of guilt for letting the ball drop more often than not, when it came to maintaining contact. Tory wasn't just her closest friend from those days, but the only person Chey had stayed tethered to from her former life. She tried like hell to ignore the even bigger stab of guilt as she leaned in close to Buttercup. Tory wasn't the only one Chey hadn't kept in regular touch with over the years.

"Living in the Blue Ridge must be quite wonderful," Tory said wistfully. "I've only been out there once, to a show in Asheville, North Carolina. Simply gorgeous."

Chey laughed and swept her arm wide. "Seriously? You live in Sedona. Possibly one of the most breathtakingly beautiful places I've ever seen. I would never tire of this view." The red rock mesas and jutting buttes, their striated lines showing the layers of the earth that had formed them, stretched out as far as the eye could see. All outlined by a cloudless sky of such rich blue, the stunning contrast rushed into her soul with a wave of awe and appreciation for what nature was capable of producing. The view was that profound.

"It certainly puts things in perspective," Tory agreed, slowly inhaling as she scanned the breathtaking vista beyond the paddock and stables, then letting her breath out in a longer sigh as she shook her head. "But an eye candy view isn't everything."

"It's certainly a good place to start."

Tory shared Chey's smile, nodding in agreement, but Chey hadn't missed that brief moment, that flicker in her friend's big blue eyes. Though they kept in touch, or Tory did, at any rate, it had been years since they'd laid eyes on one another. Some things were timeless, however, and reading Tory's every emotion as it played across her pretty face was one of them.

"What's going on, Victor?" Chey asked, kindly but directly, using the nickname she'd given her friend the first time Tory had stolen Chey's title. "Trouble in this desert paradise? You said you weren't able to keep Buttercup here, which was why you contacted me." Chey gestured to the expansive and beautifully maintained stables they were standing in. "I'm forever grateful you did, but it doesn't look like there's an issue here with room. Are they working you too hard? Want too much board for him? I know you've had nothing but kind things to say about your employers, but—" She broke off, thinking maybe it wasn't her place to push. Not that such qualms had ever stopped her before. Or Tory, for that matter.

Tory looked as if she was going to shrug off the question, but at the last second, she caught Chey's eye, and their gazes held. Tory lifted a shoulder and let it drop in a helpless sort of half shrug. "The Parmenters—the owners, my bosses—are going to sell this place and move to northern California to help out with their grandchildren. They're selling the house, the stables, the land. All of it." Her expression turned a bit bleak. "To developers who plan to turn the place into a sea of desert condos. Even if I was able to buy it, which I'm not, I couldn't compete with that."

Chey's expression fell. "Oh no. I'm so sorry. I know how much you've loved working for them." Chey might not have been good at keeping in touch, but Tory had. Chey knew what was going on in her friend's life, even if she'd generally only given a cursory overview of her own. Tory hadn't told her this, though. "I can't imagine they'll give you anything other than the most glowing reference, and you have so many contacts built up." Chey smiled. "Your e-mail and letter-writing skills must have held you in good stead where that's concerned."

Tory let out a somewhat watery laugh at that, then wiped the back of her hand over her cheek. "They've already offered to do whatever they can. They are lovely, with huge hearts, and I don't fault them for wanting to go be with family." She looked up and down the wide aisle and the row of roomy stalls that lined both sides. "One winning lottery ticket and I'd shut that developer out in a blink." She chuckled and let out a shaky sigh, all at the same time.

"You'd hate running this whole place," Chey said dryly.

The stables were just a sliver of the property Tory's bosses owned.

Tory wiggled her eyebrows. "If the win was big enough, I'd hire a majordomo for that."

"Ah. Solid business plan then."

Tory nodded and brushed at her sleeves, as if duly accepting her friend's trite apology. "Have a little faith."

They both laughed then, but it didn't diminish the sadness Chey saw in Tory's eyes. Or the weariness. Chey knew what that felt like, to have to pick up and move. Again, and then again. No matter how long the interval, or how often you did it, the process never got easier. Chey also knew that when she'd moved to Blue Hollow Falls and helped to launch Lavender Blue, she'd found her forever home. She'd been tired of traveling, tired of picking up and moving. Losing Cody had been a large part of that. Her joy was gone. Chey had long since accepted that her heart was no longer in competing. It had taken a bit longer to admit she was also tired of traveling, but she didn't know any other way of life. It had been time to find something stable, permanent. Maybe Tory was feeling the same way, and the idea of packing up and moving again was one time too many.

On instinct, Chey reached out and took hold of Tory's upper arm, gave it a light squeeze and a rub. Chey wasn't much of a toucher, so that might as well have been a bear hug coming from her, and Tory knew it. "You're going to land on your feet. Why don't you come east? Blue Hollow Falls will pull you right in."

"Lots of ranching in the mountains of Virginia, is there?" she said dryly, though she'd clearly been touched by the gesture.

Chey laughed. "Okay, maybe not. Not like out here, anyway. But there are plenty of horses and riders to go with them. At the moment, I'm the only game in town, at least where lessons and training are concerned anyway. As you duly noted, I'm also part owner of a lavender farm and we're in full swing this year, so my horse side gig is honestly just that. You could pick up my lessons and go from there. I'll help. Not that you'd need it, but I can introduce you around, vouch for you." She grinned.

"That's truly kind of you—"

"Don't brush me off, now," Chey said, a teasing note in her otherwise dead serious offer. "I'm not tossing that out there like a bone to a starving animal. You could get a job in every single state in the union, and many other countries besides. You loved your time in Canada—"

"I don't want to leave the States," she said. "That much I know. I may still have the accent, but I'm part American and a citizen here for far longer than I was a resident there. I'll admit it was a bit of a thrill when I left the circuit and traveled as a trainer, being in demand in countries other than the US. Or it was when I was younger at any rate. Now?" She lifted a shoulder. "Not so much. These shores are home to me and I plan to stay somewhere between them."

"Even better. But I'm not just offering you a chance to find work." And as Chey spoke the words, she knew the truth of them. "I'm offering you a chance to find a home." Not giving her friend even a moment to say anything, Chey went straight on. "How many of these mounts are yours?"

"Two are mine," Tory said, looking confused by the subject change. "Buttercup makes three. Why?"

"I'm buying Buttercup from you, so that makes two." She lifted a hand when Tory started to argue on the buying part. "At the very least I'm paying you back whatever it cost to get him away from those meat grinders."

Tory shuddered, but simply nodded.

"You have a trailer?" Chey asked.

She nodded. "One-horse. Had a two, but it fell apart and I haven't had the chance to upgrade again. I use the Parmenters' ranch trailer when I need anything big—"

Chey talked over her. "Fine. I'll put Buttercup in your one-horse, and leave the two-horse I hauled here. When the time comes, drive it back east for me and we'll swap back." She eyed her friend, wouldn't let her look away, and stuck out her hand. "Deal?"

"Chey—"

"You've got no family left. I've got no family left," Chey baldly stated in a way she wouldn't have done with anyone else. "Blood family, anyway. I have three close friends who are family to me now. We own and run our farm together, and it turns out that has come with a whole town full of adopted family. The Parmenters are pulling up stakes." She smiled. "I'm sure you'll write long, lovely letters to each other and you can visit over the holidays. But in the meantime, you're a horse trainer in need of a job. And a new home. And I just happen to have one of each I can share."

"You came out here for Buttercup," Tory said, but Chey already saw the considering look in her eyes, and the way her shoulders had straightened a bit. Both good signs.

"Lucky me, then," Chey said with a smile. "Twofer." She wiggled the fingers on her still outstretched hand. "Deal?"

"I don't know when it will be," Tory said. "I promised to stay until they got things completely settled here."

Chey just kept wiggling her fingers. "Stop stalling."

Tory rolled her eyes and Chey's smile split into a wide grin. Now, that was the Tory she'd gone up against in the ring.

Tory took Chey's hand in a grip that was unsurprisingly strong and deliberate. "If it will keep you from nagging, sure, I'll come east and save your sorry little tush from being so overwhelmed you can't even handle a few measly mounts." Her utterly inelegant sniffle ruined her superior tone when she added, "I don't know how you've managed to get along without me all these years."

Tory didn't let go of Chey's hand and instead pulled her

brim of her hat as Buttercup grazed contentedly in the
pasture just beyond the paddock. The old gelding still...
a long way to go, but he'd been sl...
ing weight bac...

you still l...

Tory let Chey g...

Chey's shoulders as they t... 12 ...

gonna still feel that way when I ra...at

lavender better than you and take all your st... ?"

Chey hooted. "Oh, so that's how it's going to be? We're
not in the show ring any longer, you know."

"What, you think I've grown soft and complacent over
the years?" She eyed Chey. "Have you?"

Chey looked at the horse. "You hear that, Buttercup? Big
words. She has no idea, does she?"

The horse snuffled and ducked his head, as if he was
agreeing with Chey. Chey and Tory both laughed. "I have a
witness," Chey said, looking at her friend and grinning.
"You're on."

This time around, Chey did keep in touch, albeit not
quite as loquaciously as her friend did. Three months had
passed since Chey had successfully transported Buttercup
back across the country to his new home in Blue Hollow
Falls. Spring had arrived after a particularly stubborn winter
had finally made its long-delayed exit, and things on the
farm had started to hop.

Chey's to-do list felt like it had tripled overnight, but she
took a moment, folded her arms on the fence rail, and
propped her chin on them. She watched from under the

still had
slowly and steadily put-
back on. His coat still looked pretty shabby,
but it was growing back in, and his mane, though still thin and stringy, had an actual luster to it now. Best of all, the gelding's eyes, despite being permanently clouded with age, were alert now, and focused. Buttercup wasn't a fully healthy horse—that would take a much longer period of time, if it ever happened—but he was a happy horse. She'd take that.

Her gaze shifted from the pasture they'd dedicated to the horses to the farm beyond. Row after row of lavender bushes filled the landscape all the way to the horizon, where the peaks of the Blue Ridge rose up and filled the skyline, and her heart. It was a vista that never failed to move her. Now the lavender was coming to life, the buds creating a hint of that gorgeous purple hue, and the fields were showing signs of green. "The season is coming. Ready or not," she whispered.

The sound of Foster, one of her rescues, kicking his stall door, drew her from her thoughts and she headed back inside. The rambling old stone stables had come with the farm, as had the stone and wood stable manager's house that was now her home. It had been over a year since Chey had teamed up with her three "life warrior" friends and taken on rehabilitating the farm property and turning it into both their collective home and future livelihood. This would be their first complete beginning-to-end season, with Lavender Blue Farm and Tea Room fully open and operational.

The tearoom stayed open all year, though on reduced hours just three days a week in the off season. They held special events for each of the seasonal holidays from late

October through May, but were otherwise closed to the public during that time.

Over the past sixteen months, like the rest of the property, both the stables and her house had undergone endless renovations to make them livable and functional after sitting empty and abandoned for many years. Decades of them. Given the age of the buildings, that would likely be an ongoing, lifelong chore. Chey would happily take it on.

She continued scanning the property until her gaze landed on the main house, and she smiled thinking about how far they'd come already. All four of them. Seeing Tory again had made Chey a little more reflective than she generally allowed herself to be, but these memories were all good, warm, forward-moving ones that filled her with optimism and hope. Hard to believe, from the outside looking in, that four uniquely different women, from very disparate paths, not to mention varying generations, could come together to not only forge this new life venture, but develop a bond so deep it rivaled any family unit. "And from that, we did this," she murmured, shaking her head, still finding it hard to believe.

Chey knew she didn't stop often enough to appreciate things; she was always too busy racing ahead to the next thing. She knew that came from a lifetime spent not allowing attachments to form, affections to grow, whether for a place, or the people who inhabited it. She'd always be leaving soon, so why set herself up for heartbreak and grieving over things, people, places lost?

Turned out life handed out heartbreak and loss no matter how careful you were. From that brutal reality, Chey had learned the value of investing herself—all of herself—in people, in a place, for the long term. *And look at what we've done.* They'd dubbed themselves the "fearsome foursome" the day they'd met at a grief counseling group, one they'd immediately ditched, opting to forge their own form of group therapy. That nickname had been more prophetic than they could have ever predicted. *"Fearless foursome" might have been a better fit,* Chey thought, and smiled.

Vivienne Baudin, a New Orleans-born former showgirl-turned-costume designer with her seventieth birthday on the not-too-distant horizon, had been the one who'd actually inherited the property, though they all owned a fair share now. Vivi lived up in the big main house, a part of which also served as the tearoom and, for now, the gift shop. Construction was starting on a separate shop space for that, turning the old potting shed into a unique, restored entrance to the actual shop, which would be built onto the back of it.

Hannah Montgomery, nine years Chey's senior at thirty-eight, was an artist and former children's book illustrator. She had her artist's loft and living space over the large, detached carriage house. While Avery Kent, their resident genius and the youngest of the clan at twenty-five, had what they teasingly referred to as her mad scientist lab set up in her apartment, located in the addition that had been added to the back of the main house sometime in the middle of the previous century. Four women whose paths would have likely never crossed if not for that fateful afternoon.

As fate would have it, after moving to the middle of nowhere, somehow both Hannah and Avery were now in committed relationships with what Vivi called their "better halves," and Chey wouldn't be surprised if there were wedding bells for one, the other, or both, before the year was out.

She reached over the stall door and gave Foster a good rub along his neck. "You're my better half, eh, Fos?"

The horse snorted, then lowered his nose over the stall door and started nudging Chey's pocket. She laughed and dug out the apple she had stuffed in there earlier, for this exact reason. She held it while he nibbled off a chunk. "If only men were half as easy as you. Feed 'em, water 'em, put them in at night, and give them an occasional sweet treat? I might put up with one if that were the case."

"Question is, would they put up with you?"

Chey whirled around at the sound of that British lilt. "Tory?"

Tory stepped into the aisleway and posed with a flourish. "'Tis I. Surprise!"

"Yeah, that it is!" Chey said, stunned. "How is it you can talk my ear off pretty much every other day but not mention that you packed everything up and headed east?"

"Well, I kind of took a detour, so I wasn't exactly sure when I'd get here."

Chey finished feeding an apple to Foster, then wiped her hand on her pants leg and turned toward her friend. "What detour? Don't tell me. You found someone else's horse on the blocks?" Chey had been kidding, but Tory didn't laugh.

"Not exactly," she said, then turned to look outside and motioned to someone or something. She put her hands on her hips and gave whatever or whoever was out there "the look." No one denied Tory Fuller anything when she gave them what Chey teasingly called her "Queen Victoria face."

"I hate surprises," Chey told her, frowning now. Curiosity and dread filled her in equal measure, though she couldn't have said why on the latter part. Call it a sixth sense. "Don't let her bully you," she called out. "In fact, run, run now."

Tory turned to Chey. "You were kind enough to come get Buttercup when I couldn't keep him and didn't know whom else to call," she explained. "But he's not really your responsibility, Cheyenne, and I knew you wouldn't—" She broke off and abruptly turned her attention back outside the stables.

Chey's eyes widened when Tory stamped her foot and pointed to the floor in front of her.

"If I'd told you, do you think you'd have come? Now get on in here," Tory said to whoever was out there. "Bloody hell, the two of you. I swear, if I'd known then what I know now, I'd have knocked sense into both of you years ago."

Chey had been walking toward Tory, but she stopped dead in her tracks. A prickle of pure dread—no, make that full-blown panic—raced over the back of her neck and all the way down her spine, immobilizing her on the spot. The dread turned into a tight ball in her gut, and she was very afraid she might be sick. *Dread, or anticipation?* Maybe both. Okay, definitely both. But she didn't want either of them, thankyouverymuch.

"Tory," Chey said, her voice low and as threatening as it had ever been in her life. "You did not—" She could barely get the words out. "Tell me you did not—"

"She did." And if that voice didn't set Chey so far back on her heels that it almost planted her ass-first on the packed dirt, one look at Wyatt Reed as he stepped into the stables—her stables—sure as hell did.

"Hey, Cheyenne," he said, as if an entire lifetime of anger, pain, longing, friendship, and regret hadn't filled her every waking moment since he'd walked out of her life so very many years ago. He held her gaze directly, and she owed him a direct one in return. She owed him so much more than that. But meeting his eyes was a start. And it took everything she had to manage even that much.

He didn't look angry, or mad, or sad, or . . . anything, really.

What he did look was good. So incredibly, terrifyingly damn *good*.

Chapter Two

"I didn't know," Wyatt told her. "I mean, I knew about Buttercup—not that he'd ended up on the block. I thought he was dead. I thought my—" He stopped short, looked down as he tried—and spectacularly failed—to find balance. One look at Cheyenne McCafferty and he sounded just like the ridiculous, lovesick teenager he'd been the last time he'd seen her. He was so far and away from the person he'd been back then, in all ways imaginable, he didn't even recognize that boy anymore. And he sure as hell didn't want to be reminded of him, either. He'd worked too hard to leave that kid behind. And Chey along with him.

"I'm not going to apologize," Tory said, speaking directly, and maybe a little defiantly, into the sudden, fraught silence. "Life's too short for regrets. All three of us know the truth of that in ways most people don't, and never should. I knew you both then, and I know you both now. I love you. I trust you. And I don't give either of those things lightly. We're all we have left of the unique existence we led, living on the circuit, like circus performers, just in a totally different kind of ring. No one can understand what that was like unless they lived it. Just because we chose to put that life in our rearview mirror doesn't mean we leave all of it in the dust. That life, all the good and all the bad, forged who we are, standing here right now. And I like what I see."

Wyatt lifted his gaze to look at Tory. He wasn't mad at her. He knew she thought she'd been doing the right thing. But he was far from happy with her, either. Or with this sudden twist in what had already become a rather convoluted situation. He was so far from ready for this, for Chey, he simply had no handle on what to say, much less do.

"I'm going to head out and take care of my horses and start unloading a lifetime of stuff from the back of my truck," Tory said. "I expect that will take me some time." Tory's gaze went to Wyatt first, then to Chey, her Queen Victoria face on full display. "We're adults now," she said flatly. "Start acting like it."

She strode out of the barn as if it belonged to her, which was pretty much how she'd appeared in any ring she'd stepped into from childhood on up. All tawny blond hair, bright blue eyes, and a fiercely determined, wildly competitive spirit hidden behind the biggest heart and the sunniest smile Wyatt had ever seen.

He shifted his gaze back to Chey, who looked anything but sunny. He fought the urge to smile. Some things hadn't changed there, either.

"You can't have him," Chey said quietly. She might as well have yelled it, because the words, spoken in that deadly calm of hers, made him flinch just the same. "You had your chance. He's mine now."

"I had no chance, Chey," he told her, quite truthfully. *With the horse, or with you.* "I am happy to take him, and will guarantee you he'll live out his years in comfort—"

"He already is," Chey said, and he looked directly at her then, noting that for all her quiet ferocity, she wasn't looking at him. That much was very unlike the Cheyenne McCafferty he'd known.

"As I saw on the way in," Wyatt went on, "you have a wonderful spread here. Which is an understatement. He deserves nothing less and I'm grateful to you for going to get him and bringing him here. I've got no reason to move him again, except that I'm willing if you want me to. I'll be happy to take care of his board and—"

"Don't insult me."

Wyatt lifted his hands, then let them fall to his sides. He knew he'd earned her scorn, and far worse. "Not trying to," he said, a bit of edge in his own voice now. "I'll own up to not handling my departure, or the time since, in a good way."

Her gaze swung directly to his then, eyes widened, brows lifted, her expression all but screaming, *"You think?"* That made him want to smile, too. Tory had been right, as she almost always was. Not all of the past he'd left behind was bad. The woman standing in front of him had been the very best of it.

"All of that is on me," he told her honestly, openly. "The condition of that horse, however, is not. I take full responsibility for the sins of my past, Cheyenne. I do not, however, take any responsibility for the sins of my father."

She flinched at that and looked down at her booted feet.

He wanted to take a step closer, felt the pull of her every bit as strongly now as he had as an overly quiet, withdrawn nine-year-old, in the thrall of his first-ever crush. His last, too. He stayed where he was. "I won't go into the gory details, but you knew Zachariah," he said evenly and quietly. "Knew what he was capable of."

Chey looked directly at him again, her expression now filled with the one thing he never wanted from her. Pity. "You don't have to talk about him, Wyatt. I—"

"Don't insult me," he tossed back at her, instantly sorry

when she visibly flinched again. "That was out of line," he said immediately. "I'm sorry."

"No," she said simply, then let out a weary sigh. "It wasn't. And you shouldn't be. Not for that. And not for him."

"He told me he put Buttercup down," Wyatt explained, then laid it all out there. He told himself it was because of the pity she'd shown, but he suspected the reason was far more convoluted than that. "Told me he shot him between the eyes, then sold his carcass to the meat market. Revenge for me telling him I was going to saddle up and head out."

"Wyatt—" she said in a horrified whisper.

"I had no reason not to believe him. He'd done far worse. I should have known he'd never kill something that could bring in more money alive than dead. I'd taken damn good care of that horse."

"I know you did," Chey said, abashed. "I didn't think—"

"Buttercup and our other mounts, our bulls, were the only reason I stayed with that sick son-of-a-bitch as long as I did." He looked directly at her, hating the horror and grief he'd put in those eyes he'd missed seeing so much, hating the memories he was inflicting on both of them. But that didn't alter the truth of it. "I didn't know Buttercup was alive, much less in the condition he was in, until Tory tracked me down halfway around the world. I thought I was coming here with her to rescue him."

"Halfway around the world?" she asked, looking sincerely confused. "Where were you?"

"Nepal," he replied, the corners of his mouth kicking up at her clearly shocked expression. Even as another part of him took that look as a bit of a punch to the gut. So, she truly had left him in her past. Not that his ego was such that he assumed she'd kept track of him. It was just that he'd tried—and failed—to track her down. More than once. He saw now why that had been a doomed proposition. He knew she wasn't on social media; he'd looked. Seeing her life out here, way up in the hills, he realized she'd cut herself off from pretty much everything else, too. Couldn't say he faulted her for it.

He'd only thought it because, in his case, it was very easy for anyone to know exactly where he was, to see what he was doing. A few million people he'd never even met did just that. Every day. "Country boy got a passport," he said, a sardonic note in his voice, and left it at that. If she'd wanted to know where he'd ended up, she would have found out already.

Clearly Tory had always had a handle on Chey's where-abouts but had chosen to protect Chey when Wyatt had asked for her help locating their mutual friend years back. Maybe Chey had asked after him, too, and Tory had pro-tected him as well. Not that that would have done much good, in his case. If Chey had done even a cursory search online for him anytime in the past half dozen years, she couldn't have missed him if she'd tried.

"So it would seem," Chey said, her expression unread-able now. "I'm sorry," she said, after the silence had stretched out a bit. "About Buttercup, about . . . all of that. For what it's worth, I didn't think you'd done anything to hurt him. I assumed it was Zachariah from the moment Tory told me where he was. Or that your father was, at least, at the root of it. If I was mad at all, it was that you'd left Butter-cup behind, knowing what Zachariah was capable of. I should have known better than that." Her voice softened just a hint, when she added, "It's been a long time, Wyatt, and we don't know each other now."

She let out a short but humorless laugh. "Clearly, because . . . Nepal? Really?" She shook her head, but her expression and words couldn't have been more serious when she went on. "But I do know, as well as I know myself, that you'd never be like him. You'd never hurt anyone, man or beast." She held his gaze quite steadily now, as direct as she'd been since he'd stepped into her stables. "Not physically, at any rate."

He took that well-aimed sucker punch to the gut, and the heart, and felt it reverberate deep inside him, leaving him with a sick feeling of regret. "I should have responded, Chey," he said. "To your notes, your calls. Right after I left, I just . . . couldn't. Not then." He dug his hands into his pockets, curled his fingers into fists, fists he wanted to aim at himself for the pain that had flashed through those formidably serious, old-soul brown eyes of hers. "By the time I finally pulled my head out of my heartbroken ass, I—"

"Stop," she said, quietly but no less forcefully than anything she'd said before. Then she sighed, and he saw the stiffness leave her stance. "I shouldn't have said that." A half smile curved her lips. "Some things haven't changed." Her expression sobered. "I share plenty of the blame. I hated that I hurt you. One of the single biggest regrets of my life. I had no idea how you felt, and I handled it—not well."

"It's not like you asked," he said, reeling a little at her confession. "You were honest, which is exactly what you should have been. You weren't unkind. But that didn't make it hurt any less. Probably would have been better if you'd told me off," he said, a hint of a smile surfacing. "Made me stomp off all mad at the entire female race or something."

"I was sixteen and so utterly hormone addled, I couldn't get out of my own way," she replied. "It wasn't that I didn't, or couldn't love you—I did, in all the ways that mattered to me—but I hadn't even considered that it could be different between us. You were my rock, my friend, my confidant, my partner-in-crime. You and Cody protected me and gave me a swift kick in the butt when I needed it." Her lips twitched. "We won't mention how often that was." Her gaze changed then, and even though he knew the affection that filled them was one of remembrance, not something she felt now, today, it still rocked him.

God, how he'd missed her.

"I tried to talk to you, call you. I even wrote letters." She nodded toward the stable doors. "Ask Tory how good I am at that. I suck. But I wrote them anyway. Because I hated how we ended. I wanted us to go back to how we were—"

"I couldn't," he said, as baldly and as honestly as he'd ever said anything in his life. He lifted his shoulders, searched for better words to explain. There were none.

"I know," she said, the words hardly more than a whisper. "I didn't get it then. I do now. I'm sorry, Wyatt. Truly. You know what you meant to me. Losing you was one of the hardest things I'd dealt with in my life up until then. Made it doubly hard when—" She broke off, shook her head, frowned, then shook her head again. "No, that's not fair. That had absolutely nothing to do with you."

"I didn't know," Wyatt said. "About Cody." He watched her, and she dipped her chin, kept her gaze downward. He saw her frowning again, perhaps as a way to keep tears from gathering—he didn't know. Though he couldn't imagine Cheyenne McCafferty crying. She was too tough for that.

Losing her brother, the person she loved above all else, had to have changed her, though. Worn her defenses down, at least a little. How could it not?

"I would have come back," he said quietly. "I was long since out of the country by then. I didn't find out about it until way after it had happened. Years later. I'd cut myself off from my life here pretty thoroughly. I tried to find you when I heard, but you'd left the circuit by then." His smile was rueful. "That's when I tracked down Tory and reconnected with her. She said she had no idea where you'd gotten off to."

Chey looked surprised at that.

"She was protecting you," he said. "You probably didn't want anything to do with your past any more than I did when I left."

Chey nodded. "True enough. I appreciate that you tried to find me. Don't beat yourself up over that. It's okay. I didn't expect you to show at that point."

"It's not okay," he said. "Cody was my closest friend, next to you. I would have been there. For you, for him." He shook his head. "When I left, it wasn't just your attempts to reach me that I chose not to respond to, Chey. When I say I cut all ties, that's not an overstatement. When I finally left—escaped, because that was how it felt—I didn't look back. At anything, or anyone. I couldn't if I was to have any chance of making it. Maybe you, of all people, can understand why. I felt like I was running for my life. The only way I could break free was to look ahead. Always. Only."

She met his gaze again, and what he saw now was understanding, as well as sincere curiosity. "Are you saying that when Zachariah was kicked off the circuit—you, well, you were too old to be considered a runaway, I guess—but you split from him then?"

Wyatt nodded. "I'd already told him I was leaving before they booted him. Buttercup was dead, or so I thought. We were down to our last three mounts and we only had two bulls at that time. He got thrown in jail in the next town we landed in."

Wyatt looked away, hating that, even after all these years, he couldn't remember that time in his past as dispassionately as he'd have liked. Likely because of the woman standing in front of him. She knew all about his past. She and Tory were the only ones left who knew. He never spoke of it. Not directly. Not ever. Millions of followers watched his every adventure. Not one of them knew about Zachariah

Reed. Nor would they. "For once he didn't slither back out after a forty-eight-hour hold," Wyatt told her. "The judge actually locked him up for a six-month stint. So I did the only thing I could think of. I sold the bulls and the horses—to good people—and I took that money and got as far away from that son-of-a-bitch as I could."

Chey nodded, as if she understood perfectly. And of course she did. She knew what he'd dealt with, firsthand.

"Overseas, far, I'm guessing," she said.

"It was the only way I felt safe." He smiled then, though it was empty of humor. "Early on, when I was figuring out how I was going to survive, where, doing what, I still had this overwhelming, completely irrational fear that my father would just show up, would find me, like he was some kind of omnipotent overlord instead of a sorry, violent drunk. It had always felt that way to me. He was always one step ahead of me, always seeming to know what I was going to do before I did it. I was certain he'd track me down some-how, beat me, or worse, for selling our livestock, for leaving him to rot in that county lockup instead of bailing him out."

"You were eighteen," Chey said softly.

"I might have been a man in calendar years," Wyatt said, nodding, then pointed to his head. "In here, however? I was a perennially scared little kid. I know it sounds pathetic—"

"It sounds awful, Wyatt. Because it was. The only thing that was pathetic in that whole scenario was your old man. I'm glad you got away. Far, far away. And I'm glad you told me. In your place, I would have done the same thing. And I guess, though for a different reason, I did. When Cody died, I tried to keep going, sort of in tribute to him. He'd have hated it if I'd quit because of him. I just . . . there wasn't any fun in it for me. You were gone, he was gone, Tory went off right after that to ride the circuit in Canada, then on from there to train horses in South America. Everyone I cared about was gone."

"What about your aunt and uncle?" he asked.

She smiled then, and he was relieved he hadn't inadvertently triggered another bad memory. "My aunt and uncle were still here back then. They were wonderful people from beginning to end. I loved them more than anything for taking on Cody and me when our folks died, and that bond only grew stronger over the years." Her smile grew. "We'd never have known rodeo life if not for them. Tory is right—that life made me who I am, and I'm proud of it. Cody was, too. But after he was gone, it wasn't long before I knew I was done with that life. I needed to strike out, find my own way, find a new path." Her smile edged back to dry. "Though I managed to stay on the continent while doing it."

He offered her the same smile in return. "Your aunt and uncle, are they—" he began, but she filled in the blank before he could ask.

"Both gone now." She lifted a hand to stall his reply. "It's okay. They weren't spring chickens when they took us on. They had a good, long life." Her love for them shone brightly. "They used to say they had to live forever just to keep us in line." She laughed. "I think they might have, too." Her expression shifted to one of love and sadness. "Losing Cody broke them, I think. They lost their love of rodeo life just as I did. I think they were tired, too, but they didn't know anything else."

"How did they take your leaving?"

"Oh, we all left," she said with a laugh. "I found a job where I could board our horses. I put all our gear in storage once I was settled and convinced them to take the RV down to Florida, park it on the beach for a month, see how that felt." Her smile grew. "They never left."

"I'm glad to hear it. No one deserved that more than they did."

She nodded. "They did. I got down there as often as I was able. They were pushing ninety when my uncle finally checked them both into a senior-living facility. His heart eventually gave out, and my aunt went soon after." She shook her head, let out a laugh. "She told me she couldn't leave him up there unsupervised. Passed in her sleep two months after he was gone." Chey took in a deep breath, shoved her hands in her pockets. "That was four, almost five years back now."

"We should all be so fortunate to live such a long, happy life."

"Agreed," Chey said. "And, though it might sound odd, losing them helped me deal with losing Cody. Neither of them suffered. And they loved each other so much, right up to the end." She smiled. "And probably on since. It helped, seeing people I love live their lives fully all the way to the end."

"I can see how that would be. I'm sorry they had to live through the loss of your brother, but I'm glad they were there for you."

"I wish I could have spared them that, but in truth, I needed them. We had each other to cling to, and we did." She paused, then said, "So, Zachariah, is he . . . ?" She trailed off, and Wyatt nodded, knowing what she was asking.

"Eight years ago. Pancreatic cancer. In the end, it was the one thing he couldn't beat the crap out of."

She nodded, not a shred of remorse on her face. "Good."

Wyatt had loved her for many things, but in that moment, he loved her most for that. For knowing, for understanding. For feeling exactly as he did about it.

"Did you see him again?" she asked. "After you left?"

Wyatt shook his head. "I kept track. Early on, it was for my own sake, so I always knew where he was. After a while it became habit. In the end, it wasn't a challenge." He held her gaze, knowing there would be no judgment on the son because of the father, not from Chey. "He died in a prison hospital. He was incarcerated for the last two years of his life."

She said nothing, simply nodded, as if not surprised, nor sorry for the outcome. In that regard, they were also in total agreement. If for no other reason than the longer Zachariah remained locked up, the safer everyone else was.

"Hello again," Tory said, walking back into the stables without preamble. "We're talking, we're sharing, we're catching up?" She eyed them both. "No bloodshed?" She smiled. "I'll take that as a win."

"Who, exactly, did you think was going to draw blood from whom?" Chey wanted to know.

"Fifty-fifty odds," Tory replied airily, then laughed. "Who am I kidding? If there'd been a pool, I'd have taken Chey and spotted seven points."

"Wow," Wyatt said. "I'll just pack up my decimated manhood and meet you out at the truck."

Tory walked up to him and pinched his cheek. "You would never harm so much as a hair on woman or beast. It would have been like taking candy from a baby."

He chuckled. "I feel so much better now. I think."

Tory turned, bright smile firmly in place. "I know I've arrived at your simply gorgeous farm far earlier than we'd planned, so I'm happy to find a room in town if need be. You had said that Hannah would be happy to let me lease her artist's loft, but I was thinking that—"

"First off, there will be no leasing," Chey said. "You're a guest."

Tory looked offended. "I am no such thing. I believe I

was offered a job. That makes me an employee of Lavender Blue. Or of someone, at any rate. Now, if you want to trade rent in lieu of a paycheck until I prove to you how invaluable I am, I'm happy to work out a deal. But I insist on talking with Hannah to make arrangements so she can still use the loft to paint, or whatever else she is using it for." Tory let her faux privileged mantle fall so just the honest joy and gratitude shone through. "I'm thrilled to be here, Chey. More than you can know. It's far lovelier than I even imagined. If you've no work for me now, I've planned for that. I meant what I said. I can find a room in town. I do hope I can board my horses here, but—"

"Oh, for the love of Pete, just come here already and get it over with." Chey opened her arms and Tory wasted no time rushing in and hugging the life out of her dearest friend.

Wyatt grinned, happy to relive this particular part of his childhood, as he watched the two. Chey was not at all big on public displays, much less bear hugs, which was precisely why Tory had given them to her as often as was possible back in the day. She'd called it "humankind therapy," convinced that what Chey needed was more hugs, not fewer, to make her less irascible. Wyatt wasn't any more convinced now of this plan's efficacy than he'd been then, but winked at Chey all the same when she gave Tory a kind pat on the back while staring helplessly at Wyatt over her friend's shoulder.

"I've already spoken to Hannah," Chey said. "And the place is all yours for as long as you need it. No rent—" She raised a hand, stalling Tory's reply. "Hannah is the sole owner of said loft, so it costs her nothing to do the kindness. She's not using it and is happy that you can. However, I'll give you her number and the two of you can hug it out, or whatever. I'm just the messenger."

"Thank you," Tory said. "And I would like to call her, to thank her if nothing else. Once we get things established, I'll see about finding my own place. Or whatever," she quickly added. "Thank you. Now I'll shut up."

Chey pretended to be shocked; then both women shot Wyatt a look when he laughed. He lifted both hands. "I'll just go out and help with unloading."

"I've offloaded my mares. They're tied at the post. I wasn't sure—"

"The paddock is empty," Chey said. "They can go in there for now. I'm sure they'll enjoy the freedom after the road trip. I've got stalls picked out for them but haven't set them up yet."

"I'll put them in the paddock," Wyatt said, and turned to go, then paused and turned back to them. "I'd like to go see Buttercup, if you think he's up to it. I saw him out in the field. Okay if I whistle him in?"

He'd asked casually enough, but Chey turned to him then and he saw, as few did, straight past the bluster and fierce independence, to the big, mushy heart she worked so hard to keep concealed. Chey had told him once she felt emotion made her look weak, and her rivals would use that against her in competition, both inside and outside the ring. That might have been true enough, but Wyatt had long suspected that the hardness of life on the road, not to mention the cutthroat competition, especially given her young age, had made Chey tamp down that soft heart to help herself remain tough.

She had been plenty tough, maybe too tough at times, but he couldn't fault her for that. In all the ways that mattered, she was all heart. He knew how conflicted she must have felt about Buttercup; finding him as she had must have stirred up her most protective instincts. Just as he was certain she knew how poignant and powerful the reunion between him and the horse that had been his first true friend would likely be. Despite what she'd said earlier, in the heat of the moment, he had no doubt she'd let him reclaim his horse, especially if she thought, even for a minute, it would be what Buttercup might need most.

Horses lived a long time, and their memories lasted just as long. Wyatt had no doubt his horse would remember him, by scent and sound if not appearance. He just didn't know what Buttercup would think about him suddenly stepping back into his life, especially given what had transpired since they'd last seen each other.

Chey nodded, her gaze directly on his, her serious expression signaling to him that she was well aware of the momentousness of this particular occasion. For man, and for horse. He appreciated that she trusted him to handle the reunion properly.

"Thank you," he said, hoping she could read his thoughts as easily as he read her.

He stepped outside the barn and walked over to Tory's mares. He made sure there was water in the trough and dug a few carrots out of the cooler in the trailer and fed them each a few. Minutes later they were both happily trotting around the paddock, feeling their oats a bit after the long drive. Wyatt leaned his arms on the fence and alternated between watching them and looking to the field in the distance where Buttercup was grazing. Maybe he should leave well enough alone. The old gelding didn't look so great, and Wyatt didn't want to imagine how bad off he must have been when Tory first found him, if months later, he was still looking so thin and ragged.

Nonetheless, he looked settled, content. And Chey would see to it that he had the best of everything going forward, of that Wyatt had no doubt. Maybe the best thing he could do for his childhood friend was to leave him be, not stir up past memories, past pain. *For the horse, or for you?*

He honestly didn't know the answer to that. Both, probably, though he'd like to think he was putting Buttercup's best interests first. Why reunite, stir up whatever might be in that big, majestic beast's heart, only to walk away again? The truth of the matter was Wyatt didn't know where he'd be a month from now, or a year from then. He couldn't traipse around the world, doing what he did for a living, with a horse in tow. On the other hand, he had property. He didn't have to board the horse out. He could make a life for Buttercup, a good one. But the truth was, he'd been home less than thirty days, total, in the past year.

Wyatt ducked his chin. Buttercup was better off here. The gelding knew Chey, too, and she wasn't going anywhere.

"He doesn't look so good, I know. But he'll be happier to see you than you can imagine. He's up to it." Chey came to stand beside him at the rail and rested her folded arms next to his.

A glance showed that she was looking beyond the paddock to where Buttercup was cropping grass.

"I was thinking it might be more cruel than kind," Wyatt said. "To Buttercup, I mean."

Chey glanced at him. "Because you're not staying."

She didn't make it a question, but he nodded anyway.

"I'm not offering this because I think you can't do it, but because I think I should do it. I could take him home, support him, his care, whatever medical attention he needs, for as long as he needs," Wyatt said, then turned to look at Chey directly. This close, the impact of those brown eyes of hers was like a one-two punch to his heart. "The truth is, though, I won't be there much. I'd have someone I trusted care for him, but—"

"You trust me. And I have the added benefit of knowing him as long as you," Chey said again, not making it a question or needing a response. "All that is to say that he will be fine here. You know I'll care for him like he's my own. Honestly, I already feel he is."

"He deserves you," Wyatt said, leaving the "more than he deserves me" part silent, knowing she heard it anyway. "And I'm grateful. Thank you, Cheyenne. For all of it. Truly."

She swallowed hard at his use of her full name. He'd been pretty much the only one who'd ever called her that. But he'd thought it such a cool name when he was a kid. Later, it had meant something entirely different to him; so he was the only one she let call her that.

"Maybe you're right, then," she said quietly, looking back out to the field. "Maybe best to steer clear." She glanced at him again. "For now."

Wyatt suspected she wasn't just talking about him steering clear of the horse. He nodded and left it at that.

They both watched Tory's mares in shared, if not completely comfortable silence. He spent some time taking in the full scope of the property, the row upon row of budding lavender, the magnificent backdrop of the hazy, deep blue peaks.

He debated remaining silent, simply taking the moment for what it was, and being grateful for that much. He was still reeling at the suddenness of this reunion, after so many years and endless conversations he'd had with himself about how this exact situation would play out, if it were ever to happen. And, frankly, he'd long since given up hope on that even being a possibility.

"I don't have too many regrets," he heard himself say, deciding life didn't hand out moments like this often, if ever. He'd only add to the list of regrets if he let it pass without telling her how he felt. "I used to think I should have run away, should have escaped sooner." They were both looking straight ahead, but he felt her side-glance at him, even without seeing it. "I told myself that I couldn't have saved our horses if I'd done that, much less our bulls, and I would never have left any of them with Zachariah. But it was more than that."

"Wyatt," she said, so softly he hardly heard it, even though their elbows were almost touching as they continued to lean on the rail.

"Let me finish, Chey," he said, just as gently.

He looked at her then. Given their difference in height, her face was mostly obscured by the brim of her cowboy hat, but he saw her nod. And keep her focus straight ahead, as if she was bracing for whatever he was about to deliver. He wanted to assure her he'd learned his lesson on that score. She'd gut punched him more than once today, though he didn't blame her. Beyond her shock at his sudden appearance, which he'd had no control over, he hoped to spare her from even one of the same.

"I used to dream about running, but then I'd think, what in the hell would I do out in the world alone? And how would I take care of myself, much less my animals? So, I stayed, and it was hell. Worse than hell. You and Cody and your aunt and uncle were the only good part of my life. The only thing that felt like a real family. Your friendship meant more to me than you'll ever know."

"I think I do know," she said, the words clear, but spoken in hardly more than a whisper.

He turned to face her then, still leaning on the railing. "My regret isn't that I stayed, or that I left when I did. My regret is telling you how I felt about you. I knew you didn't feel that way, Chey. Any fool could have seen that, and probably did. It was a selfish thing, blurting all that out, like by some miracle my own eyes had deceived me and you felt the same way, too, and somehow we'd be together, and the horror of my life would magically be behind me."

"There's no shame in honesty," Chey told him, sparing him a brief glance, but otherwise keeping her gaze firmly on the horizon.

For once he could honestly say he had no idea what she was thinking. But he hadn't said anything she didn't already know. So, he added the part that was new. "Maybe. But it cost me the thing I valued most. Your friendship. If I'd known it was all or nothing, maybe I'd have kept my big mouth closed. Maybe not." His smile was a brief flash. "You weren't the only one who was a bundle of hormones who couldn't get out of your own way."

He saw her lips twitch at that, and she nodded again. "Fair enough."

"I'm glad we had a chance to talk."

She did look at him then, back to being the direct Chey he'd always known, back to facing things head on. It was both a relief and had him tensing slightly at the same time. Now it was his turn to brace himself.

"Maybe it's just as well we had no warning about this meeting," she said; then she surprised him by smiling. "Less chance of us making matters worse."

It wasn't one of those half smiles, or little lip twitches. No, it was that big, broad, beautiful smile that so transformed her. And if it had been stunning at sixteen, and all the years before, all the way back to when she'd been an obnoxiously overconfident eight-year-old, the years since had somehow managed to pack even more of a wallop into it. In fact, he felt it right down somewhere very deep inside his chest. A specific part of his chest that hadn't been fully engaged since . . . well, since the last time he'd seen that smile.

He knew right then he was still in serious, serious trouble where Cheyenne McCafferty was involved.

"I know it's not the same as it was then," he said, aware he should look away, stare at the fields, the mountains, anything but those big brown eyes. "It's been a very long while. Too long. It's not like we can just pick up where we left off."

"Uh, yeah," she said with a surprised laugh. "Given where we left off." It was a testament to just how strong their bond once was that she could joke at a time like this.

He smiled, too, even though amusement was all mixed up with sadness over what they'd lost, and the lingering regret and guilt he felt for being the reason it all ended. "The friendship we had once upon a time might be beyond recovery," he said, as lightly as he was able. "We're different people now. Or, I am, at any rate."

"That much is definitely true," she said candidly.

"Meaning?"

She motioned to him, head to toe. "You've seen you, right? I mean, you are not the quiet kid with the big heart and gentle spirit I knew back then. That hidden streak of wicked humor might still be there, though I suspect not so hidden any longer." She straightened then and rested her arm on the top rail. "You are confident and definitely not shy. I wouldn't say you have swagger, not the cocky kind at any rate, but I believe you could put on a pretty believable display if asked."

He laughed at that, but he didn't deny it. Any of it. "Well, that much hasn't changed about you," he said.

"Me being blunt, you mean?"

He flashed a fast grin. "That, and your observational skills were always one of your sharpest traits. One studied look, and you could read a room, a person, a horse, you name it. I always trusted your judgment even when I didn't see things the same way, because you were so rarely wrong."

She studied him for a moment, then said, "Am I wrong now?"

"About your assessment of who I am?" He shook his head. "No. I have seen me, yes," he added with a chuckle. "And no, I don't much resemble the kid I once was. Thank God. Though I'd like to think the big heart part still applies."

She nodded, but didn't say anything more, then turned back to the fence. "Where are you headed from here?" she asked. "Back to Nepal?"

He noted she didn't ask him what he'd been doing there, or anything else of a personal nature. Beyond tying up loose ends from their past, anyway. She sounded sincere enough, but he couldn't help but think that in her mind, their little reunion had come to an end. Chey was ready to move on. Or ready for him to move on, at any rate. This was polite conversation now.

He could tell her, fill her in on what he'd been doing the past twelve or thirteen years, what his life was about now, but she didn't really want to know. And he no longer gave away pieces of himself, even the most trivial of facts, to people who didn't care to know them. Didn't care to know him. Not even for her.

Whatever he might have said in response to her question went unanswered, because Tory came running out of the stables just then, waving a cell phone in her hand.

"Hey, sorry to interrupt. Your phone has been ringing off the hook. I didn't answer because . . . not my phone. But when it kept going, I thought you might want to return the call. It's Vivi, according to the readout. She's left voice mails."

Instantly concerned, Chey took the phone from Tory.

"Thanks," she said, then tapped the screen a few times and listened to the voice mail.

"Everything okay?" Tory asked anxiously. "I'm sorry. I should have told you sooner. I just . . . wanted you two to have time to talk."

Tory looked visibly relieved when Chey's mouth curved in that dry half smile. She lifted a hand to stall more questions and put a call in. "Hey there," she said when the person on the other end—presumably Vivi—answered. "Up a creek without a paddle, are you?"

She listened for a few minutes, then said, "Hold tight. Cavalry is coming."

She hung up and looked at them. "Vivi—she owns part of this farm"—she said to Wyatt—"went paddling on the lake today. Which . . ." Chey just shook her head, looking bemused, then smiled. "Apparently she's lost her oars and can't get back to shore."

"Paddling?" Tory asked, sounding as surprised as Chey looked. "From what you've told me about her, she didn't strike me as the outdoorsy type. Lavender farm notwithstanding."

Chey laughed. "She's most definitely not. I don't know the full story, but I guess I need to go rescue her." She looked at her phone, as if trying to formulate a plan of action. "Maybe our friend Noah has a canoe or something. His fishing cabin is out that way."

"They don't have boats at the lake?" Tory asked.

Chey shook her head. "Only in the summer. Otherwise you just bring your own and use the ramp."

"I can get her back to shore," Wyatt said, wondering who Noah was and knowing it was none of his business.

Chey looked at him, surprised. "With?"

"I have some experience with alternative transportation," he said with a grin. "Trust me. You drive, I'll rescue."

Chey looked at Tory, then back to Wyatt, then shrugged. "Okay. Thanks."

Tory stepped back. "I'll hang here, start unpacking things into the loft. Call me if you need anything." She wiggled her eyebrows. "Cooler, picnic basket, blanket . . . life raft."

"Funny," Chey said, then headed toward the gravel lot and a big red, dual-wheeled pickup truck. It was parked off to the side of the stone and wood house just past the stables. Her house, Wyatt assumed. "Thanks," she told him again. "I appreciate the assist."

"Anytime," he said, and climbed into the passenger seat, wondering just what in the hell he thought he was doing. *Not leaving Cheyenne McCafferty in my rearview mirror again, that's what. Not yet, anyway.*

Chapter Three

Chey drove down the dirt and gravel lane back to one of several access points to Firefly Lake. The lake was located higher up in the hills above Blue Hollow Falls and was more accessible on foot than by vehicle. This was the road in most commonly used, so she could only hope Vivi had taken the same route. She pulled into the long, narrow parking area and sighed in relief when she saw Vivi's fully restored, cherry-red, '56 Chevy Bel Air. It was the only car in the lot. She hadn't seen anyone else on the way in, either.

"That is a beauty of a car," Wyatt said. The first words he'd spoken since they'd left the farm twenty minutes earlier.

"Don't tell Vivi unless you want an excruciating history of the vehicle from assembly line onward."

"Oh, then that's the first thing I'll ask her. She can tell me all about it while I drive her home." She caught Wyatt's fast grin from the corner of her eye, which was where she was keeping him. In her periphery.

Yeah. And how's that working out for you? Not great, she admitted. She'd bought the big dual-wheeled truck to haul horse trailers and had happily paid extra for the roomy, extended cab. After years living in an RV with three other people, she liked her space.

The cab of her truck had felt the opposite of spacious from the moment Wyatt had climbed in and pulled on his seat belt. Strapped it right across his ridiculously broad chest. Which she really, really tried not to notice, but *damn.* The term "rawboned" had been created to describe the teenager Wyatt Reed had been. If not for the long, ropy muscles he'd developed working with the steers and bulls he and his father trained and handled for the rodeo, he'd have been skinny to the point of bony.

Yeah, well, he ain't bony now, Chey thought as she continued on toward the back of the lot and the narrower road that led down to the boat ramp.

The water wasn't visible from the parking area due to the dense pines that crowded this side of the lake. It was a surprisingly large body of water to be up in this high valley pocket. Mountain peaks fully encircled the area, and as a backdrop to the tall pines and water, made for a breathtaking view. In addition to the hikers and boaters, it was a popular spot for photographers, painters, and night-sky watchers, too.

"Spectacular setting," Wyatt said. "Is the lake spring fed? Small streams? Pretty good elevation for a decent-sized lake."

"Partly," Chey said, keeping her gaze straight ahead as she steered around some large potholes and deep ruts that had resulted from the harsh winter. "But it's too big for just that. There are a few smaller streams, but its main source is Firefly Creek." It was easier talking to him about the view than delving back into their past, so she added, "Firefly runs down from the higher elevations, feeds the lake, then snakes through a few hundred acres of wilderness area and nature park that surrounds the lake, before heading down and eventually joining in with Big Stone Creek."

She rolled to a stop at the head of the boat ramp road

and frowned. The big yellow bars were closed across it, chained and padlocked. "The two creeks combine to create the heavy flow that rushes over the big tumble of boulders next to the silk mill. That creates the waterfall that gives the town its name. From there Big Stone runs all the way down to the Hawksbill River in the valley below." She said the last part by rote, like a guide reciting the history of the place to a tourist. "How the heck did she get a boat down there?" Chey said, giving voice to her actual thoughts.

"Guess the ramp stays closed till summer, too, then?"

"I guess," she said, putting the truck into park. Other than Vivi's car, the lot behind them was completely empty. They hadn't passed anyone coming in, either. "I haven't been out here since late last fall. Not sure when they close up the dock. I was on the horse trails, and they go in around the lake from a different direction." She turned off the engine and pocketed the keys. She had one hand on the door handle.

"Cheyenne," he said, in that way a person did when they wanted to say something important, and her hand froze.

He'd been the only one to call her by her full name when they were growing up. She'd always thought it sounded like she was in trouble for something, so she'd never liked it. Except when he said it. But the way he spoke her name sounded so different now. He was so different now, she supposed that was to be expected. It shouldn't make her feel sad. She'd changed, too. She supposed that's what happened when you grew up. Now if she could just find a way to not also feel all the very grown-up things that deep voice of his was doing to her, not to mention the sexy-as-all-get-out grin, and those big ol' arms and chest and . . . *whew.* Yeah, she'd really appreciate it if he'd dial all that back. Like he could. She glanced at him. "We should go find Vivi."

"It's weird," he said, his serious expression at odds with the casual way he'd spoken.

She dipped her chin for a brief moment, knowing she should just get out of the truck, go find Vivi. Leave Wyatt and whatever he was about to say behind. "What's weird?" she asked, knowing she'd never truly left him behind. What made her think she could do it when he was seated not two feet away from her?

"This," he said, and she looked over at him.

She let her raised brow be her reply, then instantly regretted it when he flashed that brash, yet somehow so down-to-earth grin. Where in the hell had he gotten that from, anyway? What happened to that sweet, quiet smile of his? It hadn't been so much shy as it had been . . . pure. And definitely not packing . . . all of that. She supposed world travel had taken the quiet and pure right out of him. *So why do you want to lean closer? Why are you gripping the door handle like if you let go, you might just grab him and see where that takes you?* "We need to go find Vivi," she said again, frown firmly in place, entirely self-directed, but if it got him to drop that grin, so much the better.

She opened the door and he reached his hand out.

"Don't," she said, and shifted out of reach, hating that there was a thread of something that sounded a whole lot like panic in her voice. Knowing he'd heard it, too. She didn't panic. Not ever. Nerves of steel, that was Cheyenne McCafferty's claim to fame. She didn't need anything or anyone reminding her that losing her brother had also taken her edge. "I'm—sorry," she added. "I just—" She broke off, sighed. She might have sworn under her breath as well. She wanted to tell him not to even dare think about smiling about that, either.

Not that he'd listen to her. And he didn't. "Remember that old mason jar we used to keep?" he asked, smiling in reminiscence. "As I recall, you used to call it the goddamn swear jar."

It was as close to how he'd looked and sounded as a teenager as she'd seen since his surprising arrival, and she felt a tug so hard inside her chest, she almost pressed her hand to it.

"How much of your allowance ended up in that thing?" he said.

She didn't want to answer, didn't want to be drawn back in. She wanted to get out of this truck, get out of this . . . whatever the blazes it was Tory had gotten her into without any warning, much less her permission. "A hell of a lot more than yours," she said, then grabbed her cowboy hat from the console, and did just that.

He met her at the front of the truck, lifting his hands to prove he wasn't going to touch her when she stepped back. "That's what's weird," he said, continuing the conversation as if she hadn't just about leaped out of the truck to escape it.

"That I still swear?" she said, being deliberately obtuse. "Actually, I don't anymore. Much." She gave him a fake sunny smile. "Must be the company."

"What's weird," he persisted, "is that on the one hand, it's like we're still in the same rhythm, the way we always used to be. Like minds, and all that."

She looked to the ground, but he waited her out, and she hated feeling like a coward. *Then stop acting like one.* She looked up, met him gaze for gaze, and wished like hell it was easier. Because it wasn't. And it wasn't going to be anytime soon, either. She tried to feel annoyed that he wasn't having any such issues. He was the one who'd thrown his heart at her feet. *But you threw yours right back in those letters . . . and he didn't even bother to reply.*

And Tory wondered why she hated letter writing.

"But it's awkward, too," he said, his gaze serious once more, his words quieter. "I guess there's no way it can't be, given . . . everything. I just wanted to say . . . I know we didn't plan this, but I'm glad it happened. And not just to clear the air. It's good to see you again."

His gaze searched hers intently, for what, she couldn't say, but she wondered about it all the same.

"Really good," he added. When she didn't say anything to that, he finally looked away. He shoved his hands in his back pockets and nodded toward the gate. "Is there another way in?"

She shifted her gaze away from his stance, which was classic Wyatt, and fought the smile that rose to her lips without a single bit of approval from her. "No," she said. "Not by car, anyway."

On the one hand, she and Tory were going to have a nice long chat about surprises and Chey's utter lack of enthusiasm for them. Today's stunt had only strengthened her position. On the other hand, what was done was done, and in that regard Chey agreed with Wyatt about having the chance to clear the air. As much as they could, anyway. Beyond that—well, she didn't really want to think about anything beyond that.

She started to walk to the back of the truck, to get the rope Wyatt had asked her to bring; then she abruptly turned back to him. And suddenly all the words burst forth, before she could stop them, much less think them through. It was just, she was tired of holding it all in. Years of holding it all in. Apparently, that wasn't something she could do a moment longer.

"Yes," she said, "it's . . . surreal. That you're standing right here." She looked up at him. "You're so different now from the Wyatt I knew. We're strangers in a lot of ways, and you even look like one, so that makes it easier. But then the old you peeks out from time to time, and it really throws me." She paused then, to take a breath, and she had to look down, gather her thoughts, because it was too late to turn back now. "I know I've changed, too. I'm definitely more settled now, and I'd like to think less impulsive, more thoughtful." The corner of her mouth curled up. "This little speech notwithstanding. I'd have said 'less mouthy,' but I think I've already given the lie to that."

A hint of a smile played around the corners of his mouth, but the honest affection shining in his eyes was all there, too, loud and clear. Affection for who she'd been to him in the past, of course, but still. It rocked her already shaken-up heart. Hard. "I guess I just . . . don't know what to do with it all."

"Who says you have to do anything?" he asked.

Now she dug her hands into her front pockets, studied the toes of her boots again. She wasn't sure how to explain it to him, or if she even should. She was just having a hard time figuring out where their reunion belonged on the grand scale of, well, everything. He'd once been her everything. Her worst mistake and biggest regret had been not realizing that, not truly understanding the full meaning of who he was to her, who he could have been in her future—their future—until after he'd gone.

Now he'd just head back out, back to whatever life he was living. And she'd keep his horse. And then they . . . what? What would they do? Keep in touch? Text? E-mail? And say what? And if they didn't, how would that feel? Would she never see him or hear from him again? Was that what she wanted?

"We should go get Vivi," she repeated, because it was the only thing she could think of to say that wouldn't make this harder than it already was.

In response, he went and grabbed the rope from the back

of the truck himself, and she led them both to a trail that wound its way down to the lake about twenty yards away. A small white gazebo was set just back in the trees, marking the trailhead for a variety of paths that converged on this spot. Inside the gazebo were benches for hikers and a big signboard that held safety and local event notices as well as a laminated map of the trails, picnic areas, and the path that led down to the boat ramp and dock. She didn't need to look at any of them. She knew exactly where the lake was. The park had horse friendly trails and she'd trailered a few of her more easygoing mounts out here so she and her students could go on trail rides together.

She reached the gazebo first and paused, then turned to look at him and waited for his gaze to connect to hers. "It's good to see you, too, Wyatt." That much, at least, was true. She might not know what would happen next, but at least now she wouldn't have to wonder any longer what would happen if she ever saw him again. She tried not to think about what it would be like after he left. *It will be like it always was, with just a little less regret on the side.*

Wyatt held her gaze for a long moment, his expression unreadable now. She hated not knowing what he was thinking. She couldn't read him the way she once did. Not when he didn't want her to, anyway.

He nodded but said nothing more. He motioned to the path to their left. "Does this lead to the dock?"

She watched as he silently and swiftly tied a slipknot loop at one end of the rope. He hadn't been a calf-roper on the circuit, but they all had rope skills. And who the heck knew what he'd learned since they'd parted ways. He hadn't gone from Clark Kent to Superman sitting around doing nothing. "If you're thinking you can lasso the boat or its passenger and tow them in, I hate to tell you, but I wasn't kidding about the size of the lake."

"Ye of little faith," was all he said, sending a brief flash of that new smile of his and a wink her way. He expertly coiled the rope and slung it over one shoulder, then motioned for her to lead the way and followed behind her.

What's with the winking? The Wyatt Reed she'd known didn't do things like that. His quietly keen observations about people and the world around them, along with the surprising discovery of his dry sense of humor, were the qualities that had initially drawn her in. That he was also thoughtful, respectful, and kind to animals had decimated her last resistance to his quiet but repeated and determined attempts to start a conversation with her. Like Tory, only nothing at all like Tory, he'd found his way in, and he'd stuck. He'd become her best and closest friend. She'd only trusted her brother more than Wyatt.

This guy, with his smooth wink and flashy grins, was nothing like the boy she remembered. She supposed that getting away from Zachariah, from the physical and emotional blows, the undermining of every last thing Wyatt had ever said or done, would have given anyone a new lease on life. Wyatt appeared to have taken that new lease and run with it. Hard.

The minute Chey stepped from the wooded trail to the first overlook, Vivi started waving. Waving with her lemon-colored, tassel-edged parasol. "Oh boy," Chey muttered, even as she lifted a hand to give a short wave in response, so Vivi would know they saw her. *Like we could miss her.*

Chey could hear Vivi shouting something to them, but she was too far away to be able to make out anything of what the older woman was trying to convey. The breeze off the lake snatched most of the words away. *Other than she really is up a lake without a paddle.* A smile twitched the corners of Chey's mouth. Any other time, once she'd established that Vivi was fine and unhurt, she'd have found the humor in pretty much every part of this. If she could just get the rest of herself to calm the heck down, stop reacting to every little thing Wyatt said or did—*like breathing*—she might have shared that comment with him.

"The docks are down the path that way," Chey said instead, pointing to a tree-lined path that obscured the view of the water. "The dock on this side is fairly short. The nature center staff uses it to tie up the few paddleboats they rent out on weekends in the summer. The canoes and johnboats are pulled up on the banks at night, but they'd all still be in storage now, I guess." Which begged the question of just where Vivi had gotten the boat. "You'll be at water level, but frankly, you won't be any closer to Vivi down there since she's all the way at this end of the lake, so I'm not sure how you—"

She broke off as Wyatt was already loping down the path toward the dock.

"Okay then," Chey said, starting off down the path as well. "You do you." She refused to run after him. Until she heard the loud splash. Then she picked up speed. The path had curved back into the trees enough that, with the new spring foliage, she'd already lost her view of Vivi. "Please just stay in the dang boat," Chey muttered.

She could only imagine Vivi's reaction to seeing who'd come to her rescue. Chey didn't even want to think about what would be involved in explaining who Wyatt was and why he was there in the first place. Vivi knew Chey as well as anyone on earth ever had. The fearsome foursome were closer than most families, tighter than sisters, despite the generational gaps in their ages. They'd shared every last thing with each other as they'd worked their way through the most difficult time they'd each ever experienced. *Almost everything.* Chey hadn't told them about Wyatt. Well, Hannah knew now, but that was only because Chey had been trying to keep her from making the biggest mistake of her life.

Hannah, Avery, and Vivienne were her family now and more important to Chey than she'd ever allowed anyone to become who wasn't related to her by blood. Not even Tory. Anyone except for Wyatt Reed. She tried not to think about where that had gotten her. She was older now, wiser, and the three women whom she trusted with her love were the same three women Chey trusted with her very soul. They wouldn't just ride off into the proverbial sunset with her shattered heart lying on the ground in pieces. *Whose heart again, Chey? Yours? Or his?*

Ignoring that question, she picked up speed, running by the time she hit the first dock, then had to do a quick two-step around Wyatt's boots, and his shirt, to keep from tripping over them and landing in the lake herself. Once she'd steadied herself, she looked out across the lake and saw he was already halfway to the boat.

"When did you learn to swim?" she wondered out loud. Chey, Tory, and Wyatt had a broader than average set of skills from their unique life, but swimming was not one of them. Not for Wyatt at any rate. Indeed, Chey knew for a fact he hadn't known how to swim. Not when they were kids, at any rate. They'd been thirteen and fourteen the summer they'd found a rope swing over a lake outside a town where the rodeo caravan had parked for a weeklong stay. It had been a sticky hot August in Oklahoma and that cool, serene surface had beckoned them like the promise of nirvana.

She and Tory hadn't wasted a second making good use of that knotted length of heavy rope. Wyatt had hung back, making lame excuses about having forgotten he had something to do. Cody had been the one who'd finally gotten

Wyatt to confide that he couldn't swim. Cody had offered to teach him, but Wyatt had opted out. Chey always suspected it had something to do with his father, though even so, she couldn't imagine what he had against swimming.

"Clearly that's changed." She was unable to look away as she watched him cleave through the choppy, windswept surface with the grace and speed of an Olympic swimmer. The rope was still looped over his head and shoulder, held against his chest and back by the force of the speed with which he was cutting across the lake. The water had to be pretty damn cold. They'd had some warm days, but the nights were still brisk.

Chey tried and failed not to notice his arms. As a teenager, Wyatt had sported lean, ropy muscles at best. Now they were sleek, and full and cut, like a man who used his body—all parts of it—to get through his day-to-day existence. And don't get her started on his shoulders. Or his back. *Jesus, Wyatt. What in the hell have you been doing?*

He pulled up next to the boat and treaded water, tossing his wet hair back as he gestured with one hand, apparently giving directions to Vivi. Even from the dock, Chey could see Vivi's delight in the sudden change in her circumstances. Chey found herself smiling, despite her annoyance. She didn't even know why she was annoyed. Wyatt had gone the extra mile and then some for a woman he didn't even know.

She watched as he made quick work of tying the loose end of the rope through the loop on the front end of the small flat boat. He hung the rest of the rope over the prow, then took off across the lake behind the boat. Chey frowned, confused, until she saw him lift a paddle from where it had floated away. He headed back to the boat, stowed it flat over the two bench seats, then took off again in a different direction, presumably after the other one.

Wyatt motioned Vivi to scoot to the center of the bench and stowed the second oar across the benches on that side, all without getting Vivi's somewhat insane—to Chey's eyes—outfit even the least bit damp. *What on earth was Vivi doing out there, and in that getup?*

Chey and Vivi watched, with varying degrees of delight—okay, the delight was pretty much all Vivi's—as Wyatt began to swim back to the dock, towing the boat behind him with the rope.

As the boat neared, Chey noted that the fringed, lemon-yellow parasol looked right at home with Vivi's lavender-streaked, upswept do, complete with ringlets framing her face. The boat was still a distance away, but Chey assumed Vivi's makeup would be stage-perfect, and possibly as over the top as the abundantly lacy, poufy-sleeved ivory blouse she had on. *She must have made that herself,* Chey thought. No self-respecting boutique in Blue Hollow Falls—heck, all of Virginia—carried something like that. Vivi looked as if she was getting ready to audition for *Mary Poppins Meets Oklahoma: the Musical.* Chey didn't even want to know what was going on with the getup from the waist down. From the boat to the outfit, to the fringed parasol, the whole situation was bizarre. Vivi was theatrical, but even for her, this was a bit much.

Chey went to the end of the dock and knelt down just in time to catch the end of the rope when Wyatt tossed it to her. She pulled the small flat-bottom boat the rest of the way in and tied it off. Wyatt climbed the short wooden ladder affixed to the side of the dock and immediately went to grab his shirt. She could see the gooseflesh on his skin. "Why would you go shirtless? It's freezing in there."

"This wasn't going to keep me any warmer in the water,"

he said as he tugged the shirt back on. "I figured it would do better warming me back up when I was done."

She almost commented on the fact that he'd left his pants on, then immediately thought better of that. "I've got blankets in the work box in the back of my truck," she told him. "If I'd known you were going to go all Tarzan on us, I'd have brought one along."

"Thanks," he told her, his tone and smile both on the wry side.

Chey couldn't help but notice how his shirt clung to his damp skin as he knelt down and helped her position the boat next to the ladder. How was it possible that this look was even sexier than his bare chest had been?

Wyatt climbed down a rung and offered his hand to Vivi. "Your three-hour tour has concluded, Mrs. Howell," Wyatt said, and Chey snorted a laugh at the *Gilligan's Island* reference.

"Why, thank you, kind sir," Vivi said, beaming as if she'd just taken a bow for her second curtain call. "However, I believe I would be closer to a Ginger, don't you think?" She closed her parasol and handed it up to Chey.

"Indeed," Wyatt said. "Now that you're not hiding behind that parasol, the resemblance is striking."

Vivi giggled like a schoolgirl and allowed him to help her up the ladder. Once she was standing steadily on the dock, in the laced-up, heeled boots she apparently thought made great boat shoes, Vivi was almost as tall as Wyatt. And though her figure might be a tad more matronly than it once was, she still carried herself with the elegant bearing of the dancer she'd been.

Eat your heart out, Ginger, Chey thought with a smile.

Vivi took her parasol back and carefully opened it once more. "I love that the sun has returned," she said, then added in a teasing tone, "but we fashion models can never be too careful about protecting our fair skin."

"It appears you were a front-runner in figuring that out if your luminous beauty is anything to judge by," Wyatt rejoined without missing a beat.

Chey rolled her eyes even as Vivi laughed gaily. "Well," she said, taking in her rescuer with a bold once-over. "I could say the sun looks quite good on you."

It was only then Chey recalled that Wyatt had been rather tan all over. She abruptly turned and started toward the shore, because that's what it took to keep her from checking out the waistband of his pants to find out if she was right about assuming there was no tan line. *Tarzan, indeed.*

"Are you going to stroll off and not introduce us properly?" Vivi called out, her tone filled with humor rather than chiding. As if she knew. *Of course she did.*

Chey turned and walked a few steps back. "Of course. I'm sorry. I thought you'd taken care of that boat-side. I was going to grab that blanket." *And cover up the eye candy.*

Vivi's eyes danced with mirth and Chey knew she hadn't been fooling anyone. Chey's mouth kicked up at the corners, because at some point you just had to own it and roll with it. "Wyatt, please meet my partner in farming and one of the dearest people in the world to me, Vivienne Baudin."

Vivi's expression melted, filling with love and affection. She lifted her fingertips to her still perfectly painted lips and sent an air kiss in Chey's direction, then turned and extended that hand to Wyatt, palm facing downward, fingers curled just so, of course. Chey was only surprised Vivi wasn't wearing white gloves, given the rest of the getup. *Probably couldn't get them to fit over all those rings,* she thought, but not unkindly. Vivi was a living, breathing force of nature. With all her flamboyance, she was the opposite of

Chey at every turn, and Chey wouldn't have her dear friend any other way.

"Vivienne Baudin, formerly of New Orleans via Broadway," Vivi said to Wyatt, commanding the dock as if it were a stage. Everything for Vivi was a stage, if she wanted it to be. "And who you would be, my dear Good Samaritan?"

"This is Wyatt Reed," Chey said, before Wyatt could respond. "We knew each other growing up. He was on the circuit with Cody and me. Oh, and Tory has also arrived today. Surprise," she added faintly.

Vivi's smile grew wider still as she looked from Wyatt to Chey, then back to Wyatt. "Sounds like a veritable rodeo reunion back at the farm."

Chey had talked with her three partners about the offer she'd made to Tory. They'd all been enthusiastic about meeting her childhood friend and giving Tory a chance to find her place in Blue Hollow Falls. Chey knew part of their excitement was due to her being the least chatty of the bunch when it had come to sharing stories of their past lives. It wasn't that she'd had anything to hide. The truth of it was, actually, that the reason she hadn't offered up her share of anecdotes was because they all featured the man presently standing on the dock next to her.

A look in Wyatt's direction caught him glancing at her at the same time. Their gazes held there for a second, and she swore he read her mind, or at least her reluctance. A slight dip of the chin and a brief, reassuring smile made it clear that her secrets, at least as they pertained to him—to them—were safe.

It was those moments, that sudden yet seemingly effortless return to the connection they'd once shared, that disconcerted her the most. It took nothing more than a glance, a look, to communicate volumes. She didn't like feeling shaken, but she couldn't seem to find level ground around him. She knew she should just accept Wyatt's presence as another thing happening, like Tory showing up early.

Except this wasn't at all like Tory showing up early. This was Wyatt. She wasn't ready for that. For him. For all the things she'd felt back then . . . and didn't want to feel now.

A glance back at Vivi showed the older woman studying the two of them openly, which was pure Vivi. She was wonderfully colorful, bold, and direct, and took care of those she called her own. If Chey knew her, and she did, Vivi had already surmised that there was a good deal of history between Chey and Wyatt. What Vivi planned to do about that was what worried Chey. Vivi's heart was always in the right place, but Chey wasn't sure she wanted to be her next fix-it project. She and Wyatt didn't need fixing. He'd be gone soon enough.

"A real pleasure to meet you," Wyatt said, taking Vivi's hand and lifting it for a quick kiss to those delicately curled fingers.

Vivi put on a bit of a swoon—maybe only partly a put-on—then glanced at Chey. "If this is what rodeo life was like, you've been holding out on us, darling."

Chey laughed at that. "Oh, cowboys can be charming, no doubt about it." She left it at that and turned to Wyatt. "You have to be freezing. The box in the back of my truck is unlocked if you want to go grab that blanket." She tossed him the keys, which he snagged easily. "Why don't you go ahead and get in the cab and get warm. I'll see Vivi to her car and meet you back there."

Wyatt took his cue and swept a quick bow in Vivi's direction. "Glad to be of service, Miss Ginger. It was a pleasure meeting you." He nodded to the boat, then winked at her. "Next time, use the oarlocks."

"And miss out on another fine rescue?" Vivi smiled. "But have no fear, there won't be a next time." She smoothed the ringlets that framed her cheeks, despite the fact that even the breeze coming across the water hadn't so much as lifted a single hair on her well-coiffed head. "It was poor judgment on my part that I came out here at all. That's on me. I learned long ago to avoid making the same mistake twice." Her quick smile was dazzling as she shot a wink right back at him. "Gives me more time to make new ones, don't you know."

Chey was struck once again by how beautiful a woman Vivi truly was. She'd seen black and white photos of Vivi at the height of her Broadway showgirl days, but even they paled in comparison to the live, in color version standing before her now, no matter the decades that had passed.

"Why did you come out here?" Chey asked her. She'd intended to wait for the two of them to be alone to get the full story, but the question was out before she could put it on pause. "You suddenly wanted to go boating? All by yourself?" Chey didn't really take the outfit into consideration. It was over the top, even by Vivi standards, but the woman didn't so much as brew tea in the morning without "putting her face on" as she called it. "And how in the world did you get the boat out here? The road to the ramp is closed."

"Well, I don't think she got all gussied up to go boating by herself," Wyatt pointed out, sending another wink to Vivi.

Chey noted that Vivi's cheeks turned a bit pink at that. Blushing? Seen-it-all, done-even-more Vivi? At least Chey wasn't the only one being affected by new-and-improved-Wyatt. The old one had turned her head quite well as it was.

"And seeing as this is none of my business," Wyatt added, "I'll head to the truck and take you up on the offer of that blanket and some heat." He'd already pulled on his boots.

"I try not to be a foolish old woman," Vivi said, all her colorful airs aside now. "But admittedly I was one today."

Chey found herself glancing again at Wyatt, who was glancing at her. Again. It was how they used to be, when talking to someone, silently communicating to each other while letting the other person say their piece. Instead of looking away, his lips twitched up at the corners, an admission that he recognized what they'd done, too. Out of habit.

Surely habits had an expiration date, Chey thought stubbornly. *And yet, here the two of you are, staring at each other.*

Chey pointedly turned back to Vivi, who hadn't missed the interplay. "I'm sure whatever prompted your outing, you had nothing but the best intentions," Chey said in sincere support, and because it was undoubtedly true.

Vivi snorted at that. "I don't think Paul Hammond would share the lofty opinion you have of me." Her smile spread to a grin, and a devilish twinkle sparked in her eyes. "At least not until he dries out a bit."

Chey immediately looked right back at Wyatt, brows lifted, then jerked her gaze directly back to Vivi, her frown self-directed. "Paul Hammond? As in the guy who owns a good part of Blue Hollow Falls? Why would you have a meeting with him out here? On a boat? You're not a boat person. A yacht person, maybe. I'm guessing it was his then?"

At least that explained how the boat had gotten down to the water. Hammond had enough money that he could have airlifted the thing in if he'd wanted to. More likely, he had a key to the padlock on the security gate blocking the road to the boat ramp. He was known to stay in close contact with the town officials and often golfed with the mayor. Chey had never met him, but the rumor was he liked to grease the wheels to expedite whatever his latest project was.

"I don't think it was a meeting," Wyatt offered quietly, with a smile of support directed at Vivi. "So much as a . . . social engagement."

Chey's mouth opened, then closed again, as she tried to process that possibility. The only person less likely to go on a date than herself was Vivienne. The older woman had made it abundantly clear from the time the four of them had met, more than a half dozen years ago now, that she'd had her share of true love and had tired of the company of the opposite sex. The man she'd loved for the better part of her life had bequeathed her the very farm they all lived and worked on.

Chey, along with Hannah and Avery, thought it was losing Harold that had ended Vivi's willingness to put her heart up for grabs again. Coming to terms with that loss was what had sent her to the grief counseling meeting that fateful afternoon when the four of them had first met.

Chey didn't want to examine too closely the reason why her own heart hadn't been in play for, oh, a dozen years or so, so she focused on Vivi. "So, a date?" she asked, her curiosity sincere. "I didn't even know you were thinking about that."

"I guess we don't share all of our nooks and crannies with each other," Vivi said with a smile directed at Chey. Vivi never bothered with being subtle. Her gaze shifted to Wyatt, then back to Chey, one perfectly penciled brow arched for emphasis.

Now it was Chey's turn to feel a bit of warmth in her cheeks. "That was my former life," Chey said. "This is happening now. I'm sure we all have stories we haven't shared."

"None of the big ones, I'd wager," Vivi said, not having to look at Wyatt this time.

Chey didn't bother trying to defend her omission or pretend that Wyatt wasn't a big story from her past. But he was from the past. Vivi dating again was very much a story set in the present. "How did you and Paul Hammond come about?"

Vivi lifted a shoulder in an elegant shrug, something only she could pull off with the profusion of pouf and frill she was sporting. "I honestly wasn't thinking about dating," she said. "I'm still not. We were both at that joint meeting Mayor Fielding held with the town council and the chamber of commerce." She smiled. "We were arguing about a proposal on how to grow the town revenue. I was arguing that we needed to find a way to honor the land, and not just build more things . . . and Paul asked me out here to see the lake, to prove a point. I demurred, because I really didn't want to sit in the middle of a lake with the sun refracting off the water and onto my skin. He upped the ante until it somehow turned into a champagne picnic lunch, and I thought, why not? Worst case, it's a nice diversion for an afternoon." She laughed at that. "I did get that part right. It was indeed diverting."

"And . . . the outfit?" Chey asked. "Was that like, part of a dare?"

"Oh hush," Vivi said, but the mischief in her eyes spoke the truth of it. "Okay," she relented when faced with Chey's patient gaze. "He might have made a few less than kind comments as to my, shall we say, flamboyant style. So I thought I might goad him a little by showing up for our 'date' in full stage regalia." She laughed. "Honestly, I didn't view it as a date so much as a comeuppance. He can be charming, but at core, he's not a pleasant man."

Chey smiled with her, but she was also worried for her friend. Vivi was smart, sharp, and had no problem holding her own, but she hadn't been in the dating world for quite some time. Then something else Vivi had said popped back to mind. "Wait, did you say 'after he dries out'?" Chey's eyebrows narrowed. "I'm assuming you don't mean he had too much champagne."

When Vivi merely smoothed a nonexistent wisp of hair from her forehead, unapologetic mirth brimming in her expression, Chey found herself once again looking at Wyatt, as if for confirmation that she wasn't wrong in assuming Vivi was saying what they both knew she was saying.

"Man overboard?" Wyatt prompted.

"In so many words," Vivi said, then twirled her parasol, making Chey splutter a laugh after her mouth had dropped wide open.

"What did he do?" Chey wanted to know, worry creeping back in once the shock wore off. She frowned and closed the distance between them. "Are you okay? Did he—"

Vivi's expression sobered some then as she waved off the question. "He . . . drew some inappropriate conclusions, regarding my former occupation on stage, and that's all I'll say. I'm perfectly fine."

Chey nodded, accepting her friend's discretion, but that didn't stop her from worrying. "And so you, what, invited him to swim back to shore?" She tried to imagine Vivienne telling the wealthiest man in Blue Hollow Falls to take a dive, and him actually doing it. What on earth could he have said or done for that to be the only option? And one he'd taken, apparently. Then another thought occurred to her. "Wait, did you . . . you didn't push him over, did you? Not that he wouldn't have deserved it for . . . whatever it was he said or did, but—"

"Let's just say money doesn't buy class," Vivi said. "I found him to be somewhat insulting. No, make that highly insulting. So, I asked him to return us to shore. He thought he could cajole his way back into my good graces." She smiled evenly. "He discovered he was mistaken."

"And . . . he just jumped overboard and swam back to shore because you politely asked him to?" Chey wouldn't have pressed, but she decided she needed to know the particulars, because she doubted someone of Hammond's stature in the community, not to mention his very deep pockets, was going to take an embarrassment such as this without some pushback, be it verbal or legal. Likely both. Chey wanted to have some idea what they might be up against.

"Actually, he might have had a bit of, shall we say, extra encouragement." She closed her parasol, aimed it at the dock, and pushed a hidden button on the handle. A long, slender blade popped out of the other end.

Chey was so surprised by the maneuver, she took a quick step back and was saved from going off the dock entirely by Wyatt's quick reflexes. He caught her by the elbow and propelled her forward. Right up close and into his personal space. Not intentionally, but intentions didn't matter. Her body's immediate reaction to said personal space did.

"Thanks," she said, then eased away from him and turned to look at the umbrella more closely while she pulled herself back together.

"One of my favorite props, kept from Broadway days," Vivi said, somewhat cheerfully, before zipping the blade right back into the umbrella tip. "I never thought I'd have reason to use the thing. Honestly, though, the joke was also on me. If I was hoping to make a bit of public spectacle, that backfired." She gestured to their surroundings. "You need an actual public to make that happen. And he did make his point, which was that this beautiful park and lake have become a drain rather than a draw for the town. Even so, I've been trying to dissuade the town fathers from the path they want to take, the one Paul proposed. But as one of only three female chamber of commerce members, and the only one who has been attending recent meetings, I've realized that they're a good old boys club with little respect for women entrepreneurs. Or women in general, I'd say."

"Maybe you need to take your parasol there to the next council meeting," Wyatt said.

"I'm tempted," Vivi replied. "As it stands, Addie Pearl, Hattie Beauchamp, and I are the only female members. All women of a certain age who were raised to understand the importance of civic engagement. What I need is for more of the women who run their own businesses—young and old— which account for over half of the artisans at the mill, to show up to these things. Addie's been trying, but honestly, I think she's grown weary of being outnumbered and out-maneuvered and has turned her energies to trying to improve the town directly through growing the artisans' guild and making a success of the mill. And she's doing a great job. Hattie is there when she can be, but running that restaurant doesn't always allow her to attend at the times Mayor Field-ing schedules these things. We need to make our voices heard in greater numbers—all the business owners, men and women—so loudly that we're taken more seriously by those old boys. As well we should since it is our endeavors that are the driving force behind the current revenue stream."

"And aye, there's the rub," Chey said, as the big picture became clearer.

Vivi nodded. "The mill and the new music center have been an overwhelming success. The wedding venue Seth added to his winery, the cidery Mabry's family is building to go along with his apple farm, and our farm, new as it is, are all doing well and bringing in much needed tourism revenue, but they aren't drawing people to the other, older town amenities."

"Meaning the services owned by most of those good old

boys," Chey said. "Like Tremaine's tax and accounting, Larry Moyes's dry cleaner. Winston's jewelry store."

"The bank, the mercantile, the hardware store," Vivi added, nodding. "Yes, yes, and yes. And that's definitely a big motivator for them in their decision-making process, though they claim, of course, that they are there to serve the needs of all the citizens of Blue Hollow Falls, not simply themselves." She sighed. "But I look around out here and it's hard to deny they have a point about the park being a liability rather than an asset. I know it's not peak season, but according to the council, this place used to be a draw year-round, and they have the photos to prove it. The nature center is always a draw, but the mayor said they've had to close it for the past three winters. Used to be folks wanted the local photographers to come take pictures here for weddings, family Easter portraits this time of year when everything is in bloom." She gestured with her hand. "You can see that is no longer the case. Not even a random hiker came through here today, and these are supposed to be world class trails. Some go all the way up to Hawk's Nest Ridge, but the town has let maintaining them go by the wayside and they're not properly marked any longer. There aren't enough park rangers to make hiking in the back country between the lake and the ridge safe anyway, from what I hear."

"The park and trails, the lake, aren't really a huge revenue stream for the area, though, are they?" Chey said. "Except for renting paddleboats and such, access is free, right?"

Vivi looked back to them and nodded. "Yes, it is, and no, it's not directly a revenue stream, but it's always been a solid indicator of tourism. And the council is saying that the lack of people coming out here to enjoy the lake area is part of what's negatively impacting the town."

"Because that means fewer people shopping and otherwise using the town amenities."

Vivi nodded. "The population of Blue Hollow Falls, in and of itself, isn't big enough to support all those businesses. It doesn't help that a lot of the locals go down to Turtle Springs and do their shopping there. Combine that with the fact that most of the tourists spend time out at the winery, our farm, the mill, and don't go into the town proper at all, and you can see the problem. So, now the council is saying that not only is it not worth spending tax dollars to maintain the park, but that there might be a better use for the land."

"Better use?" Chey said in disbelief. "Like what?" She gestured. "It's a lake. It's not like you can get rid of it."

"What is Hammond proposing?" Wyatt lifted a hand. "If you don't mind my asking."

Vivi frowned. "He thinks we should sell off this property to a big, fancy resort developer who has shown interest." She sighed. "Interest that came, I am certain, because Hammond courted it." She looked out over the lake. "I know I may seem like an odd champion, given I spent my life in sequins and feathers, and, even now, my idea of enjoying the great outdoors is standing on the porch of my house looking out over it." She turned back to face them. "But it's not just about this park. It's about the mindset of those who want to shift the focus of the town to attracting, bigger, broader commercial interests. In just the few years we've been here, I have come to know the people of Blue Hollow Falls, what they do, what they love. What we've already started building, and what Seth, Mabry, and the folks at the mill and music center are building, all of that respects the land, this place. Not corporate bottom lines and greed-motivated land grabs. Which is exactly what it will become if they start to sell out. It's what Turtle Springs is fighting against now, and losing from the looks of it."

"What is this mill, the music center?" Wyatt asked.

"One of the founding families of the Falls owned and operated a silk mill up here over a century or so ago," Chey told him.

Wyatt's eyebrows lifted. "Silk mill. As in silk fabric silk?"

She nodded. "Long history of silk production in the mid-Atlantic region back when these were colonies, not states. Anyway, the mill had long since fallen out of use when corn, cotton, tobacco, and in this area, apples became more profitable crops. A few years ago, the locals—led by Addie Pearl, who owns a chunk of the mill, and who had spent years cultivating this area as the perfect community for artisans—renovated the mill and turned it into a home for the Bluebird Guild members. The guild Addie started years ago. The various craftsmen and women, artists, and the like, had, up to then, operated separately from their own properties or small commercial spaces in town. Hannah, one of the partners out at our lavender farm, is a member of the guild. She's a painter and has had showings at the mill."

"It has, by any measure, been a success," Vivi said, picking up the story. "But it's not just the mill. The winery owner out near us that I mentioned, Seth Brogan, married a well-known folk singer from Ireland, and she instigated and funded the building of the music center, which includes an amphitheater and stage big enough to put on a variety of different productions. It's right next to the mill, which is set with the falls as its backdrop. Pippa—Seth's wife—recently added a recording studio to their winery property, and more and more musicians are coming in, from all over the world, to record there. Now they also have a wedding venue, which launches officially this summer."

"It sounds like a really vibrant, active community," Wyatt said. "Don't you think if you explained what's going on, the new business owners would join the chamber of commerce, or show up at the town council meetings?"

She nodded. "Possibly, in the future, but that takes time, and I'm afraid this is all moving far too quickly for them to make much of an impact now."

"Sounds like you all need to come together to brainstorm ways to help everyone out," Wyatt said. "Give the mayor and the council an alternate plan."

"I think I know the one person who could pull this together," Chey said, a smile creasing her face. "And she might turn the tide all on her own. Addie Pearl. Have you told her what's going on? About the resort proposal? No way would she take that news sitting down."

Vivi nodded. "You're absolutely right. If anyone can get things organized, it's Addie. No, I don't believe she knows. The council just introduced the proposal this week, and I haven't talked to her personally about it. The problem is, it was presented as a fait accompli. Hammond has everything lined up. All the council has to do is say yes and all the mayor has to do is sign the contracts. The whole project has quite obviously been in the works behind the scenes for some time. And I can guarantee you that Hammond has the majority council vote locked up." She smirked. "Paul made sure to mention that he golfs regularly with three of them and how well they've done investing in his properties. Hammond recently got another invite to join Paul's very exclusive country club out in Valley View. Four votes gives him the majority." She sighed. "The mayor could overrule the vote, or table it, but it might be too late. This solution solves too many problems at once."

"But opens the door to the eventual complete ruin of what makes Blue Hollow Falls special," Chey said. "They're thinking short term. Can't someone get the mayor to see the big picture? We have to at least try." Chey paced the short width of the dock. "Hannah and Will could talk to Sawyer. He owns another chunk of the mill," she told Wyatt. "They, along with Seth and Pippa, can get Mabry and his daughter on board. Addie will mobilize the guild members. We could have them all out to the farm and organize our thoughts, draw up a plan of action."

Vivi nodded and a spark of renewed energy replaced the note of defeat that had entered her voice. "That's exactly the right approach." She let out a short sigh. "I still worry that none of that is going to match up to Paul and his deep pockets and council influence. And my little stunt out here didn't help matters any."

"I don't know," Chey said, considering. "He must view you as something of a threat if he thought he needed to wine and dine you to his way of thinking."

"Are you saying you don't think it was my natural beauty and witty insouciance that led to his rather ardent pursuit of me?" Vivi twirled her parasol and batted her perfectly applied false eyelashes.

"Reign it in, Ginger," Chey said with a laugh. "I'm saying that while he might have been drawn to you personally— and who wouldn't be—I'm betting there was more to his pursuit than merely getting you to go on a date. He wanted to charm you and silence the opposition at the same time. Kind of a killing two birds with one stone kind of thing."

"So, you're saying he's a player," Vivi concluded, causing Wyatt and Chey to look at each other with a splutter of laughter.

"Yes," Chey said. "That would be the appropriate term. Only in this case he's not just playing the field; he wants to own the field it's being played on."

"You know, I might be able to help with that," Wyatt said thoughtfully.

Surprised, Chey turned to him. "How?" she asked, sincerely curious.

He smiled then, and it was a mix of the old Wyatt and the new, both of whom packed a punch. "Let's just say, I know a few people, too."

Chapter Four

Wyatt hadn't intended to have dinner with Chey, much less the rest of her newly collected family. Of course, he hadn't intended to offer himself up as a possible solution to their local development issues, either. *But here you are.*

Vivi had insisted he join them that evening before they'd even left the parking lot, telling Chey she expected Victoria to join them as well. In truth, he had no other immediate plans. He'd thought he was coming to Virginia to get his horse. Tory had told him she already had a place set up for Buttercup, which had been the truth. Just not the entire truth. He'd assumed that would take some time and hadn't made specific departure plans. Yet.

When Tory had tracked him down, he'd just been wrapping up production on his Nepal adventure. He was planning to head back to his croft near Mount Snowdon in Wales for postproduction and to plan out his next trip. He'd had several interesting offers from rural municipalities ranging from Africa to the Arctic Circle to one of the islands in the South Pacific kingdom of Tonga. Each one represented an opportunity to bring attention not only to the unique culture and challenge of an area, but, specifically, a targeted natural treasure, be it flora, fauna, or local topography that was under some kind of threat. For some, the threat was a naturally occurring ecological or environmental issue, but most often it was a direct threat from mankind.

He hadn't green-lighted any of them as the focus of his next livestream series. He had time to do more research and decide, as he had plenty of work to do organizing, editing, and repackaging the mass of videos from the Nepal adventure. He'd be putting the footage into a more traditional documentary form than usual, so the work he was doing could have a longer lasting impact. He'd blocked out several months for that, though the truth was, he could get it done sooner. He'd decided he wanted some time to step back, let the spotlight go dark for a bit. It had been a good while since he'd simply sat and let himself be.

He knew it was a risk with the current mentality of more-more-more, now-now-now, but he'd worked hard to amass the subscribers and followers he had. In the past few years, he'd grown his platform to a point where he'd been able to set up distribution for the permanent, hard-copy content he was now creating as a result of those livestream productions. The income from those sales paid the bills and provided full-time employment to a few core crew members. All the funding they raised went to covering their expedition expenses and directly supporting the causes they were trying to help.

He loved what he was doing, was excited about the new opportunities he was creating for himself and others, utilizing new media to draw attention to little known, but important issues.

All told, though, he'd been going nonstop for longer than he could recall. Too long. He pulled Tory's truck into the circular drive that fronted the main house on the Lavender Blue farm and parked there, as he'd been asked to do. He folded his arms on the steering wheel and took in the place. From this vantage point, he could see it all, from the main house to the stables and Chey's house, the lavender fields, and then the higher peaks of the Blue Ridge Mountains, more rounded with age than their rugged, western counterparts, but equally majestic in their own right.

He could help Chey, help this place keep its focus on the environment; that was what had drawn folks to settle there in the first place. He wasn't against growth. Development had its place in all types of societies. The key was making sure that the development was thoughtful, that it enhanced rather than diminished a place. His work shone a spotlight on the individuality of a place, with an eye to preserving it and caring for those who called it home. Man, beast, and plant life. He grinned, shook his head, and climbed out of the truck. It surely wouldn't be his most exotic location, but his followers had come to trust him. He could make it all work.

The beautiful oak and stained glass front door to the main house opened and Tory stepped out on the porch and waved, then started down the steps and across the yard toward him. He wondered what she'd think of his idea. It was obvious Tory hadn't clued Chey in to what he did for a living, but perhaps she would now. He and Tory had kept in sporadic touch since she'd first tracked him down to tell him about Cody; she followed him online and knew what he was about. Professionally speaking, anyway. Technically, he'd been the sporadic one. Tory was nothing if not a champion communicator. But the nature of his work filled in most of the gaps he hadn't.

At first, connecting with her had made him more than a little leery. Zachariah was dead and buried by the time Tory had contacted him, but even then, he hadn't felt comfortable reestablishing old ties. Mostly because it closed too many links in the chain between where he was and wherever Chey had ended up. Tory had kept her friendship with Chey and him separate, but apparently even she had her limits.

"There you are. Was wondering if you'd gone off on yet another wild adventure somewhere and lost your way back." Her expression was unreadable. Very unlike Victoria.

He opened the door and got out, leaving the bags from his errand runs on the seat of the truck. "Something happen? I thought dinner wasn't till seven." He checked his watch, which was also a compass, odometer, elevation register, and kept time in four countries. Plus, wearing one was old school, and he kind of liked that. It was only a little past five, eastern standard time in the US. He glanced back at Tory. "Sorry if you needed the truck. I didn't know."

"The things you don't know could fill volumes," she said, making him frown.

"What's wrong?"

"Chey's gone."

He'd turned to reach into the cab to grab the bag containing some rudimentary toiletries; he'd inadvertently packed his own in the bags that had gone on to Wales with his crew. He'd showered and changed in the loft Tory was moving into, but didn't want to impose any more than he had to. At Tory's surprise announcement, he immediately turned back. "What do you mean, gone?"

"Two of her rescues—horses—needed to be looked at by the local vet. Nothing serious, but now that she has her trailer back, apparently she decided it couldn't wait another day, so off she went. She told Vivi not to hold dinner for her." Tory had said that last bit rather pointedly. "I knew she wasn't going to be happy with me, pulling this little scheme, but I never figured her for a runner." She looked directly at Wyatt. "Did you two talk things out? Did it not go well?" She folded her arms.

Wyatt had to resist the urge to smile, knowing that likely

wouldn't go over well at the moment. It was just that he'd forgotten how much he liked Tory. Years off the competition circuit hadn't dimmed her focused determination one bit. He wasn't keen on being the target of said focus at the moment, but it brought back good memories. "So . . . she's gone to run an errand? Aren't you being a little overly dramatic?"

"She's not going to be here for dinner," Tory repeated, as if that explained everything.

"Does that mean I'm uninvited?" he asked, thinking maybe it was just as well. If Chey was absenting herself now after the conversation the three of them had had at the lake, then she clearly wasn't up for him sticking his nose into her business, which was a completely legitimate beef. Though she might have simply told him that.

"Of course not. Vivi extended the invite, not Chey. My point is—" She broke off, threw her hands up, then let out what sounded like a strangled shout of frustration.

"What is your point, Tory?" Wyatt asked, quietly this time. He realized now where all this angst was coming from. He wasn't too happy about it, but that frustration would have to get in line behind all the other things he wasn't too keen on at the moment. "What exactly did you think was going to happen when you surprised the two of us that way?"

"I thought you'd both act like adults," she shot back, but he could see his rather pointed comment had hit home.

"We have," he told her. "Despite the fact that we didn't ask for this and had absolutely zero time to prepare ourselves for it."

"Well, you were never going to find each other if I didn't do something," she said, arms crossed again now. But her defensive tone was matched by a look of regret in her eyes.

"That doesn't mean you get to choose," he said, gently this time.

She blew out a long breath and let her hands drop helplessly to her sides. "It just seems ridiculous for the two of you to not reestablish the wonderful friendship you once had."

"Did you ever stop to think there might be a good reason why that friendship ended?" he asked, his tone dry now. He wasn't angry, or even upset, really, but he did think she ought to consider her actions.

"Of course I have," she told him, surprising him with her straightforward response.

"And without knowing why, you—" He stopped. "Or has Chey—"

"No, she hasn't." She walked closer and leaned against the side of the truck, her defenses down now. "It's been a challenge, maintaining a friendship with you, and separately with Chey, and not being able to even talk about one to the other, to share stories, or . . . any of it. But that's what I signed on for when I tracked you both down. I realize you didn't come looking for me."

"Tory—" he said, feeling chastened.

She raised a hand, halting his response. "This isn't a pity party. My point is, I needed the two of you. I wanted you in my life when we all went in different directions. I realize that you didn't feel that same need. You were dealing with . . . getting away from your father. Chey was dealing with losing her brother, then eventually her aunt and uncle, and leaving her rodeo life behind for good. You each needed to do what you needed to do. I respected that then, as I do now," she added, then smiled at his dubious look. "I do, Wyatt."

"I know you do," he said. "It's just—"

She cut him off again. "Let me finish," she said softly. "We've all moved on from our past life together. You and Chey have each moved forward through some tragic and horrific challenges. I know you both; I love you both. I know what kind of friendship you had. I was there. I saw it with my own eyes." She smiled briefly. "Truth be told, I envied it. I was so jealous of Chey when I first met her. I mean, she not only had the best brother in the world, but she had you, too. I would have given anything for a brother or a sister." Her smile flashed to a fast grin. "Why do you think I worked so hard to make friends with you both? I couldn't make the world give me a family, so I went out and made one of my own."

He smiled at that. "And we were the better for it, Tory. We still are."

"Right?" she said with faux indignation, then they both laughed.

"Maybe I'd have gone on forever with you both being part of my life, and just hating that you weren't part of each other's. I don't know." Her smile sobered. "But then I found out from one of our old circuit mates that Buttercup was still alive and not in a good way. And I couldn't get through to wherever you were in the wilds of the Nepalese alps. So, I went and got him and called Chey. If I'd been able to keep him myself? Well, I don't know what I'd have done. I'd have told you for certain. But I couldn't keep him where I was, and I didn't know anyone else who would be willing to take him on. He was in really bad shape, Wy. I couldn't ask that of anyone else. I knew Chey was rehabbing rescues, and she knew Buttercup." She lifted her shoulders in a helpless shrug. "So, I did what I had to do. I jumped through many mental hoops trying to figure out how I was going to let you know Buttercup was alive, but was with Chey—" She groaned again. "I never could get the words right."

"You could have told us, let us decide how we wanted to handle it," he said, understanding better now the predicament he and Chey had unknowingly put her in.

"Could I?" she asked him. "I don't know. You two are the best people I know, but when it comes to each other, you're obnoxiously stubborn."

Wyatt lifted one eyebrow. "Hello, pot, I'd like you to meet kettle."

She accepted the gibe with a brief smile but continued. "I didn't want to be in the middle of that. I'm tired of being in the middle, Wyatt. I know I asked to be put there when I kept our ongoing communications separate from one another. If she'd ever so much as spoken your name, maybe I would have told her—I don't know."

"But she didn't," Wyatt said, surprised that of all the things that had been said and shared between them, this was what pinged most painfully at his heart. *What did you think, Reed? She was pining after you all these years when you flat-out shut her down?* The truth of it was, she'd been the one to shut him down first, but he'd long since stopped holding on to that sliver of indignation.

"Anyway, maybe I handled this wrong, maybe I've completely screwed up my friendship with Chey, and blown my chance at finding something up here before I even got started." She looked around. "I mean, look at this place, Wyatt. Of course, she loves it here. Who wouldn't? It's gorgeous. But if she doesn't want me here after this, I won't stay. She's worked too hard to find herself, to figure out what she wants to do, who she wants to be."

"You didn't blow it," he said. "Yes, you can be determined, but Chey certainly knows that. If she hadn't wanted your friendship, she'd have shut you out long ago. She didn't invite you here on a whim. That's not who she is."

"That was before I pulled this little stunt," she reminded him.

He shook his head. "If you think her friendship is that shallow, then maybe you—"

"Yours was deeper with her than anyone's," Tory reminded him quietly. "And look where you two ended up."

The reminder gave him a little gut punch. "That was different, Tory. And what's done now is done, anyway. Chey knows, as I do, that you were doing what you thought was right by us both. And by Buttercup. Things happen, life changes. The three of us know that better than anyone, right?" He ran a hand through his hair. "I don't know how it will end up with Chey, but you and I are okay. Right? I'm betting once Chey has a chance to step away and sort things out for herself, she'll be okay, too. That's probably why she took this run to the vet. Whatever the case, we'll sort things out."

"You won't leave until we do?" she asked.

He lifted his hands. "I can't promise that, but I'll make sure everything that can be said is said. Okay?"

She frowned, seeming surprised he hadn't given her a more definitive promise. "All right. Well, you may not feel like you owe me any favors right now, but I'd greatly appreciate it if you'd go talk to her."

"Tory, she didn't take off because she wanted to be chased down. Especially by me. I know we haven't been around each other in a long time, but I am pretty sure I can still guarantee you that." He flashed to the conversation with Vivi earlier that day, how Chey and he instinctively turned to each other, sharing and gauging their reactions to what they were hearing, just as they'd done when they were younger. He and Chey might be strangers to each other in some ways, but the core of who they were hadn't changed.

"I don't think she's sorting things out. I think she's hiding so she doesn't have to. There's a difference." Her shoulders fell then, and her expression wasn't merely worried; she looked helpless.

Wyatt knew Tory rarely let any vulnerability show, so that was no small thing.

"Okay, full disclosure," she said. "Maybe this is about me, too. I just got here, Wy, but I already don't want to leave. I adore Vivi. The stables are amazing old works of stone and wood. I can't wait to meet Hannah, who is so graciously letting me stay in her loft. And Avery, too, whom I've heard so much about. All of Chey's stories were about this place and these people and how they renewed her life. Renewed her heart after Cody died. Yes, I want all the parts of my life to come together, for her, for me. And for you, even when you go traipsing off again." She laid her hand on Wyatt's arm. "I am sorry, truly, if I messed up. I don't want to hurt either of you. You are all I have, the two of you. I know that sounds sad and pathetic, but—"

Wyatt pulled her in for a short, tight hug. "You didn't screw up anything." Then he ruffled her hair, which he knew she'd always hated—because she'd earned that much, and because she had always been the sister he never had. Bossy, intrusive, and so certain of his worth. She'd defend him to the ends of the earth and kick him right in the ass when he needed it. She had done both for him and Chey, though far more of the latter than the former, and he knew he'd never properly thanked her for it. "Wanting your life to come full circle, to surround yourself with people who mean something to you, to find a place you feel good in, where you can finally put down real roots is the opposite of sad. And there has never been anything pathetic about you. You're hopeful, and we could all stand to have a bit more of that." He let her go, then slid his hands down her arms so he could look at her. "We come from the kind of life that most people could never understand. It's true I've made friends all over the world in my travels, and some of them mean a great deal to me." He grinned. "Many, if not most of them, have lives even more weird than ours were."

"I always assumed that was the draw," she said with a laugh that sounded a bit watery. "You found your people."

"Maybe," he said, then laughed, too. "Probably. But close friendships or not, none of them, not a one, knows who I was back then, my life, or anything about it, other than that I grew up raising bulls in a family business. You know. Chey knows. That's it. You're it. And that means something."

Her eyes widened, and he saw understanding hit home, but what she said was, "Not if you're still trying to put it behind you."

"There's only so much I can do, Tor. I know I haven't said this to you, and I should have. I am very grateful you hunted me down to tell me about Cody. More grateful still that you stuck around. I don't have siblings or family, either." His smile then was genuine, without reservation. "Except you. I may not approve of, or have been particularly thrilled with your methods of bringing about this reunion, but then siblings don't always agree on everything, right?"

Her eyes grew glassy then. "So, you're really not upset with me?"

He shook his head, then took her elbow and tugged her into a hug. "Okay, maybe a little, but I'll get over it."

She knuckled him in the ribs and he winced even as he laughed and hugged her more tightly still.

"Oh, I'm sorry," came a soft female voice from behind them. "I didn't see anyone, or that you were—"

Wyatt loosened his hold on Tory but kept his hand on her shoulder as he turned, instinctively putting himself between her and the newcomer to the conversation. "No, that's okay," he said, his smile open and friendly. He dropped his hand to his side as Tory stepped up beside him.

"Victoria Fuller," Tory said, extending her hand. "Oh, you're Hannah, aren't you?" Tory's smile could have brightened a cloudy sky. "My new landlord. I'm so happy to meet you!"

The woman nodded and took Tory's hand in a quick shake but found herself enveloped in a brief hug instead. Her smile was as immediate and sincere as Tory's when the two parted. "I am, and me, too," she said with a laugh. "I'm sorry I wasn't here to greet you. I didn't know you were coming so soon. I haven't had the chance to really get in there and straighten up. I just use the place as a painting studio these days and I'm not really doing much of that out here, either."

"No, no, that's okay. Chey didn't know exactly when I'd arrive, I'm afraid. I wanted to surprise her with something of a family reunion."

"Oh?" Hannah said, then glanced at Wyatt expectantly.

"Wyatt Reed," he said, extending his hand. He didn't know what he'd expected, but it wasn't the immediate faltering of her sunny smile. Or the brief look of shock that passed over her face, followed by a quick series of expressions he honestly couldn't read, as Hannah glanced between the two of them. All he knew was that none of them looked favorable.

One thing was clear, though. Chey might not have talked about him to Tory over the years, or Vivi, for that matter. But Hannah definitely knew who he was. Or thought she did, anyway.

Just when he was about to pull his hand away, she reached for it and gave it a quick shake. "Sorry," she said quickly. "I just—you caught me off guard." She didn't say anything else.

Tory glanced between the two of them, even as Hannah was sizing him up.

"Pleasure to meet you," Wyatt said, hoping his wide smile would cut through the suddenly awkward tension. "I understand from Vivi that you're one of the artists out at the mill. A Bluebird, I think they call you guild members?"

Hannah looked surprised, but she smiled. "Lavender farmer, mostly, but yes, I am a painter in my spare time. And a member of the guild." She looked at Tory. "And in case you're worrying about the loft, being a member means I have a studio there now. I'm also pretty much set up at Will's. Now that it's getting warm, I expect I'll do most of my painting outdoors anyway. All that is to say I won't be coming in and out. My place is your place, for as long as you need it."

"Thank you," Tory said. "I can't tell you how much I appreciate your kindness." Her smile spread but Wyatt saw the determination behind it. "If it works out, I'd like to set up some kind of lease agreement, pay you rent."

"Oh, that won't be necess—"

"Trust me," Wyatt broke in, shooting a fast grin at Tory, then looking back to Hannah. "It would be better to just nod and say 'sure thing.' Save yourself a lot of time. Or she'll just start shoving checks under your door."

Tory laughed but nodded. "He's not wrong."

Hannah laughed with them, and the tension eased a bit more. "We'll work something out."

"This place is amazing," Tory told her, gesturing to the house and the fields beyond. "I can see why you all have fallen in love with living here." Her smile softened then. "It means a lot, this welcome. Thank you."

"We're happy you're here, too," Hannah said. "I know this means a lot to Chey. We're her family, so if you belong to her, then you belong to us, too."

Tory stepped in and gave Hannah another hug, surprising her again, then let her go and stepped back. "Sorry, I'm a hugger, and I just—" She wiped at her cheeks and let out a self-deprecating laugh. "It's been a long couple of months combined with a long drive here. I'm a bit punchy. I'm not usually a blubberer. Just . . . thank you. For saying that." She glanced at Wyatt. "We were just talking about family and bonds."

"I meant it," Hannah said, but didn't ask any of the questions Wyatt could see in her expressive gray eyes. "Were you heading in or heading out?" she asked, nodding toward the house.

"In," Tory said. "Vivi invited us to dinner after this morning's excitement." When Hannah frowned, Tory added, "Oh, I guess she hasn't told you that part yet."

"She just called and said we needed to powwow and could I please come out to dinner. Avery is coming, too. And Ben, I think; though I'm sorry, Will and Jake aren't able to come. They're up at the winery with Seth, pruning the vines in preparation for the coming season. The recent wet weather has them behind and I didn't think this was vital. Chey had let me know you'd arrived, so I thought I could get you settled while I was here." She looked between the two of them. "So, is there something else going on? What don't I know about?"

"I'll leave that to Vivi to tell," Tory said. "I wasn't there with them this morning, so—"

"There, where?" Hannah asked, looking more confused by the moment.

"At the lake," Tory said, then pasted a bright smile on her face. "You know, why don't we head in together and Vivi can fill you in. Then we can go up to the loft and do what needs to be done before dinner." She looked at Wyatt. "You were just heading out, so I won't keep you," she said, rather pointedly. "We'll see you and Chey back here for dinner, okay?"

"Where is Chey?" Hannah asked, then let out a short laugh. "You know what? I'm sure this will all be sorted out shortly. I won't hold you up," she said to Wyatt, then held out her hand again. "It was nice meeting you."

She met his gaze directly as she shook hands with him, and Wyatt saw untold depths there. He'd met a lot of people from more walks of life than most folks knew existed. He'd spent long hours talking to people who had seen and done things that he could only try to comprehend. Hannah's eyes had the same look of hard-earned wisdom in their soft gray depths. He wasn't sure what had happened to put it there, but he suspected she saw a lot more than most people did when she looked at him. And that wasn't even taking into account whatever it was Chey had told her about him.

"The same," he told her. Whoever this woman was, she'd been part of the group that had helped put Chey back together after losing Cody. For that alone, he'd forever think of her as an ally and friend. That he hadn't been there to do the same for Chey was likely at the root of all those questions in Hannah's eyes.

"I'll head on inside," Hannah said. "Sorry again for interrupting earlier." She left them with a quick smile and a nod.

Wyatt looked after her, wondering what Chey had told her about him. And why. Especially when he knew she'd never once mentioned him to Vivi.

He noticed Tory watching him as he watched Hannah's retreating figure. He thought she'd comment on the odd, underlying tension that had been there, even when they'd laughed together. Instead, she surprised him by changing the subject entirely. "I was in the kitchen with Vivi before you got here," she said. "She was still waxing rhapsodic over your stint as Tarzan, by the way." She shifted her stance, arms still folded, gaze directly on him. "I also heard you're going to bring the Wyatt Reed dog and pony show to little Blue Hollow Falls. Don't you think that's overkill?" She smiled. "Or is that the llama and koala show? I've lost track."

He shared her smile. "Just trying to help." He shoved his hands in his pockets and took in the view once more. "Seems like a view worth preserving." He shot her a fast grin. "Surely you agree."

Tory laughed and shook her head. "Here for five minutes and already making a place for yourself." She unfolded her arms and knuckled him in the side. "I thought that was what I was supposed to be doing."

"Looks like there's plenty of room," he said. "And you seem to be doing just fine. Hannah has already adopted you."

"So," she said, a considering note in her voice, "does that mean you're staying?"

Okay, so she hadn't changed the subject after all. She didn't sound hopeful, or even guardedly optimistic. Mostly just guarded. "Tory, you know I'm not trying to wedge myself in here, or take up the space they're carving out for you. I didn't even know I was coming to Blue Hollow Falls."

"I was teasing. That's not remotely what I'm asking, and you know it."

He sighed. "I know. And you know my life isn't here. It's not even on this continent. I'll be heading back to the UK sooner rather than later. I have a lot of work to do."

"I seem to recall your telling me after I picked you up at the airport that you were looking forward to taking a break."

"From the travel and livestream productions, yes. I have a ton of postproduction work to do from the Nepal trip and preproduction work for the next one. I haven't even decided which proposal I'm going to take. I'm simply going to do all that at home, instead of on the road. It will keep me busy for a good while, and frankly, I am looking forward to staying put for a bit."

"If you're going to stream something live from here, draw attention to the situation at Firefly Lake, that means you'll be staying on at least for the immediate future, though, correct?"

"I suppose. I'm not, as you put it, bringing the dogs and ponies." He smiled. "Or the llamas and koalas. This isn't going to be a full-scale Reed Planet production." He lifted his hands. "Actually, I shouldn't say that since I don't know what it will be. But I'm not planning to fly the whole crew here. I've just given them the summer off. Or well, sort of. But they're all working from home this summer, too. I think. Or wherever they want to work from. We don't even know what we're trying to do here yet. Just what we're trying to keep the town council from doing. I can bring enough attention to bear on the situation to at least make the council and chamber of commerce act responsibly and take all angles into consideration before they make a decision. The thing is, Vivi and her friends are going to have to come up with some kind of alternate solution, or I don't think the council will turn down the one they have in hand, no matter how good a case the townspeople make."

She smiled sweetly. "Sounds like you're the perfect person to help them figure all that out."

He shook his head. "I'll do something short, bring the heat of social media attention to the situation, then leave it up to the residents here to take it from there." He accepted her hug, and hugged her back, then said, "This is a one off. A favor for a friend." He smiled at her. "A best friend," he amended. When she gave him the Queen Victoria look, he rolled his eyes, then added laughingly, "Friends. Plural. Okay?"

She nodded, then stuck out her hand. "Speaking of which, hand me your phone."

He frowned but slid his phone out of his pocket and handed it to her.

She turned it on, then tapped on the screen for a minute and handed it back.

He looked at the screen. "What did you—"

"Directions to Dr. Campbell's place, all loaded and started for you. The vet," she clarified. "Where Chey is at present." She reached up on her tiptoes and kissed him on the cheek. "Go get our girl, will you please? She's had her alone time. We need her here. She's part of this."

Wyatt heard what she was really saying. *We need her here. She's part of us.*

Chapter Five

Chey lifted up the ramp on the back of the now empty two-horse trailer and latched it closed, opting to leave the top half doors latched open. She waved to Ben—Dr. Campbell—as he headed from the huge, red and white, gambrel-roof barn and the offices that were attached to it, back toward the white clapboard house he called home. Avery spent most of her time out here with Ben now, but apparently Chey had just missed her as she was heading back to the farm for dinner.

Which is where you should be right now, chicken little.

It was true that she needed to get both of the horses over here for a full checkup—they were recent arrivals to her growing menagerie of rescues—and she'd kept them quarantined away from the rest of the herd. It was a pain, but she could have gone another day. Or week. Neither horse was in a bad way or needing specific medical attention; she just wanted to get a full bill of health on them before introducing them to the herd.

And you needed an excuse to get away from Wyatt.

"That too," she muttered. She'd like to think she was better at rolling with things now that she'd settled down in the mountains. For the most part, she was. "So, go on and roll your sorry ass—behind—home again, and be part of the solution." She smiled at herself for self-editing. *I don't need no stinkin' mason jar,* she thought. *Yeah, you do,* her little voice added, and she chuckled. "Yep, I probably do."

She turned on her phone and sighed. She'd dawdled as much as was humanly possible and she'd still be home in plenty of time for dinner. She'd hoped to spend some time with Avery. All Chey had to do was get her started on any one of the numerous topics Avery was studying at any given moment, and she'd have been good for an hour's distraction at least.

Chey walked around the trailer to the driver side of her truck and reluctantly climbed in. She tossed her hat on the seat and raked her fingers through her hair. She really didn't have anywhere else she had to be or errands that needed running, and, frankly, she didn't want to be hauling an empty trailer all over God's creation just to kill time. And being alone wasn't really helping her think things through. What she needed was a sounding board, someone who would listen to the whole tale, then help her figure out what to do with all the things she was feeling.

She pulled on her seat belt, then picked up the phone and called Hannah, who was the only person who knew about Wyatt, knew about her past, and why they'd lost touch. She might have needed to make another deposit to the mason jar fund when her call went to voice mail. She turned on the ignition and started down the drive when she heard the ping of an incoming text. She stopped the truck, put it in park, then looked at the screen. It was from Hannah, and it wasn't subtle.

I'm at the farm. WE NEED TO TALK.

All caps.
Ah. So, she's already met Wyatt. Chey swore under her

breath, then found herself fighting a wry smile. "We're going to need a bigger jar, Wy." She let her head tip back against the headrest, closed her eyes for a long moment. Why wasn't this easier? He wasn't having any issues with seeing her. Not at all, as far as she could tell.

She opened her eyes, picked up the phone and texted Hannah back.

We do. I'll call you later.

She waited, then got a thumbs-up emoji. "Great." She tossed the phone back into the cup holder. She knew Hannah would have called her if she could have. Naturally the one person who could help her was in the one place Chey didn't want to be. She put the truck back into gear and rumbled on down the long, rutted drive that led to the main road, the horse trailer bouncing along behind her. Once there she paused, looked both ways, even though she knew maybe three cars a day traveled down that road. She wasn't looking for traffic. She was looking for divine intervention. Or at least a sign. "Any sign would be nice."

Her phone buzzed again. Another text. She glanced skyward before looking at the screen. "Thanks," she said. "I think." She scooped up the phone. This one was from Tory.

Come on back. I'm going to fix this. Promise.

Wow, Chey thought. Tory must be feeling the weight of the world for the stunt she'd pulled. She never wheedled or cajoled. She was more the delivering ultimatums, telling it like it is kinda girl. *Well, maybe you can stew a bit longer*, Chey thought. It was only fair. Decision made, she turned on the main road, heading away from the farm.

Twenty minutes later, she was driving down the bumpy,

pothole-riddled road to Firefly Lake. Once she got all the way back to the closed ramp road, she parallel-parked truck and trailer across the end of the ramp road, then picked up her phone again and texted Tory back.

At the lake. Research. Start without me.

It was the truth. More or less. If she was going to sit somewhere and think, then this seemed like a good place to do it. And if she couldn't figure out what to do about Wyatt, then maybe she'd figure out what they could do to save the lake. And Blue Hollow Falls. *Sure. No problem.*

Since her thoughts and feelings where Wyatt was concerned were just a big, indecipherable jumble, though, maybe it was better to focus her mind elsewhere and just back-burner him for a bit. She had no idea how Wyatt thought he could help.

The bigger question at the moment was what kind of help did they need? She popped open the center console and took out a spiral notebook and pen she used to keep track of business mileage and flipped to a clean page. Then stared at it. "So, how to keep the park from being sold to a glitzy resort developer. Go." She tapped the blank page with her pen. Vivi had contacted Addie Pearl the moment they'd returned from the lake. According to Addie, with the advent of the music center and the mill, developers had been sniffing around for some time now. As of yet, the developers had been in the market to buy, but none of the folks they'd approached with an offer had been willing to sell. "So, knowing they were struggling, Hammond ever-so-helpfully steered one of them to property owned by the town instead."

Clearly, the lake property couldn't sustain itself in its current iteration. It was a drain on town resources with little on the positive side to balance the scales. Aside from the fact that it was a fabulous resource no one seemed to want to use. So, one of the problems to be solved was how to make the lake and surrounding park and wilderness area a vital, necessary attraction again. "That shouldn't be too hard." It might just be a matter of refurbishing worn out equipment and sprucing up the trails, maybe updating the Web site. She made a note to have Avery look into that. Heck, find out if Firefly Lake even had a Web site.

If the council members balked at spending the money to fix the place up with no guarantee of success, and they'd have a pretty good argument there, she conceded, she'd bet between Vivi and Addie Pearl, they could get a coalition of townsfolk willing to pitch in and do most of the labor, maybe donate new equipment. Surely it could be a tax write-off or something. After all, look what they'd done with the mill. She made a few additional notes and started feeling a bit more optimistic.

She reverted to tapping her pen on the notebook, and her enthusiasm waned when she realized it wasn't going to simply be a matter of revamping the town's recreational area. Vivi had said the businesses in town were suffering the same neglect. With the new tourist draws largely outside the town proper, folks didn't have to drive through Blue Hollow Falls to get to the winery, the music center and mill, or even their lavender farm. She would have thought that the taxes being collected from the new endeavors would balance the scales, but apparently those funds weren't trickling down to the businesses themselves.

She picked up her phone and checked the time. Well, that had been a whopping ten minutes she'd spent not thinking about Wyatt. She let her head drop back against the headrest. "Go me."

Her thoughts returned to his confident assessment that he could help turn the town around. He *knew people.* She stared at the dark screen on her phone for the longest time. She'd spent the past decade-plus actively and quite specifically choosing not to look for him. Not to see what he was doing, or where he was doing it. *Or with whom. Be honest.*

That was true, also. She wished him happiness. Always had. No one deserved it more than he did. She'd hoped he'd left Zachariah behind and had struck out on his own to find what made him happy. Her good wishes for him had been sincere and unwavering. She'd cared about him deeply. Always.

But that didn't mean she had to torture herself by watching him while he was doing it. What did they call it these days? Self-care? Yes, she'd been well ahead of the trend, practicing self-care.

Only, now he was here. Where she could hardly avoid seeing him do . . . whatever it was he'd be doing. She put the phone down, then picked it up again. Her finger hovered over the screen, then finally she tapped it with determination. *You're going to find out anyway*, she told herself.

Tory knew what he'd been up to, why he *knew people.* Why he'd changed so dramatically, and all for the good, at least as far as Chey could tell. Tory had known enough to figure out how to track him down and get him to travel halfway around the world to come get his horse back. And what *had* he been doing in Nepal, of all places? When Chey had thought about him and what he might be doing, she'd pictured him with some small spread in Montana, raising cattle, maybe still raising bulls, with a few horses. Maybe go wild and add in some free-range chickens, a few goats. She'd figured at some point he'd have met someone who would love him for the amazingly sweet, gentle, and kind man he was. *Someone who'd be a hell of a lot smarter than you were and marry him when he asked.*

Somehow Nepal had never factored in to her visuals

when she tried to picture Wyatt Reed all grown up and on his own. Heck, she wouldn't have imagined him anywhere he couldn't have gotten to without a horse trailer in tow. "Possibly you were projecting a little," she murmured dryly; she'd just accurately described her own future, postrodeo.

She pulled up the search engine on her phone, then took a deep breath and typed in his name. "What have you been up to for the past dozen years, Wyatt Reed?"

To say her jaw dropped open when the answer to that question popped up immediately on her tiny phone screen was an understatement. "Reed Planet," she read aloud, that title coming up repeatedly in the first few pages of hits. *Pages.* A quick glance at the total number of hits floored her all over again. The count didn't number in the millions or even the tens of millions. "Holy jumping Sherpas," she murmured again, almost afraid to click on any of them. "What in the world did you go off and do?"

The bulk of the first string of hits were connected to YouTube videos, all of which started with the words "Reed Planet," then included whatever part of the planet he'd been visiting, where, presumably, the video had been shot. There was a clever logo of a planet, with the title emblazoned on a Saturn-like ring around it, with all kinds of beautifully drawn critters and plants and people popping up from spots around the globe. This was no small enterprise. "Clearly," she said under her breath, still scrolling through the first dozen pages of hits.

She would have perhaps guessed this was some other Wyatt Reed, but clicking on images showed that logo and his handsome, smiling face staring back at her, with a variety of background settings showing the picture had been taken in any number of the same far-flung spots noted in the titles and captions.

"Reed Planet: Wyatt Goes Wild in Micronesia!"

There were dozens of them. More than dozens. She quickly lost count.

"Well, twelve years seems like long enough to procrastinate," she said, then scrolled back to the top of the first page. "Guess we might as well start here." She clicked on the video, turned her phone sideways so she could view it in as large a format as possible, turned up the sound . . . and sat there, utterly slack-jawed and transfixed for the next twenty minutes.

He was bold, confident, and so charismatic. *And don't forget sexy as all hell.* Where was the Wyatt of her childhood? And how had he transformed himself into this? The only connection to the boy she knew, the young man she'd realized she loved far, far, too late, was the reason behind Reed Planet. She was watching a tape of what had originally been livestreamed, as it happened, while he explored the most amazing places, talking to people, going off into jungles, and down rivers, into canyons and up on top of impossible peaks. Revealing little-known issues about certain cultures, animal species who were in danger of losing their home turf, plants, flowers, foliage of all kinds that were threatened with extinction. Entire villages full of people who relied on some of those other things for their survival.

He drew attention with his broad smile, easygoing nature, palpable excitement as he talked to the camera as easily and charismatically as he did the people he was interacting with. She could see immediately why he'd gained the following he had. He was compelling, almost impossible to look away from. And he staged his streams, set them up, so that something was always happening, and the viewer was seeing it all, live and unedited, right along with him. It careened from thrilling, to funny, to touching, to dramatic and informative, then back to funny, then thrilling. She felt as if she was on the edge of her seat, front row on a roller coaster, right there in a lake parking lot in the middle of nowhere, fully transported to wherever he was, hanging on his every word, following his every action.

She was breathless when the first clip ended, followed by a string of information on where people could go to learn more, or to donate their help, whether it be in money, supplies, or in person. He was like a one-person Peace Corps for the new millennium. She glanced at the number of times the video had been watched and blinked twice at the nine-digit number. In the content below the video, she saw that millions had watched the streaming event she'd just watched on tape, live when it had happened. Millions.

"So . . . yeah," she said faintly. "I guess he does know people."

She was halfway through her third video clip when a knock on the window made her squeal and bobble her phone, all but tossing it across the cab of the truck.

Hand to her pounding chest, she turned to find Wyatt standing on the other side of her window.

Of course he was.

She'd never been less prepared to see him. Not even when he'd stepped into the quiet, dust-mote filled air of her stables that morning. Nothing about what she'd just been watching made this easier. Quite the opposite. Because this man, staring at her right now with a knowing smile on his oh-so-handsome face, was, in fact, an utter stranger to her. Whatever they figured out, whatever they decided to do about being in each other's orbits again, the absolute bottom line truth was that the Wyatt she'd known, the Wyatt she'd considered her closest, dearest, and most deeply trusted friend—and, after he'd gone, the Wyatt she realized she loved—no longer existed.

The man before her might be a bigger, bolder, better version of the Wyatt she'd known, and that was fine, good—

great, even—but this Wyatt wouldn't be sticking around in Blue Hollow Falls for long.

So, what did it really matter what happened between them now?

She looked past him and saw Tory's truck. It was empty. So, it was just the two of them. She started to motion for him to come around and get in the cab, then decided that was a far too closed-in space. She was still catching her breath and trying to reconcile the person she knew with the man standing a foot away from her. Now when she looked at him, she saw the guy livestreaming from some of the most remote places in the world, with such vibrancy and intent. She could no longer see the boy he'd been. That was a memory associated with someone else now.

She pulled the door handle and he stepped back while she climbed out and closed the door behind her. Before he could speak, she held her phone up and wiggled it. "So, Reed Planet, huh?" Her smile was as dry as her tone, but inside, she felt anything but casual.

He lifted his shoulders in a short shrug. "It just sort of happened."

Her eyes widened in disbelief. "Because people just happen to hop from Tierra del Fuego over to the middle of Antarctica one day, so they can go hang out and livestream with penguins and a handful of scientist folk who live in what looks like something built by Star Wars storm troopers."

"I was on the edge of Antarctica. Haven't made it to the middle yet."

"Ah, the Antarctic Riviera then." She waved a hand. "Sounds positively balmy. Bring a beach towel and umbrella. How are the penguins at catching Frisbees?"

"A bit flat-footed, actually."

She snorted at that. She had a thousand questions for him. In the end, she just shook her head and said, "You're clearly doing something you love very much." She held his gaze and smiled. "I'm happy for you, Wyatt." She laughed. "Utterly and completely gobsmacked, but truly happy for you. You're making a difference." That was the one thread that connected the two Wyatts. "I'm really proud of you."

"You're making one, too. Tory told me about the work you're doing, taking in rescue horses, working with kids who otherwise wouldn't ever pet a horse, much less ride one. Kids with special needs, too, who open up with your horses in ways they can't otherwise do."

"It's a few horses," she said. "And the kids aren't work; they're a pleasure and a miracle. I'm just happy I can facilitate. Nothing on the scale of what—"

"Anything anyone does to help—whatever that might be—is meaningful and potentially life changing to the living thing on the receiving end. We're not grading on a scale of who did the most. Any good being done is leaving this big rock better than we found it."

"Reed Planet," she said, with a smile and a short shake of her head. "How did it all start?"

He shrugged, then dug his hands in his back pockets. "Like most things. A complete fluke." He nodded toward the path to the docks. "Want to walk?"

She glanced at her phone. It was a few hours to dinner. She still was not looking forward to facing the cabal of her friends and their curiosity about Wyatt, but she didn't want him to miss dinner. She had no idea what he had in mind in terms of helping, but he surely had a massively huge platform from which to draw attention to their issues. She grabbed her hat and put it on, wanting the screen of privacy the brim would provide. Just in case. "Sure."

They started down the path. "Should we bring a blanket?" she asked, and he chuckled.

"Unless you plan to go for a swim, no. I'm good." His lips curved in a dry smile. "I got my laps in earlier today."

"And I was so worried that you were cold," she said, shaking her head. "That actually probably did feel balmy compared to some of the things you've done."

"Well, normally I at least have a wet suit or something, but it was for a good cause."

She just laughed, shook her head, and kept on walking.

"What?" he asked, when she didn't explain.

"Nothing," she said. "I guess I just remember you as the guy who wouldn't try a rope swing or climb on the back of the bulls you raised." She waved her hands. "I can't seem to connect that guy to the person I watched in those videos."

He laughed loudly at that. "Oh, trust me, it's a big mix of adrenaline rush and outright terror most of the time."

She sent him a sidelong glance. "Oh yeah, you looked petrified."

"That's the adrenaline talking." He lifted a hand, still chuckling when she just kept shaking her head. "I'll admit that the longer I do this, the more confident I feel about certain things, but I have a healthy respect for the risks I take. I'm daring, maybe, but I'm not reckless," he told her. "There's a difference."

"Daring, most definitely," she said, "but, yeah, I concede your point."

"It takes a team of dedicated souls to pull off what we do. I would never risk their safety unnecessarily." He smiled. "That's not to say we don't risk a lot, but we mitigate the risks in every way we can. The point is to bring that thrilling sense of discovery to the person sitting at home, with both of us seeing it, experiencing it, for the first time together. Truly together, because it's streaming live. So yes, there are unknowns, but it's not like we don't do our research before going in, wherever we're going."

Chey nodded but didn't say anything more. They walked in silence for a time. It wasn't awkward, but she wouldn't say it was comfortable. She was even more hyper aware of him now than she had been before. Now it wasn't only dealing with her physical reaction to him, her memories of how they'd been when they were younger, how they'd parted ways.

All of that was still there, but it was largely overshadowed by her visceral reaction to going on that thrill ride with him, sitting alone in the cab of her truck. It had felt . . . intimate, and wild. Like he was talking directly to her, taking her—specifically her—along with him. Which she knew, intellectually, wasn't the case. He was taking millions of others along with him. But the magic of Wyatt Reed was that he made that reality fall completely away. It was just her. And him. Thrashing through a jungle, leaping off a cliff, navigating a river that was all boulders and thrashing white water. She started off wondering things about how they worked the camera angles, but those questions were soon forgotten. He was *right there* turning to look at her, talking directly to her, as if she was next to him.

Her pulse still jumped when she relived the journey in her head. And at the very same moment, in real life, he really was right next to her, walking with her, talking to her. *Talk about surreal.*

Add to that all the rest of it. The man who'd just taken her on a thrill ride down the Amazon was also the guy she'd once confided her deepest secrets to. The guy who'd turned to her in an effort to get out from under the bloody fist of his father. The same guy who had laid his heart right at her feet.

The same guy she'd told that she loved him, too . . . like a brother. Also, the same guy she'd simply never thought of in that way. Until she'd crushed his heart, and he'd walked away, from her, from rodeo life, all of it . . . and then she couldn't think of him any other way. Her own heart broken, because she'd just let go of the best thing that had ever happened to her.

"What was the fluke?" she asked, somewhat abruptly, needing to get her mind off thoughts of them, together. "How could you accidentally launch a whole planet of you?"

They approached the dock and he tilted his head toward it, a questioning look on his face. She nodded, and they walked to the end and sat, each leaning back on one of the pilings, facing one another. She took her cowboy hat off so she could lean her head back, and set it on the dock, tucking the brim under her thigh so the breeze wouldn't blow it into the water. Then immediately missed the privacy that brim provided, allowing her to look at him without being obvious. He was hard not to look at. *He's just so damn handsome*, she thought, and shifted her gaze out to the water while he talked. As privacy went, it wasn't perfect, but at least this way he couldn't read every thought that was going through her mind as he had so effortlessly done, once upon a time.

"The fluke," he began. "Well, as I told you before, when I first got away from Zachariah, I couldn't seem to flee far enough to feel safe. It was a mind game he'd played with me, and I knew that, but I couldn't sleep, or even think clearly. So, the first thing I figured out was how to go about getting a passport. Then I worked odd jobs until I had enough money saved to get on a plane and fly away."

"To where?"

He shrugged. "It didn't matter. Just not here. I bought the ticket that would take me the farthest away."

"Which got you to . . . ?"

"I actually never made it to that first destination. I flew out of New York, and the layover was in Iceland." The memory made him smile. "Iceland. I was so awestruck. I wandered out of the Reykjavík airport . . . and never went back to catch the other leg of the flight. I hitched a ride into town. It was summer there, so the sun never went down. It was like nothing I'd ever seen, or even imagined. Honestly, I felt like I was on another planet."

"Ah," she said, nodding as comprehension began to dawn.

"I started writing down everything I was seeing and what I thought about it. I stayed with a family there and they helped me get a work visa. I worked on a fishing boat, like a trawler, and one of the men who was on the crew with me was from Greenland. Greenland," he said, his expression marveling, as if he was still hearing it for the first time.

That was his magic, Chey thought, *right there.* With everything he'd seen and done since, that memory still captivated him as utterly as it had the first time. His easy, understated confidence contrasted with a real sense of earnestness, as if he wanted you to see what he was seeing, feel what he was feeling, because it was just so thrilling, he couldn't keep it to himself.

"It was the first time I felt truly free," he told her. "I could be whoever I wanted to be. Working that trawler was the hardest, most grueling thing I've ever done. It terrified me daily, but I was doing it. Over the course of that summer, it changed me. I was surrounded by people who liked me, championed me, wanted me to succeed. And, I'm not saying I had none of that before in my life," he was quick to add. "But it was the first time I could revel in it, without having to look over my shoulder, or worry. About anything. About anyone. I know they accepted me partly because I was this kind of freak of nature to them, this skinny kid from the States who'd essentially run away to join the circus. I was a novelty at first, something to look at and point at. They marveled at my stupidity for actually choosing to do what they had no choice but to do. I had a tough work ethic they respected, though, and eventually, I became stronger, more confident; then their acceptance was earned in all the ways that truly mattered."

"You showed them," Chey said dryly.

He grinned. "I did." His expression sobered, but his eyes were still full of light, and his voice had that understated energy that made her want to sit forward when he spoke. "It was amazing to me, what I could accomplish, what I wanted to accomplish, when I didn't have to spend so much of my emotional energy navigating the minefield that was Zachariah's temper. I didn't have to plan my day around trying not to get hit."

"Oh, Wyatt—" she said softly, and it didn't escape her that he didn't refer to his father as "dad" because Zachariah had never, not ever been that.

"I'm not saying that for pity or empathy. You were there, you know what that time was like for me. You were my rock, my escape, my place to vent." He smiled again, and his gaze was filled with affection. "It took an entire fishing village in Iceland to replace you."

She smiled with him, even as her heart broke for him all over again.

"I only bring that up as a way to explain how profound that time felt for me. I could have worked on ten trawlers, doing twice the work. I truly did feel like Superman. It was life altering, in the truest sense of the word."

"I'm glad you got away," she told him. "Far enough away that you could allow yourself to be free. It sounds like a rebirth."

He nodded. "That's the perfect word for it."

"Then what did you do? After Iceland?"

"When the season ended, Femo—Johan Filemonsen was his full name, but we called him Femo because that's what his little granddaughter called him—he was going back to Nuuk. The capital city of Greenland. I asked him if I could go with him. I had a hunger then, to see more. Do more. Knowing I had a passport and just had to earn enough money for a ticket was intoxication. I could literally see anything, go anywhere. I just wanted to see this place he'd talked about, experience it. He said he could get me a job there. I planned to go back to Iceland the following summer and work the trawler again, so I had a safety net of sorts. And off we went."

"Did you ever go back to Iceland?" she asked.

He nodded. "About four years later."

"Years," she repeated, shaking her head.

He smiled. "I picked up a cheap, secondhand camera before I left Iceland the first time. Writing things down wasn't enough. The phone technology back then, at least the one I had, didn't allow for pictures, and I wanted to record the things I was seeing. I wanted to keep all of it with me as I continued onward, the sight, the smells, how the air felt. I couldn't do all of that, but pictures plus my words were a start." He looked out across the lake now, and she could see that his mind had wandered back to that time. "I had this idea that I'd become a photojournalist. Me, with my rodeo schoolroom education and GED."

"You were a voracious reader," she reminded him. "You read everything you could get your hands on, from the classics to science books, graphic novels to the history of the world. If the point of higher education is to expand your mind, I'd say your education is far more complete than most."

His smile was self-deprecating. "Thank you. I appreciate that. But it was still a pretty far-fetched dream to have."

"A kid who took off from a rodeo crew with next to

nothing, and his first stop ended up being Iceland, then Greenland? Yeah, you were already overachieving at far-fetched."

He laughed. "Well, when you put it that way. And there's a grain of truth to that. Because of what I'd already done, I felt kind of fearless. I mean, what did I have to lose?"

"So, how did you start?"

"Femo's brother lived in this tiny village a distance from the capital—you have to understand, when I say capital city, the entire population of all of Greenland is like, less than sixty thousand people—so his tiny village was the true meaning of the word 'tiny.' He was fighting to keep the halibut fishing revenue for their village. I took photos, interviewed him and others, wrote a story about it, then tried—admittedly very clumsily—to sell the story."

"Did you?"

He laughed. "No. But I knew then that I was on to something. My story did change things for the village, got people talking about the problem in a different way, and they figured things out. I didn't come up with the solution to their problem, but my talking to them about it got them to discuss it in a new way."

"If you didn't go back to Iceland, where did you go from there?"

"From my time in Greenland and Iceland, I knew I wanted to bring a voice to those the world rarely heard from. I just didn't know how. In Greenland, the direct route hadn't exactly panned out, but the goal had been reached. So I started thinking about things differently."

"Greenland certainly seems a good place to start. So, was that the fluke?"

He shook his head. "I didn't stay. I couldn't in good conscience take a job away from someone who was born there, who needed the work because they wanted to grow old and die there. I could leave, go anywhere." He lifted a shoulder. "So, I did."

He pulled one knee up and looped his arms around his bent leg, and Chey flashed back to a memory of them, sitting in the flatbed of her uncle's pickup, late at night, looking at the stars, watching the moon rise. It had become something of a ritual for them. Zachariah had usually passed out drunk by then; their chores were done. It was the only time that it was quiet, and, for Wyatt, safe. They could really talk without fear of interruption, or of anyone overhearing their secret thoughts and dreams. They'd always start off sitting just as they were now, each leaning back on a wheel hub.

Wyatt would pull up his knee like he had just now, so she could stretch her legs out. Hours later, they'd always end up lying on their backs, staring up at the moon. Talk of the day, the current gossip swirling around camp, would eventually turn to hushed recounting of their future dreams. They'd make plans for what they'd do if they won the lottery—not that they'd ever bought a ticket, but Chey's aunt and uncle often did—nonsense plans, but it had been fun, and stretched her mind, made her think about a life beyond the circuit.

"I felt so utterly liberated," he said, drawing her thoughts back to the present. "The confidence I'd gained from working commercial fishing in some insanely rough conditions, traveling through such an inhospitable terrain, meeting the most wonderful people, people who were so different from me, but at the same time, wanting the things I'd always wanted. Fairness, respect, the right to feel equal."

Chey felt that hard pull inside her chest again. She was looking at the man who'd taken her on a wild ride not twenty minutes ago, thrilling her with his brash smile, palpable enthusiasm, and easygoing assertiveness, all while risking life and limb to help others understand the complexities and challenges of living in worlds she'd never even known existed.

But she was hearing the boy she'd grown up with, yearning to simply be treated fairly, with the kind of respect that everyone should be due, just by default. That Wyatt, the one she'd laughed with, cried with, talked into the wee hours of the night with, surrounded by flickering fireflies, under full moons and galaxies of stars . . . the one she'd loved, he was still there. He would always be there.

She'd changed, too. She'd suffered a tragic loss, yes. She'd lived through the horror of watching her only sibling be trampled to death by an enraged bull whose back he'd been on moments before. Images and feelings that could never be erased. But even that didn't touch on the horror that had been every single day of Wyatt's life. His pain had been inflicted on him personally, directly, for *years*.

It wasn't that she'd pretended not to know the truth back then, or shoved it aside, but Wyatt had always been able to step outside himself in that way. Not being the poor kid with the drunken, mean-as-a-snake father, but just a kid. With her, he had been exactly that. And that's how she remembered him.

Hearing him now, though, she felt as if she'd done him an injustice. Because she didn't think about him the way he clearly thought of himself.

She blinked at the sudden moisture that gathered at the corners of her eyes. "You know, what you've been able to do," she said softly, hearing the raspy edge in her voice, "is nothing short of a miracle. Truly." She blinked a few times, then looked at him and smiled. "You really were meant to do what you do. If there's such a thing as a calling, that's what it is, what you've found."

"Thank you." He ducked his chin. "It's as good a word

to describe it as any." When he looked back up, his gaze searching hers, she was certain he was seeing all the things she was feeling for him.

"So, when the journalist thing didn't pan out, did you ever think about running for public office somewhere? With your passion for illuminating the need for change, you could be on the ground floor of making it happen."

He shook his head. "I didn't stay in one place long enough for that. And I didn't want to just try to help one place. I didn't want to limit myself to that." He grinned. "Which is the selfish part of it. Once I'd had a taste of feeling like I was on another planet, I wanted to visit the whole galaxy. Traveling suited both of those goals."

"So, how did it happen? How did you go from that dream to Reed Planet?"

He leaned back against the piling, his face lighting up as he continued the story. "I was in Uganda, maybe eight or nine months after I left Nuuk."

"Uganda," she repeated.

He shrugged. "I wanted to see gorillas."

She laughed. "As one would."

"There had been a few other brief stops between Greenland and there, with me just working odd jobs wherever I landed, still taking pictures, still writing everything down, trying to figure out how to make that particular dream come true. I'd started going to the local libraries wherever I was, like I did when we were growing up. Not for the books this time—well, not only for the books—but to use the computers to look things up, do research, figure out what I wanted to see where I was, where to go next."

"Did you learn other languages? How did you communicate?"

"Most of the time not very well," he said with a laugh. "But I figured out early on that if I made an honest effort to learn enough of the language wherever I happened to be, people would meet me halfway and try to figure out what I was attempting to say. English is spoken in more places than you could dream of, which is humbling, but I worked hard to be respectful, to speak to people in their native tongue whenever possible." His lips curved in a dry smile. "I'm not fluent in anything, and I can't read or write in a foreign language to save my life. But I'm a whiz at picking up a few dozen phrases and getting by."

Chey bet it went a lot further than that. He didn't just want fair treatment and respect for himself; he gave it to others. That's who he was. "So, the video? Or streaming, or whatever you call it. When did that start?"

"It was video first. Streaming wasn't even a thing then. It happened by accident really. The fluke," he added, wiggling his brows. "I was actually truly playing tourist for a change. I was tagging along with a sightseeing group in a protected animal preserve, so I could hear what the tour guide was saying. One of the young guys on the trip didn't heed the warnings about not feeding the wildlife. He'd snuck some crackers or something in somehow, and I don't know how, because they controlled that kind of thing. Anyway, when we went to leave one area for the next, the wildlife in question thought they'd like to keep the young food source behind with them."

"Oh no!"

"No one else had seen him slip off the side of the vehicle we were in. I didn't want him to freak out, and I definitely didn't want his parents to freak out—"

"Wait, how old was he?"

"Nine, maybe ten?"

"Oh my God, Wy."

"I didn't even really think about it. I just hopped off and went and got him. It wasn't that I wasn't scared. I was, but

I'd spent years learning how to fit into new environments, so I kind of adopted the same strategy. I stayed calm, much like the guides were, joking, smiling, you know, no big deal. Talking to the gorilla, and to the kid, acting like I belonged there." He shook his head. "The whole thing lasted maybe five minutes. Felt like a lifetime, I won't lie. My heart was in my throat the whole time. But someone in the tour group filmed the whole thing and posted it to the Internet, and it went viral, as they say now. Which back then wouldn't have meant what it does now, in terms of numbers. YouTube wasn't that old at that point. So, it didn't take as much to get noticed. I didn't even know about it until way later. I got a call from someone who'd spent a few weeks tracking me down after seeing the video, wanting an interview." He chuckled. "Instead of being a photojournalist, I got interviewed by one. I felt like such a failure; my goals were a joke."

"Hardly, you saved that kid's life."

"Maybe. But I didn't want to be the subject of a story—I wanted to tell the story, you know? Then I got to thinking, about the number of people who had viewed that video clip, and it finally clicked. I realized I was going about my dream all wrong. Why write about my experiences and try to show what was going on with still pictures, when I could bring my audience right there, invite viewers right in to experience it live and in person, or feel like they were, anyway. A lot of the comments on that video clip were about my attitude, how I came across, that people related to me, or found me funny, or easy to watch. So, as much as I didn't want to put my face on things, I thought that might be the way to do what I wanted to do and be in total control of the story at the same time."

"Pretty brilliant actually," she said.

"I realized that I didn't need anyone's permission. I

didn't need someone to hire me to do this. I just needed some decent equipment, to be willing to put in long hours while I supported myself and pursued this passion on the side. Then it was a matter of figuring out where I wanted to go, what story I wanted to bring attention to, and using my five minutes of fame to start my own channel. The live-streaming part started much later, just a few years ago, in fact. That took things to the next level, opened more doors for me and for the work I'm doing." He lifted his hands, then wrapped them back around his knee. "I haven't been home much since."

"Home," she said, still marveling over his story, but not truly surprised by any part of it. He'd finally done what she hadn't been able to do, connect the person he'd been then to the man seated before her now. She could see the evolution clearly now. He was a good storyteller. "Where do you call home these days? Not Nepal." She shot him a wry look. "Or do you still feel like you have to tuck yourself away in the most remote place possible all the time?"

He shook his head. "No, not anymore. I have a croft in Wales, near Mount Snowdon. I bought it thinking I'd start my own little farm there, something to ground me between trips. Only somehow seven years have gone by since I bought it and I never seem to not have another proposal before I've finished my current trip."

"What do you mean, proposal?"

"The work I've done in getting people to learn about various plights in far-flung places has come to the attention of a lot of small principalities and municipalities that other-wise have no voice, no beacon. I get asked all the time to come help shed some light on this story or that."

"That's . . . amazing."

"Trust me, no one is more amazed than I am at how this has all taken off. It's also a little overwhelming. I can't do them all and it's gotten increasingly harder to decide which to say yes to. I'm not a miracle worker. Some places see more benefit from the spotlight than others, but—"

"Like you said before, any is better than none. Without you they'd have no chance."

He nodded but didn't say anything else.

"So, do they pay you? These principalities? I mean, not to sound dense, but how do you keep a roof overhead? All this travel has to add up."

He shook his head. "They may comp me and my crew a place to camp, a few rooms, or something. It all depends on where we are. But we don't take compensation from them. We're trying to help them, not be an additional strain on their resources."

"So, is it sponsorships? I didn't see any ads on your YouTube channel."

"And you won't. I want the access to be immediate, not 'wait, watch this thing you don't care about, and then you get to see.' We do get sponsorships for our equipment, some clothing, a few other items and tools we use, in exchange for a credit at the end of the video version." He shrugged. "We've started selling hard copies and digital downloads of some of the trips, made into a sort of documentary. That's what I'm working on this summer, actually, for our Nepal trip. That revenue is what we live on now—me, and the few people on my crew I employ full time. Occasionally I do interviews, things like that, not to get paid directly, but to donate funds to the organization. The less overhead we have to deal with, the more we can do." He lifted a shoulder. "Otherwise, we all live pretty simply, my crew and myself. The ones who work for me have been with me from the early days. Abroad, we usually hire some locals, translators, people who can help us navigate the cultural aspects of things. And we have others who hire on for each venture, depending on where it is, what we need, whom we need. They may come and travel with us for a while, then move on when it's time to settle down. It sounds like an exciting life, and it is, but it has become pretty nonstop, and most folks need a home base, at least periodically."

"And you? Is that something you ever see for yourself? Settling down?"

His smile was more fleeting then, and she saw a hint of the weariness he'd only alluded to. "I can't do what I want to do and be home at the same time. I figure when the call to settle down somewhere is louder than the call to keep going, I'll listen to it then." A moment later, his grin was back, and the peek into that part of him was gone.

"Sounds complicated, or complex, anyway, working things out as you go, and juggling all the external things, like the documentaries, and getting them made and distributed. That by itself has to take a lot of focus."

"It is, but we kind of learn as we go. If the revenue from the documentaries starts to really pick up, then I can hire someone to take it on."

"I can't even imagine." Chey shook her head. "Where do you go next?" She wanted to know, and not know, all at the same time. Getting to know the stranger Wyatt was a lot easier than navigating the past with her old friend Wyatt. She felt like she was just getting to know this person. And she liked him. A lot.

"After the summer in Wales? I don't know yet."

"A whole summer in one place," she said, then smiled. "How will you stand it?"

"I think I can handle it for a few months."

She saw flickers of that weariness again, and wondered if, for all his enthusiasm, he was feeling a little burn out. Not about the work itself. He clearly was still deeply passionate about it. Still, how could it not take a toll? She suspected he said yes to more projects than he should, in an effort to disappoint as few as possible. "Good on you then." She let out a little laugh and said, "Self-care."

"What?" he asked, laughing with her.

She waved the question off. "Nothing, just a little private joke." Here she'd run off to Ben Campbell's place to assuage her sudden fragile sensibilities. While Wyatt was just hoping to lay his head on the same pillow for more than a few nights in a row before he jaunted off again to risk doing God knows what to be a champion for those with no voice. "Maybe the difference you need to make is for yourself this time around. Just for a little bit."

Rather than laugh the suggestion off or refute her, he surprised her and quite soberly said, "Maybe." He pushed to a stand then, surprising her with the sudden movement. He held out a hand. "Come on. Right now, we need to go save a certain town high up in the hills of the Blue Ridge."

She put her hat back on and stood without assistance, thinking she was feeling enough as it was. She didn't need his touch to bombard her already overloaded senses. "Child's play," she said with a smile. "The most dangerous wildlife you'll encounter here is an occasional black bear protecting her cubs." She smiled. "And I doubt they'll be attending any of the council meetings."

He smiled at that, but said, "Oh, I think Mr. Hammond might prove to be something of an obstacle."

Chey's smile fell. "Yeah, me too. Even if we get every artist, winery, cidery, and farm owner to come together over this, we still won't have near the clout or the financial resources he does."

"Oh, we have a very powerful resource," Wyatt said. "It's not the kind of currency with Benjamin Franklin's face stamped on the front of it. It's the kind that has millions of faces stamped on the front of it."

Chey smiled and started down the dock, liking that she didn't have to shorten or slow down her typically ground-eating stride. They'd always been well-matched that way. Now that she understood him better, reminders like that, of who he'd been, who they had been together when they were younger, felt comforting rather than disconcerting. "Good thing," she said, "because we don't have piles of the Benjamin kind."

They reached the end of the ramp road where they'd both parked. Theirs were still the only vehicles in sight. She paused at the driver's side door of her truck and turned back to him. "You don't have to stay here," she told him. "In the Falls, I mean. You worked hard for this break. A working break, I know, but . . . you should go and take it. We'll figure this out." She flashed a brief smile. "You haven't met Addie Pearl. She doesn't have a livestream, or whatever it's called—heaven help us if she ever did—but when it comes to manning the helm, she makes Vivi look like a wilting wallflower."

"Well, now I have to stay," he said, a teasing smile curving his lips, "just to meet her." Despite the smile, his gaze was a lot more direct than it had been, and far more serious. "I want to stay," he said, more quietly now. "And help."

She nodded. *And help.* He'd made sure to make that part clear. Not for any other reason. Which was a good thing. Wasn't it?

"It's your call, but—" She looked down, took a moment deciding what she wanted to say, then met his gaze again. "I'm glad we had this chance to talk, too. So I could get to know you."

"You know me," he said, equally quiet, gaze so intent.

She shook her head. "No. I knew you, once upon a time. But not now. Not since you walked into my barn. Not just because you look different. Your energy is completely different, too, the confidence you exude now, as naturally as breathing, all of you . . . it threw me. Not good or bad, just . . . I couldn't match this you with the boy I knew. You'd peek out once in a while, which was so disconcerting. Only . . . now that I know your story . . . it all makes sense. I meant what I said before—I'm happy for you, proud of what you're doing. All of this is such a good thing. It just took talking to you for it to fall into place."

"Well," he said, looking a bit taken aback, though she'd said all of it kindly, meant it kindly. "Now you know us both."

Her brief smile matched his. She nodded. "A little anyway." Their gazes met and held for the longest time, and, looking into those crystal-blue depths, she saw eyes that had seen so much now. They were no longer innocent, if they ever had been, and yet they were so deeply, utterly familiar. She couldn't stop herself from feeling a whole lot of things she really didn't want to be feeling. Childhood things, daring, adventurous things . . . very adult things. "I guess I have a whole library full of videos to watch if I want to know you better."

"That's only one part of me," he said. "You know . . ." He drifted off, then shook his head. Now it was his turn to break eye contact, look away, maybe debate, as she had, what he wanted to say. When he looked back, his gaze was more penetrating, not less, so focused, she felt pinned by it. And the way that made her feel wasn't at all bad.

"You know the me that no one else does, Cheyenne. Not even Tory knows me like you do. That's still me, too. A lot has changed, but it all came from who I was. That never changes."

She could feel the intensity emanating from him like a live, vital thing. She nodded but didn't look away. Couldn't look away. "I missed you, Wy." The words that had been dancing out to the tip of her tongue just leapt off before she could stop them. And with that breach, it was like the dam broke. "So much," she whispered, horrified she'd said it the moment the words were out. More horrified still to hear the crack in her voice. Completely done in when she felt fully formed tears sting the corners of her eyes.

"Aw, Chey," he said, a throaty rasp in his voice, too. "I was wrong to leave things how I did. Wrong to just bomb you with my feelings, then not give you time to—"

She shook her head, hard, as if willing him not to say anything else.

"I read every e-mail. Listened to your voice mails. So many times. I kept them, first because I was hurt, and mad, at myself, at you. They motivated me to move on, to better myself. Later I kept them because I knew I'd made a huge mistake." When she looked away, unable to bear the words, see the sheen that stole across his eyes, he lifted a hand, touched her chin to turn her gaze back to his. "Maybe the biggest mistake of my life."

His touch did her in entirely. The mere brush of his fingertips sent shudders of sensation rocketing to every pleasure point she had, shot her heart rate up so fast her chest pounded. She wanted to jerk away, yank open the truck door, turn the key, and drive and drive and drive. As far away from him as she could get.

"Then I didn't write you back, didn't come back, because I thought it was too late. I was a man on a mission."

"So, maybe it wasn't a mistake after all," she managed.

"It sure as hell feels like one." His gaze dropped from her eyes to her mouth and she saw his throat work. The restrained energy she felt in response to the way he looked at her, so hungrily, made her gasp. The dark pupils of his eyes instantly expanded, swallowing up all that beautiful blue, swallowing her up with it.

The punch of need she felt was so swift, her knees shook with the effort it took to hold still.

His gaze lifted to hers again, searching, wanting, needing. Oh, so very, very, needy. "I knew if I saw you again, I'd be tempted to forget all about that, and do what I should have done the moment I got your first note, telling me how you felt, what you'd realized after I'd gone."

"What is that?" she asked, trembling as an entire lifetime of feelings rose up and threatened to burst free, all at once.

As if it had been inevitable, that everything would eventually lead them to this exact moment, he slid his broad, warm, callused palms over her cheeks, sinking his fingertips into her hair, knocking her cowboy hat to the ground unheeded, as he cupped the back of her neck and lifted her mouth to his. While she did absolutely nothing to stop him.

"This."

Chapter Six

As colossal mistakes went, it was possibly the worst one he'd ever made. Worse than telling her he loved her, worse than walking away from her. And even knowing that did absolutely nothing to dampen the feeling of utter joy that filled him the moment her lips parted under his. It was revelatory, like nothing else he'd ever experienced, and it swamped him. Filling up all the empty spaces he hadn't known still existed. He was kissing Cheyenne McCafferty, and it felt like the whole world had just woken up . . . and bloomed.

Home. Finally. Those were the two words that kept echoing inside his head. He'd traveled to the four corners of the earth trying to find his place on it. When he'd kept going, and going . . . and going, he'd told himself his place was on all of it. But he'd known, had always known, his place was right here, in front of her. Wherever that happened to be.

He lifted his mouth from hers, slid his hands to her shoulders, and pulled her gently into his arms. He wanted more. So much more. He wanted it all. All of her. Her body, yes, but so much more than that. He wanted her sharp mind, her bold laughter, her teasing gibes and clever remarks, her insights and advice. *Her love.*

He rested his cheek on top of her head. "I should probably make an apology for that. But not a single part of me is sorry."

His knees might have buckled just a bit with relief when she slipped her arms around his waist and stayed in the circle of his arms. She rested her forehead on his chest, gaze cast downward. "I'm not asking for one," she said quietly.

He lifted his head and nudged her until she looked up and met his gaze. "Hi," he said, his smile meant to charm her. He didn't do a single thing to try to hide what he was feeling. "I'm Wyatt Reed. You remind me of a girl I used to know."

Relief again when she responded in kind. "Funny. I knew a guy with that same name." Her lips twitched. "You're nothing like him, though."

His brows rose. "Oh?"

She shook her head, her smile bemused, her eyes lighting up with that mischievous glint he knew so well. "He would never have done what you just did."

"Too scared?" Wyatt asked.

She shook her head again. "Too stupid."

He winced even as he chuckled. "Then he for sure didn't deserve you."

"That's what I thought."

"Good thing I'm nothing like him, then."

Her smile slid from mischievous to downright devilish. Then she shocked the hell out of him by sliding her hand to the back of his neck and nudging his mouth down to hers. "That's what I was thinking." And this time, she took him.

Colossal mistake? Or the best thing you've ever done?

Yeah, he had no idea, but he was too busy letting her kiss the socks off him to care.

She broke the kiss that time, her eyes still twinkling as she beamed up at him. "Definitely nothing like him."

"I almost feel sorry for the poor guy."

"Don't be," she said. "He turned out all right."

He ducked his head, feeling flattered and chastened, all at the same time. "Chey—"

"Don't," she said, quickly but not harshly. "I don't want to—" She broke off, shook her head, then said, "Let's just let this be . . . whatever it was, okay?"

"You mean pretty damn perfect?"

She smiled. "Well, that much was obvious."

He chuckled. "True."

"Also, I'll be sharing that swear jar with you later."

"Worth it," he said.

"We should head back to the house," she said. "For dinner and deliberation on how best to dismantle the plans of a determined, and possibly still soggy Mr. Paul Hammond."

Wyatt grimaced and said, "Yeah, I think that soggy part is going to cost us."

"Same."

He expected her to slip from his arms and climb into her truck. Once she decided on a course of action, typically the Cheyenne he knew wanted to get right on it.

Only, she didn't move. And he wasn't all that motivated to let her go. To be honest, he didn't want the chance to deliberate on the meaning of what had just happened, or what it might mean an hour from now, or tomorrow. Or the next day. On the very decent chance that once calmer heads and settled hormones prevailed, this was probably never going to happen again. He wasn't ready for it to be over, quite yet.

"Dinner," she said, not moving so much as an inch.

"We should," he said.

"I am hungry," she said. Then her gaze dropped to his mouth.

He groaned even as his body sent up a very enthusiastic yes vote. "Starved," he agreed.

"Right?"

He didn't even know who kissed whom first that time.

By the time it ended, her back was up against the truck, and neither of them were breathing particularly smoothly.

"So, I was wrong about one thing," he said, basically panting and not ashamed of it.

"Which was?" she managed, holding his waistband in a death grip, possibly as her only means of remaining upright.

"The first kiss being perfect." He braced one hand against the side of her truck, still sucking air. "Because that last one showed some marked improvement."

"I don't know," she said, her tone musing even as she clung to him for support.

He'd ducked his chin in an effort to find oxygen and turned his head to the side. "Just me then?"

She shook her head. "Not necessarily. But more research might be in order." She tipped her head back and blew a whistling breath through her lips. "Although that may have to wait."

"Oh?" he said.

"I think if we go in for another round right now, I'm either going to pass out, or . . ."

His eyebrows lifted, and one corner of his mouth twitched. "Or?"

"Do something really irresponsible in the bed of this truck."

He almost choked. "Yeah," he managed. "Point taken."

"Actually, point not taken. Which was my point. As it were."

They wheeze-laughed, and she let out a raspy squeal when he opened her truck door, picked her up, and put her on the driver's seat. He nudged her knees around so she faced the steering wheel, then closed the door. "Lock it," he told her.

"Good idea," she said through the glass, and he heard the locks click into place.

He turned to his truck, grinning like . . . well, like he'd never grinned before, when he heard the window power down behind him.

"Wyatt."

That's all she said. All she had to say. He turned, looked at her. And that's all he had to do. Three long strides later he climbed up on the running board, slid his hand into her hair, and kissed her hard, fast, and oh so very deep.

She slumped limply back in the seat when he let her go and hopped off the running board back to the ground. He scooped up her cowboy hat and plopped it on his head, shot her a wink, then whistled as he walked back to his truck.

"I don't think I should be driving under the influence," she called out as he climbed into Tory's truck. "Under the influence of Wyatt Reed."

"I think you're the bad influence, Cheyenne McCafferty."

"Yeah, well, whaddya gonna do about it?" she taunted, just like she had when they were kids, only this was so very, very adult.

He climbed in and closed the door, then lowered the window, tugged the brim of her hat down low, and shot her his own devilish grin. "Why, maybe we can discuss that over dessert, ma'am," he said in his best cowboy drawl.

"Don't you ma'am me," she shot back, her giddy grin at complete odds with the stern order.

Oh, I want to do a whole lot more than ma'am you, he thought, but for once, wisely refrained. "Dessert and deliberation," he told her. "With a side of Blue Hollow moonlight. Miz McCafferty."

She tipped her fingers to her forehead in a brief salute. "That's a date. Planet Wyatt." She started to raise her window, then lowered it again. "And I'm going to want that hat back."

Now it was his turn to taunt. "Come and get it," he shot back, then gunned the engine and peeled out of the parking lot.

Two and a half hours later, Wyatt leaned back in his chair and carefully laid his linen napkin on the table next to his now empty plate. "Miss Ginger, I can't recall a better meal in all my travels. Who knew supermodels had so many hidden talents."

Vivi beamed at the teasing and the heartfelt praise. "Sometimes you have to come home to get the food that fills the belly and soothes the soul, *cher*," she said, letting the New Orleans drawl of her childhood fill her voice.

Wyatt grinned. "I don't think there's any part of me that's not full right now." He was proud of himself for not looking at Chey when he said that. He was proud of her for being at the dining room table in the first place. He'd have bet the funding for his next project that between the lake and the farm, she'd have managed to talk herself into thinking what had happened between them a few hours ago had been a mistake.

Wasn't it, though?

He refused to give his little voice a toehold. Not yet. Yes, on the surface, it had been a phenomenally bad idea to pursue something—anything—with anyone, given where his life was. And yet, every part of him was still rejoicing. Vivi was right—sometimes you just had to come home. He was quite certain it was all going to come crashing down at some point, but he'd never felt the way he did at the moment, and frankly, he simply wasn't ready to give up on that yet.

There was still dessert and some moonlight to be attended to. Life would sort itself out. It always did. And rarely in the way he expected. *One step at a time.*

"Dessert?" Vivi offered.

"Did I see lavender-infused cupcakes with cream cheese frosting sitting out on the porch when I came in?" This from the fourth and final partner in the lavender farm endeavor.

She was the youngest—midtwenties, with dark hair, big, red-framed glasses—an enthusiastic, charming conversationalist with a scary-smart intellect. He thought she was the perfect addition to their mission.

"Indeed, you did," Vivi said, then turned to him. "In all your travels, have you ever had lavender as part of the menu?"

"I can't say that I have." They'd yet to talk about their plans for tackling the resort issue. Vivi had made it clear there would be no business talk over one of her meals. Instead, Hannah—with an affectionate gleam in her eyes—had asked Wyatt and Tory to share some childhood stories, preferably ones that featured Chey in a less than flattering light. The two had shared a few mild anecdotes, which Chey had taken as a challenge, sharing a few of her own in return. This had delighted all three of Chey's partners. There had been laughter, plenty of ribbing, and possibly some good-natured name calling involved.

He'd been surprised at how comfortable it all had been, how seemingly natural. As if the three childhood friends often met up and relived old times. When nothing could have been further from the truth. Wyatt hadn't spent much time in the States in the past decade-plus, only what he'd had to do early on so he could keep traveling on a work visa, before finally getting dual citizenship with Britain. Being stateside had never felt comfortable. Even with his father no longer a shadowy specter to be feared or loathed, it had still felt like . . . purgatory. A place that was between the two other planes of his existence, necessary but only as a holding spot until he could get on a flight to where he needed to be. It had certainly long since ceased feeling like home. If it ever had.

So today had been revelation upon revelation. Time he'd most definitely think on, sort out, analyze too much, and ultimately find a place for. Somewhere. He just didn't know what that place would be. At the moment, he couldn't imagine thinking back on this evening, spent with these people, as anything less than a wonderful memory. A highlight, for so very many reasons.

"No," he replied to Vivi. "I can't say I have. As wonderful as that sounds, though, I'm afraid I'm going to have to take a rain check." He pushed his chair back and picked up his plate and napkin.

"You don't have to clear," Avery said, hopping up. "You're company."

"KP duty is my middle name," Wyatt said with a grin, standing anyway. "You went to all this trouble—let me earn my keep."

"Vivi, you are not going to let him—" Avery began, but Hannah cut her off.

"Wyatt, have you made arrangements for tonight? We should have asked."

Wyatt glanced at Tory. "Tory said it was okay to bunk with her," he said, then looked at Hannah. "If that's okay with you." Tory had offered him her couch—or Hannah's couch, as it were—when they'd arrived. Over this delightful dinner he thought they'd gotten past Hannah's initial reaction on first meeting him, so he was surprised by Hannah's less than enthusiastic reaction to his request. He hurried to add, "I hadn't planned on staying more than the night. I'll find a place in town tomorrow."

"You'll do no such thing," Vivi said, stepping in. "I'm afraid between renovations and whatnot, we're full up here—"

"Vivi, he can use—" Avery started, but Vivi talked over her, her smile becoming brighter and more determined as she continued.

"Chey, darling," she said, as casually as you please, "you've got a fully furnished guest room. Surely you don't mind—"

"Vivi, he and Tory sound like they've worked this out—"

"Oh, the loft really isn't set up for guests," Hannah explained, looking from Vivi to Wyatt, her smile now firmly back in place. "Chey's place is much better." She turned brightly to Tory, who had been seated to her right, with Wyatt on her left. "Speaking of which, why don't we head out to the loft and go over everything since we didn't have a chance earlier." She looked at Avery. "Didn't you say you wanted to show Vivi that new extraction process you came up with?" She smiled. "Chey, you can help with cleanup, right? Then get Wyatt settled?"

Vivi patted Wyatt's hand and took his plate and napkin from him before he could get a grasp on the rapidly developing situation. "Avery and I will do this. And we'll talk business in the morning. I've already invited Addie Pearl for tea and lavender scones in the morning. Seth and Pippa will be joining us as well. He owns the winery up the hill here, and Pippa—well, I think she's going to be the perfect addition to our little quest." Her eyes twinkled. "She's got quite the following, too."

Thirty seconds later, as if by magic, Wyatt and Chey

found themselves alone on the enclosed veranda at the side of the farmhouse.

Wyatt laughed. "I wonder if they'd consider being on my next production crew. That was about the most well-orchestrated teamwork I've ever seen."

"And so subtle, too," Chey added wryly. "You know, you can bunk on Tory's couch. Hannah was just being protective."

His eyebrows lifted. "By shoving me into your bed? Protective of whom?" He chuckled. "Because I don't think anyone in there assumed that I was actually going to bunk in your guest room."

"I think Hannah was just making sure you didn't end up bunking with Tory." She made air quotes around the word "bunking."

Wyatt frowned. "Why?"

"Apparently she thought you two were an item, and she was trying to protect me by not letting the two of you spend the night together."

"First, why would she think that? And secondly, protect you from what?"

"Look, this is none of my business." Chey sighed. "I don't do gossip. And for what it's worth, neither does Hannah. The only reason she told me was because she knows our backstory. She was the only one I told about you. And I only did that because she was getting involved with someone and about to make what looked to my experienced eyes like the biggest mistake of her life. She came to me for advice, and I told her about you, about how we parted ways. I wanted her to understand why I knew what regret felt like, that I was speaking from a place of knowledge."

"You all seem so close," he said. "You never talked about us with the others?"

"We are as close as family. We are family. Like sisters from different generations." She looked out over the lavender fields for a moment, and he gave her the space and time to gather her thoughts, decide what to share. "We met at a grief counseling group a few years after Cody died. I worked a number of farms moving from the west to east, until I found a place on a farm in northern Virginia, just outside DC. I wasn't handling my grief well. I knew that. I'd tried counseling but, frankly, it just pissed me off. Don't tell me how to feel or what my grief is like." She waved a hand, let it drop. "That was on me, not the counselors. They were trying to help me, but I honestly wasn't receptive or trusting. I don't even know what made me go to that group meeting that afternoon. Desperation, I guess. I thought maybe I'd do better in a crowd, where I could listen but not be expected to participate. I don't know. A flyer at the post office was how I found out about it."

"Fate," Wyatt said quietly. "Or a fluke. I'm a firm believer in both." His smile was fleeting. "Even when it pisses me off."

The corner of her mouth lifted in a dry smile. She nodded. "I met Avery, Vivi, and Hannah there that day. We were complete strangers, but the thing we had in common was that we each instantly hated that group." She let out a short laugh. "They were very much interested in holding hands and wallowing in their grief. Not finding a productive way to live with it. We all more or less snuck out at the same time. As we stood in front of the elevator Vivi was the one who made some comment that made us all laugh. Avery started in as we rode down together, and we laughed some more. I felt better in the five minutes it took us to get outside than I had in the past three years before. Vivi spontaneously suggested we grab coffee."

She shook her head, a brief grin crossing her face. "Five hours later, we knew we'd formed our own grief group. The fearsome foursome was born. We started meeting every few weeks, then every week. We began doing things other than sitting and talking about what brought us each to that point in our lives and sharing ideas on how we were coping, finding our new normal." She lifted one hand and gestured to the fields beyond the French doors. "Six or so years later, we ended up here." She glanced at him. "This time, fate got it right."

She walked to the row of French doors that lined the outer wall of the veranda. He could see that this was the tearoom part of the farm. The deep, covered porch was lined with round tables, set with soft pastel linens. The large paddles of the overhead fans moved lazily, suspended between the exposed ceiling beams. He imagined the doors had been put in so they could all be opened to create an indoor-outdoor setting, with the spectacular view as backdrop.

"It's not that I was ashamed or angry or . . . I don't even know what, about our past," Chey continued. "We have shared some of the hardest, if not the hardest parts of our lives with each other. I talked a lot about Cody, about our relationship, our life on the circuit, my aunt and uncle. I talked about Tory, our friendship." She smiled briefly. "Our years taking turns beating the pants off each other in the ring. I don't even know why I just sort of skirted your existence." She let out a little self-directed snort. "Okay, so I know why. I didn't want to relive all that. I was having a hard enough time dealing with losing Cody. My aunt and uncle were gone then, too, and, other than finding ways to cope with losing Cody . . . I was otherwise just done talking about loss. I wanted to talk about anything else. Honestly, after a while, I didn't want to talk anymore at all."

He came to stand beside her, his gaze focused on the view just as hers was. "Understandable," he said.

"So, I listened, instead. When Vivi inherited this place and we started seriously planning to do something with the farm, it felt really good. To be forward looking. It was all we wanted, all we talked about. It was both healing and a welcome relief." She looked at him. "I always liked hearing their stories. Vivi's most of all. Still do. After a while, I could have talked about you, about us, but then I'd have had to explain why I never did before, and . . . I just didn't. I should have honored our friendship better than that. Yours and mine. And mine with them, too, I suppose. I'm sorry."

"You have absolutely nothing to apologize for. I've made a lot of close friends on my journeys. I'm very close with my full-time crew, and keep in touch with as many of the part-timers who have come and gone as I can. In all that time, except to broadly say I grew up out west and raised bulls for the rodeo, I never shared my childhood. With any of them. None of it. Partly out of shame, because of Zachariah. And for pretty much the same reasons you held back, when it came to talking about us. Those memories were mine to hold close, mine to regret. Sharing them would have made our relationship feel . . . trivial, I guess. Like something that must not matter much, because it was so long ago. Only nothing was further from the truth. Maybe I should have, maybe it would have been better to normalize it, or at least confront it, deal with it. Healthier, probably." Now he lifted a shoulder. "I just . . . didn't. It didn't feel right."

"I didn't want it normalized, either. Even losing Cody felt like that. Like if I came to terms with it, then he'd be in the past, and I didn't want that. Hannah has this amazing way of dealing with her grief. She showed me how to celebrate life by sharing it with Cody as I move forward, as if what I'm doing is with him. Not for him, but with him."

She shook her head. "It's hard to explain, but it was what saved me. Only . . . I couldn't do that with you. You were gone from my life, but not from this world. You were out there somewhere, living your life, moving on without me." She ducked her chin. "I can't explain it. I know that sounds crazy."

"No, it doesn't. In fact, it might be the best explanation I've heard for how I've felt all these years."

"I didn't talk about you with Tory, either. It was easier to just tuck you away, somewhere safe, but also somewhere I didn't have to examine. It's not that I never thought about you." She turned her gaze to his. "I have. At certain times in my life more than others. No matter how much time has passed, something always comes up that reminds me of you. Or that I'd want to tell you about, joke with you about, because only you would get the same absurd things I did."

He nodded, smiling. "It's funny—you'd think the far-flung places I've gone, where the day-to-day life could not be more different from anything I'd ever known growing up, would save me from thinking about you, remembering you. Because what on earth could I see, or hear, or eat, or . . . anything that would remind me of you?" He shrugged. "And yet it happened all the time. Used to drive me crazy."

"Used to?"

He nodded. "Somewhere along the line, I stopped trying to make you go away. I tried to accept that I wouldn't get to share these things with you, but that didn't make it less amusing, to think about your reaction, or what you would have said. So, it was like I was sharing it anyway. Just completely inside my own head." He laughed. "Now who sounds crazy?"

She turned to him fully. "No, that's how Hannah got me to see my life without Cody. She taught me how to take him with me exactly like that. To share what I was doing, seeing, feeling, with him." She looked up at him. "It just didn't work as a way to deal with losing you."

"You never lost me, Cheyenne." He lifted a hand, brushed his fingertips across her cheek. "You couldn't lose me if you tried."

"I know," she said with a wry twist to her mouth. "Because I did try." She ducked her chin then, slipping away from his touch and turning back to the doors and the view.

They stood there in contemplative silence for a long moment; then, with a laconic drawl, he purposefully shifted the mood a little. "So . . . what was this gossip? Why did Hannah think I was with Tory?"

He saw the corner of her mouth kick up. "So, I hear that Hannah caught you and Tory in a heated clinch out behind her truck." She gave him a sidelong glance. "She might have drawn a few conclusions."

That took Wyatt aback for a moment and he let out a laugh as he tried to imagine the scene from Hannah's perspective. "We weren't in a clinch," he said, shaking his head. "We were hugging, that much is true. And yes, we were having a bit of a private moment."

Chey's eyebrows lifted slightly and she turned her head. There was humor in her tone, but the expression on her face was openly questioning. "Do go on."

His smile slid to a grin. "I don't hug and tell," he teased, "other than to say that I can see why Hannah might have misconstrued things."

"Oh, I think maybe you should go ahead and tell," Chey said, one eyebrow arched, but a smile hinting at the corners of her mouth. "I'll make apologies to Tory later if I have to."

Wyatt laughed outright at that. "It wasn't that big a deal. We were talking about her bringing me here, about her separate friendships with each of us and how she'd kind of come to the end of her rope with that triangle of crazy.

When Buttercup joined the scene, she decided she was done juggling. But that's not to say she did any of this lightly. She felt awful, like she'd possibly ruined her chance here, and damaged her friendship with you and with me, no matter her good intentions. She was explaining to me why we are so important to her. I hated seeing her torture herself like that, because I know we both love her, for so many reasons. Always have. That hug was—"

"You don't have to explain, Wy," Chey said. "Thank you for being there for her. I'll make sure she knows that nothing has been ruined. I'm honestly glad she's here."

"You sound surprised," Wyatt said, a smile surfacing once again.

Chey let out a short laugh. "I am, to be honest. I'm not a big people person."

He shot her a mock look of shock and took the nudge to the ribs in stride. "Says the woman who is running a farm with three other women."

"Point taken," she allowed with a laugh. "That surprised me, too. Still does. But, you know, while our lives are far more deeply connected here than they ever were before, we also took great care to set this place up so we'd each have our own space and the ability to continue our other pursuits as well. Me with my horses, Hannah with her painting, Avery—though you haven't seen it—with her lab setup. Vivi with her kitchen." She lifted her hands and let them drop, her laughter wry. "Of course, we're not here even a year or two and now Hannah is living with Will and his son, Jake. Avery spends most of her time out with Ben—who also happens to be my vet." She shook her head. "It still all works, though. Maybe even better because we're not under each other's feet all the time. I don't know. When you're where you're meant to be, life has a funny way of sorting itself out, I guess."

Wyatt nodded, but didn't say anything. He wanted nothing more than for life to sort this out. He was starting to think maybe he didn't know where the hell he was supposed to be. Because he'd been everywhere, but standing right there, next to Chey, not even caring about the view, or where it was they were standing, he felt . . . settled. Like after running for so long, he could finally stop, and exhale.

"I'll talk to Hannah," Chey said. "So she doesn't think you're a two-timing snake destined to break my heart all over again," she added dryly.

"Thanks," he said, chuckling. "I think."

She nudged him again, but gently this time. "I think she already knows," Chey whispered. "Pretty sure they all do."

He glanced down at her. "You okay with that?"

"That you're not a two-timing snake?" She looked up at him and fluttered her lashes, which was so out-of-character it made him laugh.

He grinned. "Well, that, yes." He turned more fully toward her, took both of her hands in his, and let them dangle at their sides. "And the fact that I'm not means they also know I'm a one-woman kind of guy." He looked down into her eyes. "And it's not the woman bunking in Hannah's loft."

"They do seem pretty okay with that, given they've all but invited you straight into my bed." Her tone was teasing, but he saw the worry enter her eyes, the uncertainty, and it gave him more than a little twinge.

"And the owner of that bed? What does she think?"

"That I'm not ready to share it yet." She searched his eyes. "Wyatt, I don't mean that I don't want—"

"I wasn't asking about tonight," he said. "I'm not ready for that, either."

His admission got a surprised look from her and he chuckled. "Well, yes, we were both quite ready earlier today." His expression sobered. "I'm not talking about sex, Chey. Clearly our bodies are past ready."

"It's our heads that have to get wrapped around it."

And some other parts of us, too, he thought. He nodded. "I can't have one without the other. Even if I wanted to. Not with you. It won't just be one part of me getting involved."

He saw her throat work. "If only it were as simple as letting our bodies dictate things." She met his gaze. "It would be so easy if that was all we really needed."

Her smile was wistful this time, and maybe a little sad, and he felt a tiny fissure start somewhere inside his heart. "Maybe it would be better if I just head on out then. Back to Wales. Before we do . . . anything more." He didn't say "back home" because it wasn't truly one now, was it? He had nothing waiting for him there. No one keeping him there, calling him back. It was just an empty croft, on an exceptionally beautiful piece of land. Standing where he was right now, looking at Cheyenne, everything about his place in Wales felt empty.

The moment he'd suggested leaving, he felt her fingers instinctively tighten their hold on his, and for a moment, he felt profound relief.

"If you can help the town—" She broke off, shook her head. "I'm saying this the wrong way. What I mean is, if that's something you still want to do, for whatever reason, don't not do it on account of me, or . . . or this."

Not what I wanted to hear her say. Not, "Please stay. Stay for me."

Which, of course, he couldn't do anyway. Not long term. She knew that. And hadn't he just gotten done telling her that anything other than that wouldn't be enough?

"I'm going to head into town," he said, knowing it was the inevitable conclusion, so there was no point drawing the discussion out, causing either of them any more pain.

They'd hurt each other enough. Those few wild kisses had already ignited their mutual desire like a freshly struck match. Chey was right. If they spent any time together, they were going to end up in bed, no matter what their heads and hearts thought they wanted. In bed, up against the nearest wall, in the flatbed of her big, dual-wheeled truck, looking up at that big Blue Hollow moon.

His body responded to all of those possibilities like . . . like it responded to all things that had to do with Cheyenne McCafferty.

They stood there for several long, silent moments, as the pool of moonlight grew around them.

He heard her take what sounded like a shuddering breath; then she looked up at him, and he was stunned by the sheen he saw glinting in her eyes. "Will you be back out?" she asked, and he could hear the thick edge of emotion being held in check. "Or is this good-bye?" she said, and her voice broke just a little, when she added, "Again."

It was that little crack in her composure, the way she allowed him, unflinchingly, to see sides of her that he knew damn well she didn't show to anyone else, trust to anyone else, that did in his resolve to do the hard thing, the better thing. *The safe thing.*

"Aw, Chey," he said, and he wasn't sure who reached for whom first.

They were both all in, from the moment their mouths met, the moment their breath mingled. Lips parted, tongues dueled, there was ferocity, and not a small amount of fear. Fear that it might be the last time. Desperation, need, and want was a potent mix, and he wasn't immune to it, nor strong enough to fight it.

Her fingers were in his hair, gripping him, when she dragged her mouth from his. "I've changed my mind," she said, her voice nothing more than a hoarse whisper.

"If you're leaving anyway—and you have to, I know that—
then I'm already going to have regrets." She looked him
straight in the eye. "I want a night with you. I want to know
you, all of you. I want so much more than that, but if I'm
going to have regrets anyway, I know one of them is going
to be that we didn't at least share all we could, when we
could. That much, at least, I can quite selfishly do something about. So can you, if that's what you want. We can do
something about that together."

Every part of him knew that he should turn her down.
Knew that they were already well past playing with fire,
playing with pain, already wielding far too much power to
hurt, even though it was the last thing they wanted to do.

He could tell her all of that, and she'd know he was right.

He should tell her that. Tell her he was sorry, but he
couldn't do something that would hurt them both more in
the end. Then walk right out that door, grab Tory's truck,
and drive away. Without looking back.

He did walk out the door. In fact, he might have turned
the knob and all but kicked it open. But he picked her up
first, wrapped her legs around his waist, and buried his
fingers in her hair, taking her mouth again, and again as he
headed out. There was no pain-free way to end this, and
he wanted her more than his next breath, more than anything he'd ever wanted in his life.

He walked right out the door, not even glancing at the
truck. Instead he headed toward the lavender fields, and
the stone and log house bathed in moonlight.

Chapter Seven

Chey surprised herself by not having a single second thought as Wyatt carried her—*carried her*—across the moonlit lawn off the side of the main house, all the way out to her place, her home. It was sweepingly romantic and deeply thrilling, all at the same time. She wanted to swoon, and she wanted to tear his clothes off, in equal measure.

"It's unlocked," she said against the warm skin of his neck, the same neck she was presently kissing and biting her way along, as he climbed the steps to the porch. Her lips, tongue, and teeth made their way back to his jaw as he shifted around to open her front door, then carried her inside, closed it, and pressed her back against it a breath later.

Her legs were still wrapped around his waist and she groaned as he pressed fully against her. She'd never known she could ache to the point of physical pain for want of something. Feeling him there, so close, yet not nearly close enough, only stoked the need, deepened the ache. She gasped as he kissed his way along her jaw, down the side of her neck. She tightened her thighs around him, wishing their clothes would just magically disappear so he could push all the way inside her and turn that pain into a rocket burst of pleasure.

"Bedroom," she managed, as he dragged the collar of her shirt wide. With his teeth.

He took full advantage of the access he now had to the exquisitely sensitive skin at the base of her neck. This was raw, and thrilling, and utterly swamping her with need, but it wasn't mindless. She knew exactly what she was doing, exactly what she wanted, and where she wanted it. She wanted to feel his weight on top of her, wanted to feel every slow, controlled inch of him entering her for the first time.

She wanted it to be in her bed, where she knew she'd remember him for every single day she lived here going forward. The reality of that was beautiful and awful all at the same time, and she didn't care. She'd had beautiful and awful plenty in her life; she'd become an expert at learning how to champion the beautiful as a way to vanquish the awful. She had no idea what that would take in this case, or if she had it in her to even try. She did know she wanted more than old memories of Wyatt Reed to keep her company when she was alone at night.

And this felt like a pretty spectacular new memory to hold inside her heart.

"Across the room," she managed. "Behind you."

He straightened and slid his arms around her to hold her against him as he turned in the darkened house, with only the light of the moon to guide his way. He was big, his body hard and sinewy, and he carried her easily, confidently . . . and though she was perfectly capable of walking, she wrapped her arms around his neck, tightened her legs around his waist, buried her face in his neck, and let him.

For all the ravenous ways they'd gone after each other from that moment standing on the veranda, all the way across the yard, and up against the front door of her house, when he made it to the side of her bed, he lowered her to it, gently, with great care, and followed her down slowly. Deliberately.

Everything changed then, slowed down. Went from feeding frenzy to exquisitely deliberate and drawn-out discovery. As if he, too, wanted to be able to imprint every single second of this on his memory, to hold it as dear as she already did.

She opened her eyes to find him looking into hers, the silver light casting his face in shadows, his eyes too dark to read clearly.

"Chey," he said on a hoarse whisper, making the single word sound like both promise and plea.

"Don't stop," she said, feeling a momentary clutch of panic that he would change his mind, followed instantly by a stab of shame that she'd even consider putting her needs and desires ahead of his own. Just because she was willing to invite the echoes of this night into her home, to live with and recall forever and ever, amen, did not mean he was. He'd told her as much. She knew what she was doing, had from the moment she'd grabbed hold of him on the veranda. Maybe he was just now swimming back to the surface and realizing he couldn't risk drowning.

"I don't want to stop," he told her, brushing strands of hair from her forehead, looking at her, searching her features as if trying to memorize every detail. "That's just it," he said, leaning down to brush his lips against hers, drawing a soft, keening moan from her as she arched up against him. "I don't ever want to stop," he murmured against her lips.

He shifted his weight more fully on top of her, and he felt so very, very good. All of him, every part, filled her aching, rampaging, seemingly unfulfillable need. He touched her how she wanted to be touched, kissed her like he had known and understood the contours of her mouth forever, and knew just how to take it with his own. He was deliberate, assertive, and invited the same from her as they unbuttoned, unzipped, pulled off, peeled off, every last stitch of clothing.

She almost screamed with pleasure when he pulled her back under him and she felt the warmth of his bare skin touching all of hers. Just that alone was exquisite relief. He took her mouth like a man starved, accepting her equal hunger with deep growls of approval. Then, turning on a dime, he was gentle, and unbearably sweet, and made her throat tighten with unshed tears as he slowly made love to every single part of her like it was both a promise, and a benediction.

He was old Wyatt and new Wyatt, kissing his way down her body and settling between her thighs like a man on a very determined mission, confident he knew exactly what he planned to do when he got there. Then just before his tongue found her sweetest of spots, he slid one hand up, found hers and wove their fingers together, holding on as he took her, shuddering, shattering, over the edge.

No other words were spoken. They did all their communicating with touch, taste, and long, lingering, soul deep gazes. He took his time, rolling on a condom, inviting her to watch, then pulled her across his lap, to straddle him as he slid his hands into her hair, cupped her face and brought her mouth to his once more, somehow managing to take her, even while she was the one who slowly, deliberately, sank down onto him. Her head instantly dropped back, a low moan keening deep from inside her as he filled her, so utterly, and she couldn't keep from moving on him. He held her hips and took full advantage of the position, and her breasts, right there, at tongue level.

She wanted to slow it down, wanted to catalogue all the moments, everything he was making her feel, but it was too much, so much, all at once, and she gave in and let herself simply slide under the tidal wave of sensations.

He shifted so he could lie back, only he brought her down with him, then slowly rolled over, so he was exactly where she'd dreamed of having him, only the reality was so very, very much better. She wrapped her legs around his hips and they found their rhythm easily, keeping them both close to the edge, so close, as they kissed and nuzzled, but in no hurry to get there.

She wanted this reality to go on as long as possible, staving off the one that would come far too soon afterward.

Perhaps this had been a monumental mistake on her part after all. She couldn't have known how truly all-encompassing their lovemaking would be.

She knew now.

And she had no idea how she'd move on from this. Even as her body started that sweet climb to salvation once more, some part of her mind was already spinning off on a swirl of wild plans and possibilities about what she could do, how she could rearrange her entire life to go be with him. But then she felt him, saw him, heard him reaching his peak, too, and let herself be swept along with him. Mindfully and mindlessly, she let it all go, and simply let him and everything she was feeling fill her.

They didn't say anything afterward. Words seemed inadequate at that moment. Wyatt cleaned up; then they climbed under the covers, pulling up all the thick, weighty layers she kept on the bed year-round. Only this was so much more delicious, with his warm body and bare skin next to hers. He rolled to his back and gathered her to him. She tucked her knee between his legs and let her head rest on his chest, one arm around his waist. She felt his arms settle around her, strong, and heavy and perfect, and her eyes drifted closed. He pressed a kiss to the top of her head and she smiled as sleep claimed her. Tomorrow would be soon enough for the consequences of their actions to come crashing in. For now, she wanted all the bliss she could get.

She woke up alone. There wasn't even a muddled moment of thinking that was normal. She knew instantly what she was missing. Whom she was missing. Her heart clutched so hard at the thought that he was gone, she pressed her hand over it as she sat up and pushed her hair from her face. His shirt was on the floor, and his watch was on her nightstand. The relief was so immediate and profound, she slumped back against the pillows.

He wouldn't have done that, wouldn't have slipped away without a good-bye. Intellectually she knew that, but the moment of instinctive panic she'd felt did not bode well for when that inevitable good-bye came.

She'd slept soundly, the night through. No dreams, and better, no nightmares. They came very infrequently now, dreams of her brother on the last day of his life. But they did come. And just knowing that it was possible made dropping off to sleep a bit of a process for her. She'd long since mastered the mental list of things she went through, the deliberate thoughts she had, and didn't have, all as a means of prepping her subconscious for a dreamless night. It wasn't even something she did deliberately now; it was simply habit.

She'd done none of those things last night. It had been a very long time since she'd slept beside someone, and never in her own bed. The few times over the years when she'd been with someone long enough for sex to become part of the equation, sleeping together was rarely part of it. She preferred sleeping in her own bed. Alone. The possibility of the nightmares was part of it, but they were also a handy excuse. She always kept part of herself separate, disengaged, observing rather than fully participating. Sleeping alone was part of that. She didn't give away all of herself easily. Or ever.

Until now.

Ignoring that hard truth while she still could, she realized the gray skies outside had likely made it seem much earlier than it was. She grabbed her phone from the nightstand to see how badly she'd overslept. Her four-legged charges were not going to be happy with her. She was surprised she couldn't hear Foster kicking at his stable door.

The first thing she saw was a text from Tory, letting her know that she'd taken care of the horses that morning, along with her own.

> Seeing as your lazy posterior couldn't be bothered to get out of bed. Not that any red-blooded woman on Reed Planet or any other planet would blame you.

Chey smiled at that last part. Tory was getting what she wanted, so of course she didn't mind a few extra chores. For once, Chey didn't think she'd mind Tory being the smug Victor. That didn't stop a bit of warmth from rising to Chey's cheeks as she realized that everyone on the farm likely knew exactly how she and Wyatt had spent the night. Of course, they'd all but shoved them into bed together, so they'd be a little smug, too. And anyone with eyes could have looked across the property and noticed that there hadn't been a single light turned on in her house from the time they'd left the main house until now. So telling her friends the two had sat up and talked all night probably wouldn't fly. She grinned. That and the stupid grin she'd have plastered over her face all day. That might be a clue.

The scent of bacon and freshly brewed coffee wafted into

the bedroom from the great room beyond the open door, which was living area, kitchen, and dining room, and she immediately shouted, "Marry me!"

Wyatt had his phone pinned between his ear and shoulder as he came walking in a moment later, carrying a tray with a steaming mug of coffee and something else she couldn't make out. She was still sitting in bed, covers up to her hips, wearing nothing more than his rumpled shirt and quite probably an epic case of bedhead.

His hair wasn't sexily tousled but instead stuck out every which way, too. Totally old Wyatt—*thank God*—because the rest of him was drop-dead gorgeous new Wyatt. His jeans rode low on his hips and his skin was indeed a golden brown. Everywhere. As she now knew. He hadn't shaved, and the stubble shadowing his jaw added the perfect amount of sex appeal to the wire-rimmed glasses he was sporting. He looked like the hottest history professor on the planet. *Reed Planet, indeed.* She wanted to be a permanent resident.

He had been listening to whoever was on the other end of the call when he walked in and leaned down to place the tray on the bed, then casually shifted the phone away so he could pin her to the headboard with a hot, fast, and very deep soul kiss. He straightened, flashed her a grin and a wink as he started talking about file uploads and transportation budgets while walking back out to the great room. Leaving her to stare at his broad, muscled back and his very fine ass. She was dazed senseless by the combination of the scent of coffee and the taste of Wyatt Reed. And she was okay with that.

She slid the tray over and a soft sigh left her as she saw what else was on it. No bacon or eggs. She was apparently expected to haul herself out of bed for those. No, he'd brought her an oversized mug of jet black coffee, just the way she liked it, and next to it was a stalk of dried lavender, a tiny nest with a few downy feathers still clinging inside from its most recent inhabitants, and a small stone that she realized, upon picking it up, was an arrowhead. They'd uncovered a few of them during the renovations, and each one was a treasured gem.

There was a folded note underneath them. She picked it up as she took her first sip, then closed her eyes in abject pleasure. A deep, appreciative sigh later, she opened her eyes, glanced through the door to the main room, but could only hear his muted conversation and the sounds of breakfast being made in the kitchen.

She leaned back against the headboard and opened the note as she took a second sip.

"Don't make me an offer you're not willing to keep."

She frowned for a moment, unsure of what he meant, then closed her eyes again as she remembered what she'd shouted to him on waking up to the scent of coffee and bacon. *Marry me.*

She thought about that, about mornings like this being the norm in her life. Neither of them had traditional occupations, so there would never be those mornings of dashing about while showering, shaving, donning office wear and grabbing a bagel and a fast kiss before heading out the door for some god-awful commute.

No, her mornings consisted of getting up, admittedly early, but pulling on jeans and boots, and making her commute to the barn, and having a thermos of coffee while she kibitzed with her four-legged coworkers, before heading up to the main house to see what Vivi might be whipping up for breakfast. Hannah and Avery would roll in about then, and they'd discuss what needed to be done on the farm that day, then head out to the fields, or to town, or to whatever was required to keep the place humming.

They worked hard, all four of them, and put in very long

days, especially at the end of the growing season and all through the harvest, but it was a true labor of love. She was outdoors, where she was meant to be, in this beautiful place that was now home, surrounded by people she loved and who loved her right back. She watched the fields coming to life, knowing the lavender would grow and bloom because of what the four of them had done with their own hands. Her stables—her very own stables—and the field beyond were home to horses who had been given a second chance, a new lease on life.

She loved every part of that. With her whole heart.

Cody would be proud of her, happy for her, as would her aunt and uncle. She was exactly where she was supposed to be. Admittedly, watching Hannah and Avery each find someone to share all of that with had made her think about that part of her life. The one part she'd yet to fulfill.

Since moving to the farm, she hadn't given that part of her life any thought. She had no time, and even less inclination. Things were good. Why go muck it up with potential drama and heartache, and didn't relationships always seem to go hand in hand with both? Then Hannah had met Will, and Chey had watched her friend fall so beautifully and completely in love. Not without risk, or a fair share of drama, but the payoff . . . Chey closed her eyes, smiled. She was openly, wholeheartedly thrilled to see Hannah find her second chance at happiness, at love, and most importantly for her, family.

Then Avery had met Ben, and if that hadn't been the most adorable thing ever, Chey didn't know what was. The only thing bigger than Avery's brain was her huge heart. Turned out the same was true for Ben. They'd all taken great glee in watching the two of them figure out they were meant to be together.

"And crap, even Vivi is dating now," Chey realized,

smiling as she thought about how that particular date had ended, but still. Chey had a suspicion that while Paul Hammond had been crossed off Vivi's dance card, now that she'd unearthed it again, it was only a matter of time before new names got penciled in.

Which leaves you, she thought, *sitting in bed, while the man who spent the better part of the night making the most beautiful love to you is out there making you breakfast. Then could most likely be coerced back into bed for more of the same with very little effort on your part.*

She closed her eyes and her grip on her coffee mug tightened a bit. If only it would be, could be, that simple. Hannah and Will, Avery and Ben, they'd figured it out. *Yeah, but they all live in Blue Hollow Falls full time.*

And she was wasting what little time she had with Wyatt worrying about when she wouldn't have him near. She set her mug on the tray and got up, then carried it into the great room. He was still on the phone in the kitchen, his back to her while he stood at the stove. She gave him his privacy, as much as was possible, anyway, and set the tray on the oversized ottoman that doubled as a coffee table. She picked up her gifts from Wyatt and walked over to the big stone fireplace, where she arranged them on the old railroad tie that served as her mantel.

She had other treasures up there as well. Three massive-sized pinecones that she and Cody had collected as kids, standing upright like soldiers. An old shoe from her first horse, leaning upright, with the open end at the top, so it could collect good luck. A tied bundle of dried lavender that Avery had given each of them at the end of their first season. And a piece of driftwood and sea glass that Wyatt had given her on their caravan's one and only surf-side rodeo in Southern California. She wondered if he'd seen them this morning, if he remembered giving them to her. *Of course he had. And of course he did.*

She placed the bird nest on top of one end of the driftwood, then propped the arrowhead, point down, into a small crevice at the other end so it stood upright. She picked the sprig of lavender up and carried it back into the bedroom, leaving it on her nightstand instead.

She should brush her hair, wash her face, put on actual clothes. Instead she walked back out to the great room, one arm wrapped around her waist, hugging the soft material of Wyatt's shirt to her skin. She picked up her mug from the tray, then went to the big picture window with a view across the field where her horses grazed to the mountain peaks.

She felt him behind her before his arms slid through hers and circled her waist. He leaned down and pressed a kiss to that perfect spot on the nape of her neck, then pulled her back against him.

"Sorry," she said, still cradling her mug as she took in the view and reveled in feeling cared for by the man standing behind her. She was blissfully content with her world at that moment and wanted nothing more than for it to go on forever. "I wasn't trying to eavesdrop. I can go back in the bedroom if—"

"No, I'm done. And it wasn't anything you couldn't listen in on." He turned her in his arms, so she faced him. "In fact, it was kind of about you. Among other things."

Confused and curious, she reached out to set her mug on the small table that sat next to the big, leather easy chair, then turned back to face him. "Tell me more," she said, sliding her arms over his shoulders and toying with the curls at the nape of his neck.

He made a sound that was half growl, half purr, and she smiled when she saw his eyes darken as desire flared.

She suspected he saw the same in hers as her body leapt to life.

"I thought we'd talk about it over breakfast," he said. "Which is ready."

"Earning your keep," she said, trailing her fingertips over the nape of his neck, enjoying his visceral reaction to her touch. "I like it."

He leaned in and caught the lobe of her ear between his teeth. "I thought I did that last night," he murmured.

"Well, I like to think that was more of a mutual admiration kind of thing."

"Indeed," he said, trailing kisses along the side of her neck. "I know I was a big fan."

"Some might say huge," she replied, letting out a little gasp when he pushed the shirt down over her shoulders and nuzzled the crook of her neck, while simultaneously scooping her up and urging her legs around his waist. "I'm detecting a pattern here," she said, smiling as he let her head drop back, allowing him free reign to go . . . wherever his mouth and tongue wanted to go.

"This way I don't have to let you go while I get us where we need to be," he said, surprising her by not carrying her to bed, but simply turning and sinking down into the big leather chair, with her now straddling his lap.

"I'm assuming breakfast can be reheated," she said, and began unbuttoning the shirt she was wearing, his shirt, gleeful at the brief look of stunned surprise on his face as she slowly bared herself to him. "You don't get to call all the shots."

"Please," he said reverently, as he pulled her to him and took one of her nipples between his lips. "Call all the shots you want."

She cried out with pleasure as he took his sweet, sweet time, sliding an arm around her waist, and sinking his other hand into the hair at the nape of her neck, then using both to arch her more fully into him.

Now it was her turn to growl with pleasure as she moved against him, seeking what her aching body knew it wanted.

She reached down between them and flipped open the snap at the top of his jeans.

"My wallet is in the other room," he said as he trailed hot kisses from one nipple to the next. "Poor planning on my part."

She continued opening the front of his jeans. "I'm on the pill," she told him, her voice hoarse with need. "Regulates me. I haven't been with—I'm safe, Wyatt."

He lifted his head, caught her gaze, his so dark and full of want it took what was left of her breath away. "So am I." He held her gaze as assuredly as he'd held every other part of her. "Are you sure, Chey?"

She nodded, making sure he knew that she wasn't just mindlessly deciding this. "I don't ever," she said. "Ever." She wanted him to know she meant what she said, about risking her health, or his, but also that she was making a deliberate choice, specifically with him.

"Me either. Never, not once."

"We can," she said, "if you—I won't—don't mind. I'm not dismissing it for the sake of speed. I want—"

He stood then, still holding her, and walked them both directly to the bedroom.

Admittedly part of her was disappointed, both because she wanted to feel him inside her, with no barriers, and because she'd hoped he wanted that, too. With her. She would never make anyone feel bad over that personal choice, so she kissed him, with all the care she had for him, and made sure he knew that.

He lowered her to the bed, not quite as gently as he had the first time, shucked his jeans and followed her down without pause, his weight directly on her. She immediately wrapped herself around him, the look on his face alone making her arch up hard against him. She expected him to reach past her, for the nightstand, but instead he cupped her cheek, turned her face to his, and settled between her legs.

"Last time, you took me before we took each other," he said, his voice so deep now, the words quietly said. "This time I want to take you, feel you, all of you." He started to push inside her and she gasped, her hips jerking hard against his, as an almost piercing need clenched the muscles between her thighs. "On all of me."

"Yes," she panted, when he paused, his gaze hot and heavy on hers. "All of you. Inside all of me. Please, Wy."

Then take her, he did.

Chapter Eight

They were twenty minutes late to the meeting with Vivi, Hannah, Avery, and the rest of the assembled guests. The number of whom was rather startling. It looked as if half the town was packed around the tables in the veranda tearoom.

Wyatt held Chey's hand as they stepped up into the enclosed veranda where Vivi had set up court, so to speak. She'd put out quite the spread and everyone already had full plates in front of them. It was a good strategy, Wyatt thought: fill their bellies before making a call to action. Having been a guest at her dinner table the night before, though, he suspected this wasn't calculated. It was just how Vivi was.

Given the breakfast he'd made hours ago had been packaged up and stowed in the fridge untouched, he was grateful for it.

"Sorry we're late," he told Vivi, taking her offered hand and planting a quick kiss on the back, much to her delight. He and Chey took the two seats Vivi had saved for them at her table at the head of the room. "I was able to get a few things put into motion this morning," he told Vivi as he nodded while people lifted their hands in short waves, called out hello to Chey, and raised a few glasses in their general direction. "Thanks for sending the resort plans over. That helped a lot."

Chey responded to the various greetings with a quick nod and smile. It wasn't until Wyatt went to pull out her chair that he realized they were still holding hands. A quick scan of the room told him the gesture had not gone unnoticed. He didn't mind, quite the opposite, but this wasn't his town; he didn't have to live with these people. "Sorry," he whispered in her ear as she scooted in front of him and took her seat.

But when he started to let her go, she held on to his hand a moment longer, then glanced up and caught his eye. "No apologies," she said with a smile, the words for his ears only.

Their gazes held for a moment longer, and there was no doubt that she wasn't just talking about the public display of affection. "Good," he said with a quick flash of a grin, then edged behind her chair to get to his own. Vivi was on his right. Avery and a man Wyatt assumed was Ben, the veterinarian, sat across from them. They both offered happy greetings to him and to Chey. Avery's eyes were particularly sparkling as she took in the two of them.

Wyatt hoped Chey was ready for what appeared to be a room full of well-wishers eager to congratulate her on the apparent change to her relationship status. He hoped she was ready for it, period. He hadn't had the chance to tell her the rest of his news that morning, as they'd gotten distracted from that conversation. Twice. He had a whole new appreciation for long, hot showers now, and he'd been pretty appreciative of them before.

Wyatt pulled in his chair and nodded hello to the woman rounding out their table of six. She had just seated herself to Vivi's right, placing her loaded plate on the table and propped a gorgeous, hand-carved walking stick against the wall behind her before seating herself. Wyatt had started to stand again to offer his assistance, but she'd kindly waved him off.

She seemed to be in the ballpark of Vivi's age, but that was where the similarity ended. She was quite short, with narrow shoulders, wide hips, and skinny bird legs below. Her steel-gray hair was plaited into a braid that went far enough down her back that Wyatt didn't know where it ended. She wore a tie-dyed shirt with what appeared to be the Bluebird crafter's guild logo embroidered on the front pocket. Her faded and well-worn khaki shorts fell well below the knees and would have made her right at home in the bush country of Australia. Wyatt was intrigued by her already. Her face was lined by a life spent in the great outdoors, and her smile was ready and sincere.

He got hung up briefly on her eyes, which he swore were a lavender hue, though that might just be the lighting. Even as she smiled and said her hellos, she probed him in a swift once-over that left him feeling a little exposed. From Chey's earlier description when they'd talked about who was going to be at the meeting, he had no doubt who she was. Chey was right about one thing. Addison Pearl Whitaker didn't miss much.

In this case, that was going to be a good thing.

"Thank you all for coming out here this morning," Vivi said, rising from her chair, all flowing scarves, bangle bracelets, and a swept-up hairdo that looked painstakingly elaborate, yet suited her stage bearing to a tee. Between Vivi's lavender-streaked hair and Addie Pearl's eyes, Wyatt felt a little like he was at a table with the Blue Hollow Falls version of the Witches of Eastwick. And here he'd thought he had to travel to the four corners of the earth to find such interesting company. He grew more intrigued with Chey's chosen hometown by the minute.

"As you all know by now," Vivi said, after the various

conversations in the room trailed off and fell quiet, "it's come to our attention that there is a bit of an economic disconnect between the revenue flow that is coming through our businesses out here, and those centered in the town itself."

Wyatt knew from Chey that the assembled guests were comprised of the folks who owned the tourist draws outside the town proper. Seth, the winery owner he'd heard about, was there, as was Mabry, who owned the apple farm, as well as a goodly number of the artisans and musicians who populated the restored mill.

"One of the unfortunate side effects of the traffic flow being diverted from the town proper," Vivi went on, "to the mill, and to places like Seth and Pippa's winery, Mabry's cidery, and our very own Lavender Blue, is that the businesses in town have experienced a steady decline of tourist traffic. Our local nature park and the wilderness area surrounding Firefly Lake appear to be other victims of this significant reduction in tourist flow." She picked up a set of papers and a pair of bedazzled glasses affixed to the end of what looked like a wand.

Wyatt smiled, already enamored with Vivi's stage presence. She was truly something to behold. Addie Pearl caught his gaze as he shifted to look out over the room, studied him for a moment, then gave him an imperceptible nod before turning her attention back to Vivi. Wyatt felt Chey take his hand under the table. She slid her fingers through his and rested their joined hands on his knee. She leaned in and whispered, "You just got the Addie Pearl stamp of approval," she said. "And she hasn't even spoken to you yet."

"I'll assume that's a good thing," he whispered back, then flinched when Vivi swatted him playfully with her sheaf of papers.

"Don't make me split you two up now," she admonished.

"Not possible," he replied with a grin before thinking better of it.

That earned a series of hoots and a smatter of applause.

Vivi's perfectly penciled eyebrows lifted and she glanced at Chey, as if looking for confirmation. Chey made a shooing motion for her to get on with it, then looked out over the room in a dead-on impression of the Queen Victoria look and everyone quieted down immediately.

Tory, who was seated in the middle of the room, gave her a thumbs-up and announced, "I taught her everything she knows. My little girl, all grown up." She pretended to wipe a tear, then lifted a glass in salute.

Everyone laughed until Vivi tapped her spoon against her glass to regain the floor. Wyatt saw Chey's private smile when she turned back around to give Vivi her full attention once again. He squeezed her hand. She squeezed back.

Vivi held up her glasses to look at her notes, then lowered them again to address the room. She was at ease in the role of team leader, but Wyatt saw the pinched corners of her mouth, and knew she was more worried about this than she let on.

"This, of course, is a serious issue for the businesses in the Falls proper, but if those services fail, then it also becomes a problem for all of us. We rely on them for our own day-to-day lives. What we offer is invaluable in terms of keeping traditions alive, finding new ways to bring growth to the area, and increase tourism while still respecting the rural mountain culture that drew us all to this area in the first place. That said, the businesses in town can live without us, but the same can't be said for us without them. I feel like it's on us to come up with some solutions that will, in the end, help us all."

This was met with vocal affirmations, clapping, a whistle

or two, and a lot of murmured conversation. The way Wyatt read the room was that they all agreed with Vivi, and were potentially willing, but had no idea what they could do to help. That was Wyatt's experience in more village and tribal meetings than he could count. In that respect, he felt right at home.

"I've learned this week that the town council has had a plan proposed to them that will remedy this issue," Vivi informed them.

Everyone fell instantly silent. All eyes were once again on her.

"They want to sell Firefly Lake and the surrounding acreage to a resort developer." There was a collective gasp that seemed to suck the air out of the room. Suddenly, no one was interested in their bacon and eggs, lavender scones, and hot tea. "Now, I know many of you have been approached by various developers over the years, and you've remained united in turning those offers down. However, in this case, the town owns the property, and I'm afraid this proposal solves too many of the council's immediate problems for it to be turned down. No matter that the short-term fix might change the course of Blue Hollow Falls forever."

"What kind of resort?" someone asked. "Who runs it? Some big hotel chain?"

"Well, that's the thing," Vivi replied. "The developer, Pantheon Properties, has pitched a fully realized proposal, with subcontractors in place, and contracts ready to sign. I have a copy of the plans, and I've seen the full presentation. The change will be both expansive and transformative. However, not in the way I think we want. This won't be a modest hotel coming in and offering to upgrade the nature center, provide better trail maintenance, and better boats for the lake. Pantheon will completely change the face of Firefly Lake, and Blue Hollow Falls." She picked up the papers and used her spectacles to read from the overview she'd typed up. "I won't sugarcoat it, so here goes. They intend to tear down the nature center, take out the docks, dredge that whole side of the lake to put in a beach, then build a fifteen-story hotel, with three-story wings extending out from either side, all lakefront."

Wyatt saw the utter shock on each and every face after Vivi's blunt recitation and thought it had been the right way to handle the presentation. Go straight to the facts.

"The woods on the near side of the lake will be completely cut down, and condos will be built. The wilderness trails will cease to exist. Some of that wooded area will be retained but cleared in a way to make room for luxury cabins, A-frames, and other independent lease properties." She sighed and put the papers back on the table. "The rest of the wilderness area will be completely cleared to make way for a championship, eighteen-hole golf course."

Several people pounded their fists on tables, others shouted, and then things really got out of hand. To say an uproar ensued would have been putting it mildly.

Wyatt stood up and tried to call the meeting to order, but it wasn't until Chey stood up, put two fingers between her lips, and let loose a piercing whistle that the cacophony finally shut down.

"I know that none of us want this," Chey said to the still grumbling room as she continued to stand next to Vivi. "We know this is not the kind of growth we want in Blue Hollow Falls. Commercial resort development of that magnitude will mean other commercial ventures looking to attach themselves to it. Chain outlets, big box stores, and fast-food places won't be far behind. Now, I know each and every one of us sometimes shops in those kinds of businesses, so they have their place. But that place is down in the valley, in Turtle Springs and beyond, where they already exist and serve us perfectly fine. We live up here precisely because we don't want to live in the valley, and we don't mind driving to get those kinds of commercial services when we want them."

A young man about Wyatt's age with a stout beard and hair that fell below his shoulders, and the physical presence of a Viking to match, stood up and said, "So, what do we do about it, Chey? Point us in a direction, and we'll make it happen."

"That's what we're here to talk about, Seth," she told him.

Wyatt realized now that the Viking was Seth Brogan, the winery owner, whom he'd spoken to on the phone earlier that morning.

"I brought someone who might be able to give us some ideas on how and where to start." Chey turned and said, "I'd like to introduce—"

"Wyatt Reed." The words had been blurted out by a young man who was seated at the table to their left, behind Addie Pearl. He was a tall, lanky kid, maybe fourteen or fifteen, with thick brown hair. Next to him was a girl, maybe a few years younger than he, also on the tall side, with dark red hair and a surprisingly direct gaze. On the other side of the teen was a man in his early forties, and next to him sat Hannah. Wyatt immediately put the man and boy together as Will and Jake McCall, Hannah's new family.

Wyatt wasn't sure about the young girl, but she had no such qualms about him, apparently. Her gaze was alert and astute and she gave him a very deliberate once-over without any attempt to hide it. Unlike Addie Pearl, she apparently chose to withhold her judgment. He smiled and nodded toward her, accepting her wait-and-see approach. That surprised a smile and nod from her in return.

"I thought I recognized you," Jake said, looking a little awestruck. He turned to the rest of the room. "He's Wyatt

Reed." Will nudged his son, who stood. "Sorry," he said. "I'm Jake McCall. You're Reed Planet."

"That would be me," Wyatt said with a nod. His smile grew as he noted that the young girl next to Jake was not the least bit impressed by that revelation.

"It's a pleasure to meet you," Jake said, then looked at Chey with pure hero worship illuminating his handsome young face. "You're with Reed Planet?"

Hannah made a little axing motion across her neck and a shake of her head and Jake cleared his throat and looked back at Wyatt. "Are you going to livestream from Blue Hollow Falls?"

Wyatt nodded. "If it turns out you need it, I'm game."

"Yes," Jake said with a fist pump. Then he turned to the room as if expecting them to share his victorious enthusiasm. When he saw the sea of blank faces, he said, "He has, like, millions of followers. I've followed him for years. He goes to parts of the world no one knows about to bring attention to places that need help."

Wyatt noted that Jake's younger sidekick sat up a little straighter at that news, though her jury was clearly still on hold with the final verdict. He couldn't say why that made him feel better, but he liked people who needed all the information before hopping on a bandwagon, or off.

Now Addie Pearl rose, and if the moment hadn't been so fraught with tension and worried anticipation, Wyatt would have smiled at the disparity in height between her and Vivi. Yet the moment Addie spoke, her words quiet but firm, she commanded the room like a spiritual leader. Wyatt knew that in addition to being part owner of the mill, she was a weaver by trade. She was also, it appeared, something of a guidepost for the community. Someone they all turned to for wisdom and advice. As she stood barely more than hip high to Vivi, using her carved walking stick once more, Wyatt smiled and thought, *Yoda, you must be.*

"Mr. Reed has been kind enough to offer us his global platform," Addie said, then looked at Wyatt and gave him a broad, genuine smile. The transformation was striking. Her eyes were indeed lavender, and they sparkled with clarity and purposeful intent. He was as riveted as everyone else in the room at that moment.

"Now, I don't know that we need millions of anything," she went on, looking back toward the room. "But the collective attention of those millions might be enough to make our objections heard despite that mighty big carrot being dangled in front of the council's collective noses. Might help encourage them to choose a different solution to the problems facing our town. Our solution." Her look shifted to one of quiet confidence, with an impish smile that encouraged folks to have hope, to believe they could do this.

Wyatt had seen that exact expression before and realized then why he'd made the Star Wars connection. The vibe, the wisdom, and the calm certainty that exuded from her every pore was so utterly the same. *Blue Hollow Falls, you have the force, and she's right here before you.*

"All we have to do," Addie Pearl said simply, "is come up with one."

A clatter of conversation immediately erupted again. Addie Pearl merely lifted her walking stick and they quieted. She turned and gestured to Wyatt. "Given this young man has been involved helping countless other villages and towns solve far more convoluted problems than ours, let's let Mr. Reed speak and maybe we'll find the beginning of an idea."

She sat, as had Jake and Seth, and the room grew quiet.

"Thank you, Addie Pearl," Wyatt said, then turned to the room. "Hello. I'm Wyatt, and it's a real pleasure to meet you all. The reason I'm here—I've known Cheyenne since we were kids, and what's important to her is important to me. I haven't been here long, but I have already seen what it is about the Falls that draws you in and makes you want to stay."

Chey had let go of his hand when he stood up, but he felt her rub the toe of her boot alongside his, giving him her support.

His smile grew. "I haven't explored the town proper yet—which kind of does demonstrate how easily tourists can come up here, higher in the hills, and enjoy your farms, the mill, and the Falls, but never quite make it into town. I have had the pleasure of spending some time out at Firefly Lake."

"And in Firefly Lake," Vivi offered with a glint of humor, causing a ripple of laughter and easing the tension a bit.

"Also true," Wyatt acknowledged with a grin, seeing that word of his rescue had apparently gotten out. The twinkle in Vivi's eyes told him she'd likely been the source of that leak. He wasn't sure how wise it was to poke the deep-pocketed bear that was Paul Hammond by spreading that tale around, but it was her story to tell, and her bear to poke.

He looked back to the room. "I won't bore you with my story. You can do a quick search online and find out way more than you ever wanted to know about my adventures, trust me." He nodded to Jake and grinned. "Or Jake can fill you in."

The teen beamed and flushed all at the same time. Sidekick's vote was still pending. He nodded at her, too, and got a simple raised eyebrow in return, as if to say, "Go on." So, he did.

"I've been in situations like this many times. Admittedly usually in far more remote areas with far fewer people involved. What Addie Pearl says is true. The best solution in your case is finding an alternate solution, then putting it forth and getting serious consideration for it. This approach does two things. It slows down the decision-making process and allows everyone to take a deep breath. That gives you the time to adequately present your side and why it's important to you that the council go in a different direction and reject the Pantheon offer."

"What if they don't listen?" The young girl seated at Jake's table stood up. "Hi, I'm Bailey Sutton. What if they just go ahead and do whatever they want? Do we have a way to force them not to take the resort guy's offer? Is there a town vote or something?"

"Hi, Bailey," Wyatt said, liking her more by the minute. Young, sharp, and wanting to be involved. "Vivi—Ms. Baudin—has been attending council meetings for some time, and from what I gather, without any other plan to choose from, the town doesn't have to vote. The council members you elected to oversee your interests will decide yay or nay." He looked at Vivi, who nodded that he'd gotten it right. "Of course, you do have a say in the next election, meaning you can vote out the council members you think aren't representing you properly. When you're in between elections, like now, sometimes, if those in a position of power fear they'll lose your votes in the future, it can be an incentive to keep you happy." He lifted a hand to tamp down her enthusiasm. "However, unfortunately, what is more often the case is that they have campaign donors with deep pockets—and they have one with very deep pockets in this particular situation—and those donors are the ones the council will be most interested in keeping happy."

"Can't we have like a town meeting or something? Voice our opinion on this at least?" Bailey looked around the room, then back to him. "Loudly if we have to?"

Wyatt smiled, and there was a scattering of applause and

voiced approval for Bailey's question. "Absolutely. You can call for a town hall meeting. It's not the same as you all getting to officially vote on the proposal, but it's the next best thing. That is where you can make your voices heard. That is honestly exactly what you do."

"Only you're saying that even if we do, they're probably still going to make Mr. Deep Pockets happy, and he wants this resort, right?" Bailey asked. "Is there anything else we can do?"

"First, they can't change what they don't know you want changed, so you have to present your case. Make your opinion on this known. Second, at the town meeting, if not before, you would also present your solution. It's hard to get anyone to say no to a big shiny object that will solve all their problems if you've got no other choice to offer."

"Even if it ticks off Mr. Deep Pockets?" Bailey asked, looking more dubious and distrustful by the moment.

Wyatt nodded. "Even then. Especially then. If no one ever challenges the council members, they'll just continue to do more of whatever is in their own self-interest. Push back has to start somewhere."

"Couldn't we present this alternate solution to them directly?" This from Seth. "Or is the town hall spectacle necessary?"

Wyatt shrugged. "You could, yes. You could get petitions signed as a measure of showing town support for your plan, and the lack thereof for theirs. But nothing beats a room full of people, all with the same concern, and an expectation that their needs will be met in some way. It's more visceral." He lifted his hands. "I'm not saying be a mob. The exact opposite, actually. You can accomplish more with direct, sincere, open dialogue. Coming in hot can oftentimes trigger instant defense mechanisms, and then everyone digs in their feet and nothing gets done."

Vivi smiled. "If we show them that there is overwhelming opposition to their plan, won't that make it clear that if they go against the wishes of the majority, no amount of campaign contributions from Mr. Deep Pockets is going to help them get the vote next time around?"

"Yes, that's step one of the town hall meeting. Step two is the alternate proposal."

"I think we all know who Mr. Deep Pockets is." This from Seth. "The Falls isn't that big." He scanned the room, and Wyatt could hear Hammond's name being murmured. He looked back to Wyatt. "Rumor is he doesn't play fair. What can we do if he's got some backroom deal going?" His tone made it clear he suspected this to be the case, and the nods of everyone else confirmed he wasn't alone in that suspicion.

"Go beyond your locality, draw broader attention to your situation," Wyatt told him. "More attention brings more pressure to bear on those in control of decision making. The problem with most of the places I travel is not having a direct conduit to the outside world, not one that would draw attention to them in the way they need. You all already have those established links via your music center, your mill, and your various independent Web sites. In this case, however, because time is of the essence, gradual campaign-building from multiple sources won't get the job done in time. We need focused attention, all at once, with as many eyes on the situation as possible." Wyatt looked toward the rest of the folks in the room. "I can help with that. Take your story from a local one to a national one."

"A global one," Jake added.

Wyatt smiled and nodded toward Jake. "It's true that if

I stream from here, people from all over the world will be watching, but all we need to do is to draw attention in this country."

"How does that work?" Vivi asked. "This . . . streaming."

"It's essentially like watching a video online, only it's live. I post an announcement to my subscribers when a live event is going to happen, so they know when to tune in, then I assemble my crew—camera guys, that kind of thing— and take my viewers with me to show them what's going on. It starts a conversation, which, due to the numbers of people watching, spreads very quickly, and that usually gets notice."

"From who?" This from an older gentleman in the back. He stood. "Mabry Jenkins. I own the apple farm and cidery. What kind of notice do we want?"

"Well, normally I want attention that grows the story beyond the online conversation to one that is seen and discussed in newspapers and on television. What that does is bring the problem into a broader realm where folks who might be able to help can hear about it."

"How does that make a difference? Who out there can step in and help?" Addie Pearl asked.

"We're not looking for that kind of help in this case," Wyatt said. "All we need is the conversation itself. It becomes a news story beyond your local press, and suddenly the council is having to answer to people who can broadcast what they're doing to a much bigger audience and bring a lot more pressure to bear."

"So, we're overrun with news trucks and reporters?" asked Mabry. "If we can't shame the council into doing the right thing when they know we all oppose this resort, then why would that work? What do they care if the whole world knows?"

"Yes, it might mean news trucks," Wyatt said. "Hopefully,

yes. You are right that we're talking about Paul Hammond. If he doesn't play fair, as Seth pointed out, then the last thing anyone involved in those backroom kind of deals wants is media attention. Media attention isn't just reporters on sidewalks, it's also journalists digging, asking questions, and publishing their findings. I'm sure you have local papers you could alert to this story, but since time is of the essence and I'm already here, I'm willing to help speed up that process."

"So, what is the next step?" Addie Pearl asked.

"Finding an alternate solution," Wyatt replied. "None of this works without that." Wyatt looked at Vivi, who had taken a seat again, to see if she wanted to pick up the ball, but she waved for him to continue. "So, I do have an idea," he told the room, and there was immediate excitement. He held up his hands. "Hear me out on this, okay? The thing is, the resort really does solve the immediate town problems in the most direct way possible, both the lake property not being utilized and the reduced tourist stream into the town itself. Just not in the way you want." He lifted a hand when the grumbling started. "Not with this particular developer." He glanced down at Chey, who gave him a supportive smile. He'd told her what he was going to propose, and he had her support. He just wasn't sure if anyone else would join her when they heard his idea. "But there are other developers out there."

That definitely stirred people up, and not entirely in a good way.

He raised his hands again. "Let me explain. There are developers now who have started to realize that coming in, razing everything to the ground, and paving things over is a shortsighted plan. More and more, planners are working to preserve the environment they come into, work with the natural aesthetic of a place instead of replacing it with something prefabricated and nonindigenous. They work with the local resources instead of squandering them."

"So, you're saying a resort of some kind is going to happen no matter what?" Mabry asked.

"I'm saying a resort is on the table right now and it does tick off the boxes. Maybe there is some other way to revitalize the town, draw tourist traffic to the town center, and separately, some other way to save the lake and public grounds around it." He motioned to Seth. "I know you built your music center, your amphitheater, from the proceeds of an album your wife recorded here. There are many ways to achieve things, but, in this case, not in the time needed to keep the council from saying yes to the solution that is already right in front of them. If they are thinking 'resort,' then give them one, just one that works with the area, and preserves what is special about it."

"Why pick an eco-resort we propose if the other will offer them backdoor deals, or whatever you called it." This from Jake.

One thing Wyatt was coming to love about this town was that everyone got involved, everyone cared, young and old. They turned to Addie, their version of a tribal elder, for guidance, but at the same time, no one told Bailey or Jake to sit down and let the adults handle things. Everyone worked together here, and that gave him hope that if any town could do this in the short time left to them, it would be Blue Hollow Falls.

"It's a combination effort," Wyatt said. "You come in with a solid alternative plan that will do the best for the most. If that and your clearly voiced opposition to their planned solution doesn't turn the tide, then you go wide, and bring in the outside world, shine a brighter light. Expose the truth."

"Does it always work?" This from Addie Pearl.

Wyatt turned. "No," he told her with plain honesty. "Sometimes greed wins, or corruption wins." He looked back to the room, saw slumped shoulders. "But more often the outcome has been positive. That's why I'm able to keep doing what I do, helping where I can. Maybe there is a better way. I'm just offering this way, because it's the way I know. I am sure that you can't win if you don't play. And I think you all want to win."

"How much time do we have?" This came from Jake's father. He looked at Wyatt. "Will McCall," he said by way of introduction. "When are they planning to sign this deal? How fast do we need to cement this backup plan?"

Addie Pearl stood. "We can call the town meeting, but as Mr. Reed has said, that's better done when we have the backup plan in place, not before." She looked at Vivi. "Vivi has fought the good fight in the meeting where this project was announced, but her concerns fell on deaf ears. I'm sorry I wasn't there to support her, but I'm not surprised at this result. This situation with our town council, and with Mr. Hammond, is not new. That's why I've shifted my energies to improving this town from the outside. But Wyatt here makes a good point. You keep letting corruption go unchecked, and it just grows. We have to draw the line at a project like the one Hammond is backing this time, one that will fundamentally change the Falls forever."

Vivi stood as Addie Pearl sat down. "The council has a meeting scheduled with representatives from Pantheon in six weeks. Even if we are vocal in our disapproval, I think the majority of the council, and the mayor, will vote yes. Unless there is another option."

The spike of tension in the room was palpable.

Chey squeezed Wyatt's hand before he stood again as Vivi sat. He gave her a quick smile. He knew the people in front of him had a lot riding on this, and he hoped he was steering them in the right direction. "Now that you know the stakes, and the time frame, let's focus on that solution." He smiled, knowing the key was to keep everyone moving forward. Hand-wringing was a natural reaction, but counter-productive when the clock was ticking. "First and foremost is to find a developer who wants to enhance what Firefly Lake already has to offer. Not all resorts come with high-rise hotels, sandy beaches, and golf courses. Think more along the lines of a smaller number of rustic lodges, done as part of the natural landscape."

There were nods of approval, but some still had their arms folded, waiting to hear more.

"This area is made for outdoor sports like boating and fishing, hiking and climbing. From what I've seen," Wyatt continued, "that is a vastly underdeveloped resource. One way to get a developer interested is to dangle that carrot. The right developer could come in and grow that market. That plan encourages maintaining the lake, land, and trails as they are. Upgrading the nature center, the docks, and maybe adding in a small campground and another, smaller amphitheater, but for nature-oriented talks and whatnot, so it complements your music venue, rather than directly competing with it. If you can find someone with the right attitude and eye, this could work as wonderfully for you as your mill renovation did. And you have the mill and music center as an example of the kind of thing you're look-ing for."

The mood in the room shifted more fully then, with people murmuring and a hum of excitement building. Wyatt reached down for Chey's hand and held on to it as he con-tinued. She nodded encouragement, her expression one of optimism and hope. He looked back to the room, feeling a renewed energy himself.

Addie Pearl stood and brought the room back to rights

with a simple question. "Where do we find such a paragon of a developer?"

"I might know someone," Vivi said, just loudly enough that the room hushed. "Let me . . . think on it."

Wyatt turned to Vivi, who remained seated. He hadn't missed her diffidence regarding contacting whoever this person was. "I have good researchers," he said, so the room could hear. "I've already got them looking. I put them on it this morning."

"I don't think that will be necessary," Vivi said, and he noticed she was tucking her cell phone back into her pocket. She stood once more and addressed the room. "I've set up a meeting with an old friend for tomorrow morning." She was smiling, but there was strain around her eyes and the corners of her mouth. Wyatt didn't know her all that well, yet he was pretty sure the meeting she'd just set up had cost her in some way.

"I'll still get my guys to find a few backup possibilities—" Wyatt started, but Vivi shook her head.

"No need," she said. "I know this will work." Vivi found a more sincere smile then, but Wyatt was still concerned.

He decided he'd keep his team on it anyway. He really didn't like the look of whatever it was Vivi was planning to put herself in the middle of. Ultimately, that wasn't any of his business, but backup plans were always a good thing. *Now you just need to drum one up for what you're going to do when you have to put Blue Hollow Falls in your rearview mirror.*

Addie Pearl rose then and slid her hand in Vivi's, encouraging her to stand. "A big thank you, to our dear Vivienne. You all are relative newcomers to these hills," she said, looking from Vivi, to Chey, then Avery and Hannah. "But you are already family to us."

Cheers of support and applause filled the room.

Vivi's expression was one of gratitude, then relief when she sat and allowed Addie Pearl the stage.

Addie turned to the room. "The weather is being kinder to us now. So, I say we see what comes of Vivi's meeting tomorrow, and in the meantime, put out the word to everyone—and I mean everyone, up here and in town—to meet up at the music center amphitheater this coming weekend. How about Saturday morning? Plenty of room for everyone, and we'll see where we are then, and what we need to do next. Sound good?"

After a deafening chorus of ayes, Addie turned to Wyatt with a broad smile on her weathered face and offered him a little salute. Behind her, Bailey nodded, and Wyatt smiled. So, the verdict was a yes all around. He nodded back.

"It appears we're all on board for a trip to Reed Planet," Addie Pearl said, then looked around the room. "Let's do this!"

The room broke out into cheers and Chey surprised him by standing, pulling him close, and laying a resounding kiss full on his mouth. The cheers doubled at that, along with whistles, hoots, and hollers. So, naturally, he kissed her right back.

Chapter Nine

"Vivi," Chey said as she walked into the kitchen after seeing the last of their neighbors off. "Do you have a minute?"

"Just as soon as I scrape these plates and—"

"Hannah, Avery, and I will take care of all of that. You cooked for three or four dozen people this morning. You're officially off duty for the rest of the day." She went to the counter and poured a cup of coffee from the fresh pot Vivi kept going all day, then steered her to the big kitchen table. "Here. Sit."

"You make me sound like the family schnauzer," Vivi groused, but she sat all the same.

"Stay," Chey added with a cheeky grin, then danced out of the way before Vivi could swat her behind.

"Your young man is quite something," Vivi said after taking a long, appreciative sip.

Chey started to say that Wyatt wasn't her man, but that kiss she'd spontaneously planted on him in front of half the town pretty much took that denial off the table. She'd just been so proud of him. He hadn't simply tossed out an offer to make a little video of their situation. He'd stood up and commanded a call to action—in that lovely, charming, congenial way he had—then laid out what had to be done and how.

Watching videos of his livestreams had shown her why he had so many people following his every move, hanging on his every word. Seeing him in action today had shown her how he'd become so successful in championing his chosen causes. She hadn't thought about all the behind-the-scenes work he had to do, talking with people, finding solutions, figuring out how to showcase them, and in a way that would maximize the kind of exposure he wanted, while minimizing the kind he didn't.

"He is, indeed," she said, maybe a little proudly. "I'm glad he could help." She opened the lid of the trash can and started scraping dishes.

"I'm glad Victoria managed to drag him out here," Vivi continued mildly, "or we'd have likely never heard of him."

Chey badly bobbled the plate she was scraping and almost dropped it to the floor. She didn't know what to say to that. Because it was true.

"Not that you owe us every detail of your past, darling. But he does seem a rather significant one." She smiled when Chey looked her way. "Emphasis on the 'significant.'"

Chey smiled at that, then turned back to the dishes. It would be easier to talk if she kept her hands busy, and her gaze averted. "I'm sorry I didn't tell you about him," she said. "With Cody gone, and my aunt and uncle, it was just too much. He was my best friend, from the time we were little, until we were teenagers. He was like family to me. When he left . . . we, uh, we didn't part well."

"It appears the reuniting part has gone significantly better."

Chey barked out a surprised laugh at that, and she looked at Vivi, whose smile was warm and knowing. She merely lifted her coffee mug in a silent toast.

"I don't know why it was so hard talking about him," Chey admitted as she continued to scrape and stack plates. "I mean, I do, but—"

"Because it was left unresolved," Vivi said, her voice quieter now. Reflective. "Unless you do something to fix that kind of thing, it remains an emotional minefield that is often best left alone. I don't fault you for that, dear Cheyenne. I certainly don't."

Chey put the last plate on the stack and closed the trash can lid. She looked over at Vivi, who held her mug in both hands, as if about to take a sip, only her thoughts were clearly somewhere else.

Chey carried the plates to the sink and turned the water on to hot, and got out the rubber gloves and scrubber, all while debating what to say to her dear friend. She'd asked for a moment with her because she, like Wyatt, had seen the troubled look on Vivi's face after she'd made her appointment. Chey had wanted to find out what was going on, see if maybe they should pursue a different path. Only now she worried that she'd be asking Vivi to wander into the same kind of minefield Chey herself had avoided for years. And, yes, probably would have continued avoiding if not for Tory.

The difference was, Vivi had apparently made an appointment to willingly walk into that minefield. As her friend, Chey couldn't let her do it without at least trying to make sure she'd be okay. She washed her hands, turned the water off, then poured a mug of coffee and sat down across from Vivi.

"You know me," Chey began. "I'm not one for gentle forays into delicate subject matters, so I'm going to preface this by saying I'm not asking you to tell me whatever this story is. It's your minefield." She reached over and gently covered Vivi's wrist with her hand when the older woman set her mug abruptly down and started to scoot back her chair. "Vivi," she said, more softly now. "I know whomever you're seeing tomorrow . . . you're making some kind of personal sacrifice to do it. I'm not asking what that is, or what happened or who he is to you. I wouldn't. I'm just worried that you're putting yourself at risk. Emotionally at the very least, maybe physically, too—I don't know. After what happened with Hammond out on the lake, maybe I'm being overprotective. But we can find another developer—"

"What's done is done," Vivi said with finality, though she still wasn't meeting Chey's gaze.

"No, it's not. You can cancel the meeting."

Vivi did look at her then, and Chey's heart broke a little at the utter resignation she saw in Vivi's eyes. Even at their lowest, most grief-stricken moments, Vivi had been their cheerleader, their fierce champion. Never once had Chey seen her look defeated like this.

"I've opened that door," she said simply. "It doesn't matter if I try to close it."

"Would it help if we went with you? Strength in numbers?"

"No, this is something I have to do by myself." She sighed and set her mug down. "I should have done it years ago, quite frankly. Instead of diminishing the impact, time has merely fed its importance, and that's unacceptable." She covered Chey's hand on her wrist with her soft palm. "You know a little about that, my dear," she said, not unkindly. "Watching you and Wyatt gave me a good reason to put this piece of my past to rest once and for all."

"Will you be safe? I mean—"

Now Vivi laughed and it was a relief to hear a bit of her usual vim back in her voice. "My darling girl, did you not witness my prowess with my umbrella?"

Chey smiled at that. "Maybe I wasn't talking physically,

but I suppose that umbrella would work to abort the mission if you were feeling threatened either way."

"Indeed," Vivi said, then patted Chey's hand again before withdrawing her arm and standing, mug in hand. "I'll be fine."

Chey wasn't so sure about that, but she'd done what she could. For now, anyway.

"Speaking of minefields, where is your young man?" Vivi said as she went to the sink and pulled on the rubber gloves.

Chey didn't bother trying to take over. She knew how she was when she needed to distract herself from a challenging situation. She puttered. Like dish scraping. So did Vivi. Instead, Chey picked up a dish towel and started drying. "He's out in the stables with Bailey. She's showing him her goat enterprise."

Vivi laughed. "Now, letting those two put their heads together . . . they could solve all the world's problems before dinner." She shook her head. "You know, I was thinking earlier, when she was grilling Wyatt, that I could see her doing what he's doing. When she gets older. Saving the world."

"I was thinking president of the United States, but hey, why limit her powers to just one country?"

They laughed, then fell into the comfortable and comforting routine.

They'd moved on from plates to glassware when Vivi asked, "What are your plans when Wyatt heads off to save the whales, or some exotic plant in Bora-Bora?" She sent a side look to Chey as she scrubbed out another glass.

"I don't know," Chey said, with complete and utter honesty.

Vivi leaned into Chey, pressed the side of her head to Chey's. "You know if you want to go with him—"

"I know," Chey said, and saw she'd surprised Vivi by not immediately stating she would never dream of leaving them, or Lavender Blue. "I know I could go off and blaze trails with him, and probably have a life full of experiences most could only dream about."

They continued in silence for another few minutes, and then Vivi said, "You've already done plenty of that while growing up."

"Yep," Chey said succinctly. "And I know what I do here isn't as important as the difference he's making—" She talked over Vivi's immediate rebuttal. "He was the one who told me that if we make any positive change, even if it's one horse rescued, or one life resurrected—or four, by building this farm—then good is being put out into the world."

"You can't save it all, but your effort can make the world of difference to the ones being helped," Vivi said. "He's right."

Chey nodded. "And that's something." She picked up another glass. "It's more than that, though. I know my life is here just like he knows his life is out there. This isn't a way station for me. I'm not searching anymore. What I do here matters, to me, to us, to those horses out in the field. But more than that, it helps me. I'm the one being saved. I feel settled, and good." She looked at Vivi. "I didn't think I ever would again. That's important, too, right?"

"Most important," Vivi agreed. "Maybe it's just as well you two didn't cross paths any sooner. Maybe you were meant to find your way, find your meaning, while he found his, without anything else clouding your judgment. Anyone else." She handed another glass to Chey. "Now, whatever you decide, you'll be making choices with the full knowledge of what you want, what compromises you're willing to make."

Chey put the last glass up in the cupboard and closed

the glass-front doors. She tossed her damp towel over her shoulder and turned to lean against the counter. "Is it wrong that I think it sucks that we have to make compromises at all?"

"Sometimes the best things take a little work. Or a lot of work." Vivi let her gaze wander the room, then land back on Chey. "We, of all people, know the truth of that."

Chey pushed away from the counter and went into Vivi's arms for a hug. It was a rare thing for her to want. Maybe Wyatt had broken down that wall, too. Because this felt really good, and she wondered why she'd deprived herself of the comfort of something so easily given, and so easily received, for so long.

Vivi pressed a kiss to the side of her head and let her go. "The things we need to feel happy, and settled, and joyful are ever changing. Life isn't stagnant—it keeps changing, too. Some good, some bad, some awful, some perfect. And we change along with it. It's impossible not to. We're not the same women we were before we experienced the losses we did. And we can't go back to how we were before that, because we've been changed by it."

Chey nodded, agreeing with her.

"That's a major change," Vivi went on, "but there are dozens of tiny ones, too. And they all change the course of the river we're flowing along, *cher*." Her New Orleans drawl snuck into her voice as she draped her arm around Chey's shoulders and leaned her head to the side until it touched Chey's. "Would you have ever imagined yourself here? If someone said you were going to have to pick between barrel racing and runnin' a lavender farm back when you and Tory were busting your adolescent little tushies beating the snot out of each other in the ring? What would you have said?"

Chey snickered at Vivi's colorful description and Vivi squeezed her shoulder in a light hug. "I'd have been making a deposit in the swear jar," Chey answered, and they both laughed again.

"When you were seventeen, if someone told you that you would willingly choose to live on a farm with three women, without a single sexy, dashing cowboy in sight, you'd have called them crazy." Vivi glanced at her. "Am I right?"

Chey laughed. "All true. I guess I never thought of it that way."

Vivi let go and slipped the towel off Chey's shoulder as she straightened and stepped away. "Now things are changing again. You had to make compromises to be here, to do this. Living in the middle of nowhere, cutting yourself off from a social life with people your own age."

Chey laughed. "Oh, after rodeo life, I was perfectly happy to be around as few people as possible."

"Exactly," Vivi said. "It was a compromise, but it was an easy one to make." She smiled. "Maybe when the time comes, your choices won't feel so hard. Given you'll be choosing happiness either way."

Chey nodded and turned to scoop up her phone, then jumped with a squeal when Vivi snapped the towel against her rear end. "Hey now," she said, but she was laughing as she turned. "Careful where you aim that thing."

"Just whipping your behind a little. Now get on out there with Mr. Planet and stop worrying about this old woman."

Chey's expression sobered. "I came in here to help you and, as usual, you do all the helping."

"Oh, I wouldn't be so sure about that, *cher*. Sometimes talking things out for someone else's benefit ends up being exactly the thing you needed to hear yourself."

"Good," Chey said, wishing she believed that. "If you want or need anything tomorrow, before, during, or after, you just give us a shout." She grabbed her hat and walked to the side door that led to the veranda. "And don't you forget that umbrella, you hear?"

She left with Vivi's laughter following her out the door.

She met up with Wyatt as she crossed the yard, Vivi's advice still echoing in her ears. *You'll be choosing happiness either way.* Now she just had to figure out how to do that without getting her heart shattered in the process.

"How are the goats?" she asked with a smile.

"So very small," he said. "I have to tell you their goat tender is one very impressive twelve-year-old."

"She'll be a teenager this fall. I don't know if we're ready. Bailey is a force to be reckoned with, for sure. Young dynamo and old soul, all wrapped into one. With Addie Pearl as her guardian and guide it's anyone's guess what kind of world and how many of them she will go on to conquer."

Wyatt chuckled. "I didn't know whether to be awestruck or terrified."

"Get used to it," Chey said with a laugh. "That feeling never goes away."

He slipped his hand into hers as they walked toward her house. She liked that he just naturally did that, she liked feeling the warmth of his palm pressed to hers, the strength of his fingers woven through hers. *Tiny little things that change the course of your river.* She thought that this connection, so basic, simple, like one of Vivi's hugs, was one of those little things. "Vivi was saying she could see Bailey doing what you do, blazing new trails, saving the world."

"You're giving me too much credit," he said. "Bailey though? Most definitely. Superhero in the making. I just find things that need a little help and try to leave them better than I found them. It's not different really from what's happening here with the lake. No more important in the grand scheme of things, but vital to the people whose lives it will affect." He grinned. "I just find my battles in some really off the wall places."

They got to the front of the house and he took her by the hips and swung her up to the porch.

"Anyone ever tell you you're a manhandler?" she said.

He hopped up after her, then back-walked her until she was up against the door, all without touching her. He tipped the brim of her cowboy hat up and smiled down at her. "No, ma'am, I generally avoid handling men."

"A woman handler then?" she said, her pulse already doing a two-step when he leaned his mouth closer to hers.

"You want me to keep my hands to myself—is that what you're saying?"

She met his gaze, knowing she had a stupid, giddy smile on her face, and not giving a single damn about it. She shook her head.

"You want me to stop picking you up and carrying you off with me?" he asked, his lips drawing closer to hers, his voice a baritone rasp. "Just say the word."

She was already quivering, just knowing where this was heading. She shook her head, her gaze dropping from his darkening eyes to his lips. That mouth of his had done some amazing things to her earlier that day. "Suddenly my knees are feeling a bit weak," she said in barely more than a whisper.

"Is that so," he said. "Well, seems only right then, me being the guy who saves things." He scooped her up easily, and she didn't think she'd ever tire of it.

"Hold on to me," he said, and reached behind her to open the door. He kicked it shut behind him. "Leftover breakfast for dinner?" he murmured against the side of her neck as she threw her hat in the general direction of the kitchen table.

"It's barely past two in the afternoon," she said, tilting

her head to the side, moaning softly and squirming against him as he kissed his way down her neck.

"I know." He walked them to the bedroom. "I figure we should be coming up for air right about then."

She didn't tell him he was wrong. Didn't tell him she had a million things to do that afternoon. Not a single one of them seemed remotely important to her at the moment. "You know, I wasn't planning on paying Tory back for the low-down, dirty rotten trick she pulled on us by making her do all her chores and mine, too." She squealed when Wyatt tossed her into the middle of the bed. "But I'm not saying I feel bad about it, either."

"And here I was thinking about erecting a statue to honor her heroic deed in the middle of the town square." He climbed on the bed and started unbuttoning her shirt. "Do you have a town square?"

"You say tomahto," Chey said, then looked down at his hands as he parted her shirt, then back up at him.

He paused. "Oh, I'm sorry, is this what you meant by manhandling?" His fingers traced down the edges of her open shirt, trailing softly over her nipples.

She gasped and arched up into his touch.

He shifted his weight and moved down. "Maybe if I don't use my hands?" He flicked a tongue over her nipple, making her moan.

"Turns out I'm okay with the handling," she said breathlessly, then grabbed the front of his shirt and rolled him to his back. She smiled down at him and flicked open the first button. "My turn."

Chey decided that reheated omelets and hash browns at midnight were the best things she'd ever tasted. She was curled up at one end of her deep leather couch and Wyatt was stretched out at the other end, with his boots propped on the overstuffed ottoman.

"Thanks for the help in the barn tonight," she told him.

He lifted his mug of coffee in her direction. "My pleasure. I haven't been around horses in any regular way in a good long while. I planned to get at least two for my farm, but I don't spend enough time there to make it fair."

"Any other livestock plans?" She was proud of herself for talking about his farm an ocean away, and the fact that he'd be going back to it, as if it was no big deal.

"If you're asking whether I plan to raise any Welsh bulls, the answer is no," he said with a wry laugh. "Although Bailey has me half talked into getting a few goats to clear my fields. Also turns out she raises and breeds a type of Welsh sheep. Herdwicks. I've been invited out to see them."

"Careful, she'll have you shipping crates of them back home, too."

He smiled. "I wouldn't doubt it." He set his mug and empty plate on the ottoman and turned to face her. "I wanted to talk to you this morning, before the meeting, about the call I was on when you woke up."

She waved an empty fork. "You don't need to explain—"

"No, this part is about you. Well, about us, at any rate."

She lowered her fork back to her plate, surprised. "Us, how?"

"In any other realm, this would seem incredibly forward, but this is us, and I think we've been up front about what we mean to each other, what this means."

She leaned down and set her plate on the floor, suddenly no longer hungry. She wasn't ready for decision making. Vivi had been right—with time, decisions might be easier to make, when she knew what she was reaching for as well as what she'd have to leave behind. They weren't even close to that yet. *How long did you think you'd have?*

She supposed at least as long as it took to come up with a working plan for the lake and the town. Maybe he thought they'd done that today. Trying to quell the knot that was forming in her gut, she said, "You've decided where you're going to go next?" She sat up, pulled her knees to her chest, and looped her arms around her legs, well aware it was a defensive posture, but she needed the support. "Wy, I'm not ready yet to make any—"

"I'm not asking you to make any choices," he said. "Not now. Or ever. We'll make decisions together when the time comes. Whatever they are."

She almost went limp with relief. *When the time comes.* So not now. *Thank God.* "So what realm are you referring to?"

"The one where I ask the woman in my life if it's okay that I move in for a bit." His smile was sweet and adorable, pure old Wyatt, only with a hint of that sexy new grin flirting around the corners. "Like for the summer?"

Her mouth fell open. That was so much more time than she thought they'd have before those hard choices had to be made. Her heart filled right up with joy. *Which answers a few things about what you want right there.* "Really?"

He gave her his best new Wyatt grin. "If you'll have me."

Oh, would she ever. "Consider yourself had," she said with a suggestive wiggle of her eyebrows. "Repeatedly."

"Why, ma'am," he said, in his best cowboy drawl. "Whatever might you be implying?"

"Exactly what you hope I'm implying," she said with a laugh.

He wiped his brow. "Whew, I was worried there for a moment."

She laughed with him. "So . . . how is this happening? The whole summer?"

"I called Dom—my assistant, production chief, and all

around get-it-done guy—to tell him what we might be doing here, get him on the horn to the rest of the crew, see what we could work out in case I end up streaming from here. He was sending me a bunch of stuff from the Nepal event to edit, as well as some promotional material we're putting together for donors, and wanted to know where to send it. So, I got him to set up a post office box in town here and then I thought, well, why not just get him to pack up whatever else I need and ship that, too. Anything I was going to do on my farm this summer I could do on this one just as well."

Chey took in everything he was saying, thrilled that he was going to do this, and at the same time, sort of sitting back and watching, listening to him be this guy he was now. A guy who had production chiefs and a global crew.

"I should have talked to you first. I didn't start the call with that in mind; it just sort of happened. Then we were late for the meeting because—"

"Manhandling," she said, wiggling her eyebrows over the rim of her coffee mug.

"I'm pretty sure the woman handling part of it played an equal role."

Her smile turned smug. "I will own that."

"As you should. You're quite good at it."

She sketched a little bow, holding one arm out and dipping her chin. After settling back in the cushions and pillows, she said, "I should have told you this sooner, but you were truly incredible today."

"Yeah, I got that you might have been okay with it by the kiss you laid on me there at the end."

She grinned, not a bit sorry for that public display. "That too. But it was fun getting to see Reed Planet in action. You and Vivi cut right to the heart of things; then you got us organized and focused on a path forward, on a solution. By the time it was over, I was thinking we might even be able to do this without your having to go to all that trouble with the livestream." She smiled. "Unless that means you'd leave sooner. Then we absolutely need you to go to the trouble."

He chuckled. "I'm glad to see you're putting the needs of the many over the needs of a few."

"Oh, there are needs all right," she said, and loved how his eyes immediately went dark with desire. This was all so very easy. Planning together, working together, be it on her couch, out in the barn, or walking the fields. She liked sipping coffee and talking with him into the wee hours. This wasn't anything like their life before. They'd been kids then, and the circumstances, the lifestyle, so utterly different. But it still felt like the most natural thing in the world now. Vivi was right, Chey couldn't have imagined this with Wyatt, even though she'd spent every day with him in her previous life.

Now it was his turn to wiggle his eyebrows over the edge of his coffee mug, making her giggle. "Yes, well, I believe we'll be addressing those needs again later."

Cheyenne McCafferty. Giggling. It felt . . . glorious. Freeing. She looked at him and knew she didn't want this to end, knew there were going to be compromises in her future. *Choosing happiness, either way.* She'd have to remember that, focus on that.

"I put things into motion before the meeting, because if we do need to do a stream, it would need to happen fast, and these things take time to set up. But I agree, maybe it won't be necessary now that Vivi has the ball already rolling with a lead on another developer. If we get set up here and discover it's not necessary, well . . . we'll see what else might be worth our time on this continent. It won't be a loss."

"Do you have offers or proposals from places in the US?"

"I'm sure we do. I haven't gone over them all since leaving

Nepal." He glanced down, then back to her. "I haven't really focused on the States. Yes, there are very rural places here without a mouthpiece, but this is such a developed country, and there are so many that aren't. That have no means to get what is needed to save what needs saving."

"So, how does your Reed Planet work, in terms of helping? Crowd-sourcing, crowd-funding?"

"Both of those things. As I said at the meeting, often-times by getting the word out that there is a critical need, the right people step up. Then I can connect those who are willing to donate their time, expertise, technology, whatever is needed, to the people who can help. Other times a financial investment is the fastest way to solve a problem, which can come through crowd-funding or donations from businesses or philanthropic entities, or all three." He grinned. "It's not just kids like Jake who watch Reed Planet. It's scientists and CEOs, inventors and doctors, investment bankers, lawyers, researchers, vets. Whether it's to save a certain species by preserving their habitat, or bringing attention to a specific plant that is threatened, either by climate or habitat encroachment, or a whole fishing village that might lose its only source of revenue because the waters have grown too warm to attract the fish they catch and sell. Somebody will have a solution or know somebody who does. We don't need to be experts in any of these things. We just need to let the world know what the problem is and connect the people to make the solution happen."

"That's . . . incredible. In every sense of the word."

"It amazes me every day that it works like it does. It didn't start out the way it is now. We tried to help more than we actually did help. It took a while to really build the global community that pays attention to us now. We learned we had to go back and show people our successes, show we were making a difference. It was hard because we didn't have the resources we have now, the clout or the knowledge about how to get in to the places we needed to get to, with the equipment needed to broadcast. Back then it was me and Dom, and some locals with a camera and an old laptop we could use to upload the grainy footage we shot. These days we have satellite links and can broadcast live from some pretty amazing locations that are otherwise completely cut off. I've got Jon manning the computer part and Peli making the camera magic happen."

"So, I've seen," she said. "You make even an endangered fern seem exciting."

"What do you mean?" he deadpanned. "They *are* exciting."

She laughed.

"I'm really glad you'll have a chance to meet my crew. We're family in a different way from yours, but they're like my Hannah, Vivi, and Avery."

Chey smiled. "I'm glad, too." And she was. The more she understood his world, the more she wanted to know. "In all honesty, what do you think our chances are? Of swaying the council to our side?"

"Your town is tight knit in the best of ways. Folks coming together like they did today will be a big part of this situation getting resolved in a way that helps everyone."

"Everyone except Hammond and the council members who are apparently looking to enhance their personal bottom line separate and apart from what the town gets out of it," she said. "Frankly, that's the part that worries me most. Vivi didn't reveal what Hammond said to her, but if she forced him off that boat, it had to have been pretty bad. He's not striking me as someone who will be easily thwarted, and that humiliation had to have doubled his determination. Tripled it."

Wyatt nodded. "Most likely, but the way I see it, if we

push hard enough, they'll cave. They'll be just fine without more money. They have plenty. And they'll make more, no doubt. Just not selling out Blue Hollow Falls to do it. If Vivi's lead pans out as she seems to think it will, we'll really hit the ground running. That helps, too."

Chey looked down into her mug, thinking about her talk with Vivi earlier.

"What is it?"

She let out a short sigh. "I'm still not so sure about Vivi's contact. I mean, I trust that if she says he'll come through, he will. Whether he's a developer, or a money guy, I don't know. I do know that she never makes blind promises. She has a long list of interesting connections from her colorful and amazing life. She's pretty well-off herself, and has been for decades, so her social circles could include virtually anybody. I'm just—"

"Worried she's biting off more than she can chew? Or biting off something she shouldn't?"

"Exactly."

"She definitely wasn't one hundred percent thrilled to be putting this plan into motion, or any percent. That much was clear."

Chey agreed. "She's doing it for us, and it's clearly requiring some kind of sacrifice on her part, which I hate. I talked with her a bit about it earlier while you were out in the stables with Bailey and Tory, but she's keeping it close to the vest. I get the impression that he's someone from her past. Someone who meant more to her than a casual acquaintance or business contact." She smiled at him, but it was bittersweet. "Maybe something along the lines of what happened with us, only my guess is a lot more complicated."

"Maybe we should go ahead and get a backup in place. Dom has a few names on a tentative list. We haven't reached out, but we could. Not only because this seems to be an emotionally charged situation for her but, given the tight time frame, you may not want the whole caboodle riding on a tenuous personal situation."

"That too. I mean, mostly I'm worried for her, but yes, given the timetable, there's no room for a do-over."

"Let me talk to Dom first thing in the morning. Early morning here will be early afternoon where he is, so he'll have had some time to make calls."

"I really appreciate that. I honestly don't know what else to do with the Vivi situation. I mean, she's an adult, making her own choices, and I know how I'd feel if someone tried to step in and tell me what I should or shouldn't do."

"Do you think she's putting herself in danger?"

Chey lifted a shoulder. "Physically? I'd like to think not." She smiled. "I did tell her to take her umbrella."

Wyatt smiled at that, but Chey could see the idea worried him, too.

"You don't think she might be putting herself in any kind of financial danger, do you? Business, property? Doesn't have to mean cash."

Chey's eyes widened briefly. "I didn't even think about that." She shook her head. "But no, I get the feeling it's more an emotional minefield."

"What time is the meeting?"

"Eleven tomorrow morning. She didn't say where, but my guess is it won't be here or in town. Probably down in Turtle Springs."

"What's the nearest actual city? Somewhere a guy on the scale of what we'd need might be more likely to do business?"

"Valley View. That's just it, though. I doubt this is someone from around here. Vivi spent most of her adult life in New York. She retired after Harold died."

Wyatt sent her a questioning look.

"The love of her life." Chey lifted a hand from her mug. "Well, maybe he's better characterized as the disappointment of her life. It's a long story and, I'm afraid, not mine to tell. Suffice it to say it was that loss she was grieving when the four of us met." She gestured to the house they sat in. "He's the reason we have all of this." She smiled, her thoughts both sad and filled with affection. "Vivi had retired from the New York Broadway scene and moved to DC, where she immediately got involved with consulting on costume design for the Folger Theater and the National Ballet Company. I don't think she ever really planned to stop working, but she just couldn't be in New York any longer." Chey took a sip of coffee, shook her head. "She loves the city, but there were too many sad memories, among other things. I completely understand that. But a new town, new challenges, fresh faces, wasn't helping. She knew he'd left her this place, but she'd never come out to see it, or deal with it. She just couldn't. But after the four of us met and grew close, eventually, she did."

"Fate, kismet, or a combination of the two," he said.

"Something like that." Chey leaned back against the pillows, the memories making her smile deepen. "It started as a joke. The fearsome foursome do lavender farming. I mean, it was funny and silly and not a little insane. But in support, we all traveled out here together when Vivi came to see the place for the first time. And, suddenly, though we pretended we were still joking . . . seeing it changed everything. We were each so drawn to this place." She sighed. "We were all at crossroads in our lives, and it felt like the perfect escape. The perfect spot to start over. I don't think any one of us would have done it alone. I know Vivi wouldn't have. It was a bigger change of pace and scenery for the three of them than for me, but it was still a huge change for all of us, being in this together. Still, what did we have to lose, really?"

"Did you each invest, or is it still all Vivi's?" He immediately lifted his hand. "Never mind. None of my business, I just—never mind."

"No, that's okay. Yes, we did each invest. Vivi wanted to gift portions to us, but we each wanted a financial stake. And it's all drawn up properly. If any one of us ended up hating it, we agreed ahead of time the other three would buy her out. And if we all hated it, Vivi agreed we'd sell the farm and sail off with our share of the profits to other adventures."

"This place seems to suit each of you in your own way," he said, holding her gaze with a smile.

"Thank you. It really does. Fate was being exceptionally kind when our paths crossed. I'm glad we were crazy enough to all say yes."

Wyatt continued to look at her, affection, caring, kindness, all of the things she'd always associated with him, right there to see. She couldn't wish that the other part of him didn't exist, because it was such a wonderful, beautiful thing, this man he'd become. *Not to mention hot as hell.* And if she'd loved the boy, as a friend, as something more . . . the feelings she was already having for the man were so much deeper, far more complex.

With their shared history, that tight bond and connection created a ready-made foundation, and things were moving swiftly; she didn't know how to slow that down. Given the limited time they had, even if it was for a full summer, honestly, she didn't want to slow it down. She wanted it all, all that she could have, all they could have.

She didn't—couldn't—miss the underlying sadness she saw in him, too. She understood it, felt it. Seeing her out here, working with her, talking to her, he knew she belonged to this place and these people every bit as much as she knew he belonged to his world after seeing those videos, seeing him in action, and watching him, firsthand, helping her neighbors, her town, that morning.

They were as perfect for each other as the lives they each led were perfect for themselves. *Where does that leave us? How does that work?*

Chapter Ten

"I cannot believe we're doing this."

Wyatt glanced over at Chey, who clutched her to-go cup of coffee between her fingerless-gloved hands. Unseasonably chilly weather had made a return, along with gray skies and a gloomy forecast. She'd even traded in her customary cowboy hat for a knitted headband that covered her ears. He thought it was adorable but kept that tidbit to himself.

"At least she's not hard to follow," he said. The light turned green and Wyatt eased his newly leased Jeep Cherokee away from the curb, a few cars back from Vivi's red and white Chevy.

"I just hope she doesn't spot us. I want her to be safe, but I feel awful for prying."

"She's never seen this vehicle," he told her. "And you're incognito without your hat. We could stop and get you some sunglasses."

"Very funny," she said, but he knew the tension in her voice had nothing to do with him.

They were both worried about Vivi. Chey wasn't the only one with a gut feeling about the meeting. "Once we get to wherever it is she's going, we'll take a picture of the guy, get his license plate. I'll send it to my computer guy, Jon, and we'll see what's what."

"Whomever she's meeting is probably from out of town, so the license plate won't help, I don't think."

"Even rental vehicles require paperwork."

Her expression was both dubious and surprised. "Who are you?"

"Just a guy who likes to know what he's walking into. And you're being a good friend for wanting to know what she's walking into. It's not as if we're going to be listening in, or barging in."

"Unless we have to," she said evenly.

He chuckled, then grinned when she shot him the Queen Vic look. "What? I just think maybe you've read one too many spy thrillers."

"Says the guy who knows a guy who can run license plates and do background checks."

"Yeah, well, like I said, sometimes it pays to know who you're getting involved with."

She glanced at him now, openly curious. "Meaning what?"

"Meaning, in some of the places we go, sometimes we need to use back channels to get where we need to be, with the equipment we need to have. Other times even the totally legit local or government contacts have dual agendas. More knowledge is never a bad thing. That's all I'm saying."

"So, could you have gotten like, a bug, or something, so we could have listened in?"

He laughed outright and glanced at her. "I thought you were upset about prying."

She smiled sweetly at him. "I was just curious about the extent of your superpowers, that's all." Chey looked forward again and pointed. "She's turning left! There, next block down."

"I see her."

Chey grinned then. "Yeah, she is kind of hard to miss."

They ended up following her all the way out to Valley

View, the closest thing Blue Hollow Falls had to a nearby city. Vivi pulled in to the circular drive of a posh, five-star hotel and left her keys with the valet.

Wyatt pulled in and stopped on the other side of the fountain that sat in the middle of the circular drive.

"A hotel?" Chey asked. "Now what do we do? He could have parked anywhere. Or worse, he's staying here, and she could be going up to his room. That's not smart. Come on, Vivi."

They had been hoping for a restaurant where they'd see Vivi meet up with her guest before going in. As long as the two were meeting in a public spot, Wyatt wouldn't be otherwise concerned for her safety. Not her physical safety anyway.

The hotel was still a public space, but Chey had a point. "I know this seemed like a perfectly rational plan when we were lying in bed talking it over at four this morning," he said dryly. "Now I'm starting to think we're overstepping."

"And I'm starting to be glad we came. I mean, he could do anything in there and we wouldn't even—" Chey broke off and slid down in her seat. "She's standing out in front of the hotel," she hissed, as if Vivi could hear them thirty yards away behind a massive, noisy fountain. From inside the Jeep.

"I see her," Wyatt said, and popped open the center console.

"Does she have the umbrella?"

Wyatt shot her an amused look.

"Well? Does she?"

Chuckling, he got out Chey's field glasses, which he'd snagged on their way out the door that morning, and his old camera, which went everywhere he did. "Looks like she's waiting by the curb. Hopefully not for the valet, or that was just the shortest meeting on record." He glanced back at

Chey. "No umbrella. But I can hardly see her. The wind is picking up with the storm coming in. It's blowing the spray around."

Chey scooched up just enough to look over the bottom edge of the passenger side window. "Should we move closer?"

He shook his head and kept his binoculars trained on Vivi. "This is a pretty prime spot. Nowhere else gives us this vantage point without also being fully in the open." He had the Jeep tucked against the curb as snug as possible to allow other vehicles to still use the circular drive. He handed Chey the camera. "Here, you're on the side closest to the curb. Look like you're taking photos of the fountain."

She stared at him in confusion.

"So we look like obnoxious tourists who don't care that we're blocking part of the driveway. But keep it trained on Vivi and zoom in—" He showed her the zoom button, then handed her what amounted to his baby. "Be careful with it."

She looked at the camera, at all the dents, dings, scratches, and general abuse it had taken over the years. She glanced at him. "Really? Because you're afraid parts of it are going to fall off if I'm not?"

"Because it's been with me every single day of my adult life."

She looked at the camera again, only in awe this time. "This is the camera you bought when you left Iceland for Greenland?"

He smiled, liking that she'd remembered that detail among all they'd talked about since. He shook his head. "Close. That's the one I got right after the other one. It shoots videos. The first one didn't."

"But you still have that one, too, right?"

He smiled, nodded. "Yeah, but it stays back at the farm.

I don't use it anymore. I don't use this one professionally, just personally. It goes where I go."

"Still taking photos and writing down your thoughts?" she asked, looking charmed by the possibility.

He nodded, then grinned. "Just for myself. No photo-journalism aspirations these days."

She looked at the camera again, with reverence this time. "I was just thinking if only this camera could talk." She smiled at him. "But I guess it has. Have you taken pictures of Blue Hollow Falls? Our farm?"

He nodded. He'd taken a whole host of photos of her when she hadn't been aware. Out in the field, in the barn. Asleep next to him.

"Can I see them, sometime? And some of the others? It's okay if they're just for you. I don't want to intrude—"

He nodded to the fountain and the woman standing on the other side. "Really?" he asked, and they both laughed. "Yes, I'd love to share them with you." He didn't bother to add that she'd be the first one to ever see them collectively, from his viewpoint. "I think it's safe for you to sit up. Even if she could see you, which she can't, you'll have the camera blocking your face."

Chey slowly slid up about halfway, but enough to aim the camera through the water spouts. "She must be waiting for him. Valet would have brought her car around by now."

Just then a sleek, silver limo pulled into the circular drive and stopped right in front of Vivi. "Is that a . . . ?" She quickly held up the camera and zoomed in. "It is! That's a Rolls Royce." She snapped a few frames as a driver in a sharp black suit, complete with driver's cap, got out and stepped around to open one of the rear doors, curbside. Chey swore. "She's getting in!"

Oh boy.

"We have to follow them," she said, sliding back down

again as the limo pulled away from the curb and started around the circle, coming right toward them. The vehicle shifted to the right and eased out of the loop, heading toward the traffic light. "The windows are tinted," she said. "I can't get a picture of who is inside."

Wyatt slipped the camera from her fingers, then expertly pointed and zoomed in on the retreating vehicle, snapping the license plate.

"Will that do any good since it's a limo?"

He shrugged. "Had to be leased or rented by someone." Wyatt circled around the fountain and got into line, three back from the Rolls, just as the light turned green. He tried to keep some distance from the Rolls. Tailing a professional driver wasn't the same as tailing Vivi in her '56 Chevy. He'd driven in far dicier situations using significantly inferior modes of transportation, so it was silly to be nervous, but this was Vivi.

"Why meet at a hotel only to go somewhere else?" Chey asked. "I want to feel like I'm being an overreacting jerk who should be minding her own business, I do. But I have to say, my gut is liking this whole setup less and less the longer it goes on. I don't care how fancy his car is."

Wyatt wanted to believe this was all a harmless arrangement, too. But it did seem rather convoluted for what was, ostensibly, a business meeting. The downside about the price tag on the ride Vivi was currently in was that money often meant power, and as he was very well aware, power wasn't always used for the forces of good. In fact, in his experience, the opposite was far more prevalent. He kept that bit of info to himself.

The Rolls turned west, and Wyatt slowed to increase the distance between them as the other cars continued on straight; then he followed suit.

"This leads out to the interstate." She turned to Wyatt.

"Okay, now I'm officially worried. Where is he taking her? I mean, this is supposed to be a lunch meeting."

The Rolls turned again, and Wyatt breathed a sigh of relief. It was moving in the opposite direction of the highway now. He was forced to slow way down, as the traffic had thinned out significantly, and the road the Rolls had turned on was one lane and flat. He saw the sign next to the road the same instant Chey gasped. Valley View Airfield.

"Oh, hell no," she said fiercely. "She is *not* getting on a plane. I think this meeting has officially come to an end."

Wyatt was on the same page there and sped up.

"Best case is this is all innocent and he is some guy from her past, they took one look at each other, and are running off to Vegas or something and we spoil a romantic interlude and look like idiots, then do penance for days." She caught Wyatt's glance. "Okay. Weeks."

Wyatt didn't want to think about the worst-case scenario. He'd seen a lot more of the world than Chey had. "Why don't you text her. She knows you were worried about this. Maybe joke that you're asking if she needs a bailout call. Say something about the umbrella. Just see what she says. Maybe that will give us a gauge on things."

He continued to close the distance, but they had entered a series of roundabouts with tall statuary and foliage decorating the centers of each one, blocking his view. He temporarily lost the Rolls, but when he saw a sign for the private airstrip, he took a gamble and turned, just in time to see the Rolls turn off in the distance at the end of the road, along a row of private hangars.

"She's not answering," Chey said, then swore. "My text just bounced back. So she never even got it."

"Cell tower signal might be blocked here to keep from interfering with air traffic control."

She looked at him. "How are you so calm?"

"Experience," he said simply. "Don't worry, Chey. He'll have parked that Rolls in front of whatever hangar his plane is in, or was in, assuming it's out on the tarmac. We'll have time, so she knows—and he knows—she has company."

A crack of lightning split the sky. "Oh, come on," Chey said, flinching at the big boom of thunder that followed.

"No, that's a good thing," Wyatt said. "They won't take off during an electrical storm."

"Oh," Chey said, brightening, "good."

He finally made it through the last roundabout and turned in along the hangars. No Rolls in sight anywhere.

"Where is it?"

"Probably in one of the hangars." Several had garage style doors on the end facing them.

He whipped the Jeep into a space in front of the small double-wide trailer that served as the private terminal building. "The strip is small enough that there can't be more than one or two planes out there fueled and ready." He cut the engine and didn't even bother telling her to stay in the vehicle. "Stay behind me, okay?"

She surprised him by nodding, but he knew she wouldn't stay there if she thought Vivi was in any danger.

They went through the terminal without talking to the sole gate agent, who trotted after them, calling for them to stop. Even at a private hangar, there were security protocols, but now Wyatt's spidey-senses were tingling, too. They could claim ignorance later and hopefully avoid any serious consequences.

They burst through the rear door to the tarmac just as the Rolls driver was handing Vivi out of the backseat. They had apparently driven through the hangar and right out to the plane. Valet-to-airplane service.

"Vivi!" Chey shouted, trying to be heard over the sound

of the small jet engine and the wind that had kicked up. The rain hadn't started yet, but it was imminent.

Wyatt was surprised they were boarding, given the lightning flickering in the clouds. He reminded himself about the power dynamic that came with wealth, but air traffic controllers were hard to buy off.

Vivi had tied a scarf around her hair and was holding her hands over her ears to keep it on and, presumably, to block out the whining sound of the engines. She didn't turn around.

They were still a good twenty yards away when Wyatt very clearly heard the cocking of a gun and the shout of "Stop! Federal agent!" right behind them.

He grabbed Chey's arm and spun them to a stop, turning to face the uniformed woman who had her gun aimed right at them. They both lifted their arms, hands up. "We're afraid the woman boarding that plane is in danger," Wyatt said, figuring they were in for a penny now. Might as well go for the full pound. "With the red floral scarf."

Their federal agent didn't appear to have a partner, and Wyatt was thinking she was going to focus on them and not Vivi, but she pulled a radio unit from her belt with her free hand and barked into it to order the flight held until further notice. A moment later, the engines wound down, leaving only the sound of the prevailing wind.

"For heaven's sake, what on earth?"

Wyatt dipped his chin and shook his head. Because he knew the owner of that voice, and Vivi didn't sound like a woman grateful for a last-second intervention.

Vivi walked right past them and said to the agent, "I know both of them, Miss—" She looked at the name tag on the woman's blazer. "Agent Jarman." She eyed Chey and Wyatt both. "I can't say that I know why they've lost their ever-lovin' minds, but I can vouch that the only danger here is the full dressing down they're about to get from me."

Wyatt caught the agent trying to tamp down the urge to smile. "I'll have to ask you all to return to the terminal to answer a few questions."

"But—" Vivi began.

"Ma'am, your flight has been grounded until further notice." She glanced skyward. "Not that you were going to get liftoff anyway."

"What about the driver and whoever else is in that limo," Chey asked, speaking for the first time.

The agent holstered her gun, and Wyatt and Chey lowered their arms. "I don't need to speak to them. I know who they are. Just you three. Come," she said, motioning them to proceed to the trailer terminal.

Wyatt looked over his shoulder, hoping the gentleman, or whoever was in the car, would get out so Wyatt could at least get a good look. He was also mildly annoyed that whatever his identity, he was apparently unconcerned that Vivi was being led away by a federal agent. *Some white knight you are, buddy.*

"I appreciated you swimming halfway across Firefly Lake, I truly did," Vivi told Wyatt as they were escorted into a small, spare office, and the agent closed the door behind them. "But trust me, if and when I need a helping hand, or my boat pulled to shore, I'll be the first to let you know."

"We were afraid you couldn't let us know," Chey said.

"Are you saying he's done this before?" Agent Jarman asked, sounding newly concerned. She motioned for them to sit in the thinly padded metal chairs crowded in front of a laminate wood desk; then she took a seat behind it.

"No," Vivi assured her. "Well, yes, but I asked him to. Well, not him exactly. I asked—"

"Agent Jarman," Chey began, calmly and with a steady

smile. "This has all been a horrible misunderstanding. My friend here had a date that didn't go well recently, and so today we were a bit concerned and—"

"I assure you I am perfectly capable of choosing whom I spend my time with," Vivi said, affronted all over again. "If you recall, I had dispatched Mr. Hammond long before your arrival. I merely lost my paddles."

"Dispatched?" Jarman repeated, looking concerned bordering on alarmed now. "What do you mean, dispatched."

"She ended the date early. He swam to shore," Chey explained. "Nothing happened. Everyone was fine." She turned back to Vivi. "I was just worried. I had this gut feeling and they're rarely wrong. We just wanted to see who it was, make sure you were okay. We weren't going to interfere— but an airport, Vivi? I mean, this was a business meeting. We thought you were going to Turtle Springs; then you come all the way out here, and we thought, okay, upscale meeting means upscale restaurant. Then you got to a hotel— a *hotel*—and *then* you get picked up in a Rolls Royce, which proceeds to take you to an *airport*? Who needs an airplane for a business meeting? And where is he right now? He just watched you get hauled off by a law enforcement agent and he's not going to follow up? Make sure you're okay?" She folded her arms and leaned back in the chair. "I'm not feeling bad about my choices right now."

"I often use an airplane for business meetings," came a very deep, very recognizable voice from the doorway. "And I wouldn't dream of leaving this lovely woman to be interrogated alone."

Wyatt and Chey both turned, their mouths having already dropped open. "Oh my God," Chey whispered. "You're Grant Harper."

The exceedingly handsome, multiple-Oscar and Tony-winning actor nodded. "Every day."

Chey's head whipped around to look at Vivi. "You know Grant Harper?"

"I've worked with a number of well-known actors," she said, still clearly miffed. "You know that."

"But Grant Harper?" Chey whispered. "You gave me a hard time about not mentioning Wyatt, and you never mentioned you know Grant Harper?" Chey looked back at Grant, still goggling.

"Gee," Vivi said dryly, "I can't imagine why."

Grant stepped into the room and extended his hand. "Agent"—he paused and read her badge—"Jarman. I think we can all agree that this has been a well-intentioned, and possibly even cinematic, moment, but otherwise harmless."

"It's against the law to—" Agent Jarman began, but then he took her hand in his and covered it with his other hand, and she faltered slightly.

"If we get them to promise never to—"

"Come to this private hangar, for any reason, or they'll be arrested on sight," Jarman finished, never once taking her clearly star struck gaze from Grant's tanned face, gorgeous blue eyes, and blinding white smile.

"I think that can be arranged," Grant said. "Thank you for your kindness."

She nodded; then he let go of her hand and glanced at the three of them. "Why don't we meet in my hangar." He looked to Agent Jarman. "I will make sure they are under supervision at all times; then we'll be leaving just as soon as we're cleared for takeoff."

"But—" Chey said, only to have Grant look at her and simply smile. "Right," she said. She turned to Agent Jarman and extended her hand. "Thank you. My sincere apologies."

Jarman gave her hand a quick shake, then surprised them by smiling. "You just got me a one-on-one with Grant Harper, so . . ." Then she frowned. "Be safe out there."

Chey smiled and nodded. "Will do."

Wyatt and Chey followed Grant and Vivi. Wyatt thought about how people would often comment upon meeting a celebrity that the star was shorter, or paler, or somehow less impressive in person. A mere mortal. That was not the case with Grant Harper. He was taller than Wyatt by a few inches, and every bit as lean and fit. His sport coat hung perfectly across broad shoulders and the fitted jeans and cowboy boots suited his swagger, all of which came across as natural and authentic, rather than put on for show.

Wyatt didn't know how old Vivi was—late sixties was his guess—so Grant would be right around the same age. To say he was iconic or legendary was not overstating it. That Grant had so effortlessly maintained his dashing, movie star good looks in the way of Paul Newman or Cary Grant simply added to the dazzle.

"Please, have a seat," he said, escorting them through a door inside the hangar and into a surprisingly well-appointed lounge area. "Looks like Mother Nature is handing us a bit of a delay, so that will give us time to get to know one another. Can I get you something to drink?"

"Coffee, darling, if you have it," Vivi said, taking a seat on one of the love seat–sized couches.

"For you, anything," he said, shooting her a grin.

Wyatt and Chey each took a bottle of water from the side table and sat on the love seat opposite Vivi. Wyatt liked to think he was not the kind of guy to be star struck, but he suspected his expression wasn't much different from Chey's at the moment.

Grant carried Vivi's coffee over and set it and a tray of creamer and sugar on the small coffee table between them. He turned to Chey. "I'm sorry," Grant said, as he handed Vivi's mug of coffee to her. "I didn't get your name."

Chey immediately stood, jarring the coffee table and

almost sloshing Vivi's coffee in her haste to extend her hand. "Cheyenne McCafferty," she said. "Just Chey."

"Pleasure, Just Chey," he said with a grin, and shook her hand.

She stood there and continued to stare, then shook her head as if to clear it. "I'm sorry. I just—wasn't expecting you to be so . . . you."

"And I work so hard at trying to be other people," he said. "One of my greatest failures, I suppose."

Chey blanched. "I didn't mean—"

Wyatt took her hand and tugged her back to the couch. He'd never seen her like this and found it both endearing and highly entertaining. He stood and extended his hand. "Wyatt Reed," he said.

"Yes," Grant said, then blew his mind. "Reed Planet. Impressive how you've used our modern technology to solve the seemingly never-ending old-world problems. Perhaps we could talk at some point about ways you think I might be able to help."

And then it was Wyatt's turn to get tongue-tied. He'd talked to plenty of corporate bigwigs and other giants in their fields, including celebrities, athletes, people who wanted to help his cause. Maybe it was because he rarely met them in person, but he was admittedly caught off guard and not a little flattered that Grant Harper knew who he was and was offering his support.

"For heaven's sake," Vivi said to them both, "have a seat and stop acting like you've just seen an alien spaceship."

Wyatt grinned and Chey had the good grace to look abashed. Wyatt shook Grant's hand. "The pleasure is all mine," he said. "And yes, I would absolutely love to take you up on that offer. Thank you."

They reseated themselves on the love seat across from

Vivi, and Grant settled next to her, a bottle of spring water in his hand.

"So," Chey said, clearing her throat and sitting forward, getting her bearings back. "Did you two meet while working on a stage production together?"

Grant looked at Vivi and grinned. She glanced at him and even her perfectly applied makeup didn't hide the hint of pink that rose to her cheeks. "We met more years ago than our vanity allows us to admit," he said in that well-known baritone Wyatt had heard coming at him from movie screens all his life. Grant took Vivi's beringed hand between his, then looked back to the two of them and said simply, "She was the one who got away." He looked at her. "My deepest regret is being too young and foolish to know what was staring me right in the face." He glanced back at them. "I'm glad to see the two of you aren't making the same mistake."

Wyatt was pretty sure his momentary slack expression was a mirror image of Chey's. She looked at Vivi. "You told him? About—?"

Vivi lifted her shoulder in an elegant shrug. "There are some people between whom there are no secrets, and nothing is off the table." She leaned forward, set down her coffee mug, and sent them a knowing smile. "I assure you he takes discretion very seriously. Your story is safe with him."

"It's not that—" Chey began, then stopped and let out a short laugh of disbelief. "I'm sorry. Truly. I'm not usually like this. It's just, I feel like I left the farm and stepped into an alternate universe."

Vivi smiled. "Why do you think I adored my work so much? I got to do that every day. Only in my case I left a three-story walk-up in the Bronx and took two very un-Cinderella-like trains to get from home to fantasy-land, but I'd have traveled farther and lived in far worse for the chance it gave me, the world it gave me."

Wyatt noticed that Vivi hadn't said anything directly in response to Grant's declaration, but the fact that she hadn't taken her hand from his and had declared them to be the closest of confidants said a great deal.

"Where are you flying off to," Chey said, "if it's okay to ask?" She smiled at Vivi. "Pure nosey, star-struck curiosity now. Not interrogating your date."

"New York," Vivi said, and Wyatt noted she didn't deny it was a date, either. "Grant and I haven't been in touch for quite some time." She was smiling, but there was a world of emotion in her eyes. "He thought I might enjoy spending the afternoon at some of our old haunts." She glanced at him. "The ones that are still around, at any rate."

"That's lovely," Chey said, smiling at Grant. "Just for the afternoon?"

"Perhaps the evening, as well," Grant said, then glanced at Vivi. "If I can talk her into it."

Wyatt knew Chey must be bursting at the seams with questions for Vivi over this startling and definitely quite juicy revelation about her past. Heck, Wyatt had questions, and he'd just met Vivi.

Vivi did slide her hand from Grant's then to reach for the creamer. "I'm sure you're both wondering why I would have contacted Grant regarding our issue with the resort deal."

Leave it to Vivi to cut to the chase.

"It had crossed my mind," Chey said wryly.

Vivi glanced at Grant, as if seeking his okay to reveal his secret. He nodded, and she looked back to them. "It's somewhat common knowledge that Grant owns a great deal of property out west and spends most of his time there. Much less known is his work supporting environmental and green energy research that's being done and tested out there. He's been outspoken about our need to pay more attention to conservation and has done a great deal to raise awareness, but behind the scenes, he's been putting his money where his mouth is, and personally financing a number of different projects."

Wyatt extended his hand to Grant again. "That's phenomenal. Thank you."

Grant shook his hand, but said, "I think we all have a responsibility to give back. This planet we all live on is pretty much indestructible, but that doesn't mean it will always be hospitable. At least to us. We've documented its formation enough to know it hasn't been in the past and will likely, at some point, not be again. It's in all our best interests to make sure we're still welcome on it for as long as humanly—and I mean that specifically—possible."

"Here, here," Wyatt said.

"Some of us have bigger platforms than others," he went on, with a nod to Wyatt. "I have been vocal in trying to draw attention to various specific things we can do to improve and extend our ultimate stay here. There is progress being made."

"I had no idea you were so involved," Wyatt said, then grinned. "You may be sorry I know that now. We're—Reed Planet—is always looking for ways to bring attention to the various projects we take on."

"I imagine we can find some overlap there," Grant said. "We'll definitely talk." He glanced at Vivi again, who returned his gaze.

Grant's smile was full-on movie idol perfection. Vivi's was softer, and though maybe not tentative, also not the twinkling display Wyatt had witnessed countless times even in their brief shared history.

"Vivi tells me that you are trying to preserve a lake and local wilderness area, that it's being considered for a big, commercial resort that will increase revenue, but likely diminish the charm and general joie de vivre of your mountain paradise."

"You make it sound a lot more exciting than it is," Chey said with a laugh. "But yes. The problem is twofold. Threefold, actually." She went on to explain to him the situation.

"I've seen this happen before," Grant said. "I owned a ranch in northern California and saw the same developers-to-the-rescue dynamic happen there. What was once a stunning rustic retreat and classic western town looks more like Sacramento now than Rustling Pine Lake. And the locals, myself included, eventually packed up, sold our properties—some of them had been in the same family dating back to the gold rush—and moved further out, started over."

"We don't want to see that happen," Chey said. "But it's not exactly an environmental or green energy issue we're having. It's a topographically diverse area, and richer for it."

Grant smiled. "Vivi tells me you all just moved out there a few years ago. Your passion and reverence for your new home is good to see. That's exactly the kind of growth and support places like yours need."

"So, what would your connection be?" Wyatt asked, then explained what they were hoping for, much the same way he'd presented it to the people who had been at the farm the day before.

Grant nodded. "That's the perfect alternate plan. It just so happens that one of the organizations I've been working with is designing green-energy friendly designs for newly developing areas. It's a challenge to rework already established areas and update them to new technologies, especially when the owners don't see any need to change anything. But if we can start that way in areas with new development, we get the benefit of not perpetuating systems that drain the environment rather than work with it and enhance it, and as new communities develop and grow, they become models for showing previously developed areas why they should consider upgrading and improving their systems."

"That's . . . wonderful," Wyatt said, beaming. He looked at Vivi. "This is so much more than I'd hoped for." He looked back at Grant. "So, are you saying you think the lake property could be developed into one of these green-energy prototypes?"

Grant nodded. "I am."

Wyatt laughed. "That's incredible."

"It's not a slam dunk," Grant said. "There are a lot of particulars that will need to be hammered out between the group and your council. This won't be a typical build, and there are a lot of other variables involved that will have to be considered and agreed upon." He sat forward and braced his elbows on his knees. "I won't sugarcoat this. The big, shiny resort they already have in hand will be cheaper to build, faster to go up, and quicker to reap rewards, both for the town, and from what I hear, their own pockets if they are working some kind of back deal with the builder or whoever is financing it."

"Would you be willing to put your face on our campaign to get them to consider this alternative plan?" Wyatt asked. "Would you work with me to do that? My following, and yours?"

Grant chuckled. "We might be able to work something out."

Just then a man stuck his head into the room. "We've been cleared for takeoff, Mr. Harper," he said, then ducked back out.

Three of them stood and Chey and Wyatt both shook hands with Grant again. "I can't tell you how much we appreciate this," Chey said. "And please accept our apologies, again, for so rudely interrupting your, uh, meeting." She winked at Vivi.

"No apologies needed. Now Vivi and I won't have to spend what time we have together talking business." He offered Vivi his hand, which she took as she also stood. "Perhaps with this out of the way, I can convince you to let me take you to dinner."

"We'll see," was all that Vivi said.

She was smiling, and there was clearly a very real fondness there for Grant, but she was also obviously holding part of herself back. All the same, Wyatt had no doubt she could hold her own, and if she didn't want to go to New York, or dinner, or anything else, he was quite certain she wouldn't.

"No umbrella required?" Chey asked, apparently on the same wavelength. She wanted what was best for Vivi, and, as amazing as he seemed to be, both by cinematic reputation and in real life, she wasn't quite sure that Grant Harper was it.

"Just for the rain, darling," Vivi said, her expression reassuring. She took Chey's hand and squeezed it. "We'll talk tomorrow, hmm?"

"We will," Chey agreed with a smile and a nod, and let her hand go. "We will indeed," Wyatt heard her say under her breath.

"I expect I don't want to know what that was all about," Grant said in an aside to Wyatt as the two women left the lounge room first.

"You would expect right," Wyatt said. "But she's a woman with many, shall we say, hidden talents. So, I'd be sure to keep a gentlemanly distance until invited otherwise."

Grant chuckled at that. "Message received," he said, and clapped Wyatt on the shoulder. "And, just so you know, that was never in question. I honestly never expected to have this opportunity. I most certainly will take utmost care not to squander it."

Wyatt turned to him just before they left the lounge. "Not to speak out of turn, but as someone presently trying to do the same thing, most definitely take care." He paused, then said the rest of what was on his mind. "I'm not sure, but if her beloved new home," he emphasized, "hadn't been put at risk, I don't know that she'd have contacted you. At least not this week. I can't speak for all of eternity, but—"

"Actually, she made that abundantly clear when we first spoke," Grant confided candidly, then smiled. "Have no fear."

Wyatt chuckled. Of course she had. Vivi didn't take no stuff. Just ask Paul Hammond. "There might be some additional obstacles put in place in this deal, by someone who didn't heed Vivi's warning," Wyatt said, revealing that bit of info for several reasons. He met Grant's gaze. "Someone in a position to make things even more challenging when you step into the picture. And not because you're Grant Harper, screen legend. You understand what I mean?"

Grant frowned now but nodded.

"I'm only telling you this because I think you have her best interests at heart, and she could use your support. Whatever she ends up deciding about your second chance, I hope you will be her champion. Because we will."

"You can count on it."

Wyatt watched Grant as he walked over to Vivi, all dashing good looks and down to earth charm, every bit of it sincere.

Chey joined him and they waved to Vivi, then watched as Grant escorted her toward the open end of the hangar and out to the tarmac beyond and his waiting jet.

"What did you just say to him?" she asked.

"Why do you think I said something?"

Chey looked from the departing couple to Wyatt. "Because Mr. Harper has a very different look in his eyes now." She smiled. "Kind of the same one I see when I look into yours."

He pulled her into his arms. "Then that is a very good thing indeed."

Chapter Eleven

The following morning, Chey, Hannah, and Avery were all seated around the big kitchen table, sipping coffee and waiting for Vivi to make an appearance.

Hannah looked at her watch. "It's almost eight-thirty. I don't think I've ever known her to be down later than seven, seven-thirty." She laughed. "Or later than me, anyway."

"Her median time is twelve minutes after seven," Avery said, pushing her glasses up her pert nose and making some notes in the spiral notebook she always had at hand. "So, this is definitely an aberration."

"I shudder to think what kind of data you have on my habits," Chey said.

Avery just looked up and wiggled her eyebrows. "Wouldn't you like to know."

Chey lifted a hand. "No, no. I think I'm good."

"Actually," Avery went on, "there's been a dramatic uptick in data entry in your binder—"

"I have a binder?" Chey paused just before taking a sip of her coffee. "Like, the three-ring kind? Okay, now I definitely don't want to know. I have the most boring life ever. What could you possibly—"

"Maybe that was true last week," Avery said. "Now? With

Reed Planet carrying you off every time we turn around?"
She looked back to her notes. "Yeah, not so much."

"His name is Wyatt, and he doesn't—" Chey broke off,
and took a big sip of coffee instead. Because saying he didn't
carry her off would be a bold-faced lie. Just that morning,
he'd carried her to the shower. And then back to bed.

"Someone's cheeks are pretty pink at the moment,"
Hannah said, and gave Chey a broad, knowing grin when
she just scowled at her. "Welcome to the club," she said,
offering her mug for a toast.

Chey frowned, but touched her mug to Hannah's and
said, "What club?"

"The one where you come into the kitchen twenty minutes late looking like the cat who just had a whole bowl of
cream, and the rest of us get to grill you on who put that look
on your face."

"Yep," Avery added. "Paybacks, meet hell."

"You're all very droll this morning," Chey said, "but I'm
not the focus of this little meeting today. We're here to talk
about Vivi. I want us to support her however she needs us
to. I just couldn't tell from seeing her yesterday what that
support should be."

"I'm still trying to wrap my head around the fact that you
sat in a private lounge in a private airplane hangar, in touching distance of Grant Harper. I mean . . ." Hannah fanned
herself. "Is he really all that in person?"

Chey wasn't normally a gossip girl, or fangirl. In fact,
she'd have said she'd be the very last one to be either of those
things. The only reason she'd told Hannah and Avery about
Grant Harper was because she was worried about whatever
minefield Vivi was making her way through and wanted the
other two to know what she'd witnessed. However, there
was no getting around the fact that she'd literally stood
there and gawked at the man yesterday. There was also no

guarantee she wouldn't again if she was ever in the same room with him. She set her mug down and with all due reverence, said, "Oh, he's so, *so* much more than all that."

Hannah gave a quiet little squeal. "It's all kind of exciting, isn't it? I mean, who knew Vivi has one of the most legendary stage and film stars panting after her?"

"I wouldn't say panting—" Chey began.

"He dropped everything and flew here on a moment's notice, picked her up in a Rolls, then flew her to New York for the afternoon," Avery pointed out. "That's the definition of panting. Hollywood style."

Chey nodded, conceding her point. "I'll admit, he's definitely a full-tilt screen idol when he walks in the room. He's more impressive in person than on screen, which is saying something. So, he's a lot to just . . . take in. But then he talks to you and he's really about a lot more than that. In fact, no part of our conversation had anything to do with his career, or Vivi's, other than that's how they met when they were young."

"It all sounds so romantic," Avery said, pausing in her chart making long enough to have a dreamy-eyed moment.

"It kind of was," Chey admitted. "I'm not gonna lie." She finished off the last of her lavender scone. "I'm just not sure what happens next in that fairy tale. Or what she wants to happen next."

"Good morning, darlings," Vivi said, sweeping into the room as she spoke, all casual and show stopping at the same time. Her hair was swept up in a flawless chignon, the lavender streaks perfectly accentuating every curve. Makeup, also flawless. Multiple bangles jingled at her wrists, with matching tasteful accoutrements around her neck and dangling from her ears. All of this glamour had been paired with very casual duck pants, a blue and white striped boat shirt, and canvas flats. Yet she still managed to command the room with the aplomb of a red-carpet entrance. "That coffee smells divine. I'm so sorry I wasn't down earlier to brew you all a pot."

She poured herself a cup and turned to face them, leaning her hip against the counter. "You're all here bright and early. I can't recall the last time we all four managed that. I suppose you have our charts for us, Avery, with our schedules for the week? I can't believe how fast time is just flying by. There's so much to be done before our official spring opening, but it's so exciting, isn't it?"

Chey, Hannah, and Avery just looked at her. "Really, Vivi?" This from Chey. "If you think you can go waltzing off to New York with a full-on screen idol and not at least share some of the—"

"Good morning, ladies," came that singular baritone from the kitchen doorway. "I hope I'm not intruding. That coffee smells pretty amazing."

"Oh my," Hannah said as Grant Harper walked right into their kitchen. She barely managed to bobble her mug back on the table instead of dropping it straight to the floor.

"Good morning, Mr. Harper," Chey said, giving Vivi a "well, well, well" look of admiration and outright curiosity. She was proud of how she held it together this time, especially when this encounter was easily as shocking as the first time she'd met him. "Welcome to Lavender Blue. This is Hannah Montgomery and Avery Kent," she said, motioning to each. "The other two partners in our farming endeavor."

"Grant, please," he said, and nodded at Hannah and Avery, flashing that legendary smile, ocean blue eyes on full twinkle as he did. "Pleasure to meet you all."

He wore faded jeans, a blue pullover that was just the right amount of snug across those broad shoulders, and he was barefoot, Chey noted, as he crossed the room to accept a freshly poured mug from Vivi. All of that was devastatingly sexy and made her want to go find Wyatt and jump him immediately.

"I won't intrude," he said congenially. "I know you all have a business to run here. I haven't seen the whole setup in the daylight as yet, but the view from the window upstairs was pretty spectacular." He turned to Vivi. "I've got some calls to make before our meeting later. Let me know when you're ready." He stole a scone from the plate on the kitchen table, then shot them a devilish wink and lifted his mug in a salute. "Have a good day, everyone." And he was gone.

Once Chey recovered from the tidal wave of *oh my* that was Grant Harper, she noted there had been no kiss to Vivi's temple when he took the coffee mug from her, or any little affectionate byplay between the two. In fact, they hadn't so much as touched each other. But the way he'd looked at her when he'd crossed the room toward her was so steamy it could have peeled the old paint off the walls.

"So," Avery breathed, "that's going to take some getting used to."

Hannah nodded faintly, still looking at the doorway he'd exited through. "Hubba and hubba, then hubba some more." She fanned her face.

"He was born for the big screen," was all Vivi said, though she'd said it with a smile.

"So," Chey said, then looked to the door, then to Vivi. "Um . . . ?"

Vivi took her seat at the table and placed a scone on a napkin in front of herself. "Not one of you has an inch of room to talk about my relationship development choices, but if you must know—"

"They didn't sleep together." This from Avery. "The

window with the view to the farm is the guest room window," she explained, when they turned to look at her. "Why would he be in there if he hadn't slept in there?"

Hannah and Chey looked to Vivi for confirmation.

She carefully stirred a dollop of cream into her coffee and said, "I will neither confirm nor deny." Then she looked up at them and, finally, the twinkle was back. "Let an old woman have some mystery."

"Old woman, my fanny," Chey said. "Have you seen him? I mean . . ."

"Why yes," she said, with full Vivienne Baudin sparkle. "I have."

Hannah sputtered her coffee and Chey let out a hoot of laughter, then put her fist forward. "Right here," she said, and Vivi fist-bumped her, then surprised them by doing the explosion finish, which made them all laugh.

"Bailey," she said, when they looked at her in surprise. "I like to stay hip."

"You have Grant Harper in your bedroom," Hannah said. "I'd say you are currently the epitome of hip."

"Yes, well, it's not so simple as all that," she admitted.

All three of them folded their arms on the table and leaned closer to Vivi. "What's the story?" Chey asked. "In general. I mean, we're not asking you to kiss and tell."

"Oh, you most certainly are. And fair's fair, we did the same to Hannah and Avery, and I'm about to want the same from you." Vivi propped her elbows on the table and rested her chin in her hands, then batted her perfect lashes. "Pray tell, what's life like on Reed Planet?"

Hannah and Avery turned to her. "Right! Yes, we need more." Then they mimicked Vivi's pose.

Chey waved her spoon, then stirred a little sugar into her coffee. Avery always made it too strong. "Oh, no. There will be no distraction from the topic at hand." She paused, then caught their collective gaze and smiled. She let her head dramatically fall back. "Except to say life on Reed Planet is ah-mazing." She straightened while they cheered. "Okay," she said, and turned to Vivi. "Now you." She lifted her hand. "I'm not asking for details. I'm asking how you feel about him being back in your life. He said you were the one who got away and I know you haven't communicated in a very long time. Yet he literally dropped everything and came running the moment you crooked your little finger. And you knew he would. Because you were pretty certain yesterday that our problem would be solved."

Chey laid her hand on Vivi's wrist. "We just worry about you, is all. We don't want you putting yourself in a personal situation you would otherwise avoid, just to help the town. We will find another way. Nothing is worth being where you don't want to be. We worked too hard to get here, to put our lives back together." Chey knew Vivi and the other two realized she wasn't just talking about being in Blue Hollow Falls.

Chey sat back and Vivi sighed and studied her coffee for a long moment. They gave her all the time she needed.

She kept her gaze on her coffee when she finally spoke. "Grant and I . . . it was quite the whirlwind romance when we first met. And it was a very long time ago." She paused and still, no one spoke, realizing she needed time to tell this her own way. "I fell madly in love with him, and I think, at that time anyway, he simply fell madly in lust with me. His star was taking off; he went from the chorus to understudy to star in the blink of an eye. I was still in the chorus and happy to be there, thrilled for his successes."

Chey could see where this was going and her understanding must have shown on her face, because Vivi looked up at her, then nodded.

"He was suddenly the darling of Broadway; then he got

his first movie role, and the gap that had sprung up between us grew to a canyon seemingly overnight. He was given so much attention, with people literally throwing themselves at him, and not just women. Movie executives, Broadway producers, television people." She set her spoon down, having stirred her coffee about to death. "To his credit, he honestly remained the same wonderfully thoughtful, charming, and down to earth man you see right now. It truly didn't go to his head. But he was overwhelmed, certainly. It was a steep, fast learning curve. In the end, he didn't think he could juggle everything and give our relationship the time it deserved. I never felt he thought less of me because his star was rising and mine was simply twinkling along where it had always been."

"He was honest with you then," Hannah said. "That speaks well of him."

Vivi smiled and nodded. "He knew he needed to go live his life and experience what was coming at him, unencumbered, as it were. But even though I saw it coming, the breakup was awful, and my heart was utterly shattered. He had ended things about as well as he possibly could have. It was just that we wanted two very different outcomes for our love story, and it was hard for my heart to accept that, because we'd been so wonderful together."

"How long did it take him to realize he'd screwed up the best thing that ever happened to him?" This from Chey.

"You see, darling, that's just it. I don't think he screwed up. I think what he did was the right thing. I didn't realize it at the time, of course, but looking back, I know that to be true. If we'd stayed together at that time in our lives, we'd have become very different people to each other, and I doubt either one of us would have loved who we would have become. It was a thrilling time, just an incredibly demanding one. I had my own dreams, my own goals. Yes, I wanted to marry him. Yes, I wanted the white picket fence with him, but I didn't want to be Mrs. Grant Harper in terms of my professional goals. Becoming his wife, at that point, in that day and age, would have ended my career, most assuredly."

"That must have been a very hard decision to make," Hannah said softly.

"I was so heartbroken, but I wasn't mad at him." She laughed. "It would have been easier if I were." She picked up a scone, then put it back down. "We did stay in touch while he was still in New York. It made things harder on us both, but we couldn't seem to help ourselves. We were just the best of friends."

She looked at Chey then, and they shared a smile. Chey knew Vivi was thinking of Chey's childhood with Wyatt. Some comparisons were inevitable.

"When he finally left New York for good, for Hollywood, and moved to California full time, we broke contact completely. Or, I guess I should say that I did. I knew I had to, for my own healing. There were no cell phones or social media and the like in those days. Calls were long distance and expensive. It was an easier time, compared to now, to cut things off. Though, admittedly, it felt horrifically lonely." She smiled at them. "And then things did begin to take off for me. In my desperation for a distraction from my sadness and my loneliness, I think I was more daring than I might have otherwise been. I pushed harder to get noticed, and instead of waiting for things to happen, I worked to make them happen." Her smile spread and that twinkle came out once again. "And they did."

"Good for you," Hannah said. "Sometimes the best love story is the love we discover for ourselves. Sometimes we have to put our own love story first, before we can love someone else."

"That is absolutely the core of it," Vivi said, "though

it took years and two failed marriages to figure that out. Despite all of it, I've regretted that Grant and I met at the wrong time, but never that we parted at the time we did. It was the right thing to do then."

"Did you ever think of contacting him later in your life?" Avery asked.

"Oh, many times," Vivi said. "I married not long after he starred in his first movie. Absolutely a rebound situation, as you know. We've talked about it before, but losing Grant was the reason I ran off and did it. And why we ended that union before our second anniversary." She waved her hand. "You know about both my marriages; we've covered this ground before, when I told you about Harold."

Harold Wolff III had been the dominant love interest of Vivi's life, or the one who'd been present in her life the longest, Chey thought now. Which wasn't to say he'd been the love of her life, as Chey was beginning to suspect, though that's what they'd always assumed. They also knew Vivi had divorced her second husband after a decade of marriage. That union had been more of a love story than the first, at least in the beginning. The marriage had long been strained, though, due to her inability to have children, and eventually fell apart completely when he'd abruptly announced he was expecting a child with another woman.

She'd been in her late thirties, maybe a half dozen years after her second divorce when she'd met Harold. He'd been one of the new benefactors of the chorus line production that Vivi had been headlining at the same Forty-Second Street theater for several years. Sort of a Rockettes kind of show. She had been doing some costume designing for the production as well and met Harold at one of the promotional functions put on by the theater.

They'd hit it off straightaway and he'd always made it a point to see her when he was in town. The thing was, in addition to being almost fifteen years her senior, Harold was also married. His wife had been put in a convalescent home after a car accident had left her comatose, with little to no chance of recovery. Harold took his vows seriously, and in all the years he and Vivi were close, he'd never once strayed across the line. Not so much as a peck on the cheek. Of course, according to Vivi, it was obvious to them and everyone around them that they were madly in love with each other.

Chey knew over the course of their close relationship Harold had often urged Vivi to go find someone else, fall in love and get married for good, but after her two failed attempts, she simply wasn't interested in playing that field. Instead, she poured her frustrations and her passion into her career. Eventually she'd been forced out of the lead roles as she grew older and had turned to her design business full time. In the end, that career had become her true claim to fame, and she'd known great success.

Chey, Hannah, and Avery had poured over scrapbooks and albums filled with photos and articles and magazine layouts showcasing her work. She designed mostly for Broadway, but also for Hollywood on occasion. She professed that she'd been surprised when movie producers had sought her out, had noticed her designs for the stage.

Chey couldn't help but wonder now if Grant had played a role in at least initiating those contacts. Having met him, seeing the way he looked at Vivi, with such admiration and respect, she would bet on it.

As to Vivi and Harold, their relationship ended in tragic circumstances, which she'd always maintained she'd deserved for pining after a married man.

Harold had flown from his home base in Chicago to New York to see the opening night of Vivi's first major Broadway production as lead designer. That same night, Harold's wife had suffered an aneurysm and died. Despite the fact that Harold could have done nothing to prevent what happened, or saved her had he been there, he couldn't forgive himself for not being by her side, as he would have been if he hadn't given in to his desire to share in Vivi's big triumph and flown to New York to surprise her.

Rather than being freed by the loss of his wife, Harold had been drowned in overwhelming grief and guilt, causing him to abruptly end things, leaving Vivi devastated.

She'd even swallowed her pride, opting to fight for what they had, and sought him out, all but begging him to reconsider and at least give them a chance. He'd refused even to see her. He'd passed away two years later, almost nine years ago now, without their ever seeing or speaking to each other again. It had been grappling with his loss, her unresolved anger, fear, guilt, and grief that had sent her to that counseling group the day they'd all first met.

They hadn't been friends for long when Vivi confided she'd gotten word from an attorney in Chicago that Harold's estate had finally finished probate and that he'd left her something.

The four of them were seated that very morning at a table in the middle of her inheritance. It was no surprise that it had taken a few more years after hearing of the bequest before she'd even been willing to go look at it.

"Why?" Hannah asked Vivi gently. "Why didn't you seek Grant out? Either when Harold was begging you to find someone else, or after his wife passed and he hurt you so terribly."

Vivi shook her head. "I couldn't."

"But—" This from Chey.

Vivi interrupted her. "It's hard to explain, but I cherished what I had with Grant. It was, by far, the happiest and certainly the healthiest love affair I'd ever had. Yes, we were very young, but the mutual respect, love, and admiration we shared and showed one another from beginning to end was actually the most mature relationship I'd been in." She picked up the same scone, set it back down. "Harold . . . our love story was so complicated. He was a sanctuary for me. In all ways." Her smile was bittersweet. "I knew I couldn't have him, so he was perfect. He couldn't hurt me, he couldn't leave me, so I could trust him, love him." She let out a short laugh. "Of course, I was so very wrong about both of those things. But while I was in it, I felt so free, and so very mature. I was having this grand career, a powerful man loved me and I loved him back. I admired him even more deeply for his dedication to his wife." She shook her head. "I mean, just listen to that, will you?"

"Vivi—"

Her smile turned sardonic. "As we know, it took a good deal of counseling to understand it was really more a co-dependent relationship that we each used as a crutch. So we wouldn't have to make the hard decisions about how to have a truly fulfilling life, or a real relationship." Vivi reached out and took Chey's hand and Hannah's hand, and Avery laid hers on top. "After Harold left, after he died, and I started to really examine my life, my choices, while trying to get a handle on my grief, I felt like . . . well, like such a failure, like I was damaged goods."

"Vivi," Hannah whispered.

She shook her head. "Now I know the truth about all of that, but then? The very last thing in the world I'd have done was to dare assume Grant Harper would want anything to do with me, a woman who'd pined after a married man for so many fruitless years, only to be ditched by him when he was finally free. How pathetic I would have surely seemed to him. He was doing so well. I would never intrude on his life. I felt I'd had my chances. When I moved here with you three, honestly, I was at peace."

"He never married," Avery said, then guiltily held up her phone. "I just did a quick look at his IMDb. His Internet Movie Database file," she clarified when Chey merely looked confused. "Sorry. I was just curious."

Vivi shook her head. "He never did, no."

"Because of you?" Hannah asked gently.

Vivi sighed, then let out a short, self-deprecating laugh. "Even I'm not vain enough to believe that. He was my perfect love, I suppose, but surely that was a romanticized fairy tale of youth."

"How did you know he would come?" Chey asked. "How long has it been since you've spoken? All the way back to when he moved to California?"

Vivi shook her head. "No. We've been in touch. Well, not directly, but I guess you could say professionally, though very, very infrequently. I'd sent him a note to congratulate him on his first Oscar nomination. I thought it was very mature of me. I was with Harold then, so it seemed a decent thing to do. He did the same whenever I reached a career milestone. We never spoke, never saw each other. Just a card with some flowers or a bottle of champagne. So, we both knew we kept tabs." She looked down, and Chey saw the brief smile.

"What," Chey chided. "What is that smile?"

"Well, the cards were really pretty generic, though he'd usually address me by the nickname he had for me, and I always called him Cary Grant instead of Grant. Some silly joke that started . . . well, I don't even recall now why, but we thought it was endlessly amusing."

"What did he call you?" Avery wanted to know. All of them wanted to know.

"Daffy," she said, then laughed when their mouths collectively dropped open.

"Daffy?" Chey said, sounding almost affronted.

"It was short for daffodil. My favorite flower."

"Aw," Hannah said, and they all melted a little. "That's so sweet."

"So, he'd send the cards to Daffy and you'd send yours to Cary Grant?" Avery asked.

She nodded. "One of the last cards he sent, he wrote, 'The one who got away, my only true regret.' And he signed that one, 'Love, Grant.' Now, I thought he was just being a charmer, but I admit, it did stick with me."

"Did you give him a signal like that?"

She shook her head. "I only sent maybe one after that. If I'm being honest, I think his card spooked me a little. I didn't want to even contemplate a thing like that."

"You wanted another safe relationship," Hannah said. "Even more distant than before."

Vivi lifted a shoulder. "Maybe. Probably," she added with a rueful laugh. "Though I didn't think of it like that. I didn't think of it as a relationship in that way. It was kind, and just . . . sweet, I guess. Those memories made me happy, not sad. I would never have done anything to risk them. To take a chance on adding to our story in a way that could ruin all that had come before."

"So, why did you?" Avery asked. "Risk that, I mean. We could have found another developer."

Vivi smiled wistfully and a bit of spark was back in her eyes now. "I honestly don't know what possessed me." She lifted her hand, palm out, when they each gave her a dubious look. "Maybe I was looking for an excuse? I don't know. He hadn't been on my mind or anything. It wasn't until Wyatt started talking about environmental developers.

Then I couldn't not think about him. I knew what he was involved in; I still kept tabs."

Chey wiggled her eyebrows and nudged her gently with an elbow. "See? Even after you both left the industry, you two couldn't stay out of each other's orbits."

"Maybe, subconsciously, it was seeing you and Wyatt together after such a long separation? I don't know. That was honestly not the kind of reunion I was hoping for. I thought it would just be business, and we were old now, and we'd meet, and it would be sweet, maybe even bittersweet; we'd rehash old times. Then talk business."

"Really?" Chey wanted to know. "Is that what you truly hoped for? In your heart of hearts? You knew he'd come. I mean, you were certain of it. All based on that one note? You couldn't have been that certain and not think it would be more than just two old pals catching up."

"Okay, fine, fine," Vivi said. Then she relented, and let them see the hope that was really there. "Maybe I secretly wanted him to do exactly what he did. Which is utterly ridiculous." She folded her hands on the table. "The honest truth is, the moment I did it I was terrified and so angry with myself. I'd broken the one promise I'd made myself. After all that time, too. Why on earth would I take a risk like that now?"

"Because you're happy now," Hannah said simply. "You're here. You've done the hard work and you've come to terms with your life. You're whole."

"If you look at it that way, it's the perfect time," Avery said. "You could probably chart it."

"Maybe," Vivi said, clearly touched by their assessment. "It was still a ridiculous risk to take."

"From great risks come great rewards," Chey said. "Or something like that."

"Not in my experience," Vivi said drolly, and they all

laughed. "But I can hardly turn the clock back now and undo it, can I?"

"Would you want to?" Chey asked, truly curious. All of this, of course, had her thinking of the course of her relationship with Wyatt, past and present.

"What are you hoping for?" Hannah asked. "If you could have any outcome?"

"Says here he's largely retired from acting and does mostly philanthropic work. Not really in the limelight unless it's to help one of his causes," Avery said, reading from her phone. She looked up at the silent pause. "What? I'm trying to give you salient information to help with your decision making. I'm just saying that she wouldn't be getting into some Hollywood whirl if they got together."

Hannah put her hand over the screen on Avery's phone. "I'm asking about the choice her heart wants her to make."

"No, it's okay," Vivi said. "And to answer both of your questions, I don't know what I want. That's why I agreed to meet him in Valley View. It felt more, I don't know . . . neutral. I didn't want him here, in my new hometown. My life here is mine."

"Well, that's kind of an answer," Chey said, pointing upward toward the ceiling, to the obvious, given he wasn't just in her new hometown of Blue Hollow Falls, he was inside her actual home.

Vivi's complexion did take on a bit of a pink hue. "I didn't know about the New York trip until he pulled up at the hotel," she trailed off. Then she finally relaxed, all the tension leaving her at once. When her smile came now, it was the most beautiful thing to behold. "But I'm really, really glad we went."

The four of them all joined hands again. "Then that's as good a place to start as any," Chey said.

Vivi nodded. "That is how I'm looking at it." She turned

to Chey. "So, now that we have my future mapped out, my darling girl, let's discuss yours."

There was a knock on the frame of the kitchen door. "I am sorry to intrude again, but Daff, it's time for us to head into town."

Chey grinned. "Saved by Grant Harper. Again."

Grant smiled, clearly not knowing what he'd done exactly, but happy to be of help. "My pleasure. And I promise to have her back as soon as I'm able," he added dryly. "No need to send the cavalry."

Chey had the good grace to blush at that. "Please, take your time. We'll be right here if you need us, though," she told Vivi on a laugh.

Vivi winked at them as she took Grant's arm, then turned and wiggled her eyebrows just before gliding out the kitchen door.

Chey called after them as they walked down the hall to the front door. "I changed my mind! Have her back by ten. And not a minute after."

"No hot-rodding in the Chevy," Hannah shouted, getting into the spirit. "Drink responsibly."

"And use protection," Avery added, then raised her arms to protect herself when Hannah and Chey tossed scones at her.

"What the hell, Ave?" Chey said, but they were all laughing.

"It's proven that STDs can happen, even at their—" Avery began, and Hannah just put a scone right into her mouth.

They heard the front door close, then the sound of the Chevy engine being excessively revved and laughed all over again as they sank back into their seats.

"No way he doesn't sweep her off her feet," Hannah said with a deep, wistful sigh.

"Oh, I think she's done been swept," Chey said.

"Can you imagine the wedding?" Hannah asked, clearly sailing off along with them. "Right here on the farm?"

Avery picked up her pen and notebook and said, "Can you imagine the guest list?"

"Oh my God," Chey said. "Let them date a minute before you marry them off." She scooted her chair back, snagged her chore chart from Avery's stack, and beat it out the side door before they could stop her. Not that they tried. All the talk about great love affairs and fairy tale weddings would have normally had Chey making snarky comments and exiting stage left anyway.

They didn't need to know that when Hannah so wistfully commented on the fairy tale wedding, the visual that immediately came to Chey's mind wasn't of Vivi walking down the aisle toward Grant Harper. No, the one taking that long, rose-petal-strewn walk had been her, and the smiling, handsome man waiting for her at the altar was the same one crossing the yard to her right now, a wide, sexy grin on his beautiful face.

Chey never thought she'd be the one mooning over wedding planning, much less saying "I do." Yet, at that moment, she couldn't figure out how she was going to make peace with a future that didn't include those two words . . . and saying them to this amazing man.

Compromises and choosing happiness. Maybe those choices were becoming easier to define after all.

Chapter Twelve

Wyatt stood backstage at the amphitheater with Dom and two other crew members who'd flown in to help with the livestream. He gave the thumbs-up to Peli, who was running the camera. She silently counted him down, then flipped her thumb from down to up.

Wyatt went straight to the hundred-watt smile as Peli zoomed in on his face. "Hey there, Reed Planet," he said. "As announced a few days ago on our site and social, we're doing something a little different with the stream this time around. I know you all are dying to find out what I'm doing in the States. This project is different from what I've done in the past, and yes, it's my first time streaming from the land of my birth, but this project and this place is important to someone who is very important to me. I've known her my whole life, and . . ." He wagged a finger in front of his face. "I know what you're thinking now."

Peli pulled back out so a bit of the scene behind Wyatt now showed on screen.

Wyatt's grin went wider, if possible. "And you'd be right. But more on that later. Right now I'm going to take you out on stage with me at this amazing amphitheater up in the Blue Ridge Mountains of Virginia, in a beautiful place filled with some beautiful souls, Blue Hollow Falls. We're about to propose a really interesting solution to a problem they've been having, one we hope will start a big conversation here in the States on how to move forward with better environmental initiatives and green energy plans."

He started backing toward the curtain that would part to reveal the stage, the crowd seated beyond, at an angle that also caught the restored mill with the mountains, shrouded in the blue haze that gave them their name. "You're going to meet some cool folks, including a few big surprises." He pushed his face closer to the camera on those last two words, then shifted back. "Then we're going on walkabout up here in the mountains. I'm going to show you this amazing century-old silk mill, which has been renovated and turned into an artisan center. Yes, they grew, harvested, spun, and milled silk up in these hills once upon a time, dating back to the time of King James of England. News to me, too!"

He could feel his energy level revving along. He loved doing this and was excited about the work they'd be doing today. He knew the people watching him could feel that, too. "We'll check out the Falls that give this mountain paradise its name, then go on safari back into the woods to a truly incredible, recently restored Victorian style greenhouse that I just found out about. They grow endangered exotic orchids there and are working on getting them off that list. More on how you can help with that later, too. We'll be seeing it together for the first time and meeting the woman who runs the whole program. Honestly, this place will mesmerize you like it has me."

Dom started to pull the curtain slowly back.

"So, come hang with me while I talk to the good folks in BHF and introduce them to some interesting people you're going to want to know." He leaned in again and lowered his voice. "There might be a little entertainment involved as well. Because we're in the mountains, in an amphitheater with some world class musicians on hand, who celebrate the music born in these hills. So, of course we are going to let them do that." He moved back again. "After our walkabout, we're going off air for about an hour or so, then we'll be streaming live this afternoon direct from the land of Firefly." He moved closer to the camera. "More on that later, too." He motioned over his shoulder with his thumb. "You ready? Let's do this."

Peli was a little bit of a thing, slender, just flirting with the five-foot mark in height, and had the flexibility of a rubber band. She was a wonder at catching all the angles, covering the stage like a cat. Or a ninja. She backed onto the stage first, crouched low, capturing Wyatt from that angle as he walked out on the amphitheater stage, then slowly panned around to capture the full vista as he viewed it. Wyatt knew she'd continue to move around the stage, and him, as everything he did and said was beamed simultaneously to phones, tablets, laptops, computers, and television screens worldwide, while it happened. She had an amazing eye for composition, and for not making folks dizzy while keeping up with the action.

He waved to the filled amphitheater and Peli lifted her hand in a quick wave as the murmur of surprise filtered over the crowd, before they started clapping in support of Wyatt. There were easily ten to twenty times the number that had assembled days ago on the veranda at Lavender Blue.

Jake, who had played his fiddle many times on that stage and was familiar with the setup, handed a microphone to Wyatt. Then the teen went to sit at the edge of the stage with Bailey, who had also offered to be stage crew that morning. She turned her phone around so Wyatt could see she was watching his livestream, while watching him. She gave him a grin and a thumbs-up, which he returned.

"Hello, Blue Hollow Falls," Wyatt said, turning to the crowd. "I hope you don't mind," he said, and motioned to Peli, then waved to her camera, "I brought a few million of my closest friends with me today."

A delighted roar erupted from the crowd and it took a minute or two before things settled down. Wyatt laughed and said, "So, this is different for me. For one, I'm not usually on a stage, and normally, folks can see me doing what I do, but I can't see them. I'll admit, I think it would be pretty cool to have people cheering me on like this, in person, while I'm at work. Whaddya say? You all want to head out with me?"

More cheering, people laughed, a few hooted and whistled.

Wyatt turned his attention forward now, to the folks of Blue Hollow Falls, and let Peli do her thing, trusting she'd capture what was happening in a way that kept his viewers invested and intrigued.

Wyatt gestured to Addie Pearl, who was seated with Chey, Tory, Hannah, and Will a few rows back in the center. Avery and Ben were just behind them. "Thank you to Ms. Addison Pearl Whitaker," he said, "and all of the artists up here in the mill, and the rest of the farm and business owners up here, for helping to spread the word to your neighbors and friends about today's meeting." Folks cheered and hollered, and Wyatt laughed, guessing they were maybe going a little over the top, because they knew they were live on air now.

He then motioned to Hattie Beauchamp, who owned Bo's, the restaurant in town; Cyrus Flagler, who ran the library; Moira Brogan Walker, the new local attorney-at-law; and a few others, who all ran businesses or worked in the town proper. "I'd also like to thank everyone whose livelihood is down in town for showing up today as well.

This affects everybody in Blue Hollow Falls, and it helps for everyone to be part of the proposed solution."

Hattie, who was a town institution—her restaurant was one of the oldest businesses in the Falls—stood and waved, then beamed at the huge round of applause she received. "Go on now," she told Wyatt when she was seated once more, like a queen rightfully claiming her throne.

Wyatt had stood before many a village council or remote area tribunal, and he'd seen close-knit communities before. He supposed he was surprised that one here in the States could be this tight. Which was silly and shortsighted of him. It was both heartening and heartwarming to witness it firsthand.

"I know the rumors have been flying around about this whole resort deal. We've come up with a plan that is more in keeping with what Blue Hollow Falls is all about. We hope you'll support it and let the town council know about it at the town hall meeting set for next week."

That remark was met with more applause and cheering, and a few folks even lifted signs that said, LET'S TURN BLUE HOLLOW GREEN! He caught Bailey giving a thumbs-up and knew where that campaign had gotten started. He loved all of it.

"Okay, on the big screens we put up to the left and right of the stage you can see the plans up close as they're explained to you. For this, let's welcome Vivienne Baudin, part owner of Lavender Blue Farm and Tea Room, as well as a renowned green developer who's done remarkable work in both Australia and the UK and is now branching into the US with our project, Mr. Bryan Westley. And the man who made it possible to bring all of this about so quickly. You maybe have seen him here or there before . . . Mr. Grant Harper."

To say the crowd went wild as the three introduced guests

took the stage was an understatement. Wyatt moved to the side of the stage after kissing Vivi on the cheek and shaking the gentlemen's hands. Peli brought the camera up to Wyatt. "I told you this was going to be a new adventure, and we're just getting started."

Vivi waved to the crowd, completely at home on the stage, as was Grant. Bryan looked a little out of his element, but gamely smiled and waved, enjoying the vibe of genuine enthusiasm and excitement. Grant turned to Peli, who had moved back on the stage, and gave a little salute to Reed Planet. Wyatt laughed as he noticed Bailey pretend to swoon. He'd been surprised to discover that Bailey was both a lover of old music and old movies. Old to her, at any rate. He'd caught her and Grant earlier as they'd been setting up the event and doing the walk-through, taking selfies together and laughing. He'd seen them both signing and exchanging notes and wouldn't be at all surprised if, when Grant went back west, he had a few goats in tow.

While Peli was focusing the stream on the folks on stage, Wyatt checked in with Jon, his other crewmate, who sat in front of two computer screens, overseeing the commentary flow online in response to the livestream. Jon gave him the thumbs-up, then lifted his thumb higher again, indicating that the conversation flow was up and climbing higher. All good news. Folks were staying with him.

Wyatt scanned the crowd to wave to Chey, only to see her seat was empty. Tory waved at him instead, then made the "raise the roof" motion with her hands, which made him laugh. He felt a tug on the back of his shirt and turned, right into a lip-smacking kiss from Chey.

"Seriously, I hope you have some free time later, because . . ." She kissed him again, then grinned. "Let's just say when you are on, you are so very, very *on*."

Wyatt checked on Peli, made sure she was still working the

stage presentation, then tugged Chey more fully backstage and showed her his idea of being *on*.

"Yeah, now you're just showing off," she said a little breathlessly when he let her go again.

"Something tells me you'll keep up just fine."

She laughed. "Wow, this is all really exciting." She looked around backstage, waved to Dom and gave a thumbs-up to Jon. Then she angled herself so she could look out to the stage and waved to Peli, who gave a thumbs-up with her free hand, while keeping the camera on Grant, who was talking about their plan for Firefly and the town. "How is the stream going?"

Chey had met the crew earlier that day during the walk-through. Wyatt had explained the whole process to her and she'd been sincerely interested in how it all worked.

"Are people staying on even though you're not in some exotic place?"

"Staying," he said, "and growing."

She smiled, delighted. "That's great!"

He nodded. "And don't sell Blue Hollow Falls short. This is a slice of life most don't see, so it's just as unique and interesting as some exotic setting. With the history of the place, with the mill, and the greenhouse—I'm so glad Bailey mentioned that—the lake and wilderness area. It's all right in the same pocket." His smile was a bit sheepish. "I guess I wasn't giving my homeland enough credit all these years."

"Well, your homeland is happy to have you back and showing it off a bit."

He pulled her close again. "I might have kind of sort of let Reed Planet know that I might be kind of sort of more than friends with a certain someone who introduced me to this mountain paradise."

"You did?" Chey said, with mock disdain. "Who is she and where can I find her?"

Wyatt kissed her again, more softly this time, but more intently, then held her gaze when he lifted his head. "Right here."

Chey smiled, and he saw all the things he wanted to see, all the things he was feeling himself, in those beautiful brown eyes.

"I've never once mentioned anyone in my life, other than my crew. So folks are going to be a little curious." He made a "wee bit" motion with his finger and thumb.

Chey frowned. "Wait, are you saying you want me to be on—"

He shook his head. "No, not at all. I just thought you should know. Speculation will be rampant." He grinned. "Fortunately, it's not like they're all here."

She gestured to the crowd. "Oh, I'd say the population on your planet has grown substantially today."

He laughed, then tugged her back into his arms. "Yeah, but they already know who that special someone is." He leaned in and whispered, "I recall someone going full on PDA with me at a breakfast meeting earlier this week."

"Right," she said, with a soft smile. "That."

"Gosh, you two are as ridiculously adorable as Bailey said you'd be," came a voice with a distinct Irish lilt just behind them. "And I hate to interrupt, truly I do, but I'm quite late and want to make sure we're all set up."

Wyatt and Chey turned to find Pippa MacMillan—now Pippa Brogan, Seth's newly wedded wife, standing behind them. Bailey and Jake had ducked backstage again as well and were walking up behind her.

Pippa placed her hands over her flat abdomen. "I'm afraid the mornings haven't been too kind to me of late."

Chey looked from Pippa's hands to her face, her own lighting up. "Are you saying you're—?"

Pippa's face split in a wide grin as she nodded. "I am," she said, then hurried to add, "but you can't tell anyone."

Chey hopped over and gave her a delicate but sincere hug. Wyatt was happy for Pippa and Seth, and happier still to see Chey turning in to a hugger before his very eyes.

"Seth and I want to wait until I'm a bit further along before we make a big to-do of it. That's why I couldn't make the meeting earlier this week. Mornings are a beast, I'm afraid. So sorry. But I'm happy I can contribute today." She lifted the fiddle she held in one hand.

"I knew it!" came a whisper behind Pippa, and she turned to see Jake, who was holding a mandolin and bow, and Bailey, who was looking smugly triumphant. Bailey stuck her hand in front of Jake's face, palm up. "Pay up."

"How did you even know?" Jake asked, still looking stunned. "How could you possibly know? Did you tell her?" he asked Pippa.

Pippa, delighted, shook her head.

"I breed animals for a living," Bailey said, giving him a pitying look. "I know things." She wiggled her fingers and Jake dug into the pocket of his jeans and fished out a five-dollar bill.

They both turned to Pippa. "I promise, not a word," Bailey said, and made a zipping motion with her fingers over her lips.

"Your secret is safe with us," Jake agreed.

Pippa just laughed. "I don't know why I thought I could keep anything a secret in Blue Hollow Falls."

Wyatt had spoken to Seth about maybe adding in a brief performance after the presentation, to build on what he'd hoped would be the positive vibes of the meeting at Lavender Blue. He'd talked with Pippa over the phone, but this was his first time meeting her. She was petite, with an infectious smile, but nothing about her personality was delicate. He'd liked her from their first conversation and had been so gratified to discover that since the breakfast meeting, she and Seth had been looking into the work he'd been doing. They'd asked if maybe they could put heads together to see if there was any way Pippa could help, either in the US or in the UK, with her fans.

It was exciting, first hearing from Grant Harper, and now a world-famous Irish folk singer jumping on board Reed Planet with her inestimable help. New opportunities would come from this, and it was invigorating to think about.

He felt Chey slide her hand into his and tried not to think about how he was going to make all these new opportunities work with his plan to keep this woman by his side, and also be by hers. That plan was still a work in progress.

He got a signal from Dom that Peli was coming to him and stepped back on stage to engage with the livestream and watch as Bryan and Grant finished up their presentation.

"Blue is the new green," Wyatt told the camera. "Am I right?" Peli panned to the crowd as they cheered the conclusion of the presentation, then swung back to him. Wyatt crossed the stage and shook hands with Grant and Bryan, then took Vivi's hand and knelt as he kissed the back of it, which sent everyone into a new round of cheers and applause.

The three waved as they exited the stage, with Grant heading over to Peli to talk with Reed Planet directly, something he'd asked Wyatt if he could do. "Hell yeah," had been Wyatt's response. Prompting Chey to pick up Dom's empty coffee mug and proclaim it their temporary swear jar. Everyone had laughed and agreed they'd need something bigger than a mug.

Wyatt turned to the crowd while Grant worked his Hollywood magic with the Reed Planet followers. "So," Wyatt said to the crowd, "what did you think?"

The cheering was loud and unified and left him with no doubt that the Blue Hollow Falls town council was going to have its hands full sticking to their Hammond-proposed deal. He'd thought about contacting Hammond, giving him a heads-up on what they were going to propose. Maybe they could all come to an agreement to work together and not even have to make the council pick a side. Vivi had dissuaded him from doing that, saying it would just give Hammond time to build his defenses.

It was impossible Hammond and the council wouldn't hear about it anyway. Wyatt had filled an amphitheater to talk about it, for God's sake. It was hardly a secret. Still, Addie Pearl had posted a few of the guild members at the entry points to the mill and music center, just so they'd have a heads-up if Hammond or any of the council had decided to show up at the festivities. Fortunately, that hadn't happened.

"Now, before I head out to show off your beautiful mountain paradise to those few friends of mine I told you about earlier, I was thinking, you know, since we're all out here enjoying this beautiful spring day together, sitting in an amphitheater that was built to showcase the music born in these hills, maybe we should celebrate that tradition." He smiled. "And maybe music from a bit farther abroad as well. Like . . . Ireland?"

A hush had fallen over the crowd, then murmurs swelled in anticipation, finally bursting into thunderous applause as Pippa walked out on stage, waving her bow to the crowd. They clearly adored her. She was joined on stage by Jake, and Jake's father, Will, along with a few other local musicians who played and taught classes at the mill.

Peli moved to cover the musical performance for the stream and Wyatt slipped off stage behind the curtain once more.

"I can't believe you put all this together in less than a week," Chey said, having to lean close so he could hear her above the music and the whole crowd singing along quite exuberantly with Pippa and Jake.

"Everyone wants this to work," Wyatt said. "It really all fell together. I just played ringmaster."

"You're quite good at it." She looked on stage at the musicians playing, then out to the spectators, all on their feet dancing and singing. Then to the mountains beyond. "It's a really special place. I'm glad I can share it with you."

He moved behind her and slid his arms around her waist, and they watched together. "Very special," he murmured against her hair, and smiled as she settled back against him.

"Do you think this is going to work?" she asked, so quietly he almost didn't hear her. He wondered if she'd meant to ask it out loud at all.

He didn't know whether she meant their alternative plans for the resort, or whether she meant the two of them being together, so he answered both at the same time. "Yes," he said. "This has too much going for it not to work. Might take some figuring out, but all things worth having are worth a bit of grit and ingenuity, don't you think?"

She turned in his arms and looped hers around his neck. She searched his eyes and he thought maybe she was hoping he was talking about them, too.

He bent his head, kissed her, then whispered in her ear, "This is going to work, Cheyenne. I'm not going to make the same mistake twice. If you want me, I'm all in."

She shifted to look at him, her eyes full of so much want and need and hope, he spared a second to wonder if he could live up to all that. He knew he would die trying. "I want," she said.

From behind them, Dom said, "Sorry, man," and Wyatt turned, sliding his hand into Chey's as she moved next to him. Dom smiled. "We're going to have to come up with a new schedule if you two are going to do this together."

Wyatt laughed and Chey blushed, but laughed, too. "I'm getting out of here now. I promise. I've got to get back to the farm. The guys are coming to work on the gift shop addition, and I've got to get them started. Vivi and Grant are driving Bryan to the airport, so I agreed to ferry Tory, Jake, and Bailey over to the lake for the big barbeque after you finish up streaming from there. Seth and Addie Pearl will get to the lake early, along with Hudson—a chef at the mill—to start grilling." She looked at Dom. "So, you should have smooth sailing with your emcee here," she said, then leaned closer to Dom and added, "We all know it's really you running this gig."

Dom, who was shorter than Chey by a good half foot, and a half dozen years younger as well, adopted a reverent expression. He pulled off his black beanie, then took her hand, leaned down and kissed the back of it. He looked to Wyatt, the hand clutching his beanie still over his heart. "See, I knew it, bro. She gets me. She totally gets me."

Charmed, Chey laughed and Wyatt shook his head. "How easily they abandon me."

"I'm pretty sure Dom here will come running the minute we actually need to have someone in front of the camera." Chey nudged Wyatt. "Somebody has to put the Reed in Reed Planet."

"Well, if you insist," Wyatt said with an air of modest humility.

"Oh boy," Chey said wryly, and kissed his cheek. Then she looked around and her smile was one of excitement. "One week till the town hall. Looks like we've got a running start. Thank you." She looked at Dom. "Thank you all."

Dom buffed his fingertips on his T-shirt, then nodded, put his phone to his ear, and mouthed "call me" before

Wyatt pretended to boot him away. Chey was still laughing as she walked further backstage toward the rear exit.

Jon was signaling to Wyatt to come and post a few comments before the set was finished, but Dom put his hand on Wyatt's arm as he turned. "Man, I don't like to tell anyone his business, but don't screw that up, you dig?" He nodded toward the exit door, which was just now closing behind Chey. When Dom looked back at Wyatt, all trace of teasing was gone, and in its place was the old-soul gaze that had led Wyatt to hire Dom in the first place.

The guy might be only partway into his second decade in life, but Wyatt was pretty sure this wasn't Dom's first go around on the planet. "I'm working on it."

"Yeah, we'll be happy to help with that," Dom said. "I'll talk to the crew, see who can relocate where. Whatever. Be happy. Okay? Otherwise, what are we doing this for?"

Wyatt was caught off guard by Dom's serious declaration. "To make the world a better place?"

"Yeah, well, she makes your world a better place."

Wyatt didn't disagree. "You've been around her for like a half a minute."

"Oh, dude," Dom said, shaking his head with a pitying look. "We knew about five minutes after you got here. Before we'd even met her. Like, the first time you checked in. Seeing it in person is just confirmation, bro." He nodded for Wyatt to get over to Jon. "They're on the last song of the set," he said.

Wyatt headed over to where Jon was set up, and Dom called out behind him, "We're all entitled to make our world a better place, too, man. Don't forget that."

Chapter Thirteen

Chey turned onto the same access road back to the lake that she and Wyatt had taken what felt like a lifetime ago now. That fact was made even more surreal because it had only been one week since she'd come out here for the barbeque after witnessing Wyatt in full Reed Planet action.

Between then and now, the formerly rutted and potholed dirt road had been freshly graded, and now had a layer of gravel on top, making the drive in smooth and easy. The grass had been cut, and the fence bordering the nature center had been given a new coat of paint. All spearheaded and funded by Grant Harper and accomplished with a lot of volunteer hours from her friends and neighbors.

Chey knew the town council was not happy that the locals had taken it upon themselves to do the work, or that Grant had personally contacted the county clerk in charge of issuing the appropriate permits. It still hadn't been exactly one hundred percent on the legit side of how things were done—they technically needed council approval for the upgrades—but they figured the council could hardly complain that all the improvements to the lake property they'd been neglecting for years had all been done for free. They hadn't added anything new or changed anything.

Chey tried not to think about the fact that if the council

had its way, all those improvements the townsfolk had slaved over would be moot, as the fencing and nature center would cease to exist, and the road she was on would be widened to four lanes and paved.

She was heading back toward the picnic area where the town hall meeting was to take place and was pleasantly surprised when she ended up having to park quite a distance away. The place was crammed with cars, trucks, and even a tractor or two. "Or ten," she said, smiling and shaking her head. No doubt there were horses tied up somewhere as well, and maybe a golf cart, too. "Classic Blue Hollow Falls." And she loved every part of it.

Everyone had come out for the town meeting, and she couldn't be more thrilled about that. The council had thought they'd congregate at the lake as kind of a dual town meeting and groundbreaking ceremony. Vivi, Chey, and everyone else had been perfectly fine with that plan. What was up for grabs was exactly which project they'd be breaking the ground to build. What better place to decide than here?

Her smile widened when she spied the phalanx of news trucks and their big satellite dishes, parked way up close to where the impromptu stage and stands had been set up. Everything was coming together as they'd hoped. "Thank you, Reed Planet and Grant Harper," she murmured. Their story had indeed gone viral.

The only hitch in their plans had come when Chey had been delayed back at the farm by a sudden and inexplicable power outage. She'd had to stay behind and sort that out and was mildly annoyed that she was late, but Wyatt, Vivi, Addie Pearl, and Grant were all already here, and they didn't need her to get things started. Still, she didn't want to miss any part of it.

She had to back up to find a place big enough to fit her

dual-wheeled truck, but finally got it pulled in and parked. She slid out, plopped her hat on her head, and turned to close the door.

"We need to talk."

Startled, both by the sudden intrusion and the menacing tone, Chey whirled around, having to put a hand to her hat to keep it from flying off. "Mr. Hammond," she said, surprised, but putting a polite smile on her face while staring down the scowl on his. "Nice day for a town meeting, don't you think?"

Hammond was a good bit taller than she was, about Vivi's age, and ruggedly built, with tailor-made suit jackets that hid the beginnings of a paunch. His hair was silver and his eyes a hard blue. She wasn't sure if his face was just built into a permanent scowl or if that was more of an indication of his nature.

He reached for her arm when she went to move past him, and she stepped back swiftly out of reach. So swiftly he looked momentarily surprised. Years spent barrel racing and dodging handsy cowboys still held her in good stead. "I beg your pardon," she said.

He took a menacing step forward and she could see the sweat beading up on his forehead. "You're going to be begging for more than that if you don't pay close attention to what I have to say."

Chey went very still. "You're going to want to be very careful here, Mr. Hammond," she said, standing her ground. Not that she had much choice, with the truck at her back, but she held his gaze openly and steadily. Something else she'd learned to do at a young age. Rodeo life was not for the naive or faint of heart, and innocence died early on.

"Your man is way back there at the staging grounds," he said, and the smile, when it came, made her skin crawl. "He won't be pulling one of his fancy rescue maneuvers today."

"Oh, I won't be needing one," Chey said, not bothering to hide the edge in her tone. "Vivi wouldn't have either if you'd behaved like a gentleman." Her hand was already in her pocket, and she palmed the rather large pocketknife she always carried with her, as pretty much every farmer and rancher did, though not usually for personal protection. "Take a step back now and say your piece. I'm listening." She held his gaze. "Unless of course you think you need to bully a defenseless woman just to make a point."

"You're about as defenseless as a snake in the grass," he said. "Rallying your troops, trying to shut down my resort."

Chey lifted her brows. "Your resort, is it?"

"It will save this town," he said heatedly.

"So will mine," Chey countered.

"You tree huggers have no idea what this town needs. And you, you've lived here no more than a minute and you think you know what's good for us? This resort will help all those people you've got so twisted up, thinking we're trying to screw them out of house and home, when we're doing the exact opposite."

"What you're screwing them out of is the place they call home," Chey said. "Significant distinction. We just want everyone to have the chance to live a decent, happy life."

"Well, we can make sure they live a hell of a sight better than decent."

"Not everyone is looking to make a fortune, Mr. Hammond. Not if it means losing their way of life in the process. If they'd wanted that, they could have moved down to Turtle Springs, or out to Valley View, or sold out to any one of the developers who have been sniffing around up here." She tilted her head to the side. "Seems like the one most interested in making a fortune out of all of this is you. And I'm guessing a majority vote of the town council stands to benefit personally as well?" She shoved her other hand in her back pocket, all laconic, laid-back cowgirl, using the stance as a cover to fiddle with the cell phone that was stowed there. She double pressed the button on the side, then slid the screen twice and pressed, hoping she was doing it right.

"If you're just looking to make some money off the deal, you could invest in our project," she told him. "We have the full support of the community. Join us instead of creating this division and peddling your distorted truth of what folks' lives will be like once that resort is built. You may not make the windfall you'll get from whatever deal you have with the guy building the Taj Mahal of resorts, but you'll do well enough and have the added benefit of being a town hero. I mean, how much more money do you need?" She noted his eyes dart away and he shifted his stance. That was when she realized this wasn't about greed. It was about desperation.

Hammond didn't just want whatever money he stood to make from his side dealing. He needed that money. Badly, if the amount of sweat beading up on his forehead was any indication.

Hammond did take a step closer then, and she saw the anxiety mingling with his utter contempt. Her pulse was racing, and she wasn't nearly as calm as she was putting on. She doubted he'd do anything to her with the entire town in screaming distance, but she really wanted to get this little tête-à-tête over with. Desperate men could do desperate things, and she didn't plan on sticking around long enough to find out what those things might be.

Hammond's voice was low and ugly, and just this side of spitting when he said, "You're going to head on up to that stage and pull your pretty boyfriend aside and explain to him that there won't be an alternate plan put up for a council vote today. We have the contracts in hand, and we will sign them in front of God and everyone this very afternoon. And all the aging celebrities in the world aren't going to save your sorry, whiny little asses. You get me?"

"Why would I do that?" she asked, because she honestly wanted to know. "You're not even asking nicely. Are you offering me part of the pie? What?"

He barked out a laugh at that, then shot a wad of spit at the ground, just missing her boots. "You may not care about money or power." His sneer went from nasty to downright twisted. "Not surprising, I suppose. Poor little rodeo girl can't manage to hang tough when her brother gets stomped because he thought it was a good idea to get on the back of a bull with a cinch around its nuts."

That shocked Chey back a step. It was such an unforeseen attack, she couldn't hide her response.

Seeing her falter only lit up his ice-cold gaze. "Oh yeah, I did a little search on you. On all of you. Come out here and farm all the goddamn lavender you like. But stay out of my business, out of town business, you and that old whore showgirl and freak show genius. The only normal one of you is the painter, and she's going to her grave thinking about her dead kid."

At Chey's gasp and stunned look of disbelief, he did pause.

"I'm sorry for her," Hammond said, appearing to realize he'd crossed one line too many, though there was zero contrition in his voice. "Hell, I'm sorry you lost your only kin." He spit again and doubled down. "But sorry don't take care of this town."

Chey had gone stock still as he'd spewed his venom. First in utter shock and disgust, then in an effort to reign in the overwhelming urge she had to take the knife out of her pocket and stick it somewhere lethal. "What happened to make you such a vile man?" she asked, barely getting the words out, her jaw was clenched so tightly. "You have every advantage, all the money, all the power you crave."

He laughed in her face and his breath smelled like sour chewing tobacco, making her flinch and her stomach heave. "Nice don't get you where I am, missy. Nice don't get you shit. When I first got wind of your little scheme, I thought you all would dance around and sing 'Kumbaya' and talk a good game but fall far short of putting your little plan together. You surprised me, I'll admit. But you're all too damn nice." He sneered the word. "The world I live in doesn't reward nice. And that's what will bring you down. You don't know how to play dirty." His grin was gleeful. "But I sure as hell do."

Chey tried hard to focus on pity and not rage, because he was certainly a pitiable man. "I'm good with being the nice one, if getting where you've gotten means behaving like you are right now." She put her hands on his chest then and pushed. Hard. Caught off guard by her sudden move, he stumbled back a few steps and took a swing at grabbing her wrist, but she was too fast for him. When he righted himself, she was holding her knife in front of her. "Don't," was all she said.

He blinked, clearly caught off guard by that, too. Then he laughed, amused by her display.

She calmly flipped the knife so she held the blade end between her fingers, then lifted her hand. "If you don't think I know how to stick a pig, and at such a close range, try me."

He seemed surprised by the cold edge in her tone now and kept his eye on her knife, but he was clearly not cowed. Chey didn't care what he was, she just wanted him gone.

"You'll tell everyone that the deal has fallen through," he said, pointing his finger at her as he spoke.

She balanced the knife and he did take a step back. "Or?"

"I will ruin your little video star boyfriend."

The threat was so unexpected, and so utterly insane, Chey laughed outright. "Seriously?"

Hammond wasn't happy with her reaction and even less with her sarcasm. He took a step forward.

"Neck or heart?" she pondered out loud, shifting the knife direction slightly.

He stepped back, but then he laughed, and there was a new note there that sent a slice of cold fear straight down her spine. This was no idle threat he was making. And given he'd dug into her background, it only made sense he'd done the same with Wyatt. Still, she couldn't fathom how Hammond could hurt Wyatt, no matter how much money he had. Or if he had any at the moment, which, given his desperation, was also up for discussion.

"And your plan would be?" she asked evenly.

"A little rumor here, an innuendo there. Could be anything, any story that paints him in a bad light. Stealing, fraud." He shrugged. "Sexual assault is big these days."

Her eyes widened, the threat was so bizarre. "And your proof would be?"

"Aw, honey, now I don't need any proof. I just need to pay someone a lot of money to say whatever I want her to say. There's lots of nice reporters over there. I'm sure they'd love to get that scoop. Make sure all his little basement dwellers hear about it and change channels right swift." He lifted his hands and made little exploding motions with fingers. "What do they call it, going viral? I'll use his own army of tree hugger idiots against him." He took another step back when she made a step forward, the knife quivering now in her hand. "And sure, he can sue me, but the damage will be long done by then." He smiled. "I'll even cover his court costs. Consider it a nuisance fee."

Years in the ring had also given Chey something that you couldn't fake. Moxie in the face of significant opposition.

She lifted a shoulder. "I don't mind that plan so much. Then he can stay here with me instead of traveling all over the world." She smiled. "One of my biggest problems solved actually. Thanks."

He simply smiled at that, and if Chey had thought Hammond couldn't look any more cruel or vicious, she'd been dead wrong. "Sweetheart, you really are way out of your league. But nice try."

"Be that as it may, unless you want to spend the rest of your life seeing the world out of one eye, let's not test just how nice I actually am." She advanced on him.

"I'm giving you the easy way out," he said, but lifted his hands as he stepped back. "But I'm perfectly happy to take what I worked so hard to get the hard way."

Chey merely lifted an eyebrow.

His smile was downright vulgar now. "I heard you had a bit of a power outage at your place this afternoon. Slowed you down getting here." He lowered his hands. "Be a real shame if anything else happened to that farm. Or anyone on it."

That froze her right on the spot.

Hammond chuckled. "See what I mean? You have no idea what I'm capable of. This is why you need to think bigger picture, sweetheart. Power and wealth come in mighty handy when things need to get done," he said. "Now, it's been real nice chatting with you, but I don't want to be late to my own party." He lifted one hand and gestured toward the field where the meeting was going to take place, making a big showy gesture. "Ladies first."

It took everything Chey had not to accidentally stick him in the ribs as she walked by. She wasn't sure what part she hated most, that he'd actually put fear into her, or that he'd purposely culled her from the herd because he saw her as the weak link. She had two vulnerable spots in her life now.

Wyatt and Lavender Blue, along with the people she loved who lived there with her. Would Hammond actually go so far as to hurt one of them? More likely, he'd hire someone to burn the place down, or, as he said, destroy their reputations and with them, their business, rather than physically harming them. Things that didn't involve him getting his hands quite that dirty but delivered the desired result.

As she walked, hating with every fiber of her being that he was walking behind her, she played out the scenarios he'd laid out. Then she remembered her phone. She slid it from her back pocket, not caring what he thought.

"No phone calls now," he said.

"Who would I phone?" she called back to him. "The police? The fire department? I'm assuming that won't do me any good. Someone as powerful as yourself would have them in your pocket." She played to his ego as she looked at her phone, then tried not to slump in defeat when she saw that while she'd managed to get the camera turned on, she hadn't gotten it to the video setting as she'd hoped. Recording their conversation had been the only solution she could think of. Even muffled, it would have been something. She did, however, turn it on now.

"Don't think about sending a heads-up text, either," he said.

"What good would that do?" she chided him. "You've threatened to burn down my house and destroy Wyatt using his subscribers against him. What text is going to fix that?" She angled the phone up close to her shoulder, just out of his line of sight, hoping she'd baited him into saying something, anything, incriminating.

"Well, now you're just making stuff up, honey," he said, and she suspected he was well aware she was recording him. "Here I offered you an escort and you're saying all kinds of crazy things. Have you had a little something to drink? Maybe you're on medication to deal with all that pain and tragedy in your past. Terrible thing," he said, sounding sincere. "No one would blame you a bit, of course, but I know they can mess with your mind."

She shook her head. *Oh, he's good.* Disgusting and terrifyingly evil, but very good at it. She'd bet he'd had lots of practice. And to think Vivi had been out with this asshole in the middle of a lake, with no one around for miles. Thank God they hadn't come up with their alternate resort plan until after that. She shivered, thinking of all the things that could have gone so terribly wrong that day. That Vivi had made him swim to shore, Chey was certain, was also why he'd chosen to target Lavender Blue specifically with his threats. She was just thankful Grant had been with Vivi pretty much the entire time since then, or he'd have likely tried to extort her. Or worse.

Chey slid the phone halfway into her back pocket, so the camera at the top remained uncovered, video still recording. Then she lifted both hands up, the knife still in one of them, though she held it butt end now. "No texting," she said. "Happy now?"

"No, but in about an hour from now, I plan to be very, very happy." This last part was said far too close for comfort. She could smell his breath again and tried not to flinch. He snagged her phone from her back pocket, turned it off, and handed it to her. "Amateur hour. Now come on."

He took her elbow in a bruising grip and steered her toward the stage. She didn't give him the satisfaction of trying to yank free, knowing it was doubtful she'd succeed. They were only a dozen yards from the stands and the picnic area, both filled to maximum capacity. Apparently, he was no longer worried about the knife now that they had an audience.

They had to walk through the gauntlet of media trucks

to get to the back of the stage, which wasn't much more than a deck with a podium on it. "Show time," Hammond breathed, then shoved her forward a step, letting her go as they arrived.

And that's when Chey got an idea. *Showtime, indeed.*

"Hey, you made it," Wyatt said, hopping down and coming over to her.

Hammond had walked to where three of the five council members were standing, all three of them men, one of whom was Henry Bassett, the lead councilman. All three looked very relieved to see him. *Good.* Now she knew who else was in their developer's pocket.

Wyatt leaned down to kiss her as she folded her knife and tucked it into her pocket.

Seeing that, he frowned, then followed her gaze to Hammond. "Everything okay?" he asked, then really looked at her for the first time. He started to turn them both away, but she slipped free.

"I can't explain it all right now," she told him, "but I need to do something. Before we get on stage. Could you snag Vivi and Grant, and meet me over where Hammond and the councilmen are standing? I'm going to get Addie Pearl."

"What's going on, Chey?" he asked, looking truly concerned now.

"Just your standard small-town corruption and extortion," she said, then smiled and kissed his cheek in case Hammond was watching her. "But we're about to take care of that. Or at least a good chunk of it." She started to go, then turned back. "Hey, is Peli here?"

He nodded.

"No streaming, but do you think she could maybe wiggle in somewhere inconspicuous and put a lens and maybe a mic on our little meeting?"

"Sure, but—"

"There's no time to explain. We need to do this before they get on stage," she said. "Just . . . please trust me, okay?"

"Absolutely," he said, "always."

Chey and Addie Pearl merged with Wyatt, Grant, and Vivi just as the three councilmen and Hammond turned toward the stage.

"Hello," Chey said to the foursome. "I thought you all might like to meet Wyatt Reed and Grant Harper," she said with a broad smile. She could feel the heat of Hammond's glare coming at her from the side. She spied Peli behind the bushes just in back of them. She gave Chey a quick thumbs-up, then ducked back down. Chey corralled the group closer to the bushes as they made their introductions and shook hands.

"We really need to get this going," Hammond said, striving for a convivial tone, but the strain was there on his face.

"I know, I know," Chey said, "but there was a small matter I needed to discuss with the councilmen first. Can we get the other two of them over here?"

The three older gentlemen standing beside Hammond looked surprised.

"It's important," she told them. "It's about the proposal we were going to make today."

She saw Hammond's shoulders relax the moment he heard her use the past tense in reference to their plan. *Good. The better to catch you off guard with.*

"Let's move a bit more out of the way, shall we?" she said. "This really needs to remain private."

Vivi was looking at her questioningly now.

"Is there a problem?" Grant asked her, openly concerned now, too.

"I'll wait until we're all gathered before—here we are," she said, as the remaining two members of the council joined them, also both men. The mayor, Tom Fielding, stepped over to join them as well. *Even better.*

They all had expectant expressions on their faces, clearly happy about what was happening in the park that day. There was more shaking of hands, and greetings with Grant and Wyatt; then they looked at her.

"It's come to my attention that there is a serious problem with one of the proposals today that I was unaware of until I just spoke with Mr. Hammond out in the parking lot."

Now Hammond frowned. *Oh, you're going to do a lot more of that when I'm done.*

"What seems to be the problem, Ms. McCafferty?" asked Henry. "And which proposal are you referring to?"

"Yours," Chey said, looking directly at him and the other two councilmen who had been standing with Hammond earlier.

Hammond took her arm. "Be careful," he warned, but for the first time, he looked truly worried. He clearly wasn't expecting her to stand up to him.

"I believe you've threatened me enough for one day," she told Hammond, then slid her arm free and looked at the surprised faces of their little gathering. She held her hand up when Wyatt stepped forward. "I got this," she told him, and he must have seen something of her current mood in her eyes because he stepped back . . . and smiled.

Chey looked at the council members who were not involved, at the mayor, and at Vivi, Grant, and Addie Pearl, and said, "It seems Mr. Hammond here is very concerned that your proposal must go through today. To the extent that he cut the power to my house to delay my arrival, then ambushed me by my truck, threatened to destroy Wyatt's career, and possibly harm myself, Vivienne, Hannah, or Avery, along with our farm, if I didn't agree to shut our proposal down."

All eight faces, Wyatt's included, went momentarily slack as what she'd said hit home.

"Now see here," Hammond interrupted, his face turning red, "I will not have you slandering my good name with these ridiculous assertions and bold-faced lies."

"The only lies being told are the ones you threatened to tell the media in order to get Wyatt's fan base to turn against him." She looked at the group. "I am a firm believer in the rule my aunt taught me at a very young age. The best way to find out what's going on in the dark is to shine a bright light on it."

Henry stepped up. "Ms. McCafferty, I'm not sure what in the world would prompt such an outrageous display," he said, all benevolent kindness and avuncular understanding. "Now, I've known Paul Hammond my entire life, and I can state—"

"—that you are in on this, too?" Chey finished for him. "Good, at least we have that on record." She then looked at the other two men standing there. "I don't know what you've got going on with your little side deal, and frankly, I don't want to know. The amount of sweat dripping off Mr. Hammond's brow out in the parking lot would indicate that he needs an immediate influx of cash and this deal is where he's going to get it. How much do you three stand to make?"

"That's enough," Hammond shouted, then immediately lowered his voice when a hush fell over the part of the crowd closest to them. "I don't know what kind of medication you're on, but you've clearly messed up today's dosage. You sound a little off your rocker, sweetheart. So, I'll just say this once: cease this sad little display right now, and I won't drag you into court. Clearly you're under enough strain as it is."

"No," Chey said, turning on him, her expression as

fierce as it had ever been. "You cease. You cease threatening me and the people I love, and this place that I love. You said I underestimated you?" She gestured to the field full of people. "No, Mr. Hammond, I'd say you're the one who underestimated me. Look what we've been able to do in just a few weeks." Then she gestured to the media trucks. "You said you'd pay someone to pretend she'd been assaulted by Wyatt, or defrauded by him, and use the media to spread those filthy lies. Well, I can use the media, too. But not to spread lies and filth. How about I call one of those journalists over here and ask them to dig into your financial dealings with Pantheon, and everyone else associated with this deal. See what they can find out."

"That will be quite enough." This from Henry, who now looked rattled. "Let's call the sheriff over here and see if he can escort Ms. McCafferty into town, where she can make a full statement, following proper protocol. We'll let the police do their job and investigate your claims," he said, sounding kind, but Chey saw the cold depths in his dark eyes. He was not happy with her. Not one bit.

Good. She wasn't too thrilled with him either at the moment.

He looked at Chey. "Now, I'm willing to just overlook all of this if you want to go on home and take care of whatever it is you're struggling with." He looked at Vivi and Grant, who both still appeared a little shell-shocked by what had so rapidly unfolded. "Perhaps you could help her out? I'm so sorry for the burden you've clearly been under, my dear," he said to Chey. "All of this must have taken a far bigger toll on you—"

"There's no toll, Henry," she said. "Except the one you're about to pay." Chey merely turned toward the media trucks, put two fingers in her mouth and—Hammond yanked them back out.

"Don't you dare," he threatened, the red in his face darker still as rage consumed him.

She turned on him before Wyatt could get between them. "No, don't *you* dare. Did you honestly think you could hold this whole town hostage to get yourself some tidy pay out? Let's talk about what you've gotten yourself into, because desperation is not a good look on you."

People were starting to pay attention to their little group. Even a few reporters at the end of the media line were looking their way. Hammond saw this and turned on her. "We were one week away from getting it all done," Hammond hissed, his composure finally breaking down completely. "One week." He jabbed a finger in her face. "And you have to come in here with your idiot ideas and get everyone all riled up. One week, and we'd have had this all sewn up. But no—"

"Paul." This from Mayor Fielding, who'd finally snapped to it. He turned to Henry and the other two men. "Whatever is going on here, let's take a step back, maybe table all this for now, and sit down somewhere and get to the bottom of—"

"No," Hammond spluttered. "This has to go through today." His gaze swung to his three compatriots. "Sign the damn contracts, Henry. Jesus Christ, just sign the fucking contracts. Don't you understand? We're going to lose goddamn everything."

One of the councilmen standing next to Henry started to back away, shaking his head. "This isn't how it was supposed to work," he murmured, looking more than a little distressed.

Henry turned to him. "Carl, don't let her rattle you, she's just—"

"She's not the one rattling me, okay?" he said, his voice

rising. "It's one thing to help grease the wheels a little in return for a favor here or there—we all do that."

The mayor turned then. "What did you say? What wheels are you greasing? We don't do that. Not in this—"

"Shut the hell up, Carl," Henry hissed. "This isn't the place for—"

"No," Carl said, looking like a man who had come to a decision. "No, I won't. This was wrong and I should never have let you bully me into it, Henry. You can tell my wife whatever you want about my, uh, extracurricular activities. It's not worth going to jail for." He swung back to Mayor Fielding. "It's a kickback scheme," he began. "We help smooth the permit process and maybe look the other way when some materials being used aren't exactly what's stated in the contract, and we get gratis office space in the lodge. We can lease it out and keep the rent as payment—"

Henry grabbed Carl's arm and jerked him around. "What in the ever-loving hell are you doing?" he hissed.

Carl yanked his arm free, only to have Hammond lunge at him and tackle him to the ground. The third councilman began to back away, only to have Henry lunge for him, and seconds later, a full-on brawl erupted between the men.

Wyatt and Grant started to step in to try to pull the men apart, but the mayor waved them back as the sheriff's deputies rushed over to take control of the situation.

In the end, the media swarmed the melee as all four men were arrested on assault charges. As they were being cuffed and taken away, Mayor Fielding said, "Officers, could you please detain Mr. Hammond, Mr. Bassett, and Carl Thomas until I can come down and give my statement? Your detectives may want to have a little chat with Mr. Thomas regarding the statements he made to me today. I'll be in to give my full account shortly and things can proceed from there."

"You will be very sorry you did this, Tom," Henry snarled as one of the officers started to walk him to the waiting cruiser. "I'll be calling my lawyer, and you can expect a very nasty, very expensive set of lawsuits, both against this town and against you personally. I take my position on the council seriously, and—"

"Oh, I don't think you'll be seated on this council any longer, Henry. Or you two, either," Fielding said, looking at Carl and the other man, who were also now in custody.

"We're elected officials, Tom. You don't have the power to—"

"One of the various codes—I'll have to go look it up to get the exact number—allows me, if any council member behaves in a manner that is considered a direct threat to the well-being of the town or any individual residing in the town, to demand your resignation, and you have to tender it. Then there's the statute—I'll get the exact verbiage—but essentially, if you have acted unethically or defrauded us, you're also done. You can expect a letter to that effect to be coming your way as soon as I get it drafted."

"It's not just Henry you have on your back, Fielding. I'm not going to take this lying down," Hammond started in as he was being led away. "I'll bury you in lawsuits and cost you every dime you've ever made."

"Oh, I think we will all be calling our lawyers, but let's wait and see on who will pay for what," Fielding said.

"Your word against ours, Tom," Henry said, looking more than a little desperate now.

"With all these witnesses?" Fielding said. "Hardly. Not to mention Carl there has already confessed."

"Wait," Chey said, and motioned to Peli, who climbed through the bushes and handed Chey a little memory card to the very shocked expressions of their collective little group, as well as the men being hauled away.

"It's all on there," Peli said.

"Awesome," Chey said, and grinned. "Thank you." She quickly trotted over to one of the police officers. "I think this will give your investigators a great place to start," she said, then walked back to the group.

The reporters all raced back to their news vans, and it looked like there would be quite a parade heading to the sheriff's department. A few remained behind, looking anxious to speak to the mayor about what had just unfolded.

"Separate cars," Fielding called out, and the sheriff's deputies nodded. "The last thing we need is time for them to concoct some wild story," he muttered. He looked deeply troubled by what had just unfolded, but appeared to do his best to shake his worry off as he turned back to Chey, Wyatt, Vivi, and Grant. "Well, I expected today to be exciting, but I admit this wasn't how I thought it would play out."

Wyatt pulled Chey close and hugged her, and they both waved to Peli, who headed back to the crowd, camera in tow, where Dom stood waiting for her. Grant had a protective arm around Vivi's shoulders as well.

"Are you okay, Chey?" Vivi asked, clearly still trying to process the swiftly unfolding events.

She nodded. "Oh, I'm very fine, now."

Wyatt kissed her temple and said, "The natives are getting pretty antsy out there." Word had spread through the crowd about the fight that had broken out and the vibe had turned from festive and hopeful to restless and concerned. "I'm going to hop up on stage and get the crowd under control."

Grant looked at Vivi. "If you're sure you're okay, maybe I'll give him some help."

Addie Pearl took Vivi's other hand. "We're fit as fiddles," she said. "You all go on and we'll sort things out with the mayor."

Once they were gone, Addie, Chey, and Vivi turned to Mayor Fielding.

"What happens now?" Addie Pearl asked.

"I suppose we'll have to delay the council vote," Vivi said, looking distressed.

Fielding shook his head. "No, we're going forward." Looking resolute, he motioned to the remaining two councilmen. "Something positive is going to come from all this. We're going to need that to hold on to once all this gets out." He took a deep, steadying breath, then put a determined smile on his face. "We all reviewed both plans before arriving today, and yours is a solid and much needed solution to our problems." He turned to Addie Pearl. "Thank you for sending the plans to me. I appreciated the heads-up."

"I knew calmer heads would prevail, and I wanted your support, Tom. I knew I could trust you to do right by them, and us." Addie looked at Vivi. "I'm sorry for going around you all, but Tom and I go way back, and—"

"No," Vivi said. "Of course, we trust your judgment." She looked at the mayor. "Don't you need a majority vote—" Vivi began.

Fielding nodded to the two councilmen. "I believe we require a minimum of three members on any given vote, and I have the authority to stand in when needed, so we have our quorum right here. Now, technically, yes, we will have to ask for and process the resignations, then take an actual vote, but I think we're all in agreement we won't be working with Pantheon."

The other two council members shook their heads and smiled, looking a bit dazed themselves by what had unfolded, though not exactly upset by it. It didn't look as if

Henry Bassett was held in all that high regard by his fellow councilmen on either side of the issue.

"We'll make it official in the next few days," the mayor said, "but since we're all here, I say we go tell the good people of our town that we're going to start turning Blue Hollow Falls green."

Vivi and Chey both let out a hoot of joy and hugged, then all three of them shook the mayor's hand before heading over and climbing the steps to the makeshift stage.

Wyatt looked at Chey, who gave him a private thumbs-up. Wyatt looked at Grant, grinned, then said into the mic, "It looks like we have some news to share."

Wyatt and Grant moved back to make room for the mayor, the council members, Vivi, Chey, and Addie Pearl.

"Mr. Mayor," Wyatt said. "Over to you." He handed Fielding the mic.

A tense hush fell over the assembled crowd as the news reporters who hadn't followed the cruisers drew closer to the stage, microphones outstretched.

"I am very pleased to announce that both projects have been examined and considered, and by a simple majority vote, and the overwhelming support of all of you," he added, and the cheers started to erupt, "Blue Hollow Falls will soon be enhanced by a wonderful new resort and event center."

He paused and Chey swore she could feel every collective breath being held until they heard the words they wanted to hear.

"Why don't you tell them." And Fielding handed the mic to Grant.

Grant nodded, took the mic, and turned to face everyone. "I'd like to announce that we are now, officially, on the grounds of the Firefly Lodge and Wilderness Resort!"

And the crowd, as they say, went wild.

Chapter Fourteen

"What's the verdict?" Chey asked as Wyatt ended the call with the mayor and put his cell on the nightstand, then rolled back over to face her. "Were charges filed?"

He pulled the pillow back under his head and tucked her up against his body. "Oh, so many charges," he said with a chuckle. "Hammond alone has fourteen counts against him, including money laundering, conspiracy to commit fraud, the actual fraud, tax evasion, and well, the list goes on and on. Apparently, he's been in deep for a good long time. I don't think even the priciest lawyer will get him off, and I'm not sure he can afford one anyway. Sounds like his buddies on the council will be joining him."

"Good," she said. "Well, it's not good. It's awful. I can't believe we had that level of corruption right here in our little burg. I mean, those guys all grew up here; they have families. Some of them have been here for generations. I feel awful for them."

"Thank goodness Carl Thomas had a sudden bout of decency or who knows what they might have gotten away with," Wyatt said.

"I don't think it was decency so much as deciding his wife divorcing him for finding out he'd been fooling around was a lesser evil than going to jail. And he might not escape that, either." She shook her head. "It's going to sting this entire community for a good long time. I know folks love Mayor Fielding, and he's handled this about as well as anyone could, with a steady hand and keeping everyone calm, but this happened under his watch. It's going to take a while to earn everyone's trust back."

"True," Wyatt agreed, "but with groundbreaking on the lodge in just a few weeks, and so much good to come from that, hopefully that will gain a lot of goodwill back for the mayor and the remaining council members. It will help make the road forward easier for everyone. I heard Addie Pearl is considering running to fill one of the vacant council seats. That would be a slam dunk, I'd think. Go a long way toward making folks feel like there's accountability."

Chey chuckled. "Yeah, I don't see them getting anything by Addie Pearl." She sighed. "I tried to talk Vivi into it, but I think things between her and Grant are happening kind of quickly."

He rolled forward and kissed her. "You say that like it's a bad thing," he teased.

She kissed him back. "Not at all, actually. I think they're really good for each other. Vivi smiles like a giddy schoolgirl pretty much all the time, and Grant looks like he's walking around on cloud nine." She wrapped her arms around Wyatt's neck. "But I suspect that will mean she'll be traveling west."

Wyatt lifted back in surprise. "Permanently?"

Chey shook her head. "No, I can't see that happening. She wouldn't abandon us, and she loves it here, loves what she is doing. I don't see her giving that up for anyone. But I can see her working some kind of compromise."

"What about you?" he said, shifting back to his side and propping his head on his elbow.

"What, would I give up Lavender Blue and Blue Hollow

Falls for love?" His expression faltered briefly, but she held his gaze when she answered, and he could see she meant what she said. "I would hope that's not a choice I'd ever have to make."

Wyatt wasn't sure what to say to that. Not that he planned to ask her to make such a sacrifice, but it seemed a pretty hard line to draw. He'd been grappling with the same issue, though, and he wasn't sure he'd answer the question any differently.

Chey nudged him to his back and snuggled next to him, sliding her arm over his chest. "Let's not talk about that," she said softly. "Not today."

Wyatt didn't want to talk about it ever, but he knew that conversation was going to happen sooner than later. That he had another eight weeks or so in the Falls felt like forever right now, but the time was already passing at breakneck speed. He felt inextricably bound to her, from their childhood together all the way up to this very second, and he had absolutely no desire whatsoever to do anything to break those ties. He only wanted them to be stronger, wrapping their lives ever more securely together.

But it was a Saturday morning after a couple of very long, tumultuous weeks, both leading up to events by the lake a week ago, and the scandal that had kept the grapevines buzzing ever since, what with the arrests and revelations. Tory had said she'd take on the barn chores that morning, allowing them a lazy lie-in, at least until Hannah and Avery arrived and another day on the farm began in earnest. He liked learning about lavender growing and all the processes, how to make the variety of products they sold. Avery had offered him a tour of her mini lab, which was the processing area now, where she'd laughingly said the lavender magic happened. He was looking forward to seeing that.

Wyatt had gone out to bring Tory coffee when he'd

gotten up to brew a pot earlier, along with some of the muffins Vivi had sent home with them the night before. Grant had stayed in town after the fallout the previous weekend, remaining at Lavender Blue with Vivi, supporting her and lending his assistance where he could as things progressed out at the lake. Wyatt felt the same way Chey did about their burgeoning relationship. It looked good on both of them. But he was seeing the whole world through some pretty rosy glasses these days.

He smiled, thinking about Bailey, who had been in the barn with Tory, tending to the goats. When he'd come in, she'd been in the middle of asking a million questions about the days when Tory and Chey competed against each other and whether Tory could teach Bailey how to be a barrel racer.

Wyatt thought he'd let Tory spring that news on Chey, who he knew had been giving Bailey riding lessons for some time now. He couldn't imagine there was much Bailey couldn't make happen if she put her mind to it, so he expected he'd see barrels being rolled out into the training ring quite soon.

He hadn't been in the Falls that long, but he already felt like he was part of the ebb and flow of life there. And that didn't alarm him in the least. It was settling and grounding to feel that he was part of something stable and permanent. His life had been none of those things now for as long as he could remember. He'd been so busy, cramming thirty hours of living into every twenty-hour day, and enjoying every minute of it, he hadn't even known stability was something he was missing, or that he was wanting, until he had it.

It wasn't that he missed his empty croft in Wales. This was an entire life being handed to him here. He'd been welcomed like a long-lost member of the family, and he'd come to care about these people quickly. Not because they were important to Chey, but because he truly liked them.

He wanted to take up Jake on his offer to show him the winery and the grapes he was growing and learning to press; he wanted to see Seth and Pippa welcome their first child into the world. He wanted to learn more about the exotic orchids he'd seen the previous week, and talk to the artists in residence at the mill, watch them ply their various trades. And those were just the people. He was itching to put a kayak on Big Stone creek, hike up into the rugged mountains above Firefly Lake, take up Addie's invite to explore her area up in Hawk's Nest Ridge, see the majestic birds of prey who had given the place its name.

And so much more.

The problem was, wanting all of that hadn't stopped him from wanting the life he already had. He hadn't even begun the final edits on the streams from Nepal or looked through the set of requests Dom had narrowed down to the "next pick" list and sent him just that morning. Wyatt was excited to look through them, meet with Dom, Jon, and Peli, along with the rest of the core crew, and see what worked for everyone. Then it would be time to assemble the rest of the team, dive into all of the paperwork and other planning that went into setting up the actual trip.

He had a few weeks, tops, before he had to have at least the initial stages underway if they had any hope of being prepped and ready to go come fall. Harvest season at Lavender Blue. He didn't want to miss that, either. Or miss watching Chey and her friends celebrate their first full, beginning-to-end lavender season.

He thought about Dom's words. *We're all entitled to make our world a better place, too. Don't forget that.*

How did he straddle both, keep both? He wanted his work, and he wanted to have a life here with Chey. When

Pippa had laid a hand on her belly and told Chey she was expecting, the look on Chey's face had been everything. Wyatt wanted that for her, for them. Wanted to put his hands on her belly and know life was blooming and growing there, a life they'd created together.

"Where has your mind wandered off to?" she said softly, drawing lazy circles on his chest with her fingertips.

"Just thinking about last weekend. How amazing you were," he said. She was right. Now was not the time to find solutions to unsolvable problems. He shifted and lifted her chin and kissed her. "You were pretty badass."

"I was pretty terrified," she told him. "I can admit that now. But I was more pissed off than I was scared, and I knew the only chance I had was to confront him in front of everyone in a way that would guarantee he wouldn't be able to retaliate without everyone knowing what he'd been up to."

"Want your own superhero stream?" He wiggled his eyebrows. "I happen to know a guy."

She laughed. "Yeah, I like the boots, but I don't do capes. And don't get me started on the spandex Underoos."

He barked out a laugh at that, then rolled and put her on top of him. "I don't know, I think you could do the cape."

"I don't even wear dresses," she said.

He pulled her down and kissed her. "I'd just take them off you, so probably just as well."

She smiled against his mouth. "Because they'd look that awful on me?"

He rolled her to her back. "Yeah, that's totally why."

She toyed with his hair. "I should be getting up and showered and out in the fields."

"I know," he said, kissing his way down the side of her neck. "Dom sent me the list of contenders for our next stream a few days ago, and I have to get to that today." He nuzzled the spot by her nape that he knew she loved. "But I could help with the shower part."

She went still, and not because he'd licked an erogenous spot. He replayed what he'd just said and closed his eyes. *So much for not ruining the moment.* He just wasn't used to filtering what he said to her.

"Sorry," he said, "I wasn't thinking."

"No," she said, and turned her face to his. "It's okay. It's silly to pretend this isn't what it is. I know that."

Now he frowned and pulled back just slightly. "What do you mean, 'what it is.' What is it?"

"Don't do that—that's not what I meant." She sighed when he didn't say anything, then immediately struck an exaggerated pose, baring her neck to him. "Can't we please continue with the ravishing, dear sir?" She glanced at him from the side of her eyes, still holding the pose. "Don't make me get my cape."

He smiled at that, because he couldn't not smile. And he wanted, badly, to just pick up where they'd left off. He knew what she'd meant. Mostly. It had just thrown him to hear her give voice to the same concerns he'd been having, only in a way that seemed to indicate maybe she'd come to some conclusions already. And her conclusions didn't include the two of them figuring this out.

He waited a beat too long to respond and she lowered her arm and shifted back around so she could look at him fully. "What I meant was—"

"It's okay, Chey," he said quietly.

"What I meant was," she repeated deliberately, "we have the next month or two to play house, and while it would be lovely to think that it will be this way forever and ever, we both know it's not. August will get here, and you'll have to go, and we'll have to figure out what that means. So, this"— she gestured between the two of them—"is going to change.

Meaning it's temporary, until we figure out stage two. So, it's silly to pretend that change isn't coming." Then she smiled at him. "But it's sure fun to try." She slipped out from under him. "Shower time. Come, wash my back."

He wiggled his eyebrows. "In that order? Seems backward, but—"

She threw a pillow at him and he caught it and threw it to the floor, then took her hands and pulled her up as he rose to his knees, so they were both kneeling on the bed, facing each other. "I love you, Cheyenne McCafferty," he said without preamble, just put it right there. Right out in front. "And this feeling is way stronger than the love I had for you back once upon a time."

She'd been about to grab another pillow, but went still, then turned to him. And it was wonder he saw in her eyes. And surprise. And most importantly, joy.

"You really say the damnedest things," she said faintly.

"Did I mention? Dom got us a swear jar. It's the size of a butter crock," he said dryly. "In fact, I think it was a butter crock. Between the two of us, we will cover my airfare for years."

"Yeah, well, you keep talking to me like that, mister, and I might just—"

He pulled her into his arms. "Just love me back, Chey," he said, looking into her eyes. "And we'll be fine. You know that, right? We're going to be fine."

She nodded, and then a slow smile curved her lips. "No more pretending then, I take it?"

Now he did grab a pillow. This was so not how he'd seen that declaration going. And yet this was so much better than anything he'd imagined. Cheyenne was real, the real deal, inside and out.

"Yeah, enough with that stuff," he said, as if they'd decided to blow off paying for cable. He made a *pfft* sound.

She copied the sound. "Yeah. No more of that." She tilted her head. "So, does this mean no more carrying me into the shower? 'Cuz I kinda liked that part of the fairy tale."

"Ah," he said, pretending to seriously ponder the question. "Yes. That." He braced one hand on his chin, then ducked down, scooped her over his shoulder, and in one smooth move was off the bed and heading to the bathroom while she squealed and kicked her legs.

"Yeah, under the no-pretending rules, this is the only certified mode of transportation."

She reached down and pinched his ass. Not gently.

"Hey now," he said.

"You want to reconsider that rule then?" she asked, trying not to laugh. Failing.

He reached into the glass-enclosed shower stall, which was fast becoming one of his favorite parts of her house, and flipped on the huge pan-sized shower head, then stepped in, taking the brunt of the just-warm water on his back as he let her slide down his front. "I don't know," he said, as steam started to billow. "I rather like the dismount."

"Point taken," she said, gasping when he scooped her up, then turned them so her back was against the tiles. She gasped and arched into him as he moved between her thighs.

"Oh, not yet," he replied. "Very soon though. First things first." He nudged her head to the side. "Now, where were we? Oh right. Coming first, then back washing." He started kissing his way down. "Check."

Chey was twenty minutes late meeting up with Hannah and Avery in the main house kitchen.

"I'm sensing a pattern developing," Hannah said wryly.

"Given you're speaking from personal experience with

this matter, I assume you know the answer to that," Chey said sweetly.

Hannah's eyes glinted mischievously. "Come to think of it, I do," she said, then waved a hand. "Carry on."

They both laughed and at the same time reached for a plate mounded with cookies.

"Wow, Vivi's been busy," Chey said, picking up an oatmeal raisin.

"Grant flew out this morning. I suspect there might be a lot of baked goods in our future. At least until he comes back."

"Better happen soon or I'll be buying all new jeans." Chey closed her eyes in bliss as she took a bite. "Although, I could use a few new pairs. My God, this is amazing. I'm ravenous."

"Can't imagine why," Hannah said, and laughed when Chey gave her a little kick under the table. Her expression matched Chey's a moment later when she bit into a chocolate chip and macadamia nut. "See, this is why I wear flowy dresses and skirts," she said, humming a little as she chewed. "Hides all kinds of sins. And cookies. So many cookies."

"Wyatt and I were just talking about dresses this morning," Chey said. "Maybe I'll surprise him."

"You should," Hannah said, not even bothering to ask how that topic had come up.

Chey picked up her second cookie. "I thought we were meeting in the barn to go over storage and the drying setup for the bundles we want to sell this season and to get our daily to-do charts from Ave."

Avery whisked into the kitchen just then and tossed printouts at them as she slid into her seat. "Be careful what you wish for."

Chey checked her watch. "Twenty-five minutes late."

She wiggled her eyebrows at Hannah. "Looks like Wyatt and I got some competition."

"It's not like that," Avery said primly, then picked up a cookie and took a bite. "This is amazing. How did she know? I'm starving."

Hannah and Chey looked at each other and said, "Oh, it's exactly like that," at the same time, then laughed.

Hannah put her hand, palm up, above the middle of the table, and the other two joined in for a three-way high five, then wiggled their fingers before lowering their hands to the table.

Chey took another bite. Moaned. "We may have to jog a few laps around the barn later, but I'm game."

"Vivi said she wanted to talk to us in here before we headed out to the barn," Avery said.

Chey frowned and paused midbite. "Did she say why? Is everything okay?"

"Maybe it's to talk about the news," Avery said. "You heard about Hammond being arrested and charged?"

"That happened so fast," Hannah said.

"Well, there were enough journalists on site that it was a race to see who could get the dirt first," Avery said.

"Wyatt talked to the mayor this morning," Chey said. "Apparently the district attorney had been trying to nail Hammond for years. He just needed some leverage to get someone to flip."

"That's where the media attention made the difference," Avery said. "I heard the developer was also being looked at for various shady practices by the DA in his state, and with the added pressure of Hammond's takedown being so public and the media feeding frenzy that followed, he caved."

Chey nodded. "Things moved fast after that."

"As well they should have," said Vivi as she sailed into the room in a cloud of lavender chiffon and black pencil-leg pants. "I'm just thankful we won't have some prolonged public harangue." She poured herself a cup of coffee and took a seat at the table with them. "We need to move forward." She beamed. "It's all very exciting really, this new lodge, and all the potential. Grant and I were up half the night talking about it." She reached for a cookie. "Sorry I'm a bit late. Oh, my goodness, I'm positively famished this morning."

Hannah, Chey, and Avery shared a look, then burst out laughing.

"What?" Vivi asked. "What did I say?"

The three lifted their cookies. "A toast to the twenty-minute rule," Chey said.

"Well, more like the twenty-to-thirty-minute rule," Hannah added with a wiggle of her eyebrows.

"I'm not sure what you three are talking about," Vivi said primly, taking a tidy bite of cookie. She took a sip of coffee to wash it down, then shot them all a wink and a rather devilish smile. "But I have a pretty good idea." She took another bite of cookie and made a humming sound, and they all cracked up laughing.

"Well," Vivi said, after she finished and dabbed the corner of her mouth, "let's get down to business, shall we?" She turned to Avery. "You've got a notebook and pen? We'll need that."

Avery had both. When didn't she?

Vivi folded her hands on the table. "So, it appears we've got ourselves a lavender farm, and a new home, and new friends all around us. We couldn't have asked for more." She smiled. "And yet, each of us has found more."

Chey knew what Vivi meant, and she and Hannah and Avery shared a smile. "It appears that way, yes," Chey said happily.

"Well, I don't know about you all, but I don't plan to lose

this farm, or any of you, or to leave Blue Hollow Falls." She lifted a hand to stall their reply. "That said, I also don't plan to lose Grant, now that he has so miraculously ended up in my life once again." She held each of their gazes in turn. "I assume you feel much the same about our home?" Her smile deepened. "And your men?"

Chey grinned. "I think we can safely say yes to both."

Hannah and Avery both raised their hands. "Aye," Hannah said.

"Good. We're partners in this," Vivi went on, "and we're family, both in and outside Lavender Blue." She reached out her hands, bracelets jingling against the table.

Avery and Chey each took one of Vivi's outstretched hands, then reached their free hands to Hannah, who clasped them both.

"So, I want us to come up with a plan that allows us to continue doing what we love here. We just got started," she added with a bright smile. "And I can't tell you how excited I am to see how things go this season." She squeezed Chey's and Avery's hands. "A plan that also allows us to figure out a way to be with the men in our lives." She looked at Hannah and Avery. "Now, I know the two of you have been making that work for a while now. Hannah, you're the most settled of the four of us, and Will is in the Falls full time, so it's been a wonderfully smooth transition for you."

Hannah's smile was soft and full of such genuine happiness, it made Chey's heart fill right up. No one deserved that joy more than she did. "It has, yes. Remarkably so."

Vivi turned to Avery. "I know you and Ben have done much the same, seeing as our farm and his aren't so far apart. But I know he wants to travel and continue doing his work with his prosthetics development, and you want to be able to join him, at least from time to time."

"I do, but not at the expense of the fearsome foursome."

Vivi lifted their joined hands. "That's what I aim to do, dear. Figure out a way where we all get what we want with as little compromise as possible. I don't want your joy, or mine, to come at the expense of something or someone else."

Chey nodded. "I love where you are going with this, Vivi, but with Wyatt, it's not just the occasional corporate trip or research symposium. His whole life is on the road."

"Doesn't he have a farm in Wales? I think I heard him mention it at the picnic grounds when someone asked."

Chey nodded. "He does, yes."

"Seeing as his work takes him all over the world, couldn't he swap a farm in Wales as home base for a farm here in Virginia? Or keep both?"

"He hasn't stayed at his farm in Wales for more than four days at a stretch since he bought it years ago. This summer was to be his first long term stay, and that was just for two months." She smiled. "And look how that worked out."

"But he's staying here, right?" Hannah asked. "For the summer? I mean, that part hasn't changed?"

Chey shook her head. "No, that's still the plan. He's slated to be here until August, which is going to come way too fast." She looked at the three of them. "Dom gave him the list of final options for their next mission, or case, or whatever you want to call it. So, things will start to swing into motion soon; then it's just a matter of time before he heads out."

"Have you talked about it?" Avery said. "Do you know what he wants? He seems to really like it here, and I don't mean superficial like, but sincere like. He's already one of us, Chey, with everything that happened, with the lake and the lodge." She smiled. "He found his space here even faster than we did, and I thought we did pretty well."

"I know, right?" Chey said with a dry tone. "And we have

talked about it. I know he wants this, and me, and us." She was well aware she hadn't responded to his declaration of love with one of her own, but she didn't want her first time saying those words to be a "yeah, so do I" declaration. What he'd said to her had been reverent and beautiful. And funny, sweet, the perfect mix of old Wyatt and new. She wanted her moment to make him feel equally cherished. "He also wants the life he has now, and seeing him in action, watching some of the videos of the things he and Dom and the team have accomplished, I can't imagine him walking away from any part of that. And even if he did, then walk away to what? Helping us on the farm?"

"Would he consider doing fewer of them a year?" Hannah asked. "Strike a balance of some kind? Maybe there are things he could do in between to raise awareness in some other way?"

"Would you want to go with him?" Avery asked. "Some of the time?"

Chey let go of their hands and picked up her coffee mug. "I know it would be a once-in-a-lifetime opportunity, like, every single time." She paused, then said, "I would have been perfectly fine never doing things like he does. I don't have that kind of bucket list. But I also know how it has made me feel to watch him here, doing what he does—and for that?" She nodded vigorously. "I would love to be with him, truly with him, to witness everything firsthand and share it all with him."

"Well," Vivi said, "this has been very illuminating." She smiled, and there was something private about it, something she was clearly thrilled with.

"Wait, wait, wait," Chey said. "What about you? Grant lives across the country."

"Yes, darling, but he has his own plane. Several helicopters, too. Now, I realize he's not on a farm down the road like Ben, or close to town like Will and Jake, but he can be quite mobile if he sees fit." She beamed. "And I believe he will."

"Yes, well, he seems to have no problem whisking to Valley View and taking you to New York for lunch. I guess we just have to expand our minds to understand that kind of life."

Avery propped her elbows on the table and rested her chin in her hands. "Do you want to go west? Hang out on his real estate out there?"

Vivi nodded. "He has real estate, as you call it, all over the world. And yes, I'd love to see all of his properties." Her smile was fond. "I do have a bucket list."

They all laughed with her. "You should check off every item," Chey said.

"Well, that's the plan, but it won't happen fast. For two retired people, we're both very busy. He's serious about the work he's doing to promote green energy and environmentally sound new development. It keeps him busy as the farm keeps me busy. He travels a great deal and I'm afraid I'd find that dreadfully boring. I think we can strike a balance between our high season here and his work travel. And focus our work time so we can travel for pleasure, be out west, as well as be here together."

"So, you've talked about this already?" Chey asked.

Vivi nodded. "Haven't you?"

"Not specifically, though I think we may have opened that door today."

Vivi covered her hand. "Well, darling, Grant and I have. Talked about you and Wyatt, I mean. It's not my place to say. Grant has some ideas for Wyatt, but that's for them to discuss."

It should have terrified Chey how quickly her heart leapt

to her throat at even the whiff of a prayer that there might be a solution.

Vivi squeezed her hand. "Be hopeful," was all she said.

"I'll be choosing happiness either way," Chey said, repeating Vivi's wisdom. "You were right about one thing. The more time we spend together, the more I know what I'd be willing to risk, or to do, for us to have a chance."

Avery tapped her pen on the spiral notebook. "So, why do I need this notebook?" she asked.

Vivi sat up straighter and took on an official air. "I want us to go through our calendar year here, with an eye toward what is demanded from each of us, each month. First column will list our obligations here on the farm. Second column will list our outside obligations. Your working with Ben and Hannah, your painting, Chey with your horses." She smiled. "Then we go through once more with an eye toward the key times we would want to spend with the men in our lives, or family, as is Hannah's case. Those can't-miss times."

"And?" Chey said.

"And we see if a glimmer of a schedule starts to emerge, one that allows each of us to have what we need. Yes, there will be compromise, but there are other options that can aid our cause. Like Tory being here to take on some of the workload with the stables and horses," she added. "We plan to hire seasonal help for the gift shop, and to wait tables in the tearoom. Then there's the lavender production itself, the cutting and such, and the classes. We decide which of those things we want to do, and which we'd be comfortable hiring out. Like the classes. I know we each enjoy them, but we can occasionally farm some of them out as needed to facilitate the other things we want." She turned to Avery. "Then we let you do your thing and make us some charts, see what we can do."

"I can do that," Avery said happily.

Vivi nodded, content with where this was going. She looked at all of them. "It's a start. Without compromising our happiness, or the quality of the experience we offer here to our customers and visitors, I think we can keep what we love, but we adjust where we can, so we can also keep the people we love."

Chapter Fifteen

Chey needed to be more of an optimist. They'd spent another hour that morning in the kitchen, making lists and columns, so many columns, and Chey wanted Avery to chart them into oblivion if it meant finding a workable solution. But she'd left really uncertain that was possible. It seemed too complicated trying to make sure they all got what they wanted. Even hiring out part of the farm workload—she just didn't see it coming together without someone making fairly major sacrifices.

She recalled Vivi's veiled comment that Grant had some ideas about Wyatt's future, but she couldn't count on that for anything. Their column-making meeting had been a week ago and Wyatt hadn't heard anything from Grant. They knew he'd flown Vivi out to his ranch for the weekend, wanting her to spend time in his home as he had hers. Hannah had covered the tearoom hours, which were reduced for a little while longer, until Memorial Day weekend. With lavender season underway, Tory had been taking on more and more of the stable management and was already teaching classes and bringing in new students after Bailey started talking up the whole barrel-racing thing. Chey had never once thought about teaching that particular skill. It wasn't something she saw herself doing again. It was part of her past now. But she'd sure enjoy watching Tory take it on.

So, things were changing, even without their deciding anything concrete. Some things were simply solving themselves as they happened. Chey had hoped that maybe they could just take it one thing at a time, like Vivi going to Montana, or Wyoming, or wherever she was, and Hannah covering for her. And Tory taking on the stables, freeing up Chey to get her farm work done with time leftover to explore as yet unseen parts of Blue Hollow Falls with a guy who was making her appreciate it in a whole new way.

But she knew it wouldn't always be that simple. Wyatt and Dom, Jon and Peli had decided on their next adventure. They were going to Canada, near the Arctic Circle, to focus on a threatened plant that was vital to the food chain for a host of mammal species. Fixing the plant sustainability problem could result in removing numerous animals from the threatened and endangered list.

Actually, it had been Sunny Goodwin, who owned the greenhouse and was the horticulturalist working with the rare and endangered orchids, who had put her head together with Wyatt's after he consulted with her on some of the methods she'd discovered for propagation. Together, they thought they might find a solution for the plant problem. Chey was pretty sure Wyatt had also chosen that particular project because part of the plan was to transport plant specimens back to Blue Hollow Falls and Sunny's greenhouse, where she'd be joined by two specialists who'd agreed to come out and help test her theories and track the plant development from there. Which meant a chunk of the adventure would take place right in Blue Hollow Falls, and Wyatt would do all the postproduction work from there, too, while setting up the next trip.

She was touched and grateful that he'd done his best to

keep their two orbits as connected as possible on his first venture out since they'd become a couple. But Chey knew his projects wouldn't all be like that. There were only so many connections he could make between his work and her home. Their home.

Ultimately, Chey was glad they'd done all those charts in the kitchen that day. Not because they'd yielded any plans yet, but because talking about what she wanted for herself, putting her thoughts into words, had helped her to solidify what she wanted, what she'd be happy to compromise on, and what she'd hoped she wouldn't be asked to do.

And then she'd laughed at herself as she walked out to the barn that afternoon, because once Planet Reed was done in Canada, and Wyatt flew off to God only knew where next, for who knew how long, she was pretty sure she'd be the Grant Harper in their situation. If Wyatt so much as crooked his finger, Chey would be on the next plane to wherever he was and thrilled for it.

And in the end, that had been answer enough for her.

It had taken some time to put her plan into motion, but now the day was here. And it was time to take the plunge. Hopefully, a figuratively speaking plunge, but whatever it took, she'd do it.

Laughing at that thought, Chey turned her truck onto the road that led back to the boat ramp to the lake. Ground had officially been broken and the park was officially closed to the public for now, but other than a crew beginning to clear the land on the opposite side of the lake where the lodge would be located, not much else had happened.

She'd gotten permission from Bryan for her little mission today. The road back to the boat ramp was open, and when she arrived lakeside and parked her truck, she saw someone else had come through for her, too. There was a rowboat tied to the dock. She smiled. "Thank you, Grant Harper."

She climbed down out of the truck, then took a minute to adjust the flowy, floral print dress she had on. *Thank you also, Hannah.* It had bunched up around the waist and the belt had gone a little sideways. "The things we do for love," she muttered as she got it all straightened out. How did people wear these things day in and day out?

She went around to the passenger side, grabbed the big covered basket and towel from the seat, along with her cowboy hat and the other item she'd borrowed, then tucked her keys under the mat and headed to the dock.

It took a bit of finagling to get everything in the boat, as well as herself. She was never more thankful that she was alone and the park was otherwise closed, because she was fairly certain she'd flashed most of the wildlife in the area several times going up and down the little ladder, trying to keep her skirts from blowing up while simultaneously not flipping the boat over. Perhaps cowboy boots had also been a poor choice of footwear.

She sat on the bench seat until the boat stopped rocking, then organized the oars while silently wishing part of the exploring she and Wyatt had done included boating. It was on the list, but they hadn't gotten that far, yet.

"But how hard can it be?" After a few attempts to sync the motions of the left and right oar resulted in a lot of water slapping and not a little splashing, she finally got the hang of it and headed out to the middle of the lake.

The sky was blue, the sun just the right amount of warm, and the usual breeze off the lake surprisingly nonexistent. The water looked like glass and reflected the mountains, clouds, and sky. Satisfied, she pulled her cell phone out and sent a text, then stored it away without waiting for a response. She made sure she was well out in the middle of the lake . . . then she purposely let the oars slip from their locks and float away on the glassy surface.

"Now, that is love. And trust," she said; then she picked up the borrowed item, and opened the umbrella she'd borrowed from Vivi, giving the fringe a little shimmy as she settled in to wait.

Wyatt's cheeks hurt from grinning all the way to the lake. His smile only slipped when he pulled in and didn't immediately see Chey's truck anywhere in the lot. Then he spied the ramp road open and went from grinning to singing. One of Pippa's tunes he couldn't get out of his head. And didn't want to.

He saw the boat well out in the lake when he made it to the dock, and if he hadn't already decided to ask her to marry him, seeing her out there in a dress, with Vivi's crazy umbrella, sealed the deal. He quickly stripped off his shirt, and this time, his pants, and made a clean dive into the water.

Chey was twirling the parasol when he popped up next to the boat. "You seem to have lost your oars," he said, as he tossed his wet hair back from his face.

"Why I declare, it was so clumsy of me," she replied in a terrible southern accent. "They were so big and heavy, I could barely manage. What with my little parasol and all." She twirled it again, a little snicker escaping despite her best efforts to look fragile and stranded.

He swam out and retrieved the oars, then swam back and stored them the same way he had with Vivi.

"Hold on to the bench," he told her, then as gently as he could, gripped one side and levered himself into the boat.

"Why sir!" she said. "Why, I thought you would tow me to shore. I believe you've gotten water all over my dress."

He sat on the bench seat opposite hers. "Well, I hate for you to be all damp. I believe I mentioned before that I'd be happy to help you out of your dresses. Anytime." He slid the oars in the locks and accepted the towel from her.

"What a kind and gentlemanly offer," she said dryly. "But I fear I burn easily. So, I'm just going to sit here and enjoy you in those snug boxer briefs. And all that delicious tan."

He wiggled his eyebrows. "Why, I believe you're flirting with me, ma'am," he said, taking a turn with the drawl.

"You wouldn't be wrong," she said, then laughed. She opened the big basket stowed in the back and took out a pair of his shorts and a shirt and handed them to him. "I can't be held responsible for what I might do, so you'd better cover up."

"I've heard about women like you. Impulsive and lacking all self-control." He grinned. "I like it."

She batted her eyelashes, making him laugh. "Hungry?" she asked. "I had Hattie pack us a picnic lunch."

Wyatt thought his eyes might have rolled back in his head just a bit. He and Chey had eaten at Bo's twice now and he was already planning some kind of homage to Hattie's cooking in his next stream.

"I am now."

"All that swimming," she said. "Works up an appetite."

He smiled, then slowly ran his gaze from her boots to her umbrella. "That's one reason for it."

She held the front of her dress closed with her hand, despite the fact that it was buttoned up to her neck.

He just made a growling sound and she laughed.

"Don't even," she told him when he shifted off his seat. "We'll both end up in the lake."

"I'm already wet," he said, "and I know you can swim."

In response she handed him the container of Hattie's fried chicken. "Down, boy."

"Yes, ma'am," he said, then settled back on the bench

and let out a long, blissful sigh after opening the lid and taking a deep breath.

She handed him a thermos of Hattie's iced tea, a side of potato salad, biscuit, and a plastic fork; then she settled back on her seat looking suddenly a little nervous.

"You aren't eating?" he asked.

She shook her head. "Butterflies," she said, as if that explained it.

He paused then. "Because?"

"Well, I brought you out here today because you're my drop-everything-and-go person. I text you, say I need you, and I know you'll do whatever you can to get to me."

He thought about that, then grinned and nodded. "That about sums it up, yes," he said. "Though I do call an exception if I'm like, on a glacier or something, but the minute they can get me off, I'm on a plane, boat, helicopter, whatever it takes."

Smiling, but still nervous, she reached in the bag and pulled out an envelope. "Well, I wanted you to know that I'm your drop-everything person, too." She handed it to him.

He opened it and slid out a small blue paper folder made to look like an official passport, and a key. He opened the folder to see a smiling photo of her stuck inside, and grinned.

"I haven't gotten the real thing back in the mail yet, so Avery made that." The sweetest blush rose to her cheeks. "But I have applied. For a real one. My first passport ever. I hope you'll help me fill it up."

Surprised and touched beyond measure, he looked from the folder to her. "Chey—"

She lifted her hand. "I'm not done."

He realized now why she looked nervous, and his heart filled right up. His smile softened. "Please, go on."

"I know we each have our paths to follow," she told him.

"And there will inevitably be times when we have to be apart, maybe for longer than we'd ever choose to be. I just want you to know that when I can work it out, I want to go with you. And when you're not traipsing the globe, I hope you'll see that"—she nodded at the key in his other hand—"as the key to your home." She smiled. "Though we never actually lock it. And, technically, that's not even actually a key to the door, because I don't think I have one."

"A symbolic gesture as it were," he said, feeling his eyes prickling a bit with emotion. She thought she was so tough, but she was so damn sweet.

"Indeed," she said. Then she laughed and let out a shaky sigh. "So, Wyatt Samuel Reed, formerly of our life on the circuit, and now with dual citizenship in Reed Planet and Lavender Blue, I hope you already know that I love you with all of my heart. And you'll be taking that with you, everywhere you go, whether I'm with you or not."

He slid carefully to his knees in the center of the boat between the benches, so he was right in front of her. He picked up her hand and looked into her eyes. "I do, Cheyenne Rosemary McCafferty. I do."

She let out a shaky breath when he kissed her hand, specifically her ring finger. He was already planning to make sure he put a ring on it before leaving for Canada. Then he leaned in, tipped her hat up, and slid his hand into her hair. Smiling into her pretty eyes, he kissed her.

"I'm all in," she whispered, then opened her eyes when the boat wobbled. "With you. Not the lake."

He laughed. "No, I'd rather we stay all in the boat, too."

She held on to the front of his shirt, tugged him in for another kiss. Her hat fell off and landed in the open basket.

He started to take the kiss deeper, but the boat wobbled again, and they broke apart, laughing, as he slid back to his seat. He retrieved his meal and nodded to her. "Okay, now you fill up a plate."

"Yes," she said with a relieved laugh. "Now I can eat. I'm starving."

"You take care of that, and I'll tell you my news."

Her eyebrows lifted as she settled in with her plate. "News? Did you hear from Dom on the paperwork from—I can't pronounce the name without mangling it—the village you all are going to?"

"No, not yet. We've hit a snag there, which is par for the course, but we're working on it. No, this is actually much, much bigger news." He smiled. "Maybe the second-best news I've gotten ever. That thing you just said being the first."

"You mean the 'I love you' part?"

He placed a hand to his heart, and she giggled. "Yeah, that. Please say that as often as you want." He hadn't repeated those words to her since his declaration that day, because he didn't want to pressure her in any way. He knew how she felt and wanted her to work through things at her own pace, her own way. He should have known she'd make it memorable. "And it's doubly great, because I love you, too, so now we can both be super sappy about it and it'll be okay."

"Oh, well, that's good to hear, because otherwise, I would have held back on the sap." She grinned. "No, I wouldn't," she admitted, laughing. "Oh my God, if Tory could see us right now, she'd be smug into the next century."

He chuckled and lifted the tea thermos in a toast. "Earned, though."

"True," Chey agreed. "So, what's the second-best news you got today?"

"A call from Grant Harper."

Her eyes widened. "Like, 'the call' call?"

She'd told him about what Vivi had said, about how she

and Grant had had some conversation about Wyatt, but as the days had gone by without word from him, they'd started to joke about it, not really thinking anything would come of it.

"He didn't say a word to me when I asked him to help get this boat out here."

Wyatt looked around. "You know, I just now realized that with the park closed now, there would be no boats. He's turning out to be a pretty stand-up guy all around."

"Well, he's Vivi's drop-everything guy, but he loans out," she added dryly. "So that's nice."

"Oh, nice doesn't begin to cover it."

Chey's eyes widened at that. She set her plate aside and leaned forward, hands clasped under her chin. "Okay, okay. Tell me, tell me. Did he miraculously solve all of our problems and make things in fairy-tale land last forever and ever?"

That had been part of the joke, too. So Wyatt took great joy in simply saying, "Yes."

She laughed and had already started to say something, then caught the look in his eyes. "Wait. You're serious."

"About as serious as it gets."

She looked stunned. "How? I mean, what could he possibly have done to do that? Is there even—"

"He set up a foundation with a global initiative to take on projects like the ones I've been streaming. So, I won't have to stream to find help or financing, or any of it. The foundation will fund what's needed. He's financing it, along with a whole team of folks he's put together. Fellow philanthropists." Wyatt took her hands in his. "He wants to accept all of the proposals on our short list, Cheyenne. Do all of the things." Saying it out loud brought a rush of gratitude that had his eyes prickling again, just thinking of what they could accomplish. It was overwhelming, in the very best of ways.

She blinked, then blinked again. "But . . . how? There is only one of you, so how could you do all—"

"I will write up proposals for the projects we choose, then the foundation will underwrite them. I will assemble a team—hopefully Dom and Jon, and even Peli will stay on, but I haven't even gotten to that yet. I wanted to tell you first. We will do the same research, work on finding the solutions, all the things we did before."

"But you won't have to travel all the time," she said, sounding a bit breathless with shock. "And you can do all of them? That's just . . ." She stared at him, speechless.

"There will be some travel. I will have the flexibility to send people to the various locales to work with the locals and set things up, oversee them, and hopefully in this case, those would be the actual folks who can solve the problems, not just me, trying to drum up awareness and support."

"Wait, so you're like . . . HR for the foundation, and the face of the brand, or—"

"No. I'm running the foundation, Chey. All of it. Grant heads up the board along with the other trustees who are helping to fund it but . . . it will be my baby."

"That's . . . incredible. But what about all your followers, what about Reed Planet?"

"I haven't thought all of that through yet, but the streaming we do now will end once the foundation is up and running. I'll find a way to bring everyone who has been so supportive along somehow, though, with new content. I'll create some new directions, new goals, and who knows what doors will open. I won't walk away from my followers, though, not ever." He grinned. "And I know for certain that Reed Planet won't die, because that's the name of the foundation." He shared her look of amazement. "I know, right? I'm feeling pretty optimistic about the whole thing."

"You know what? So am I. And it feels really good." She nodded toward the blue folder he'd picked up again. "So, does this mean no stamps on my fake passport?"

"I'll still want to go see the places, meet the people, to fully understand what's happening. More like in an ambassador role, though, for the foundation. Before or during, maybe after. I can't be in all places at once, but each trip would be fairly short." He held her hand. "And much, much easier for you to come along. We can put real stamps on your real passport." He dropped his head and held their joined hands up. "Would you consider being my, uh, ambassadress?"

She laughed. "Is that even a thing?"

He looked up through his lashes. "I'll make you a cape and everything."

"Well, if there's a cape, then I'm in." She motioned to the dress she was wearing. "I've clearly learned never to say never."

He lowered their joined hands, and peered up again, one eyebrow raised.

"Yes, yes, I accept," she said, laughing, then paused when he settled back on his seat. "Wait, I forgot to ask. Where will this foundation be headquartered? Out west with Grant? Can you like, telecommute, or do your work from here? I mean, you wouldn't really need to be on site for all of the—" She broke off, then deadpanned, "I'm already sucking at the ambassadress thing, aren't I?"

He shook his head, even as he grinned. "No, not ever."

"I'll do better when I have a cape. I know it."

"I'll hold you to that," he said, laughing. "Actually, though . . ." He gestured to the lake and land beyond. "This is the new home of Reed Planet. Grant talked with Bryan and the architect. They have to clear it with the town council, but they're hoping to build the headquarters out here."

"Like, here, here?"

"Yep, this very here right here. Bryan has his eye on a spot behind the lodge on the far side of the lake, so it doesn't impede the view. It won't be a big building, but we will need a conference room, and a few offices for core staff. We'll likely have folks flying in from all over when we're putting teams together for each project, so having the foundation near the lodge works out well."

"I don't see why the council wouldn't approve. It can only mean more good things for Blue Hollow Falls."

"I think so, too."

She smiled at him. "So, I totally didn't think this whole boat idea through, because I want to launch myself at you and kiss you and basically jump up and down for joy, but preferably without any drowning."

Wyatt immediately picked up and positioned the oars and started rowing them to the dock in swift order.

"What about our picnic?" she said, holding her hat on her head as they cut across the smooth surface.

"I thought I was the drop-everything-and-go guy. You say it, I make it happen."

Her smile was wry. "I can see I will have to be more specific about when I'm just wishing and when I really need you."

He pulled up to the dock a few minutes later, then let her hand him up the basket and the rest, and finally helped her from the boat. Then he promptly picked her up and spun her around, right there on the dock.

"That's more like it," she said, wrapping her arms around his neck as he set her feet back on the dock. "And who am I kidding?" she said, and tipped her face up to him. "I will always need you."

Epilogue

"Does Vivi know yet?" Chey used the pitchfork to toss more hay into the stall, then turned to get another load.

Tory moved the wheelbarrow closer to the stall she was mucking out. "I don't know. Bailey said she heard Addie Pearl on the phone with the mayor, talking about Grant wanting office space separate from the foundation offices, so what else could that mean?" She crossed her hands over the end of the rake handle and rested her chin on them. "Bailey's quite certain he's moving here full time and the ranch will become their vacation home."

"One of his vacation homes," Chey said. "And if Bailey thinks it's happening, it's a done deal as far as I'm concerned." She laughed when Tory sighed.

"It's all so romantic. All the good ones are officially taken," Tory said.

Chey finished spreading the last of the hay and walked out of the stall. "I shouldn't point this out to you, and I don't want to get your hopes up, but the four of us were single when we moved out here two years ago. To the middle of nowhere. Leaving mankind and, basically, men, behind. Or so we thought." She laughed. "People pair up so fast up here, it would make your head spin." She snapped her fingers. "Maybe the new lodge should use that as part of their brochure. 'Blue Hollow Falls is for lovers,'" she said, marking each word overhead with her hand.

Tory covered her ears. "Why would you tell me that? You've jinxed me for life now."

"I'm just sayin' is all I'm sayin'," Chey drawled. "You'll see."

Tory groaned. "Doomed, I tell you." Then she smiled sweetly. "That's okay. When I'm old and have adopted all the barn cats, I'll just move into the spare room with you and Wyatt." She batted her eyelashes. "It's the least you can do for this poor old maid."

"Careful," Chey said on a laugh. "I'll get Avery to start making charts for you."

Tory laughed. "Hey, I don't knock her charts. She's got a whole system set up for me now with the classes and field duties." She finished her stall and rolled the wheelbarrow to the wide double doors that opened off the rear of the stables. "Did Bailey tell you we're putting up barrels this week? I swear that child is like a duck to a pond with anything she puts her mind to. If it wasn't so amazing to watch, it would be frightening."

"Oh, it's both of those things. And yes, she told me. I'm happy she's learning." She grinned. "And happier still that you're the one teaching her."

"I don't mind," Tory said. "It's like the best of the good old days."

"Speaking of good old days," cut in a deep voice from the other side of the stables. Wyatt came strolling in and walked over to give Chey a quick kiss. "You ready?"

"I am," she said, with a smile. "How about you?"

He lifted his hand. "I brought two apples. Granny Smith. Used to be his favorite. Thought that might help."

Chey put her hand on his arm. "He's not going to need

any help. Now that he'll get to keep seeing you, this is going to be the most wonderful reunion ever."

"You sure he's not going to associate me with what happened to him? I mean, he probably thinks I abandoned him. I did abandon him. I just didn't know it."

Chey took his hand. "Stop stalling." They waved their good-byes to Tory, who had gone back to mucking out stalls, and walked out the rear double, then headed toward the fence that ran along the back field.

When they got close, Chey stopped and leaned on the railing. She didn't look at Wyatt. She knew he had a tumult of feelings about this and gave him the time to work it out on his own.

Wyatt palmed the apple. Then he walked to the fence and looked out across the field, to the gelding grazing there.

Maybe it was the wind, carrying Wyatt's scent, but Buttercup lifted his head, scented the air, then snorted.

Wyatt whistled, the whistle he'd always used for his horse. Just for his horse. It came out a bit weak and strangled the first time. Chey had a lump in her throat the size of that apple already, so she was surprised he could whistle at all.

Wyatt cleared his throat, then tried again. It was clear and pure this time, and Buttercup immediately turned his head. And without taking so much as a second, he immediately trotted toward the fence, toward Wyatt, his ears forward and, Chey swore, a skip in the old boy's step she hadn't seen once in all the time he'd been at the farm.

Buttercup stopped several feet from the fence, his hooves digging into the soft dirt. He regarded Wyatt for a long minute, then dropped his head, snorted.

"I didn't know," Wyatt said, talking to the horse. "I didn't know." His voice broke and Buttercup walked to the fence, put his nose over the rail, and let out another rumbling snort.

Wyatt didn't reach out, didn't touch him. Instead he held out the apple.

Buttercup didn't look at the apple, he just swung his head toward Wyatt and snuffled.

Wyatt reached out a hand and stroked his mane, tears tracking down his cheeks. "I'm so sorry," he said, on a choked whisper.

Then Buttercup dropped his head down and Wyatt finally put his arms around the horse's neck. Chey saw his shoulders shaking as he kept his face buried there.

Chey smiled and wiped away tears, but they kept trickling out. She quietly made her way back to the barn. This was between the two of them. She paused when she reached the stable doors and looked back, then smiled when she saw Wyatt offer the apple again, one arm over Buttercup's neck. The horse nibbled, then bumped his nose against Wyatt's pocket, looking for more.

"You got your drop-everything guy back, Buttercup," she said. *And we all got our drop-everything-to-be-there home.*

CATCH ME IF YOU CAN
Donna Kauffman

IF IT'S TUESDAY, THIS MUST BE SCOTLAND

All Tag Morgan wants to do is help settle
his father's estate so he can get back to properly
cataloguing his Mayan ruins. So he's caught
quite off guard to discover that:

A) His father had holdings in Scotland
B) The property now belongs to Tag

Leafing through his father's correspondence with
the property's overseer, one Maura Ramsey,
yields even more surprises. His father's letters
reveal a warmer, kinder man—nothing like the harsh,
cold disciplinarian Tag remembers. Surely it has to do
with Maura, whose writing is filled with a dry wit
and an infectious charm that keeps Tag reading
all night. By the time the sun rises, Tag knows
he's going to Scotland to find this woman
who has so thoroughly captivated him . . .

FERN MICHAELS
HOME SWEET HOME

USA Today **Bestselling Authors**
DONNA KAUFFMAN * MELISSA STORM

*What makes a place feel like home? A mother's embrace,
the warmth of new friendship, a sweet reunion—
all can be found in these unforgettable stories . . .*

THREE'S A CROWD * Fern Michaels
This Mother's Day will be the first in three years that
Samantha Stewart has spent with her parents. And she's
bringing a very special gift—the baby granddaughter
they've never met. Sam's work as an overseas reporter
was exhilarating and dangerous. Now she's seeking
stability for little Caroline—and answers for herself—
and finding them in a homecoming full of surprises . . .

BLUE HOLLOW FALLS: NEW BEGINNINGS
Donna Kauffman
The moment she set foot in Blue Hollow Falls,
Dubliner Katie MacMillan felt right at home.
Back to help with her sister's pregnancy, she's
contemplating her own future, especially when she
confronts Declan MacGregor, her childhood tormentor
and first crush. This Blue Ridge town was supposed
to be a new beginning, but can it
also be the setting for a second chance?

BRING ME HOME * Melissa Storm
For Hazel Long, spending time with her bedridden father
is bittersweet. There's comfort in the friendship offered
by other hospital visitors—and the kindness of a
handsome male nurse. And when Hazel's father begins
to tell her the story of the mother she barely knew,
it's an unexpected chance to bond, and a lesson
in making the most of each new day.

Connect with Us

Visit us online at
KensingtonBooks.com
to read more from your favorite authors, see books
by series, view reading group guides, and more.

Join us on social media

for sneak peeks, chances to win books and prize packs,
and to share your thoughts with other readers.

facebook.com/kensingtonpublishing
twitter.com/kensingtonbooks

Tell us what you think!

To share your thoughts, submit a review,
or sign up for our eNewsletters, please visit:
KensingtonBooks.com/TellUs.

Books by Bestselling Author
Fern Michaels

___**The Jury**	0-8217-7878-1	$6.99US/$9.99CAN
___**Sweet Revenge**	0-8217-7879-X	$6.99US/$9.99CAN
___**Lethal Justice**	0-8217-7880-3	$6.99US/$9.99CAN
___**Free Fall**	0-8217-7881-1	$6.99US/$9.99CAN
___**Fool Me Once**	0-8217-8071-9	$7.99US/$10.99CAN
___**Vegas Rich**	0-8217-8112-X	$7.99US/$10.99CAN
___**Hide and Seek**	1-4201-0184-6	$6.99US/$9.99CAN
___**Hokus Pokus**	1-4201-0185-4	$6.99US/$9.99CAN
___**Fast Track**	1-4201-0186-2	$6.99US/$9.99CAN
___**Collateral Damage**	1-4201-0187-0	$6.99US/$9.99CAN
___**Final Justice**	1-4201-0188-9	$6.99US/$9.99CAN
___**Up Close and Personal**	0-8217-7956-7	$7.99US/$9.99CAN
___**Under the Radar**	1-4201-0683-X	$6.99US/$9.99CAN
___**Razor Sharp**	1-4201-0684-8	$7.99US/$10.99CAN
___**Yesterday**	1-4201-1494-8	$5.99US/$6.99CAN
___**Vanishing Act**	1-4201-0685-6	$7.99US/$10.99CAN
___**Sara's Song**	1-4201-1493-X	$5.99US/$6.99CAN
___**Deadly Deals**	1-4201-0686-4	$7.99US/$10.99CAN
___**Game Over**	1-4201-0687-2	$7.99US/$10.99CAN
___**Sins of Omission**	1-4201-1153-1	$7.99US/$10.99CAN
___**Sins of the Flesh**	1-4201-1154-X	$7.99US/$10.99CAN
___**Cross Roads**	1-4201-1192-2	$7.99US/$10.99CAN